Werewolves are difficult.

I mean, you can count the good werewolf movies on two fingers. Of all of the horror characters, there's just not enough *there* there. There are plenty of tropes—full moons and curses and silver and all that—but those tropes don't give you a story, they don't tell you who your character is. Which is another problem with werewolves.

That Sean Lewis and Caitlin Yarsky have created a mythos, not just whereby werewolves are compelling and dangerous but also represent enormous social and gender issues, is only part of what makes COYOTES a meaningful addition to horror literature but also a monstrously fun read.

Sean has done some serious fracking of werewolf legend, lore, and association to come out with this impressionistic mythology for the world of COYOTES. Religion, allegory, folklore, fairy tale, and popular culture combine to make a rich story that feels like there are hundreds of layers to be uncovered. Sean and Caitlin mix up creation myths and too-immediate, real stories about border crossing, real-life "coyotes" and disappearing women, and teenage girls with katana blades, to create an emotionally impactful thrill ride.

COYOTES is told with immense empathy. Sean and Caitlin clearly love Red and the Victorias. It's apparent in every line of dialogue that is both human and heroic. It's clear in Caitlin's art, which draws every character as a unique individual—Red is a girl becoming a woman. She's skinny but strong. You could swim in her eyes. Abuela is all sharp angles and spittle. Duchess has weight, a strength that comes from her center. And while Sean and Caitlin have no sympathy for their devils—the wolves and men who turn to coyotes in their wolf-pelts—they do make their villains unforgettable characters with their own motivations and desires and their individual looks (that lava wolf!).

And, in the most difficult medium for it, COYOTES excels as a horror story. This can only be because both Sean and Caitlin have done the work. They've dug deep and asked what scares them and bled that truth onto the page. The harrowing stories of women disappearing at the border are layered with the symbols of horror. Sean recognizes in himself the monster that men can become and makes it the central metaphor of his story. That takes guts.

Speaking of which, there may be no one better than Caitlin Yarsky at organic horror. Her coyote transformations, her scenes of violence and bloodshed, are upsetting and beautiful. Her lines are so clean, her colors so thoughtful, that you want to pause on every page and consider it as a work of art. Then you realize you're looking at a giant wolf covered in spikes with dead humans hanging off of them. So, turn the page.

Then turn the next one and the next one. Then start again, because there's so much to discover beneath the mantle of COYOTES that just these eight issues should keep you busy for years to come. Then, if we're lucky, just when we think we have it all figured out, Sean and Caitlin will find each other again and create something more, something new, something magic. And, though it'll undoubtedly be difficult, they'll make it look easy.

—*Ben Blacker is the creator of Hex Wives from Vertigo Comics, which is about witches, a much easier horror trope than werewolves.*

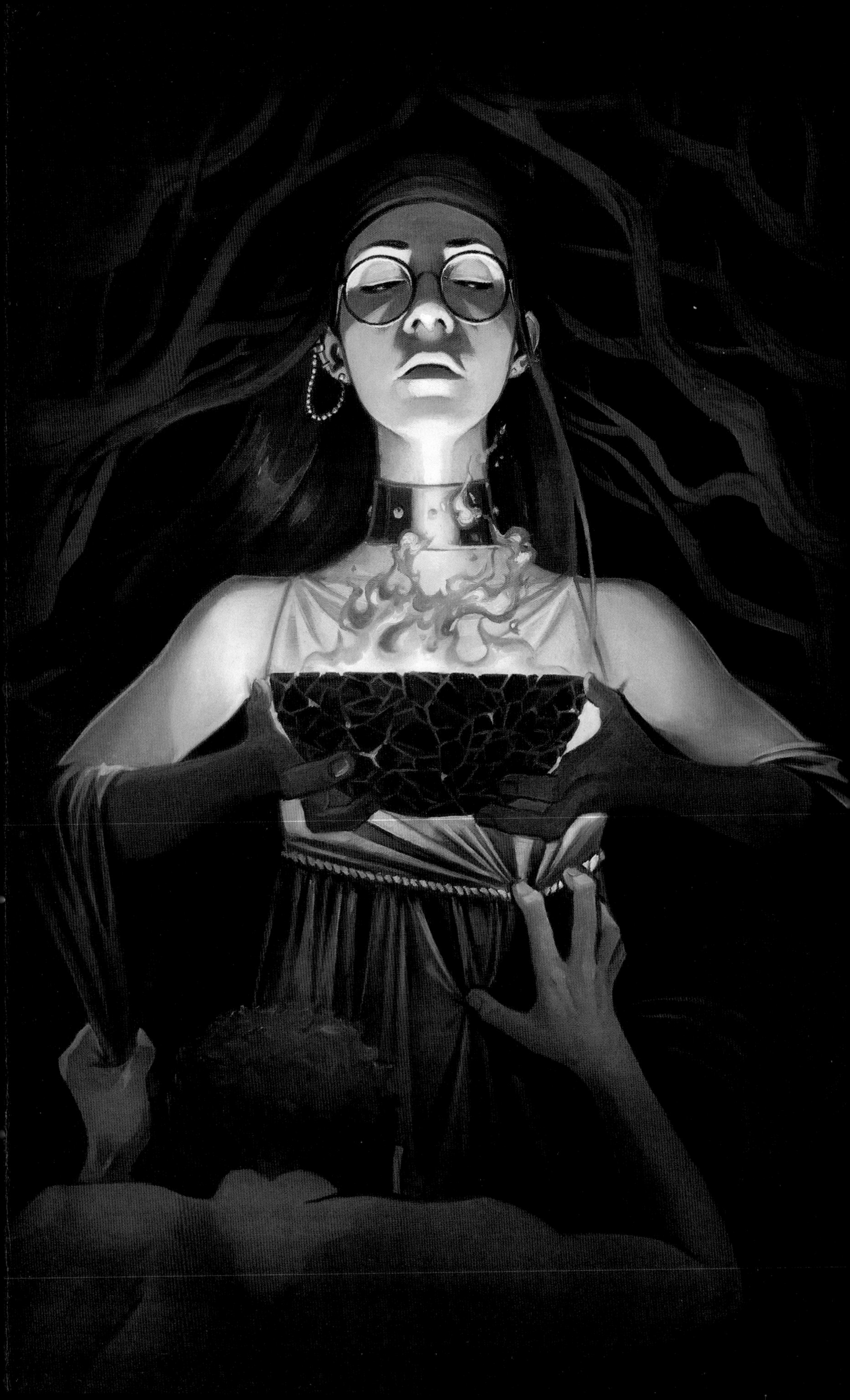

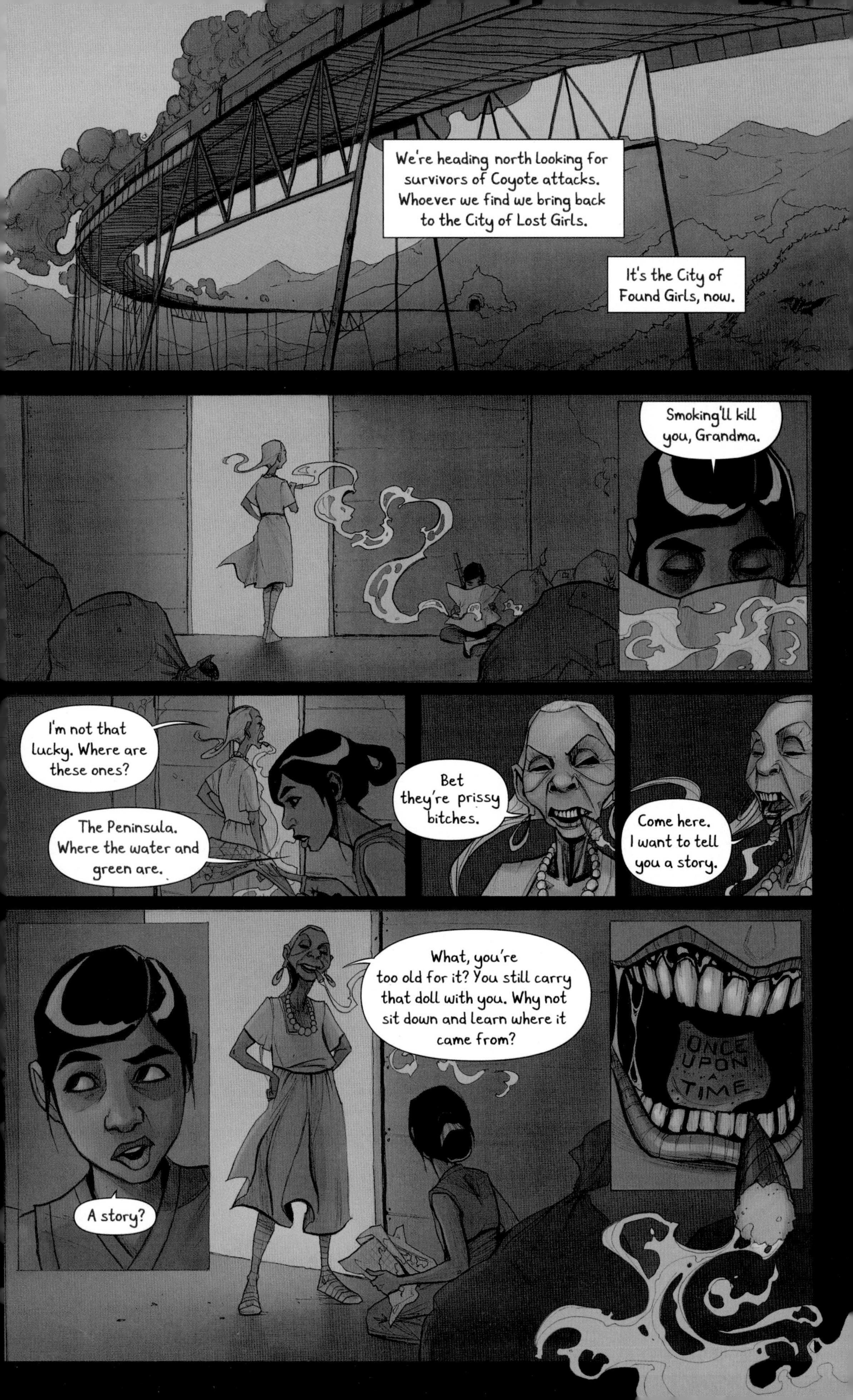
We're heading north looking for survivors of Coyote attacks. Whoever we find we bring back to the City of Lost Girls.
It's the City of Found Girls, now.
Smoking'll kill you, Grandma.
I'm not that lucky. Where are these ones?
The Peninsula. Where the water and green are.
Bet they're prissy bitches.
Come here. I want to tell you a story.
A story?
What, you're too old for it? You still carry that doll with you. Why not sit down and learn where it came from?
ONCE UPON A TIME

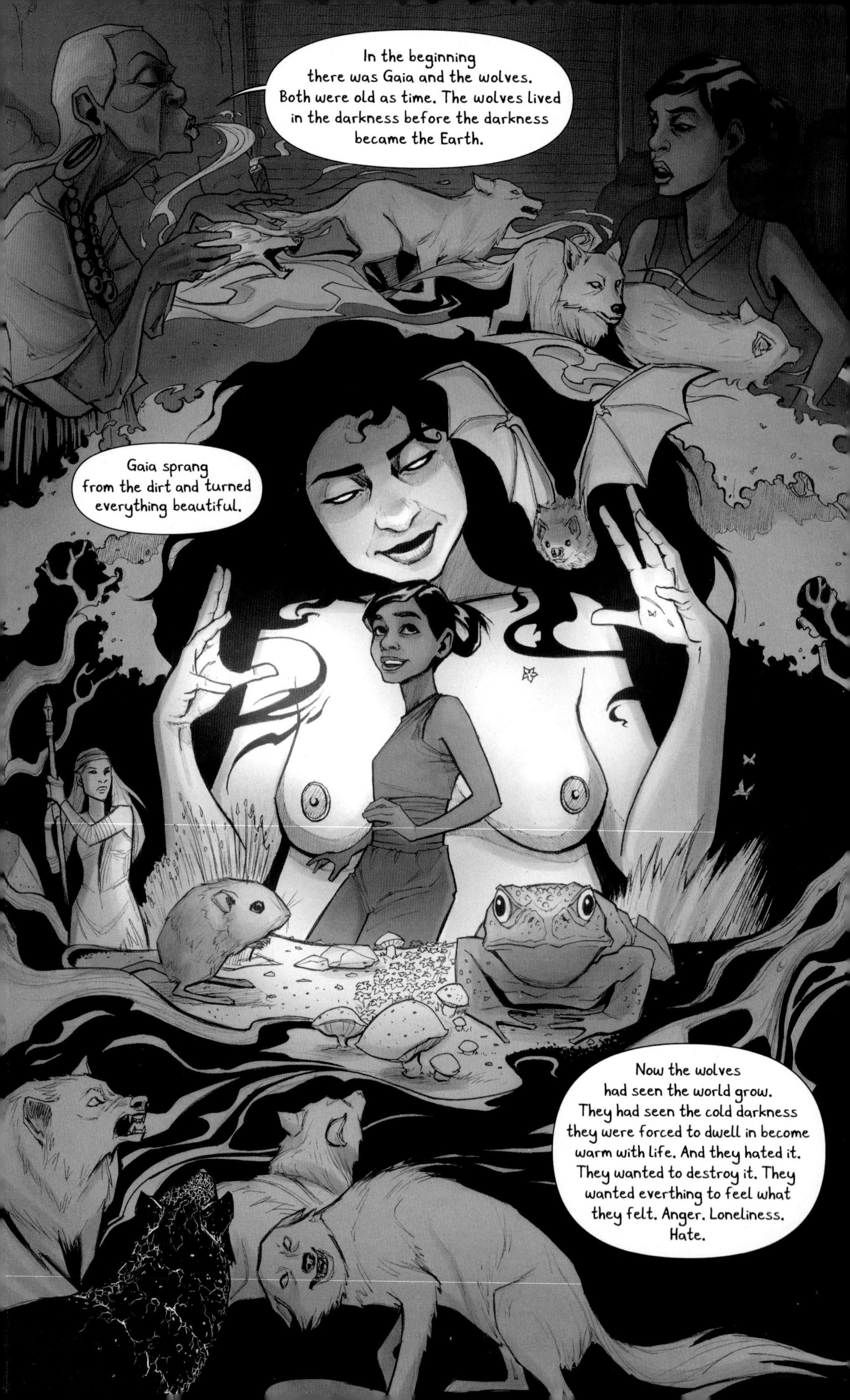
In the beginning there was Gaia and the wolves. Both were old as time. The wolves lived in the darkness before the darkness became the Earth.
Gaia sprang from the dirt and turned everything beautiful.
Now the wolves had seen the world grow. They had seen the cold darkness they were forced to dwell in become warm with life. And they hated it. They wanted to destroy it. They wanted everthing to feel what they felt. Anger. Loneliness. Hate.

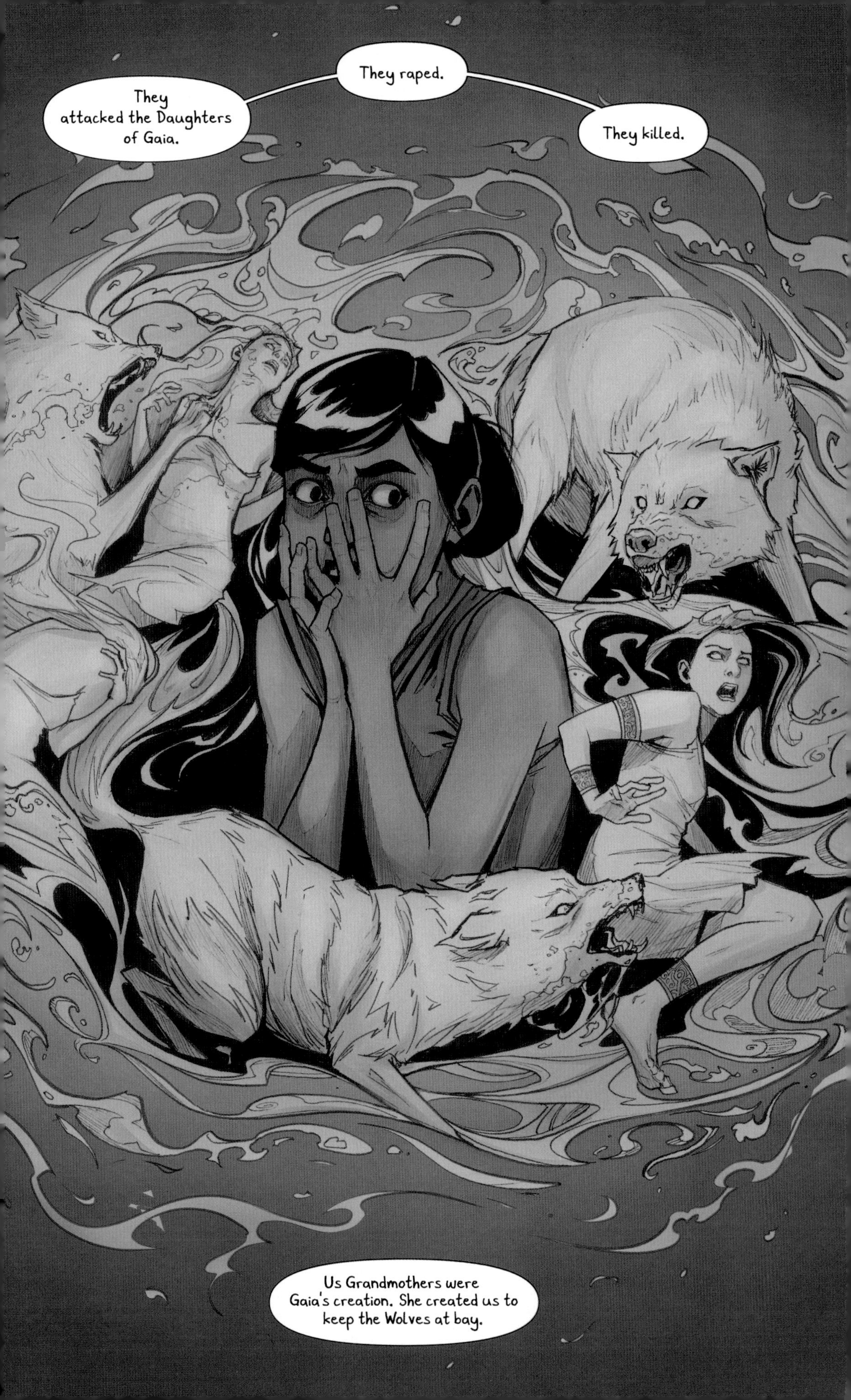
They attacked the Daughters of Gaia.
They raped.
They killed.
Us Grandmothers were Gaia's creation. She created us to keep the Wolves at bay.

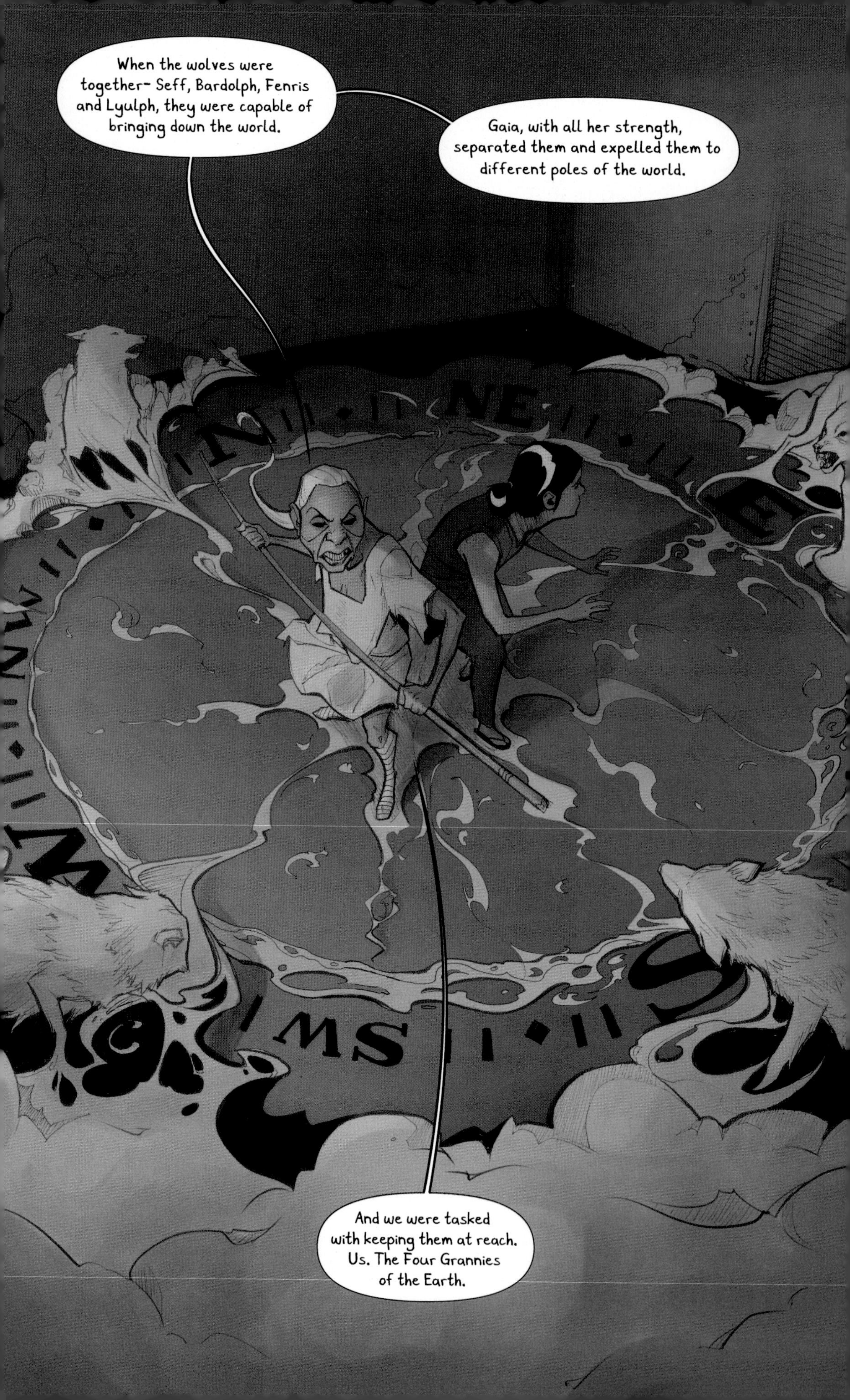
When the wolves were together- Seff, Bardolph, Fenris and Lyulph, they were capable of bringing down the world.
Gaia, with all her strength, separated them and expelled them to different poles of the world.
And we were tasked with keeping them at reach. Us. The Four Grannies of the Earth.
NE
MS

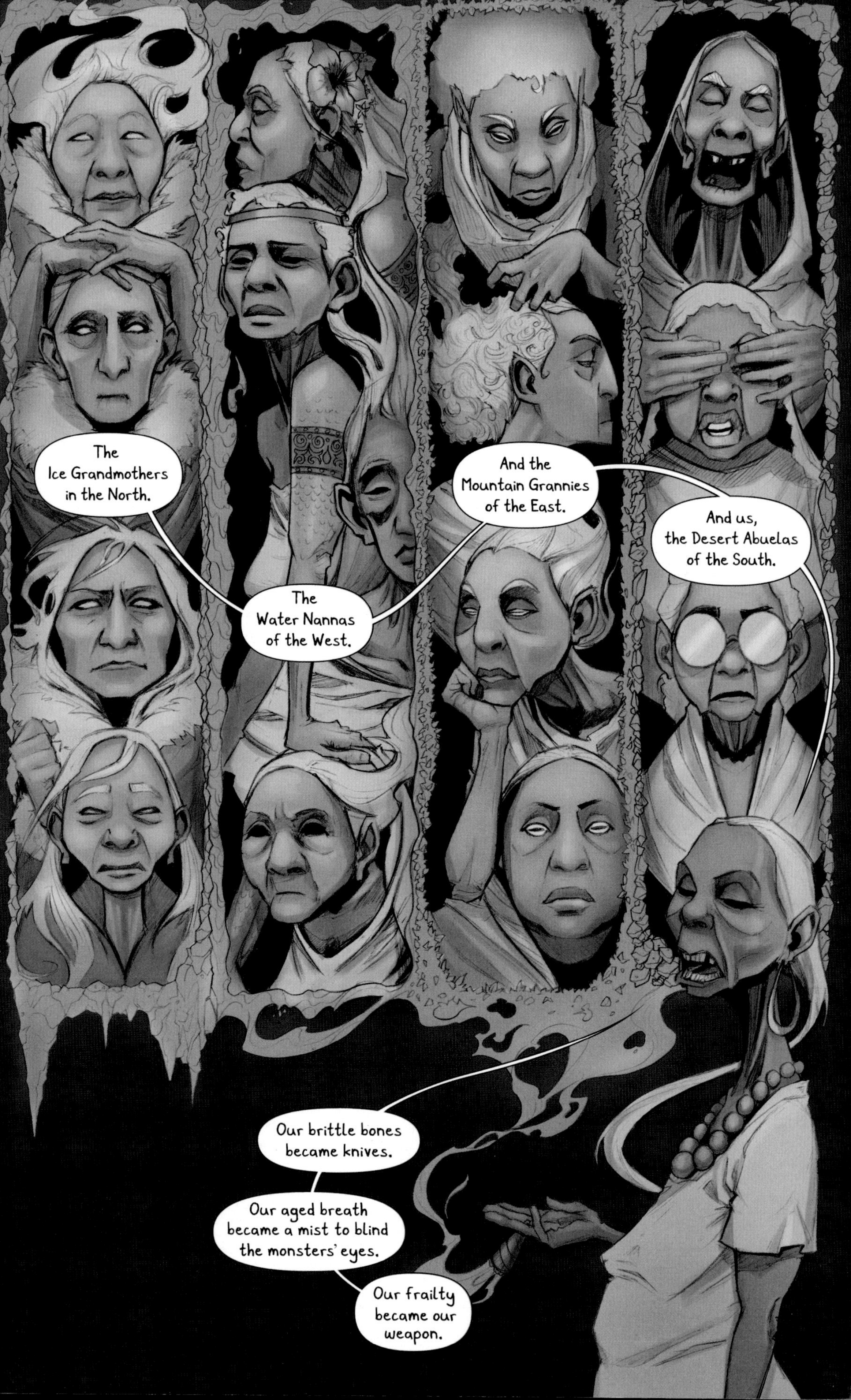
The Ice Grandmothers in the North.
The Water Nannas of the West.
And the Mountain Grannies of the East.
And us, the Desert Abuelas of the South.
Our brittle bones became knives.
Our aged breath became a mist to blind the monsters' eyes.
Our frailty became our weapon.

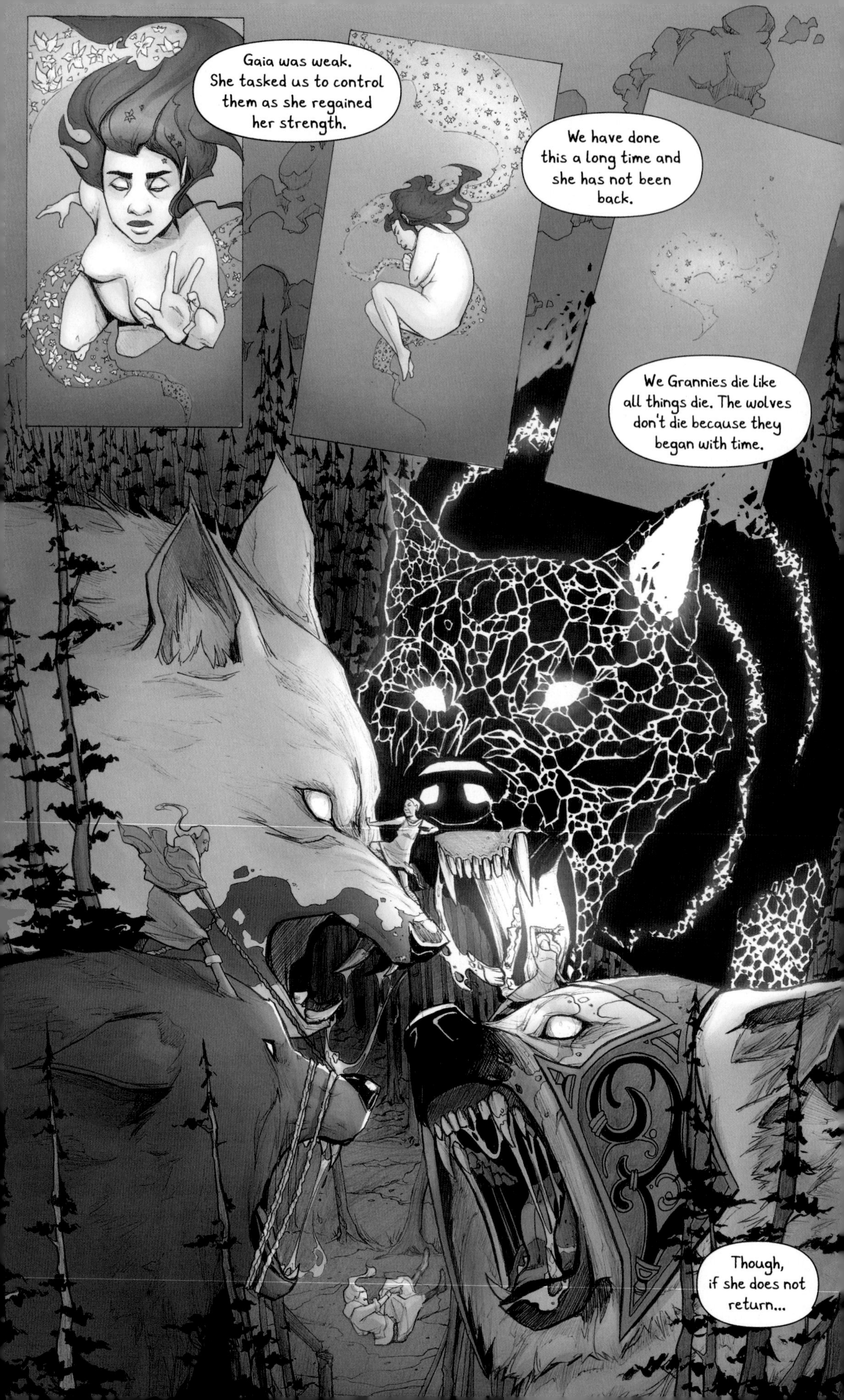
Gaia was weak. She tasked us to control them as she regained her strength.
We have done this a long time and she has not been back.
We Grannies die like all things die. The wolves don't die because they began with time.
Though, if she does not return...

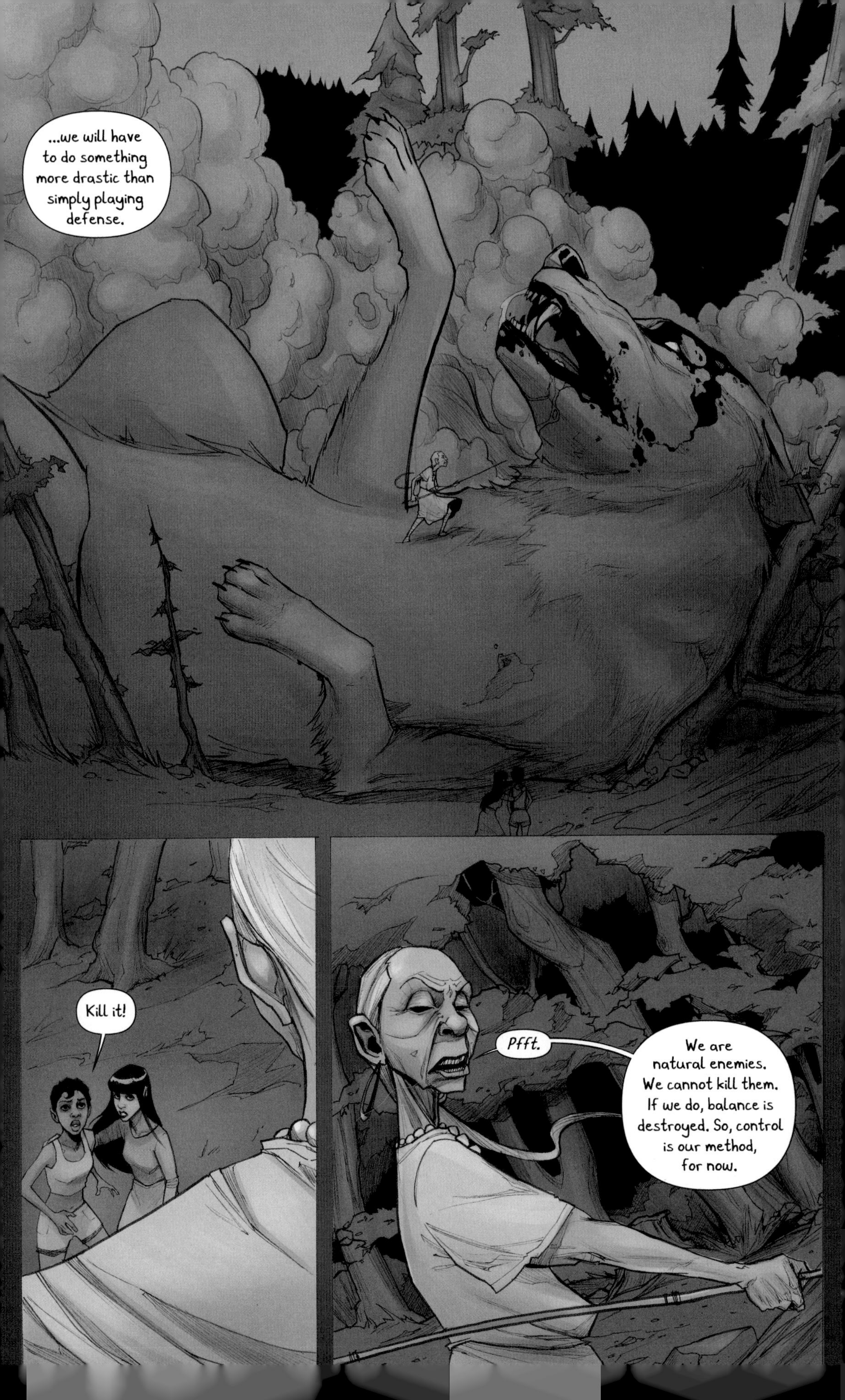
...we will have to do something more drastic than simply playing defense.
Kill it!
Pfft.
We are natural enemies. We cannot kill them. If we do, balance is destroyed. So, control is our method, for now.

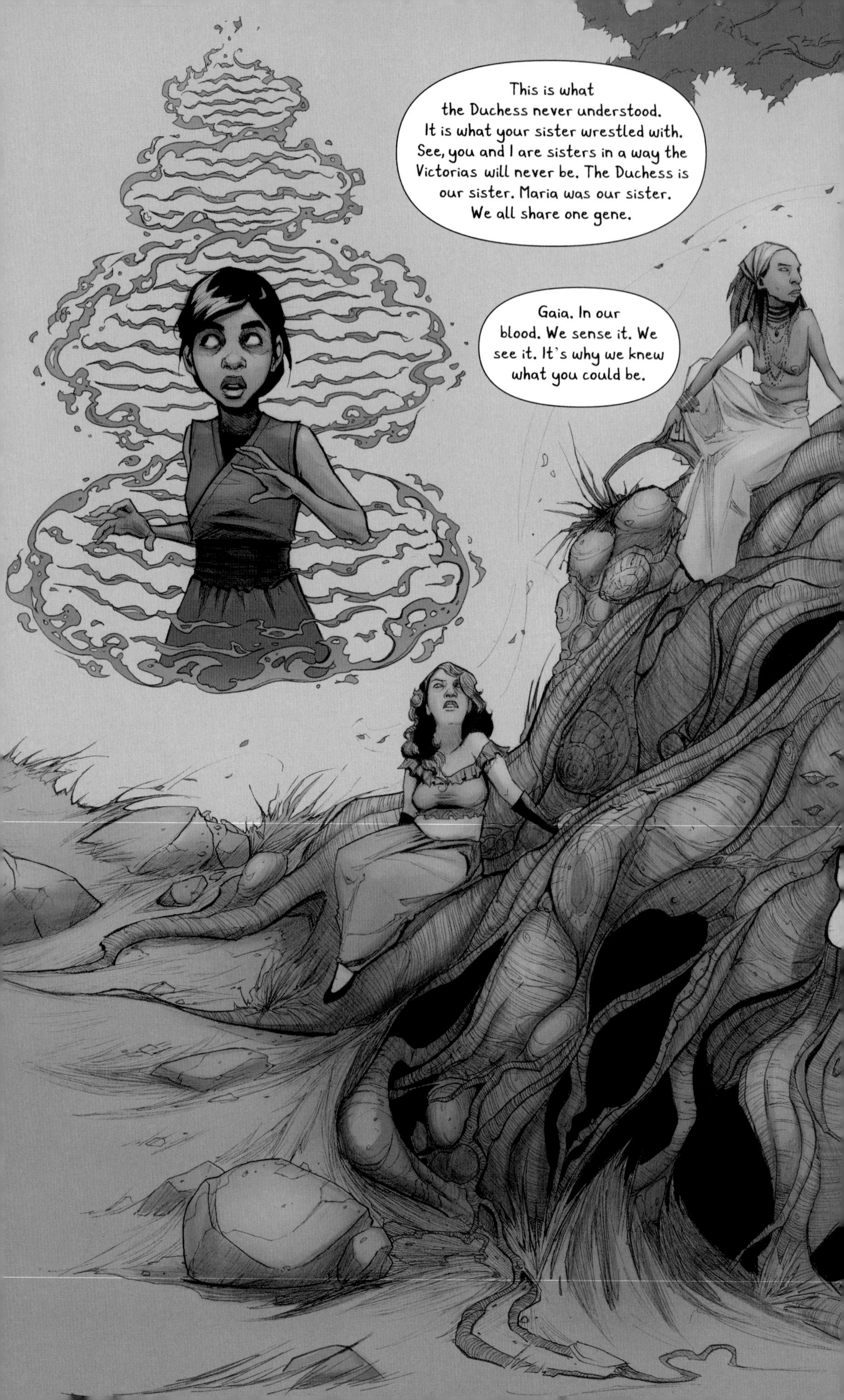
This is what the Duchess never understood. It is what your sister wrestled with. See, you and I are sisters in a way the Victorias will never be. The Duchess is our sister. Maria was our sister. We all share one gene.
Gaia. In our blood. We sense it. We see it. It's why we knew what you could be.

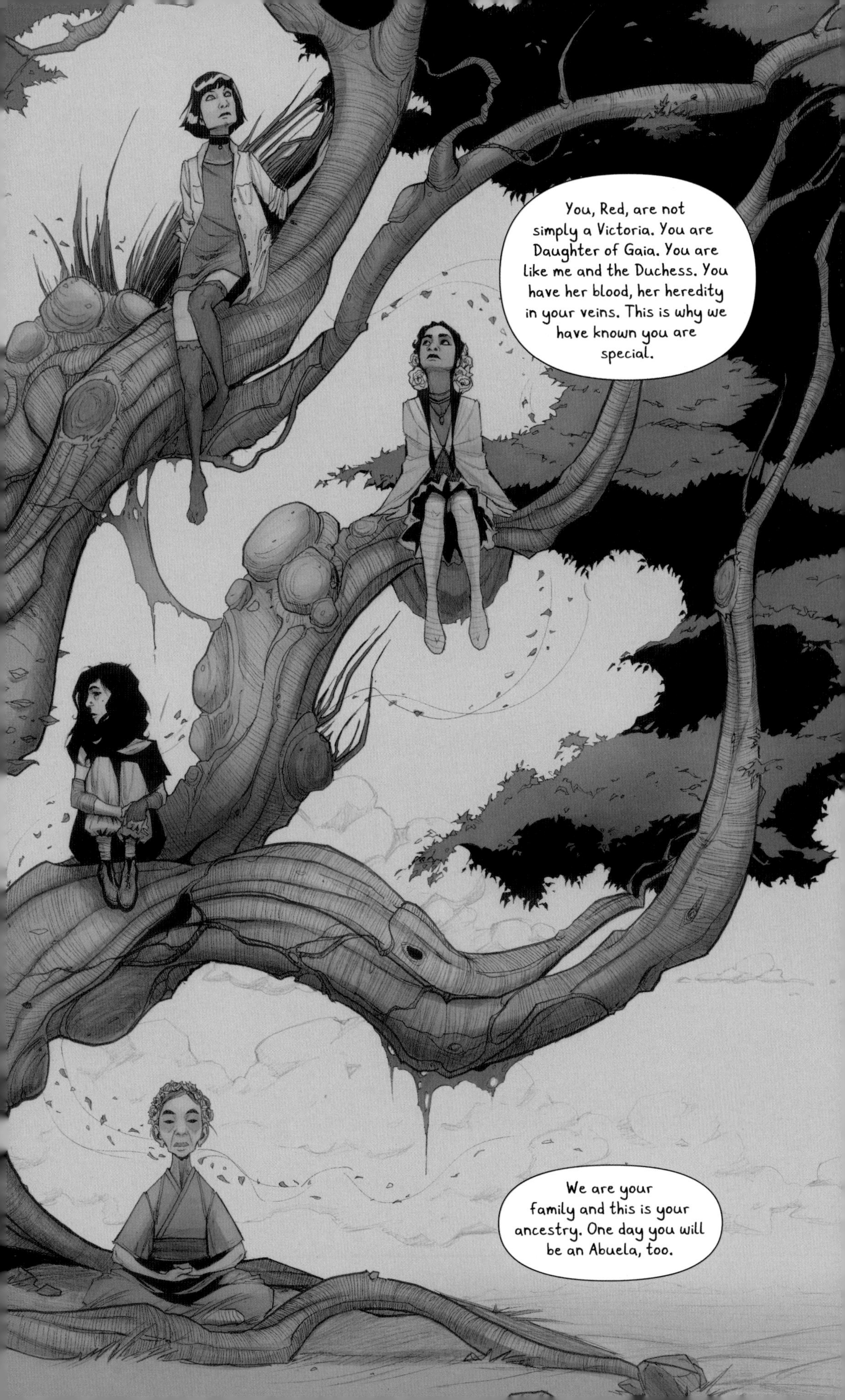
You, Red, are not simply a Victoria. You are Daughter of Gaia. You are like me and the Duchess. You have her blood, her heredity in your veins. This is why we have known you are special.
We are your family and this is your ancestry. One day you will be an Abuela, too.

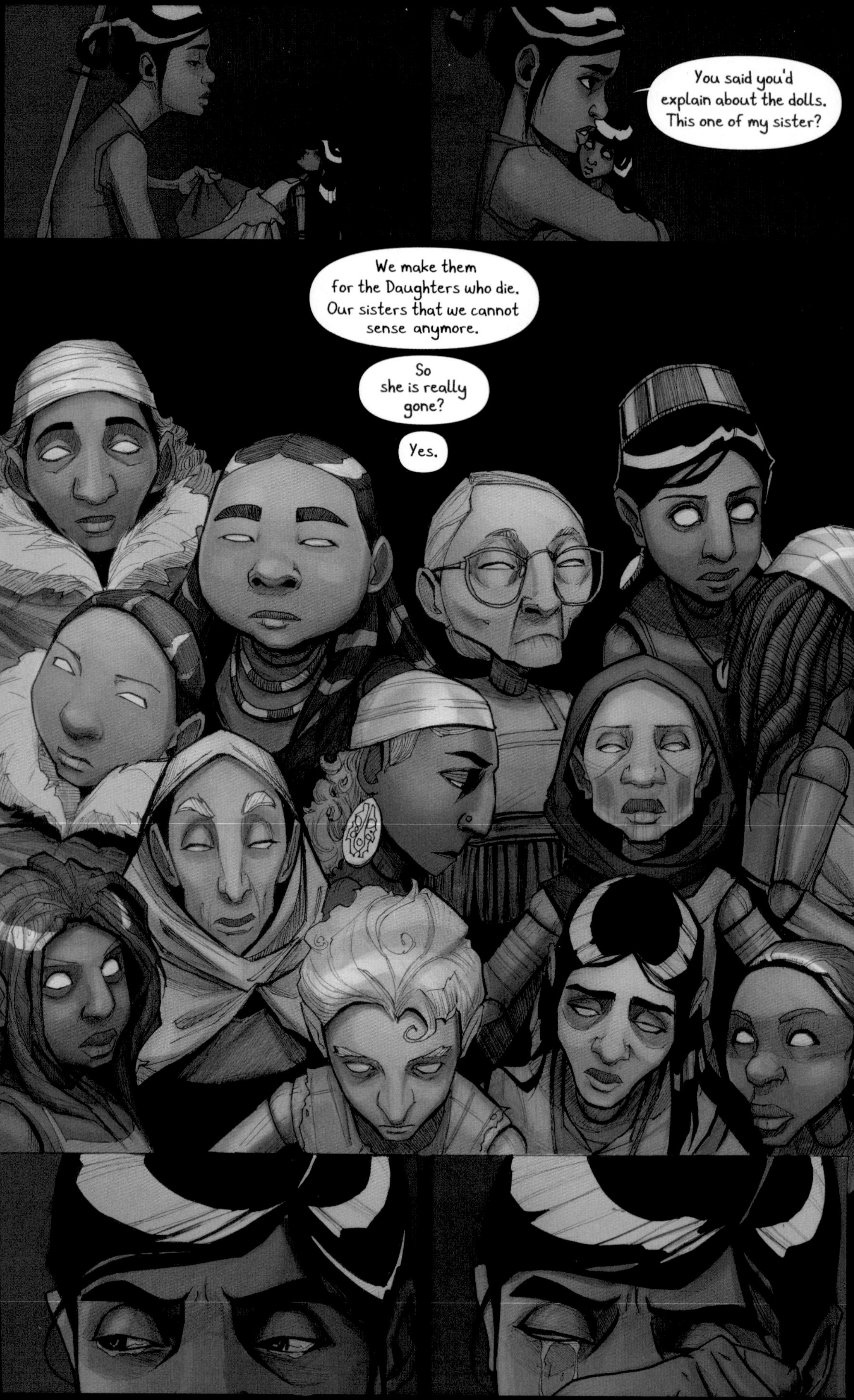
You said you'd explain about the dolls. This one of my sister?
We make them for the Daughters who die. Our sisters that we cannot sense anymore.
So she is really gone?
Yes.

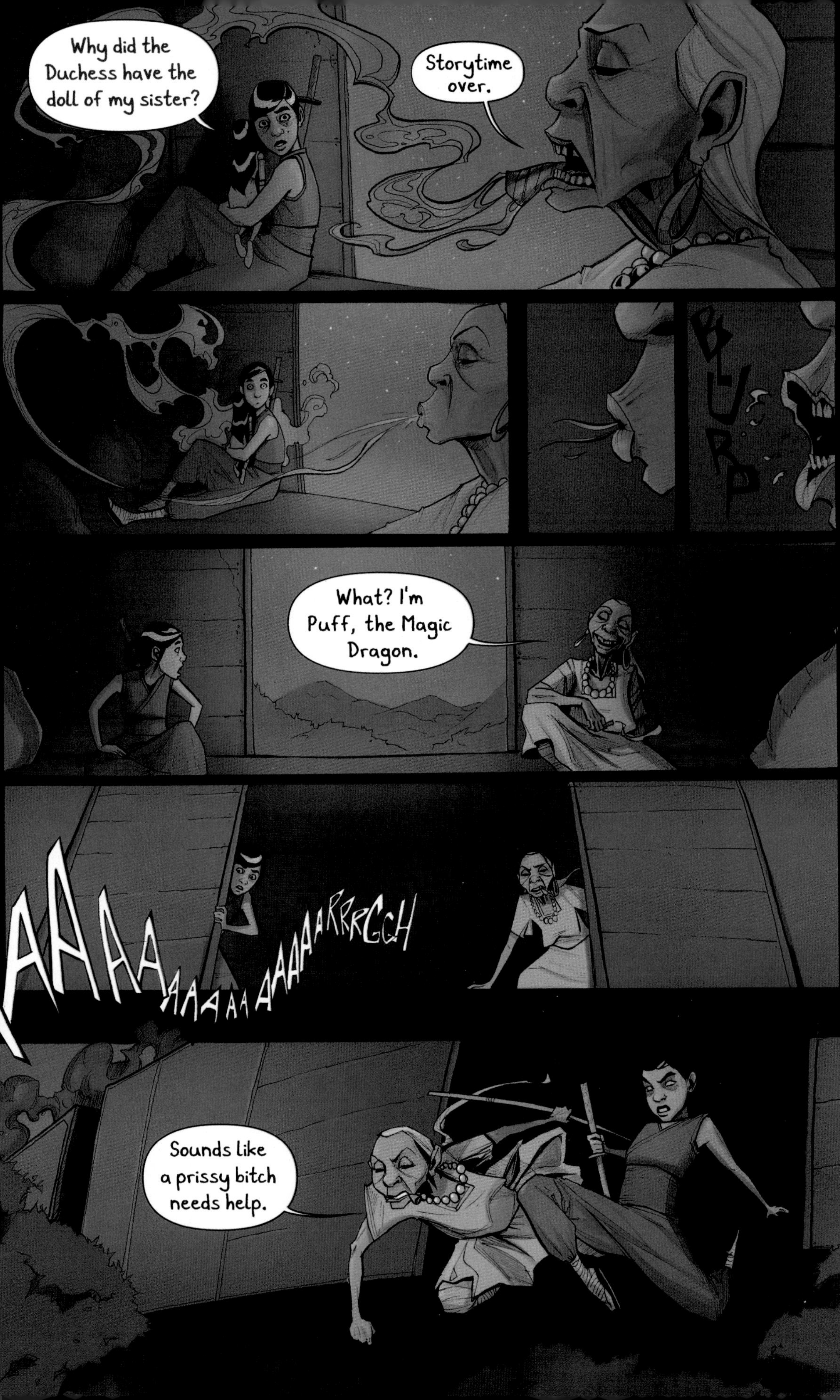
Why did the Duchess have the doll of my sister?
Storytime over.
BLURP
What? I'm Puff, the Magic Dragon.
AAAAAAAAAAAAAARRRGCH
Sounds like a prissy bitch needs help.

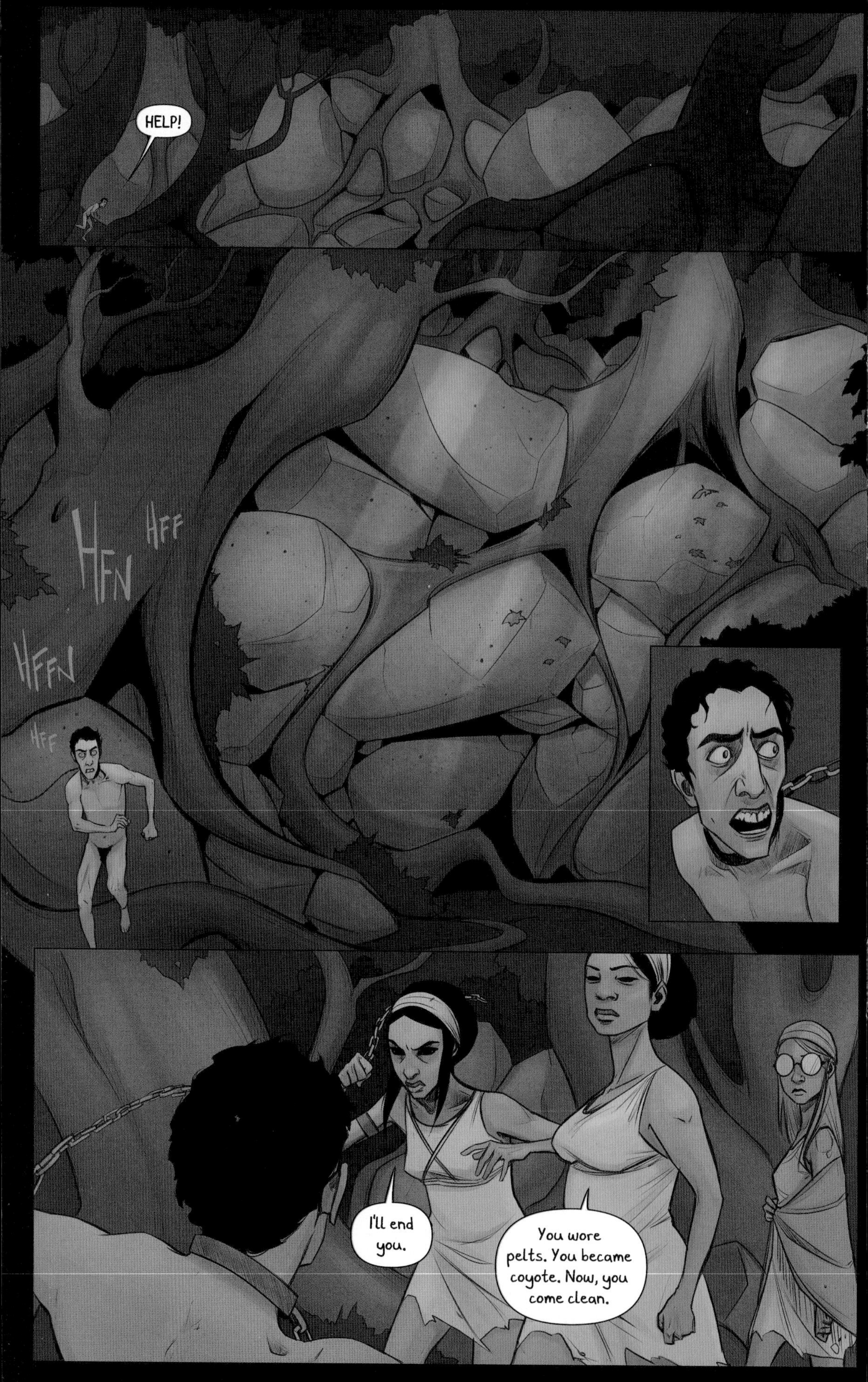
HELP!
HFF
HFN
HFFN
HFF
I'll end you.
You wore pelts. You became coyote. Now, you come clean.

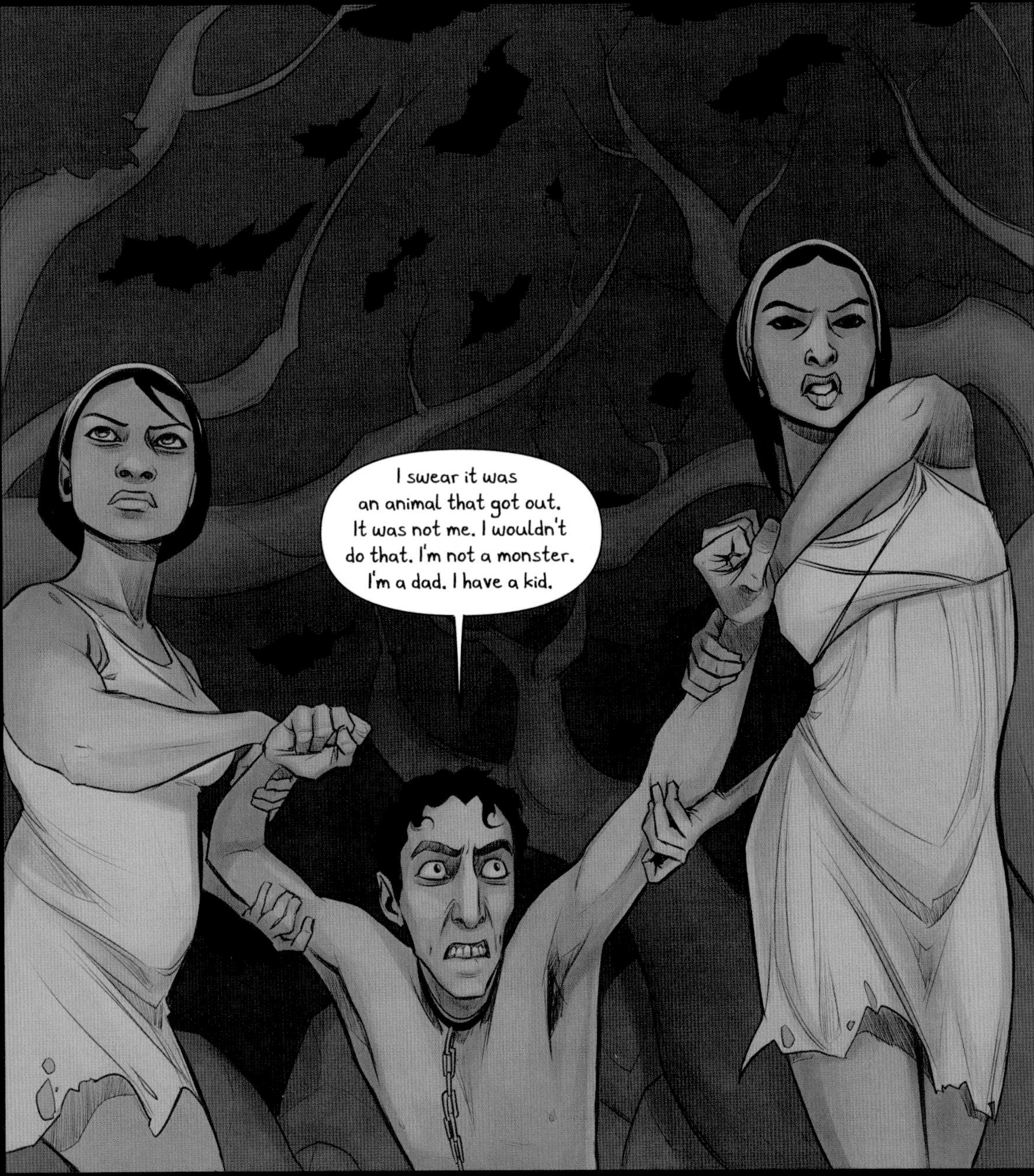
I swear it was an animal that got out. It was not me. I wouldn't do that. I'm not a monster. I'm a dad. I have a kid.

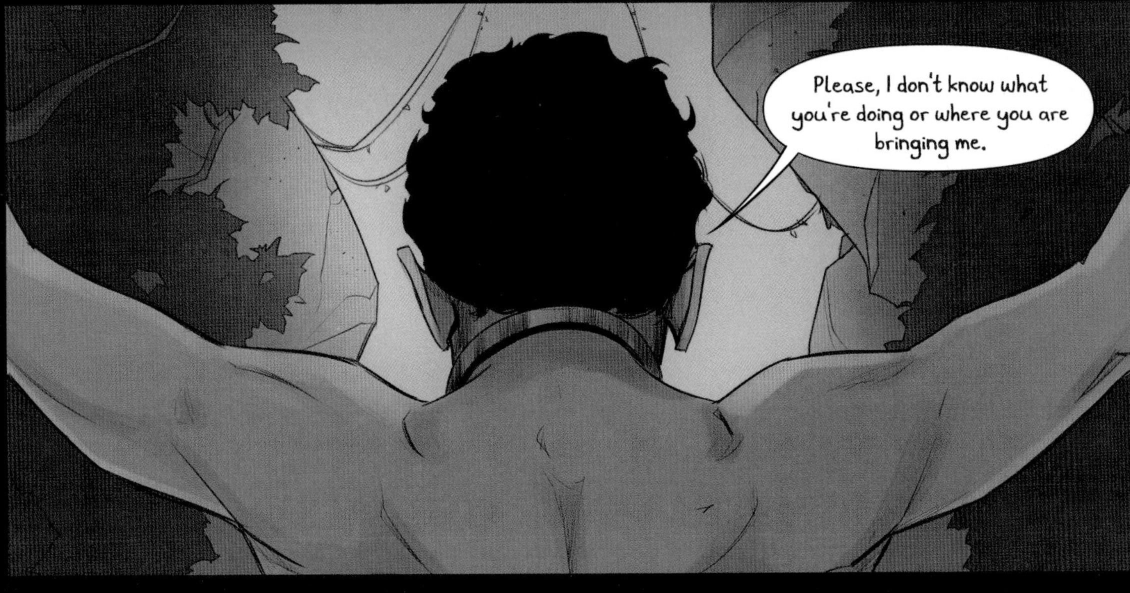
Please, I don't know what you're doing or where you are bringing me.

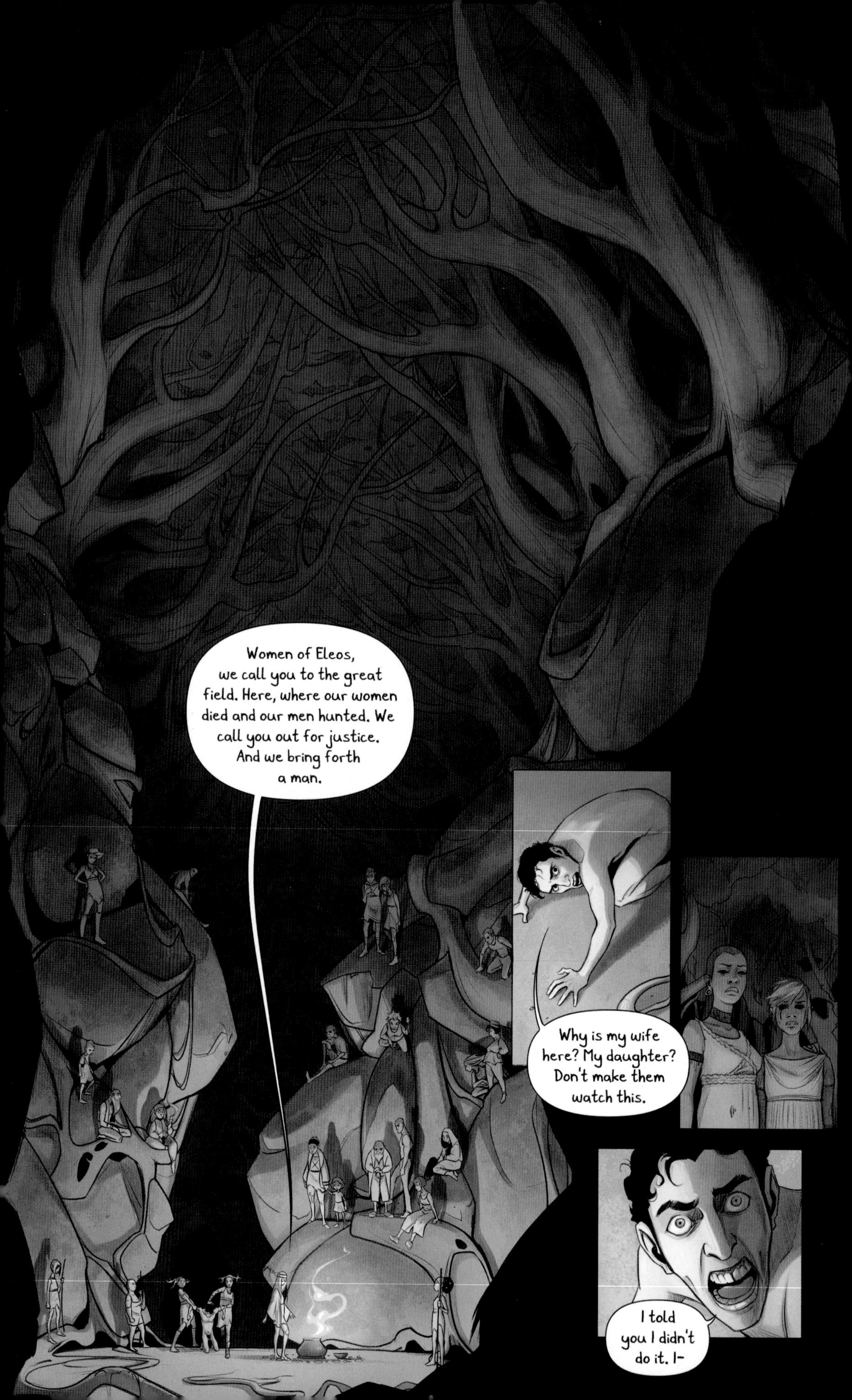
Women of Eleos, we call you to the great field. Here, where our women died and our men hunted. We call you out for justice. And we bring forth a man.
Why is my wife here? My daughter? Don't make them watch this.
I told you I didn't do it. I-

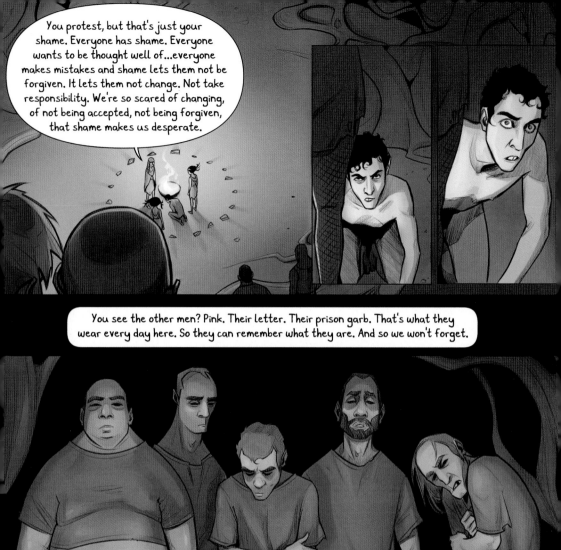

You protest, but that's just your shame. Everyone has shame. Everyone wants to be thought well of...everyone makes mistakes and shame lets them not be forgiven. It lets them not change. Not take responsibility. We're so scared of changing, of not being accepted, not being forgiven, that shame makes us desperate.

You see the other men? Pink. Their letter. Their prison garb. That's what they wear every day here. So they can remember what they are. And so we won't forget.

Eleos is the Goddess of Mercy. And I am Olive. Otherwise known as her fucking hammer.

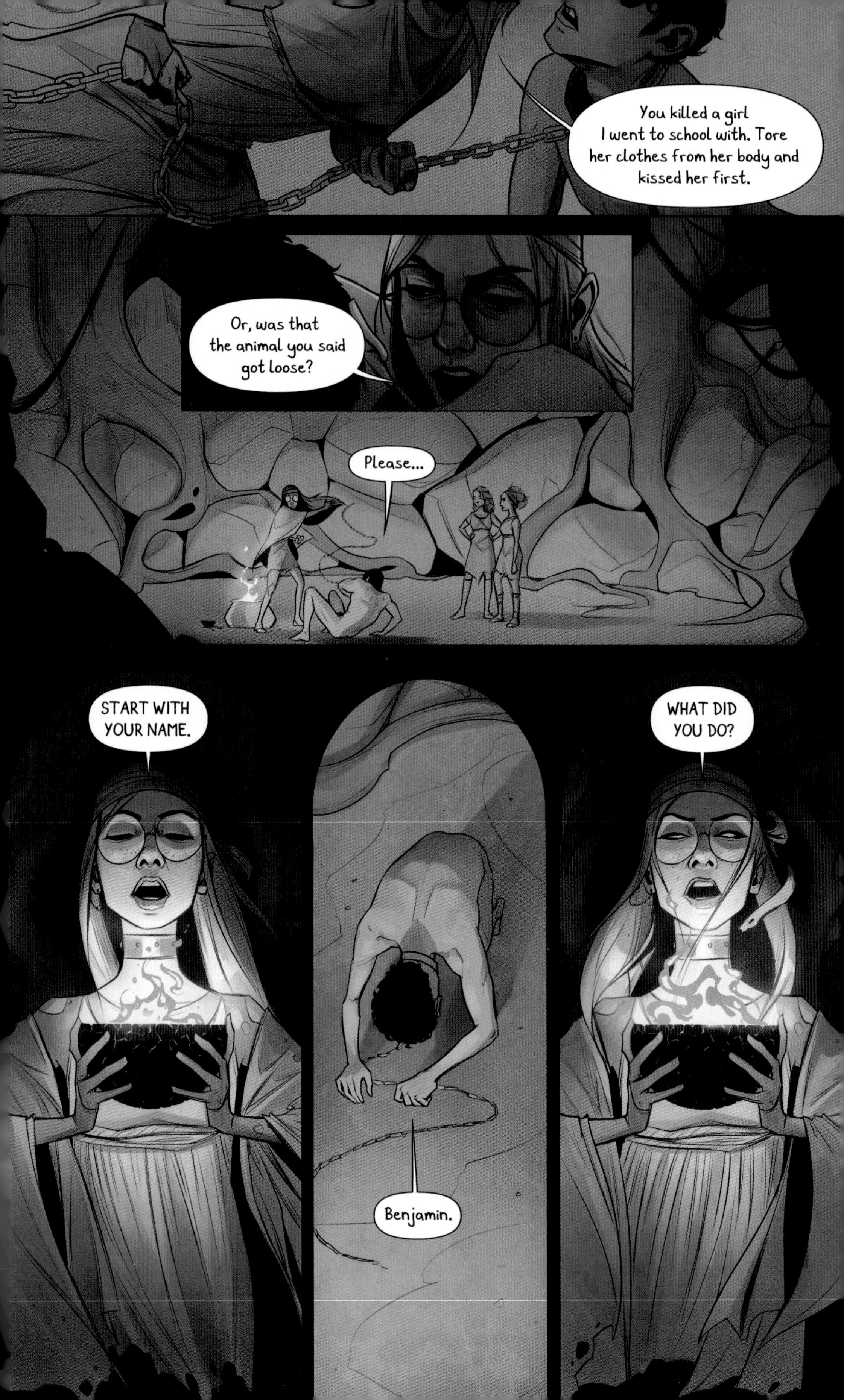
You killed a girl I went to school with. Tore her clothes from her body and kissed her first.
Or, was that the animal you said got loose?
Please...
START WITH YOUR NAME.
Benjamin.
WHAT DID YOU DO?

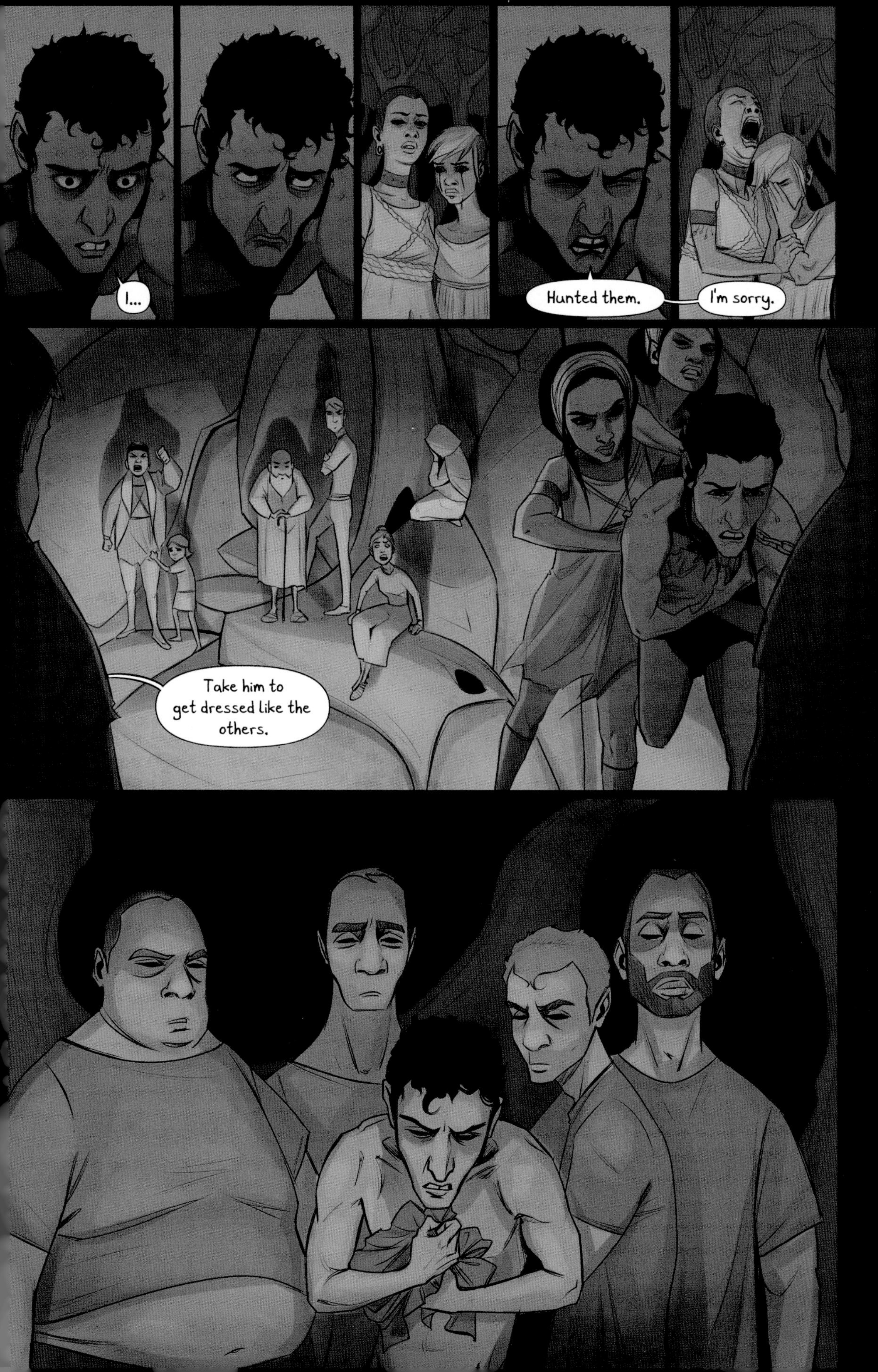
I...
Hunted them.
I'm sorry.
Take him to get dressed like the others.

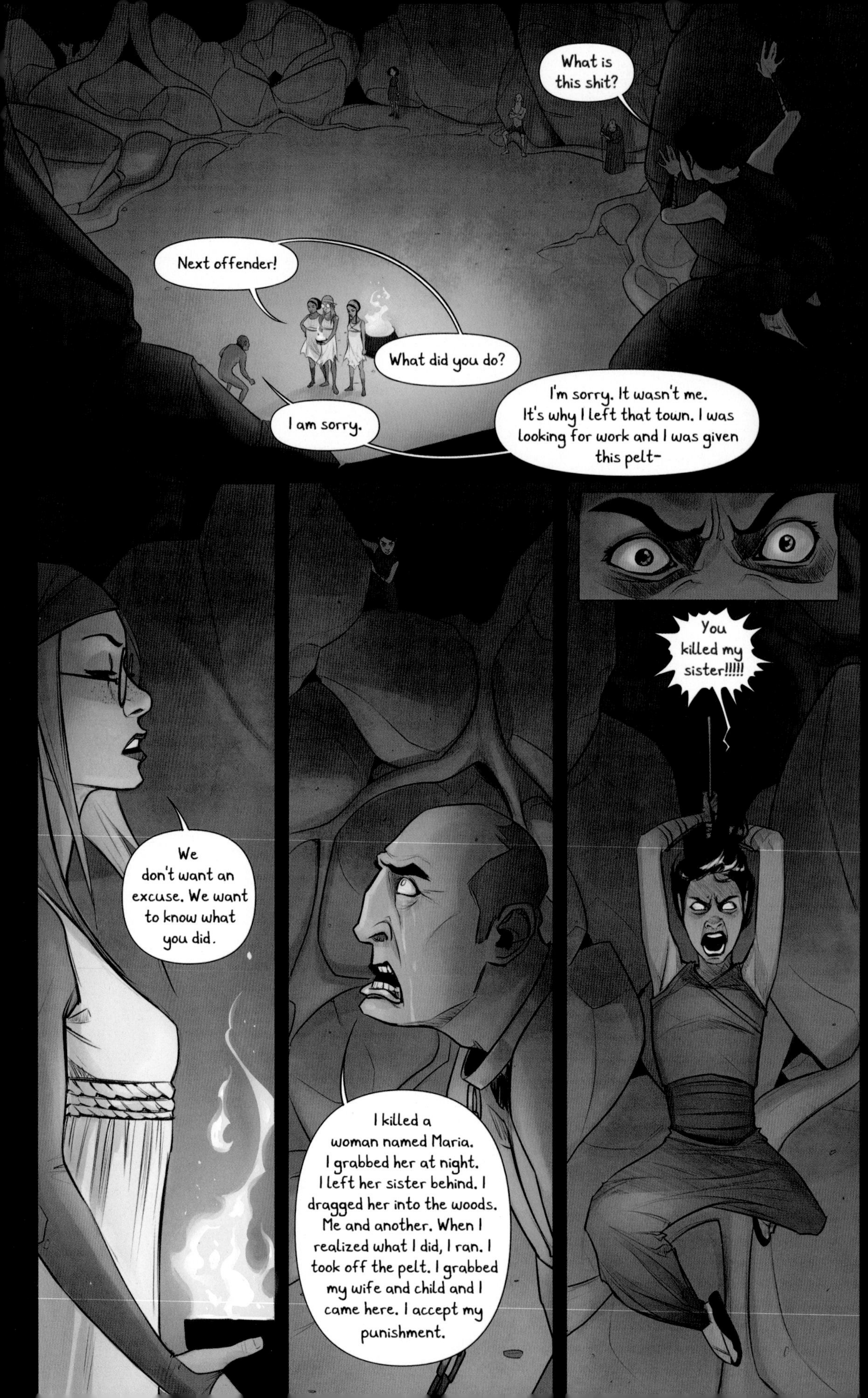
What is this shit?
Next offender!
What did you do?
I am sorry.
I'm sorry. It wasn't me. It's why I left that town. I was looking for work and I was given this pelt-
We don't want an excuse. We want to know what you did.
I killed a woman named Maria. I grabbed her at night. I left her sister behind. I dragged her into the woods. Me and another. When I realized what I did, I ran. I took off the pelt. I grabbed my wife and child and I came here. I accept my punishment.
You killed my sister!!!!!

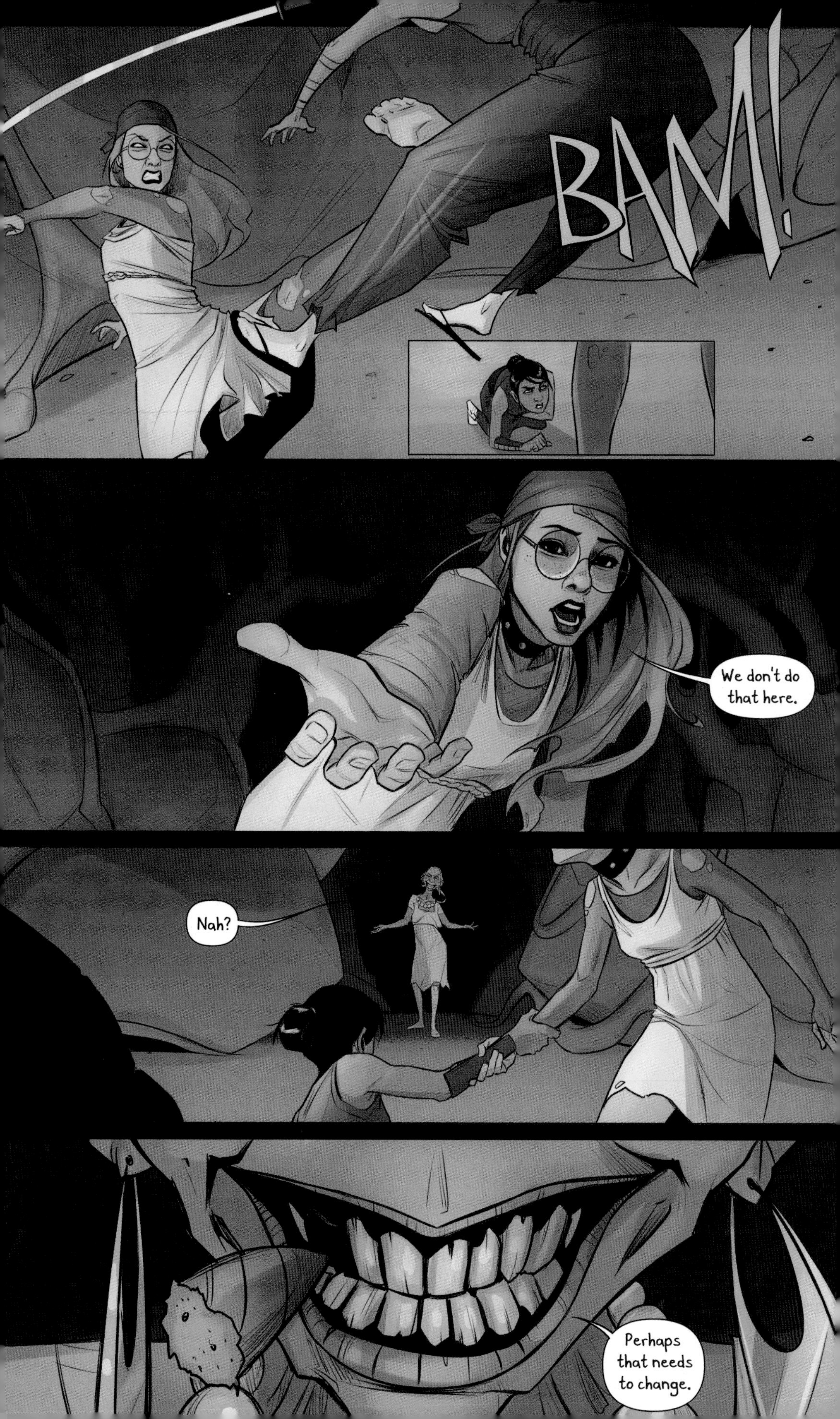
BAM!
We don't do that here.
Nah?
Perhaps that needs to change.

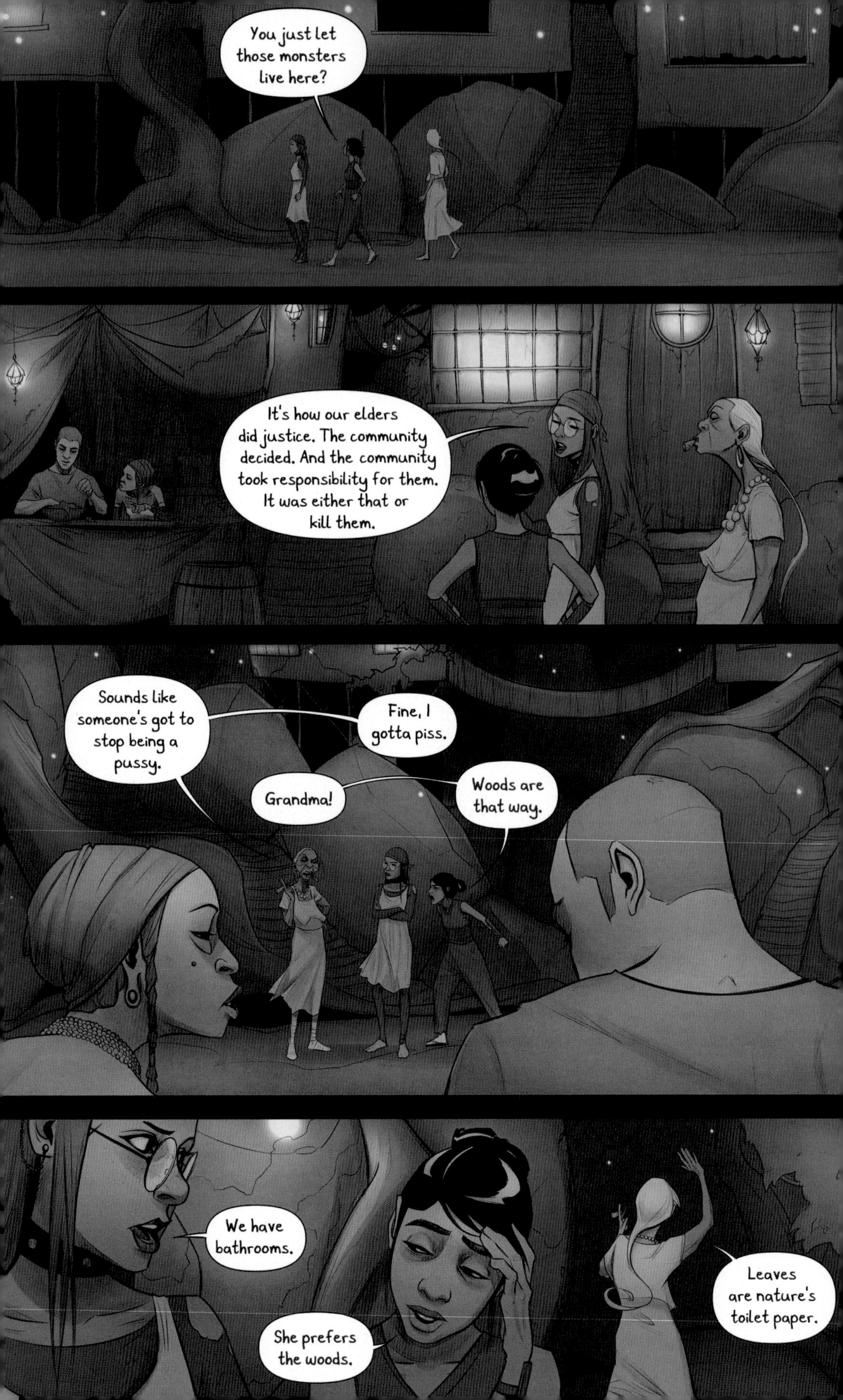
You just let those monsters live here?
It's how our elders did justice. The community decided. And the community took responsibility for them. It was either that or kill them.
Sounds like someone's got to stop being a pussy.
Fine, I gotta piss.
Grandma!
Woods are that way.
We have bathrooms.
She prefers the woods.
Leaves are nature's toilet paper.

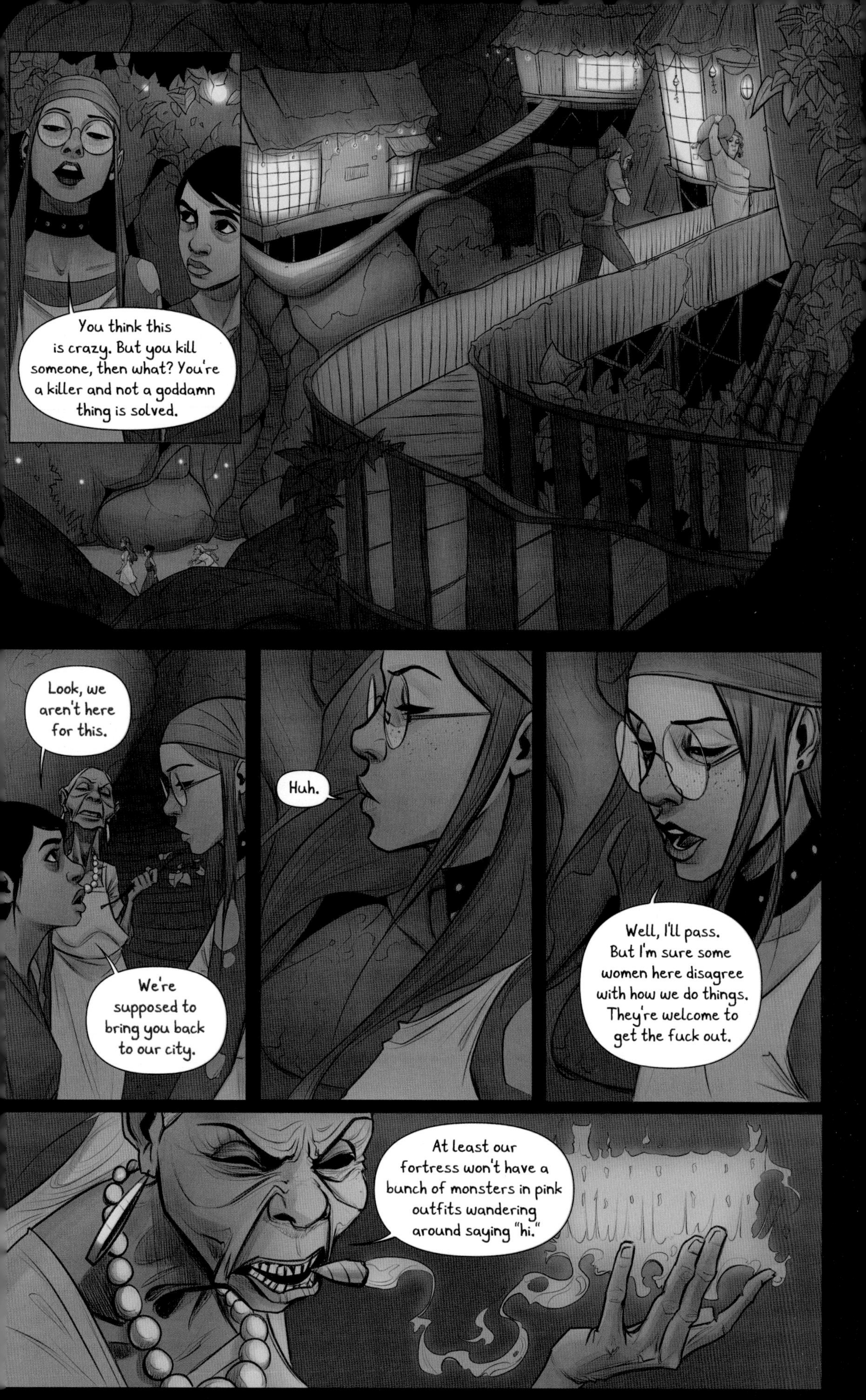
You think this is crazy. But you kill someone, then what? You're a killer and not a goddamn thing is solved.
Look, we aren't here for this.
We're supposed to bring you back to our city.
Huh.
Well, I'll pass. But I'm sure some women here disagree with how we do things. They're welcome to get the fuck out.
At least our fortress won't have a bunch of monsters in pink outfits wandering around saying "hi."

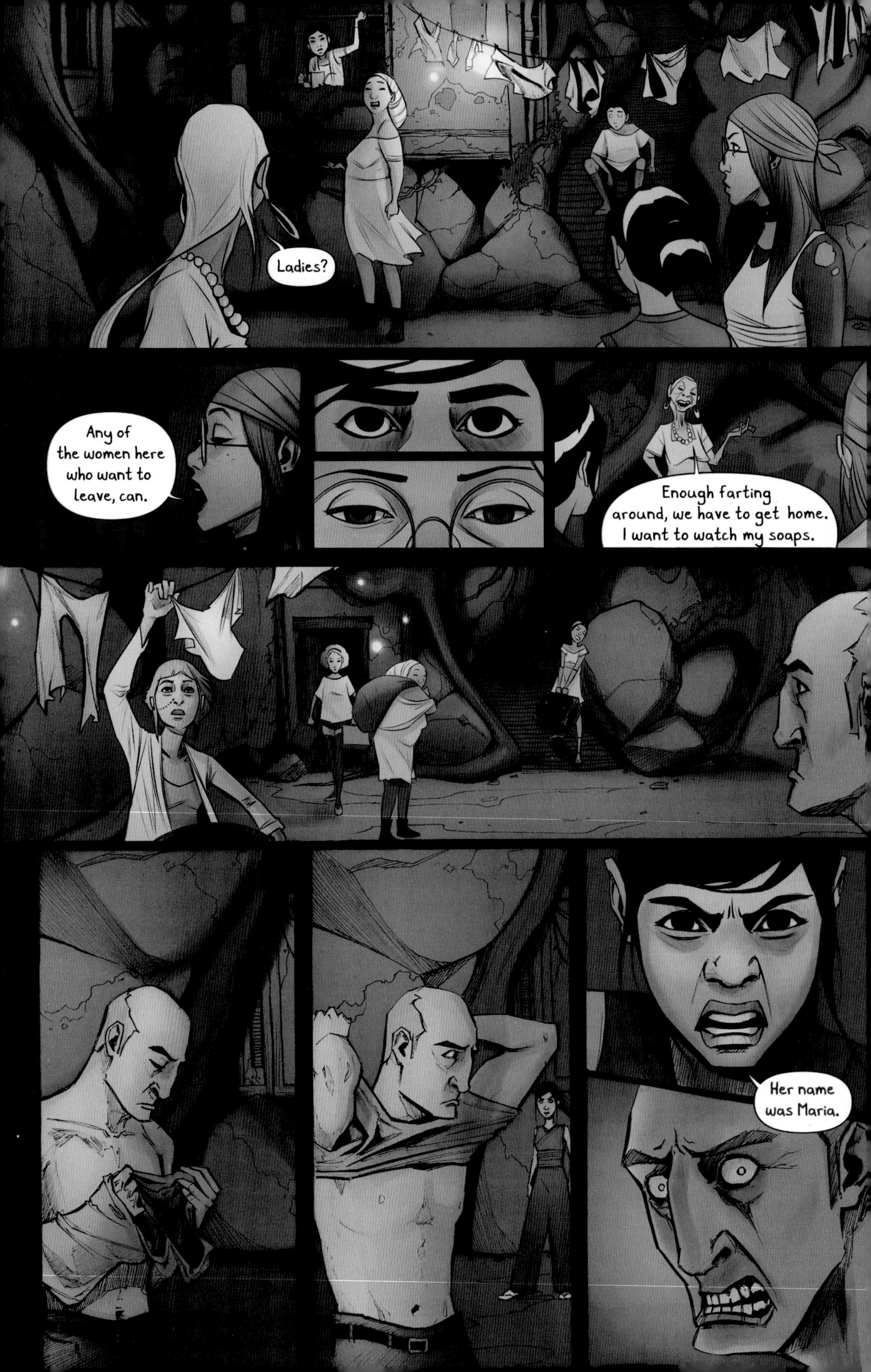
Ladies?
Any of the women here who want to leave, can.
Enough farting around, we have to get home. I want to watch my soaps.
Her name was Maria.

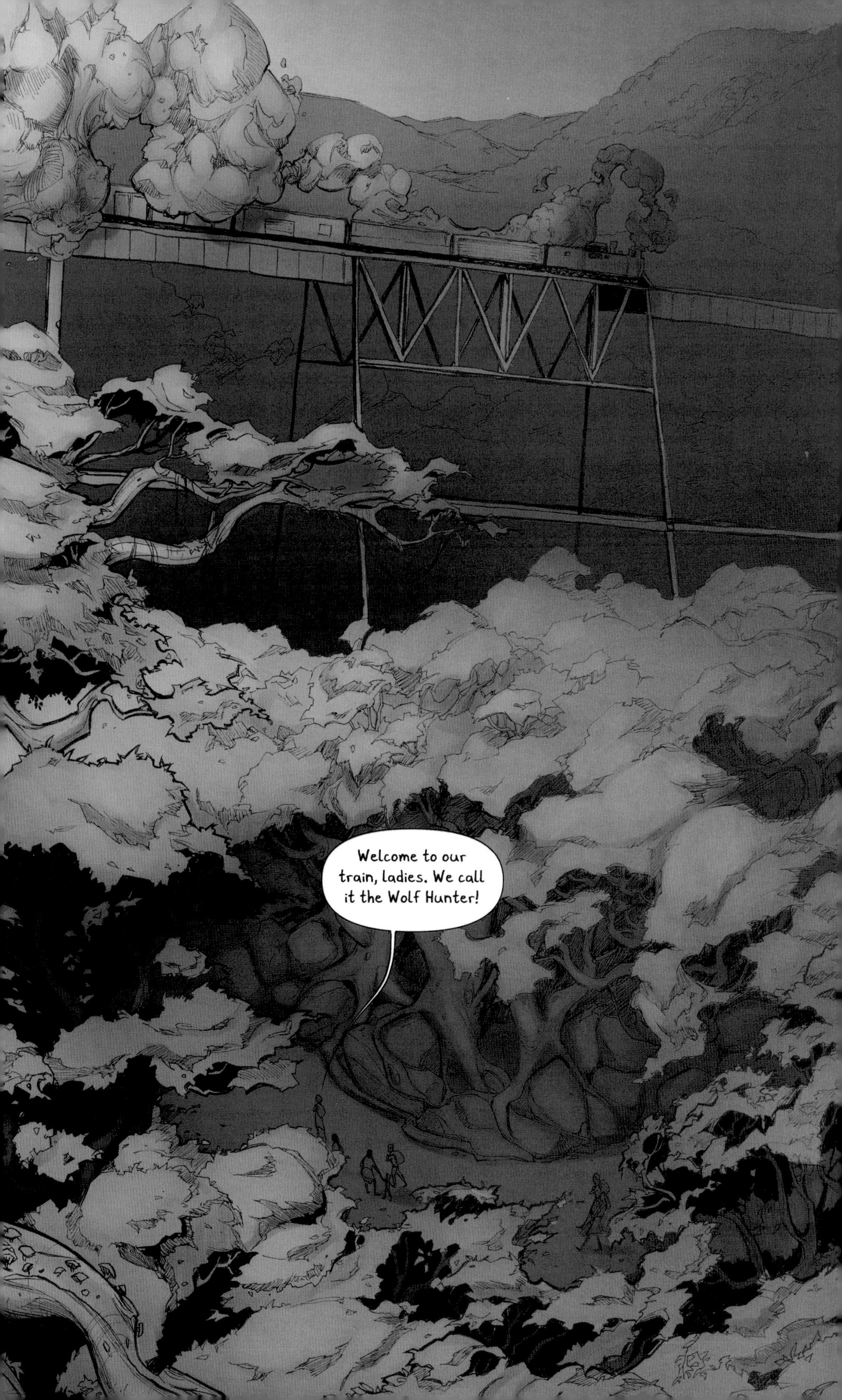
Welcome to our train, ladies. We call it the Wolf Hunter!

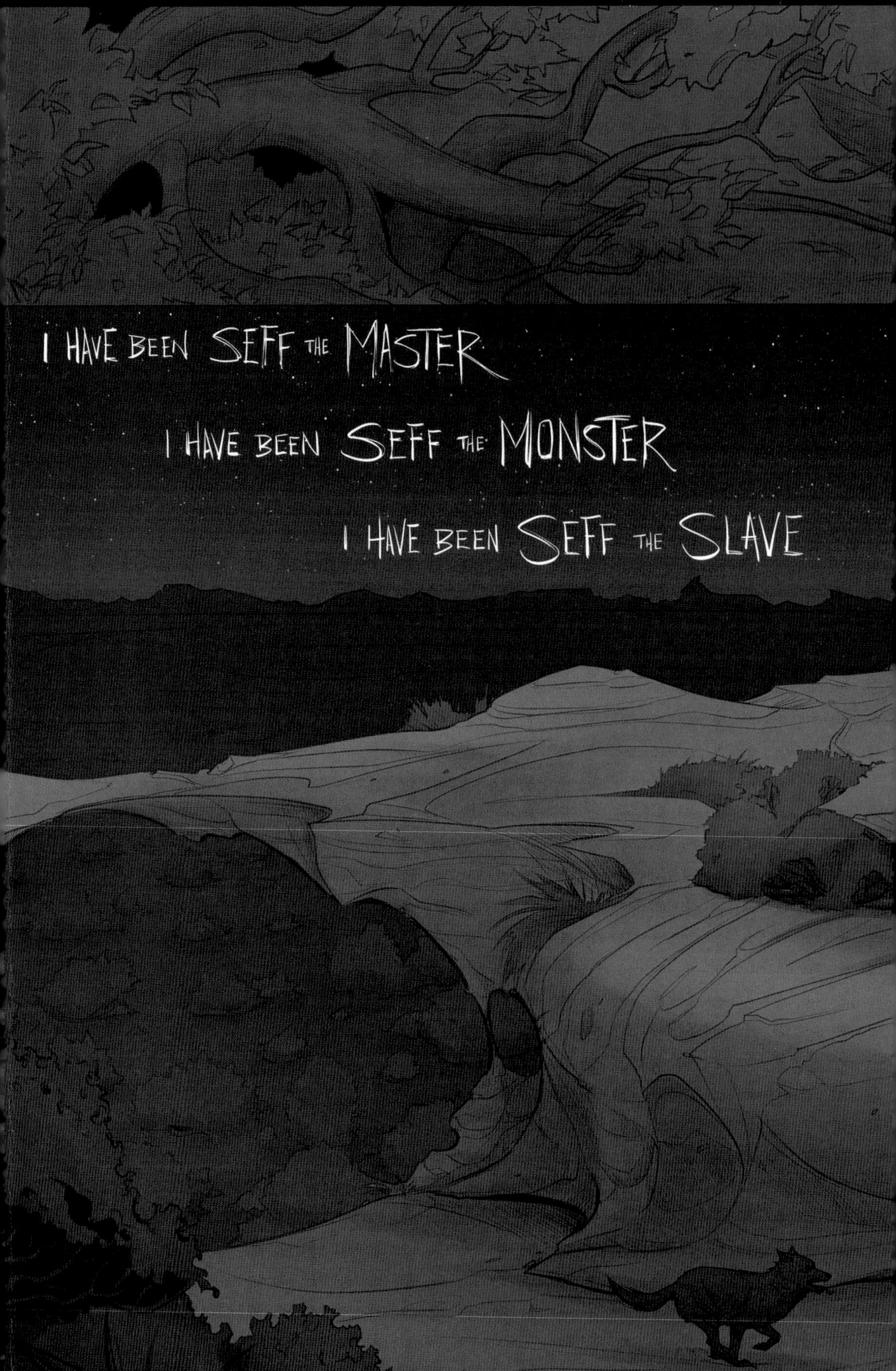
I HAVE BEEN SEFF THE MASTER
I HAVE BEEN SEFF THE MONSTER
I HAVE BEEN SEFF THE SLAVE

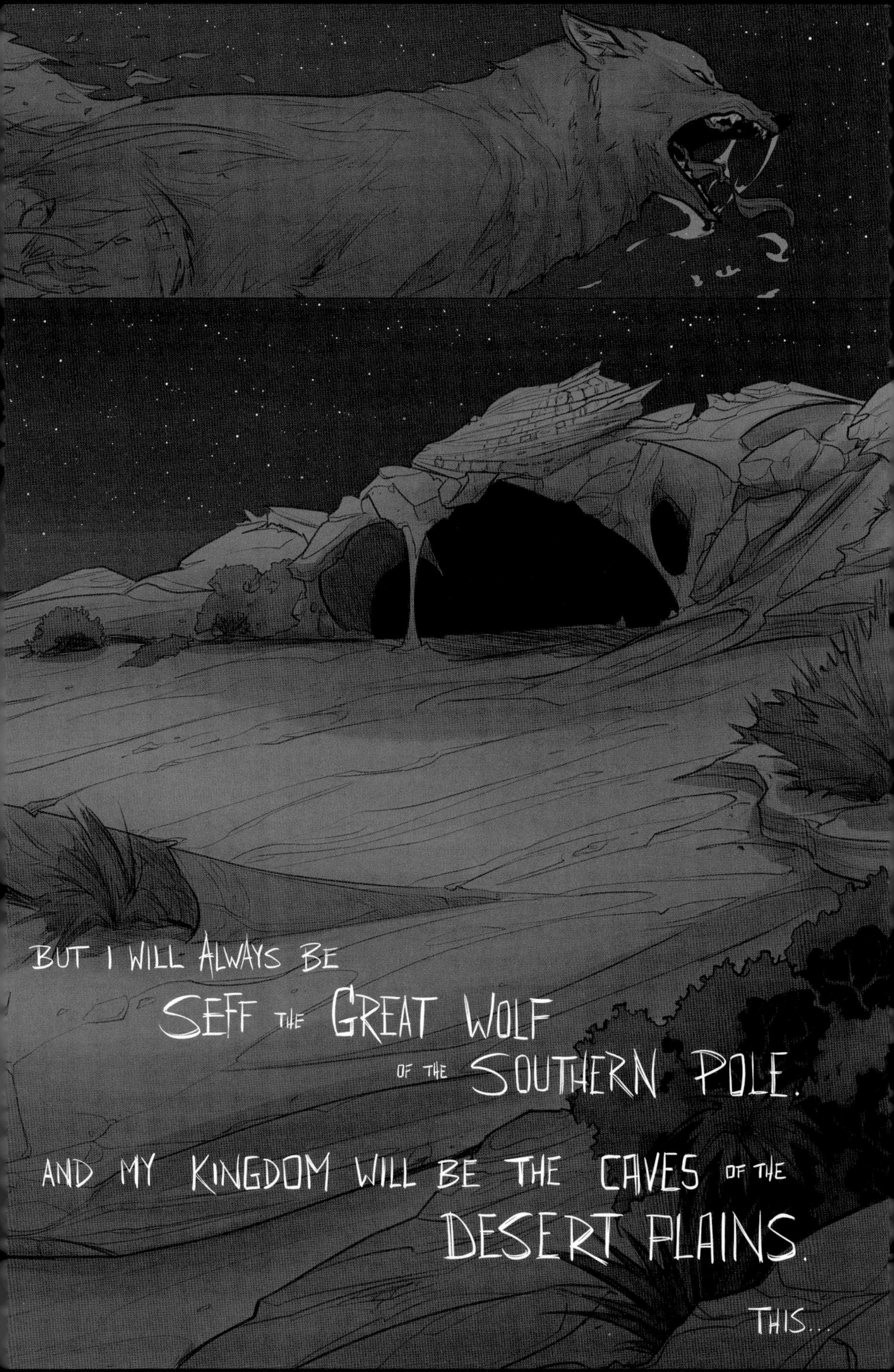
BUT I WILL ALWAYS BE
SEFF THE GREAT WOLF
OF THE SOUTHERN POLE.
AND MY KINGDOM WILL BE THE CAVES OF THE
DESERT PLAINS.
THIS...

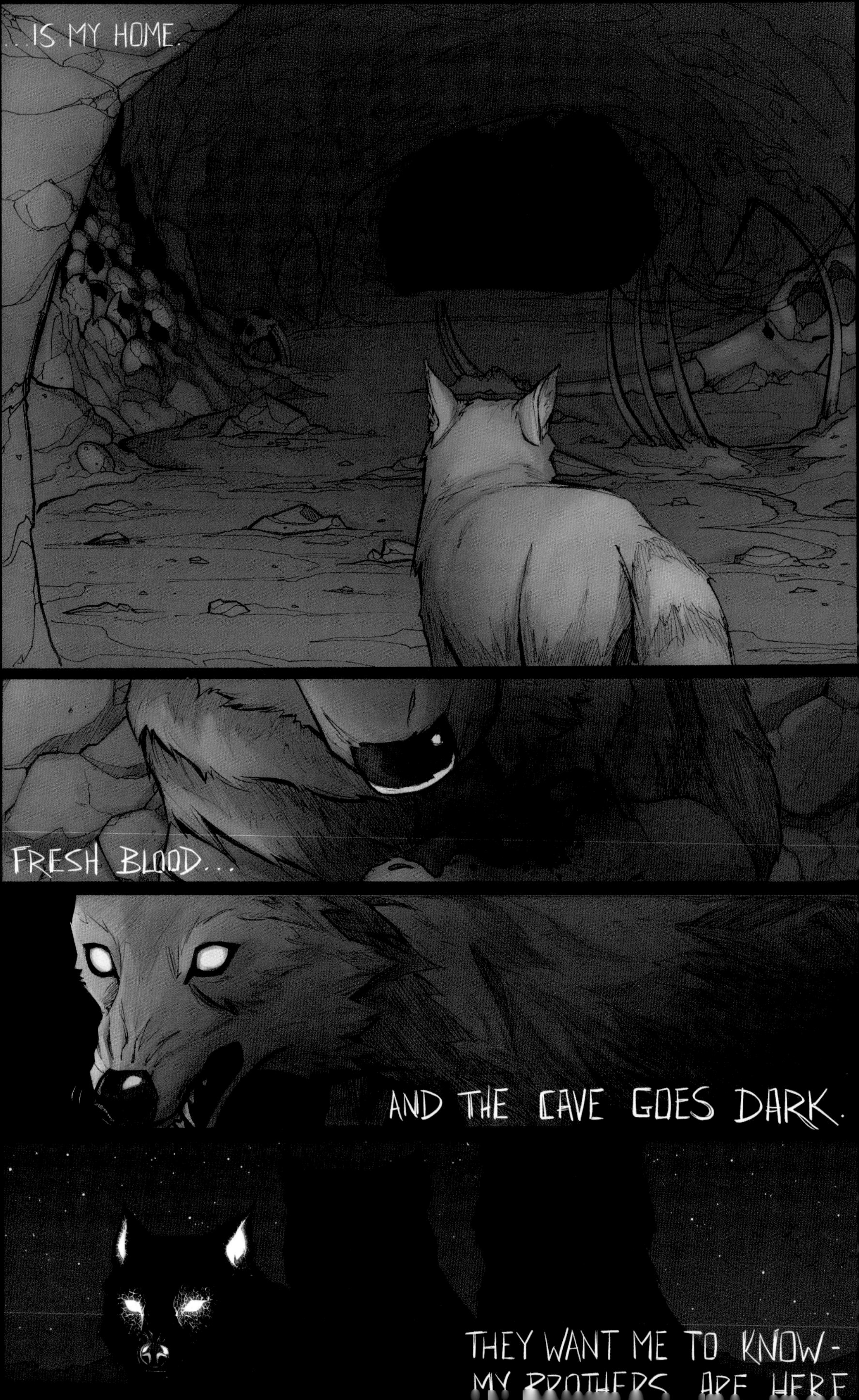
...IS MY HOME.
FRESH BLOOD...
AND THE CAVE GOES DARK.
THEY WANT ME TO KNOW-
MY BROTHERS ARE HERE

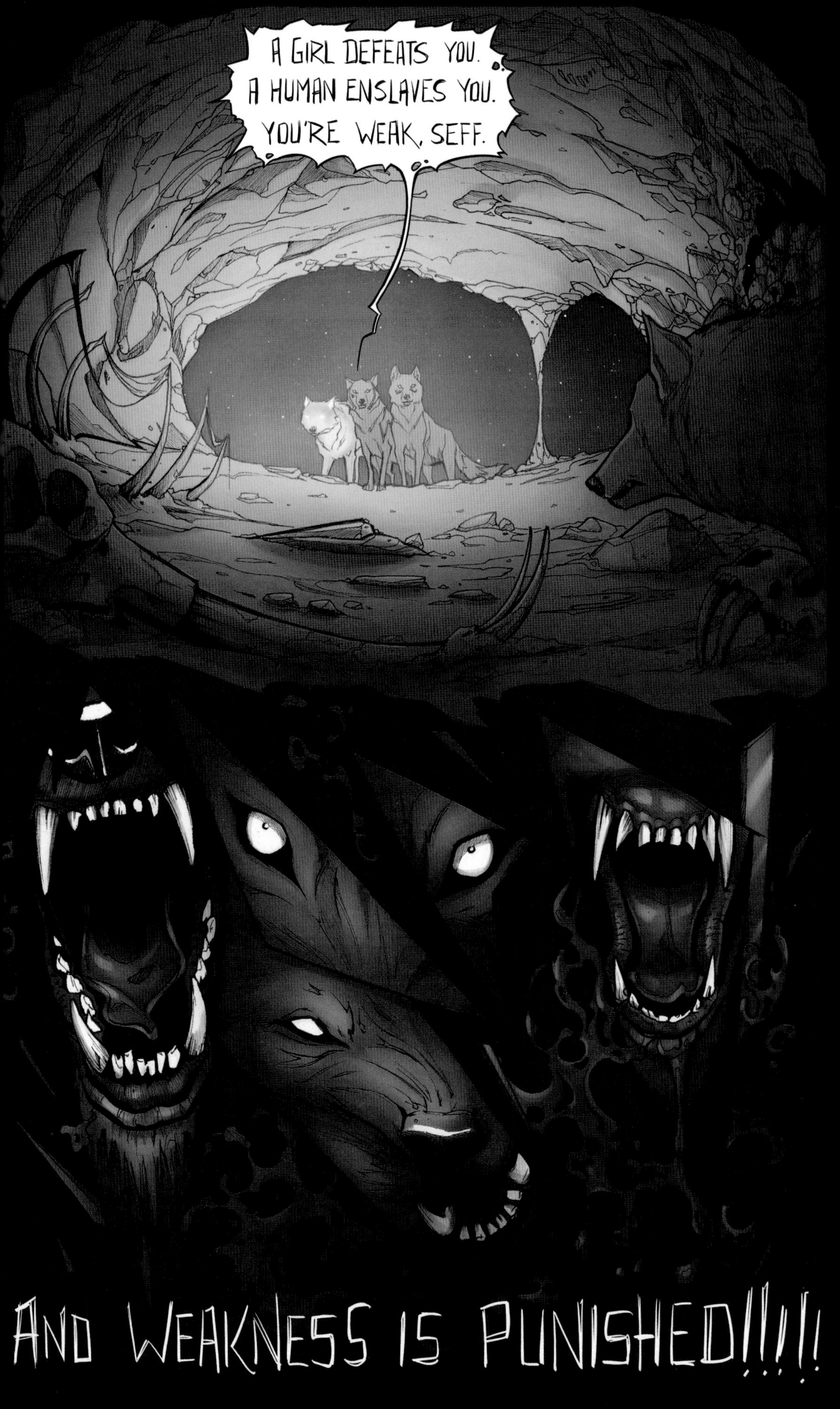
A GIRL DEFEATS YOU. A HUMAN ENSLAVES YOU. YOU'RE WEAK, SEFF.
AND WEAKNESS IS PUNISHED!!!!!

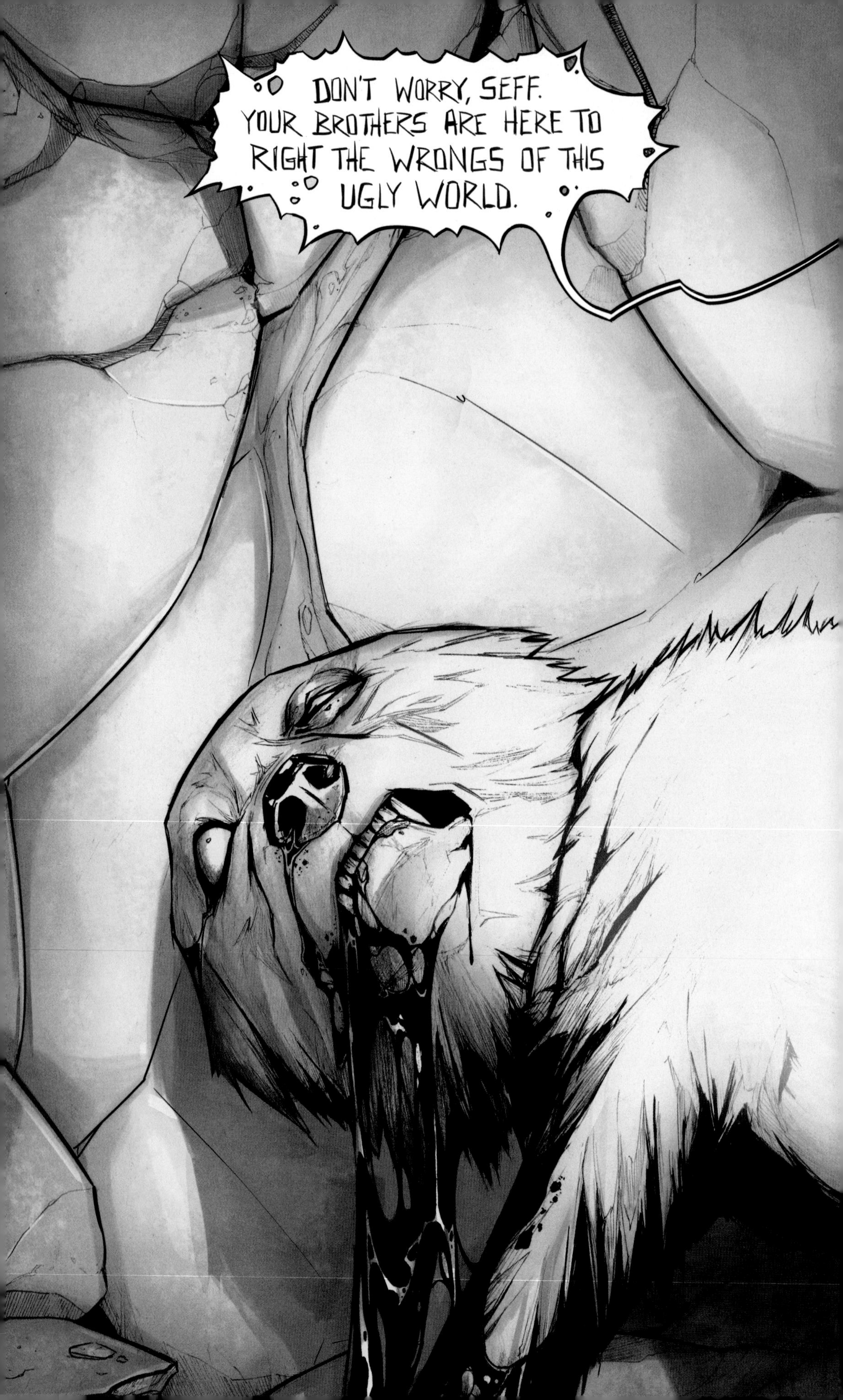
DON'T WORRY, SEFF. YOUR BROTHERS ARE HERE TO RIGHT THE WRONGS OF THIS UGLY WORLD.

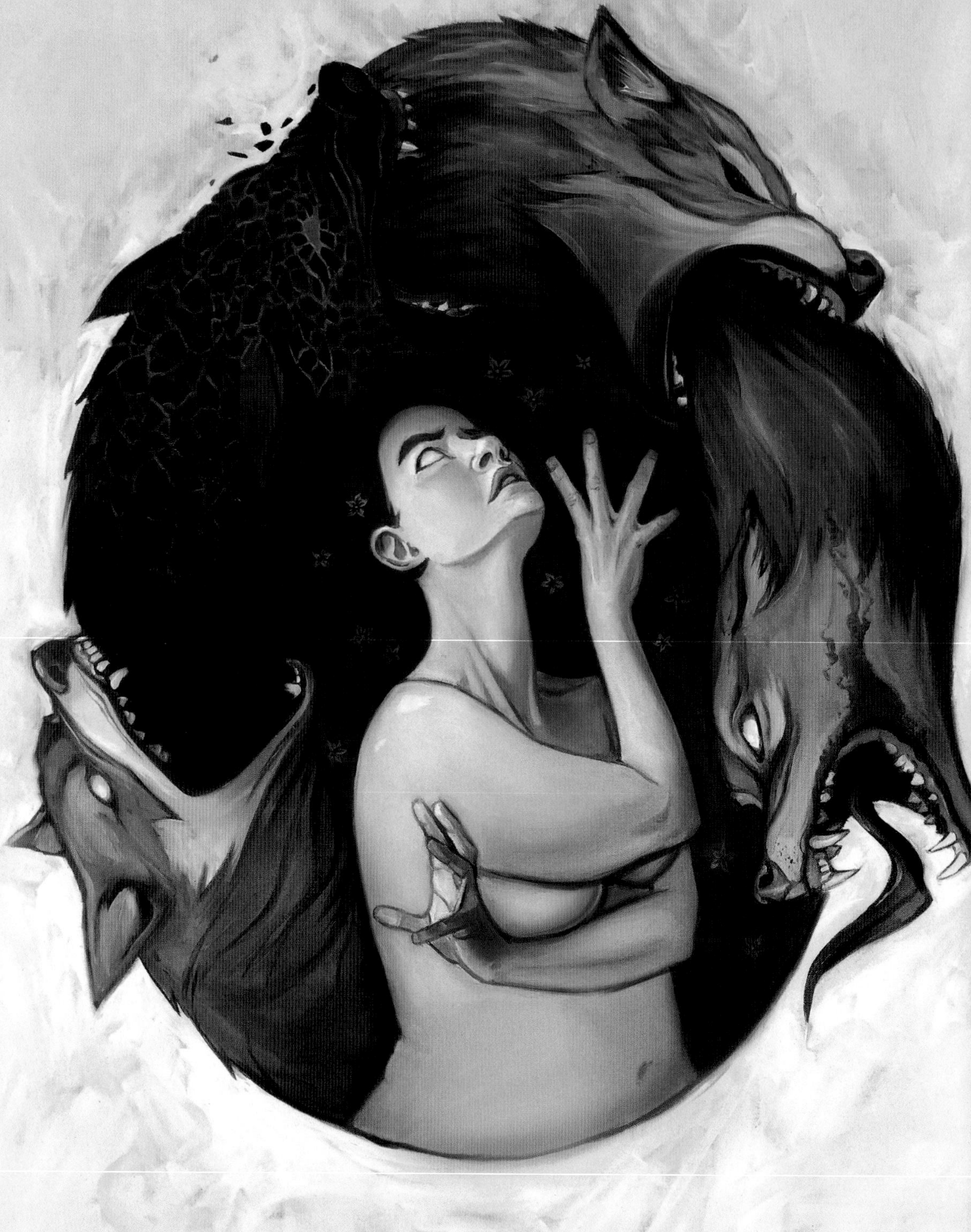

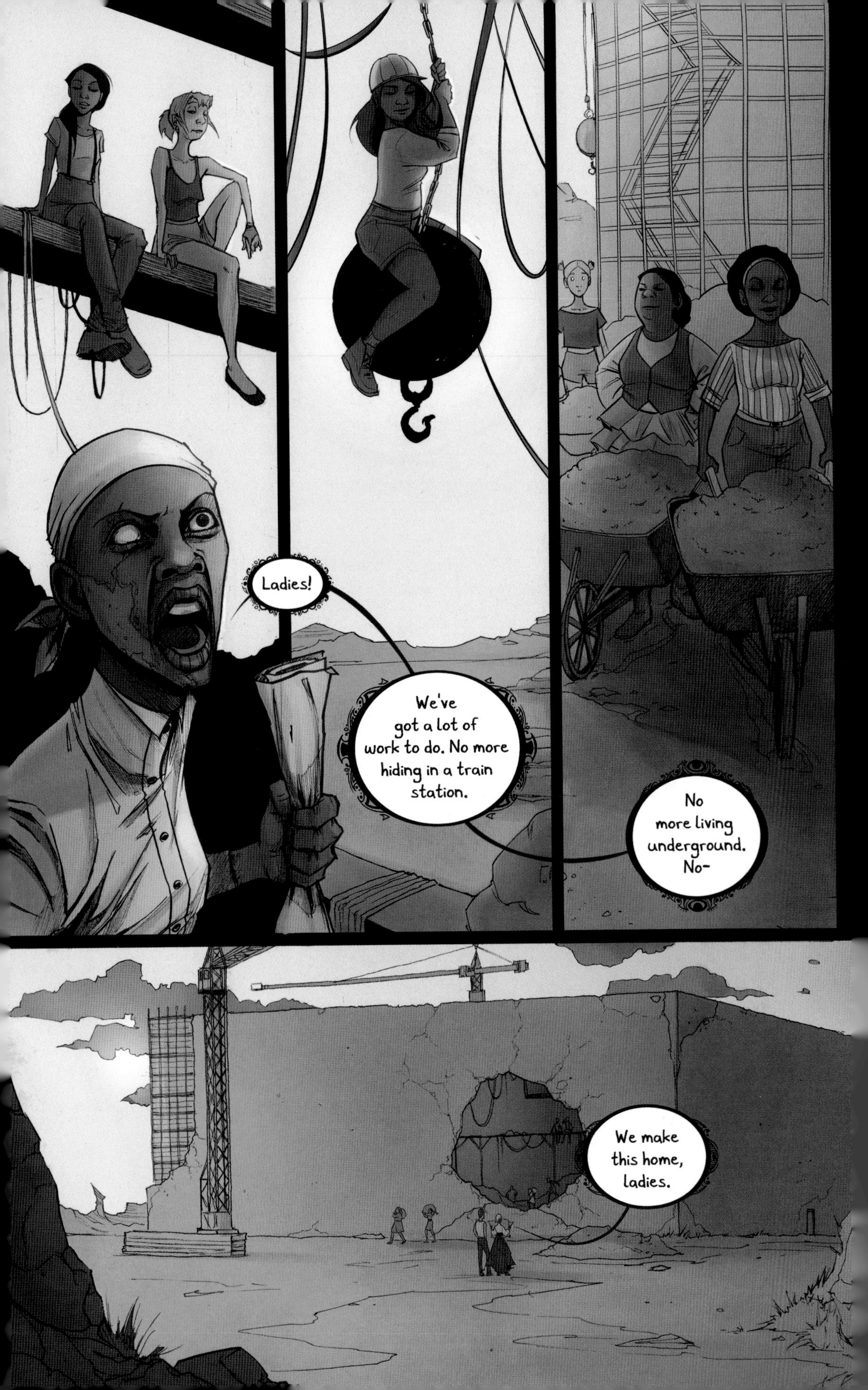
Ladies!
We've got a lot of work to do. No more hiding in a train station.
No more living underground. No-
We make this home, ladies.

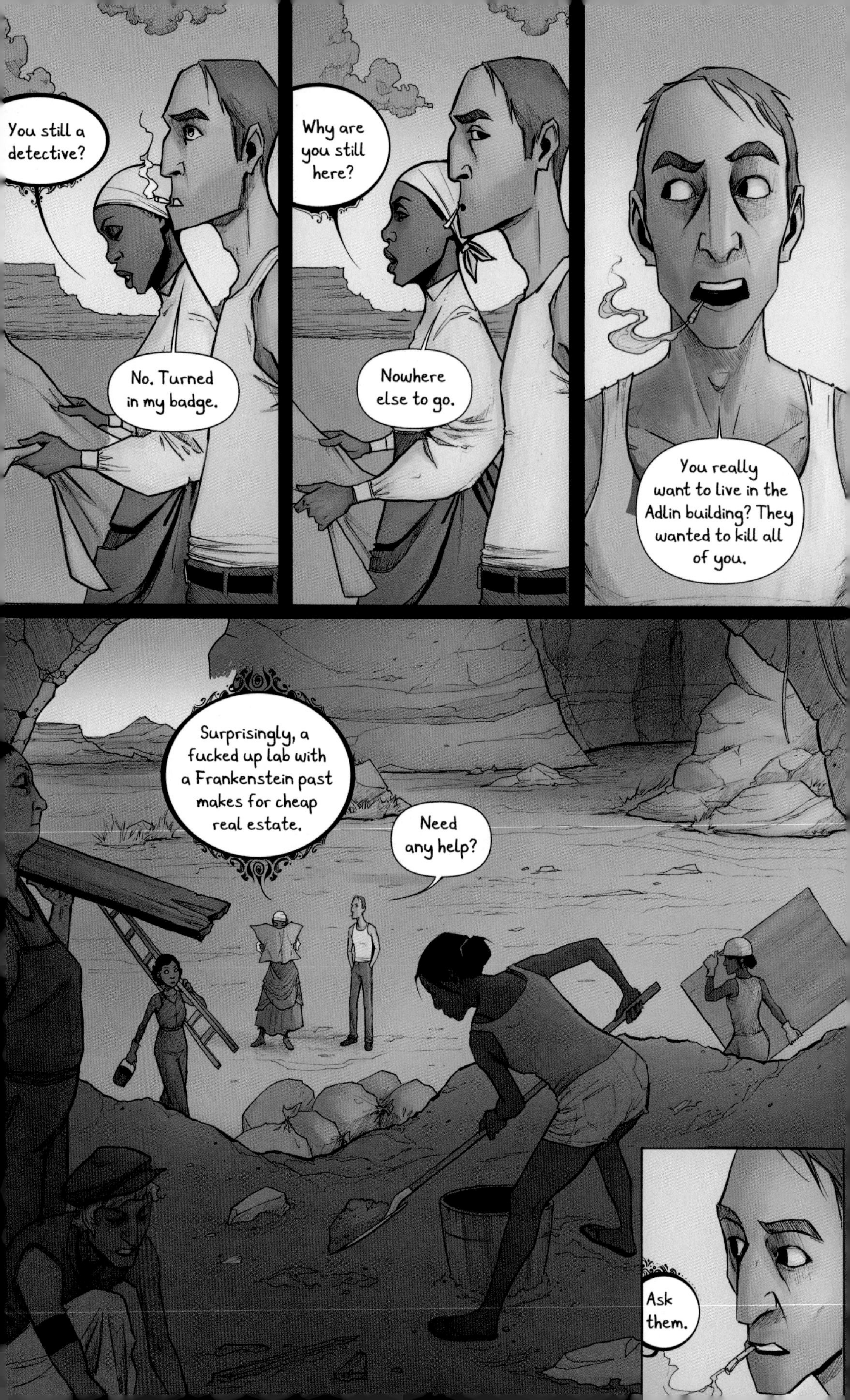
You still a detective?
No. Turned in my badge.
Why are you still here?
Nowhere else to go.
You really want to live in the Adlin building? They wanted to kill all of you.
Surprisingly, a fucked up lab with a Frankenstein past makes for cheap real estate.
Need any help?
Ask them.

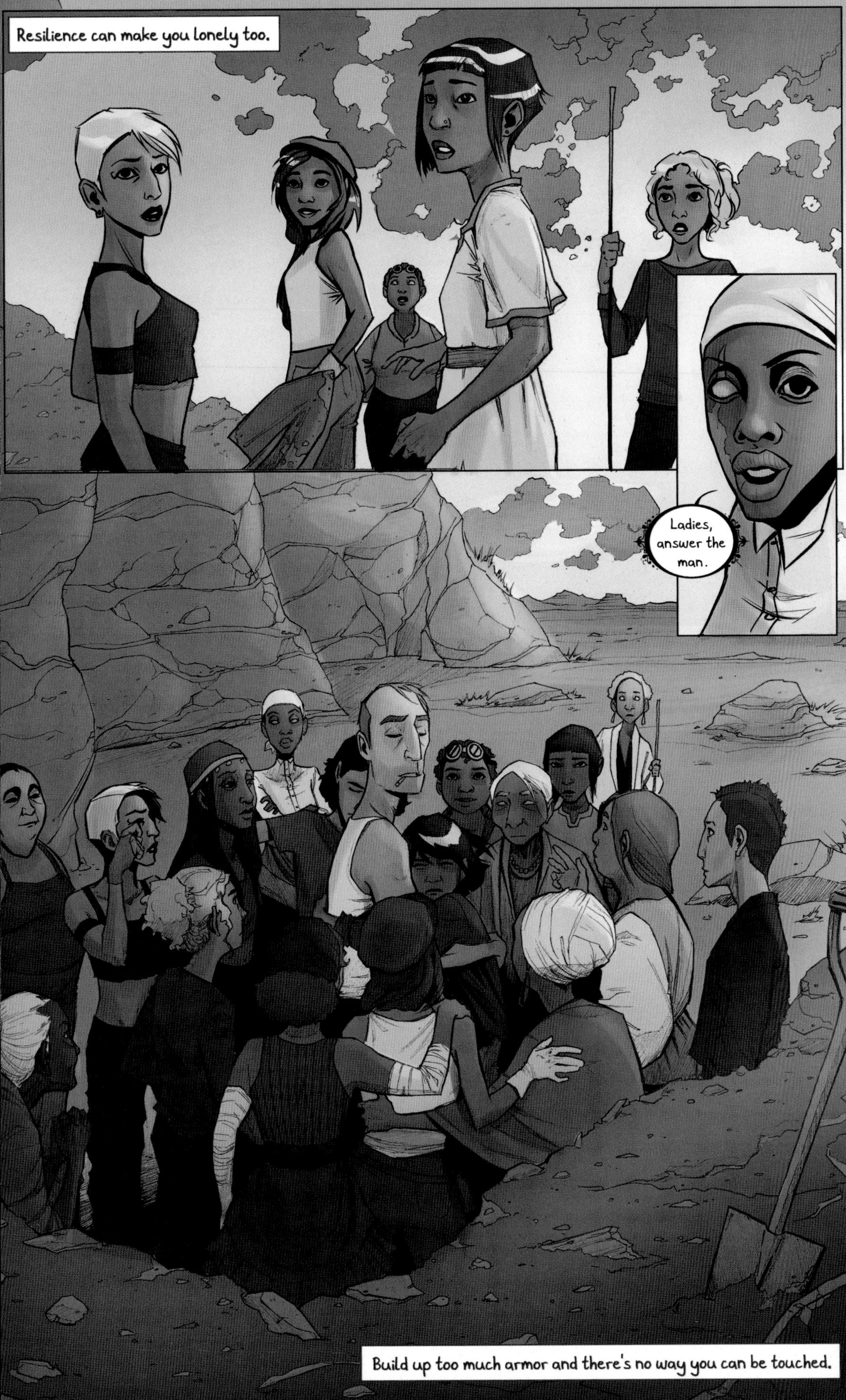
Resilience can make you lonely too.
Ladies, answer the man.
Build up too much armor and there's no way you can be touched.

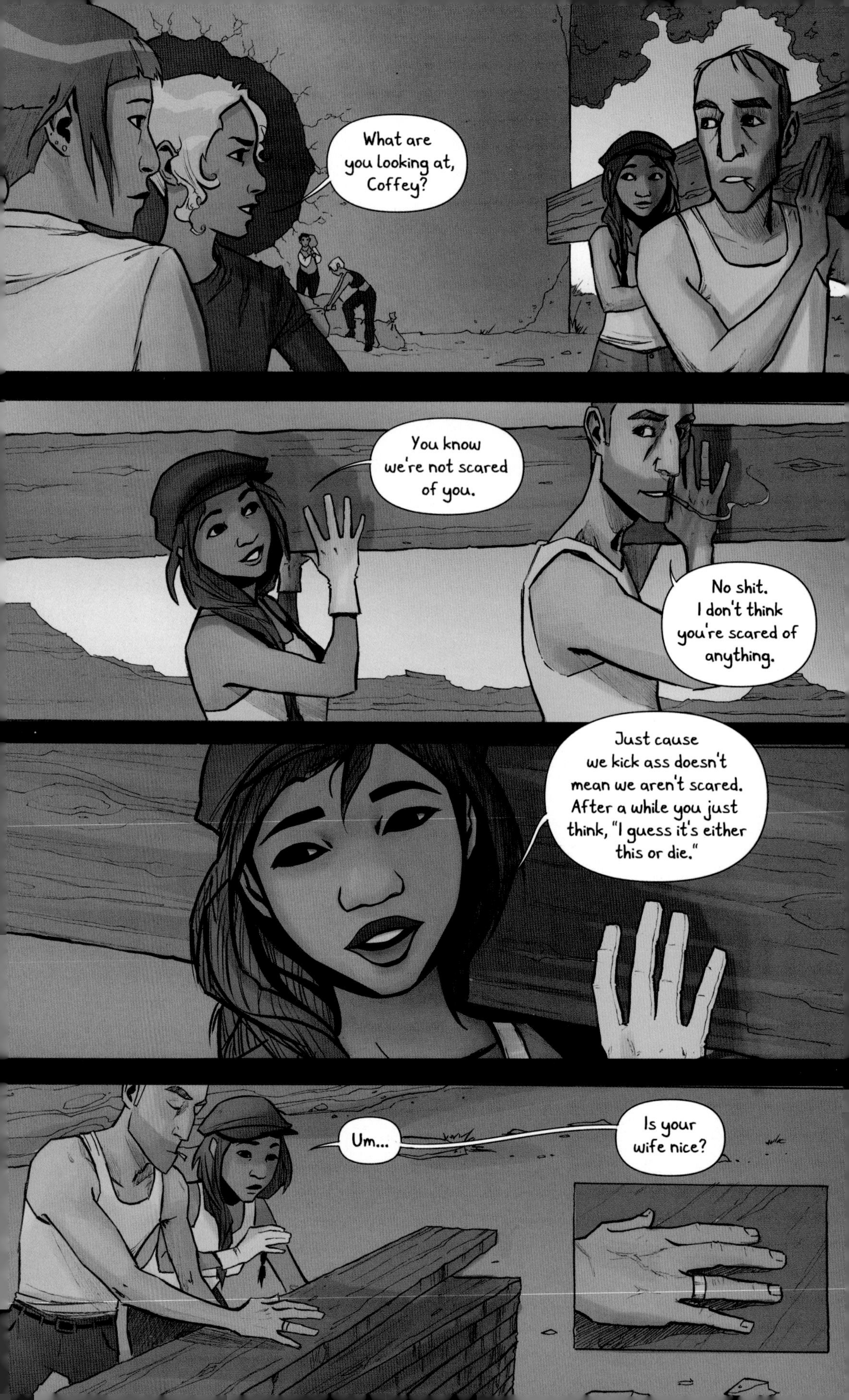
What are you looking at, Coffey?
You know we're not scared of you.
No shit. I don't think you're scared of anything.
Just cause we kick ass doesn't mean we aren't scared. After a while you just think, "I guess it's either this or die."
Um...
Is your wife nice?

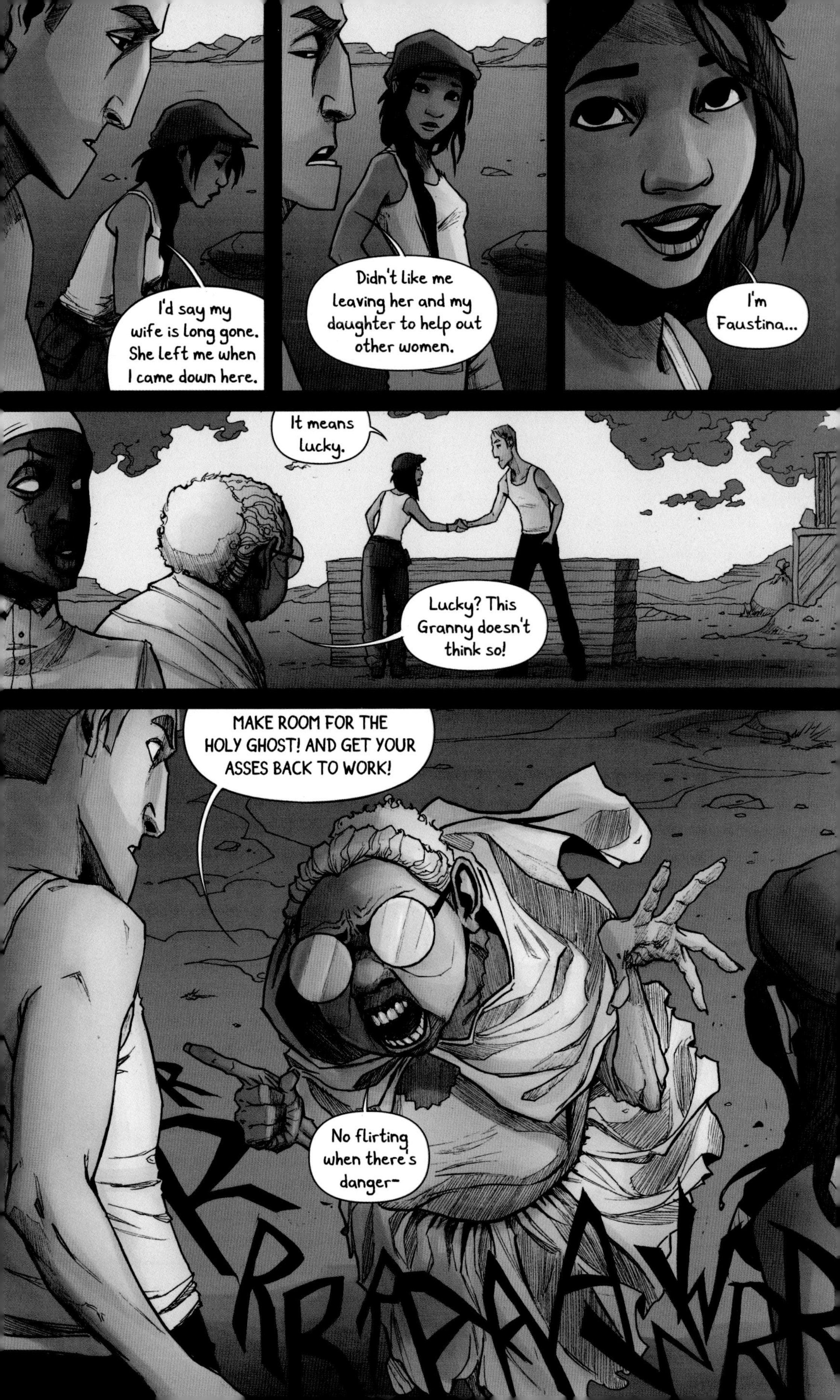
I'd say my wife is long gone. She left me when I came down here.
Didn't like me leaving her and my daughter to help out other women.
I'm Faustina...
It means lucky.
Lucky? This Granny doesn't think so!
MAKE ROOM FOR THE HOLY GHOST! AND GET YOUR ASSES BACK TO WORK!
No flirting when there's danger-

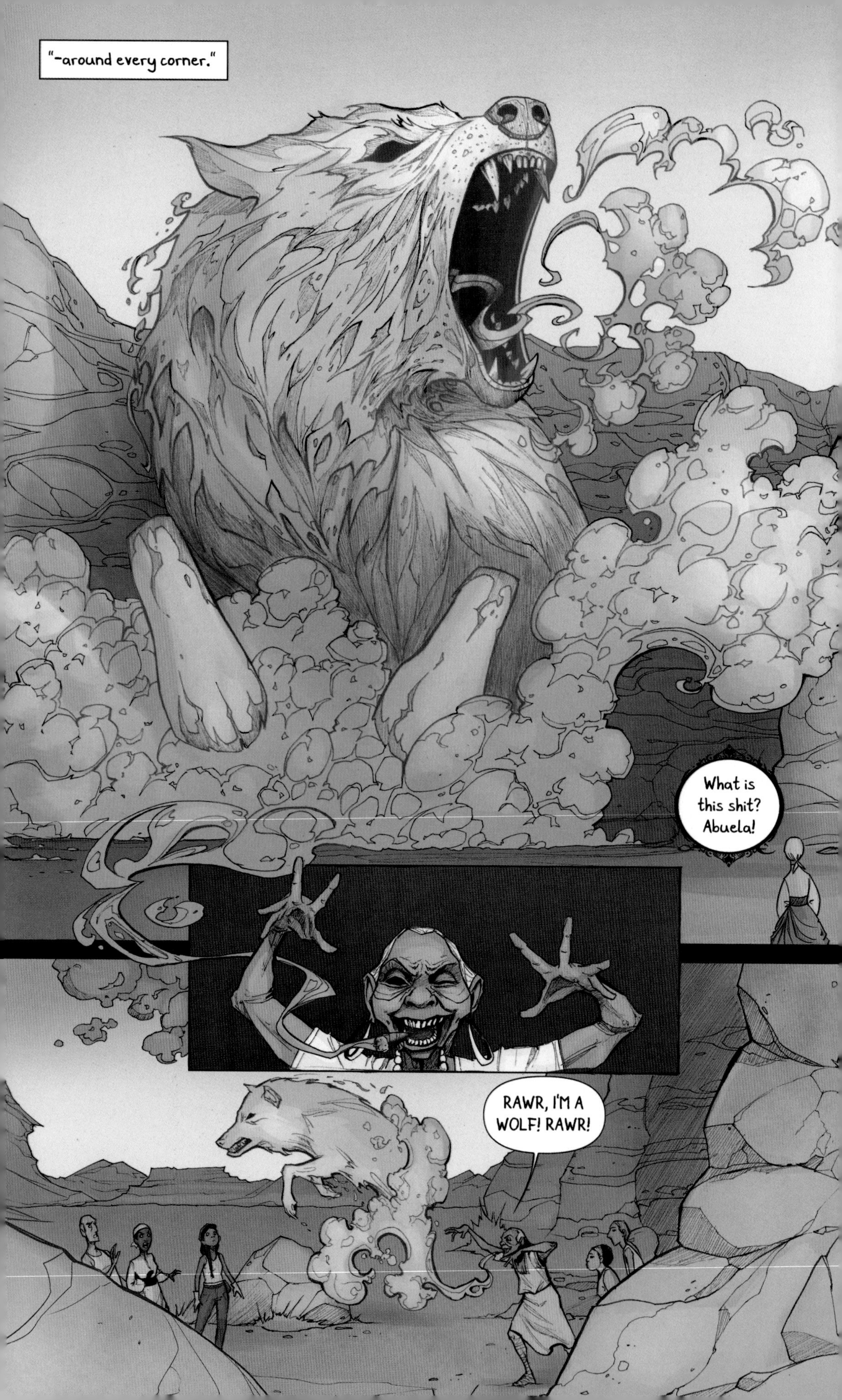

"-around every corner."
What is this shit? Abuela!
RAWR, I'M A WOLF! RAWR!

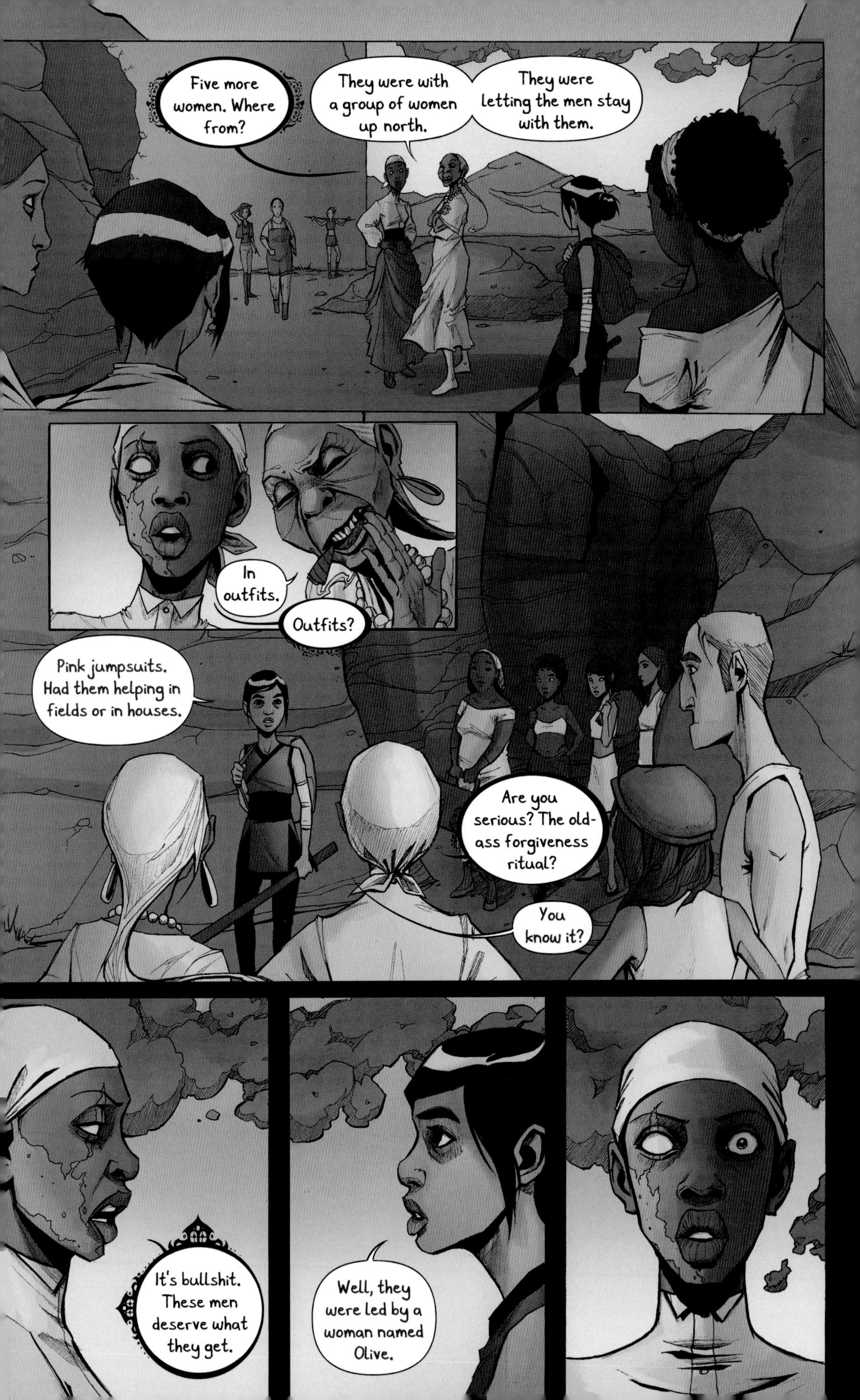

Five more women. Where from?
They were with a group of women up north.
They were letting the men stay with them.
In outfits.
Outfits?
Pink jumpsuits. Had them helping in fields or in houses.
Are you serious? The old-ass forgiveness ritual?
You know it?
It's bullshit. These men deserve what they get.
Well, they were led by a woman named Olive.

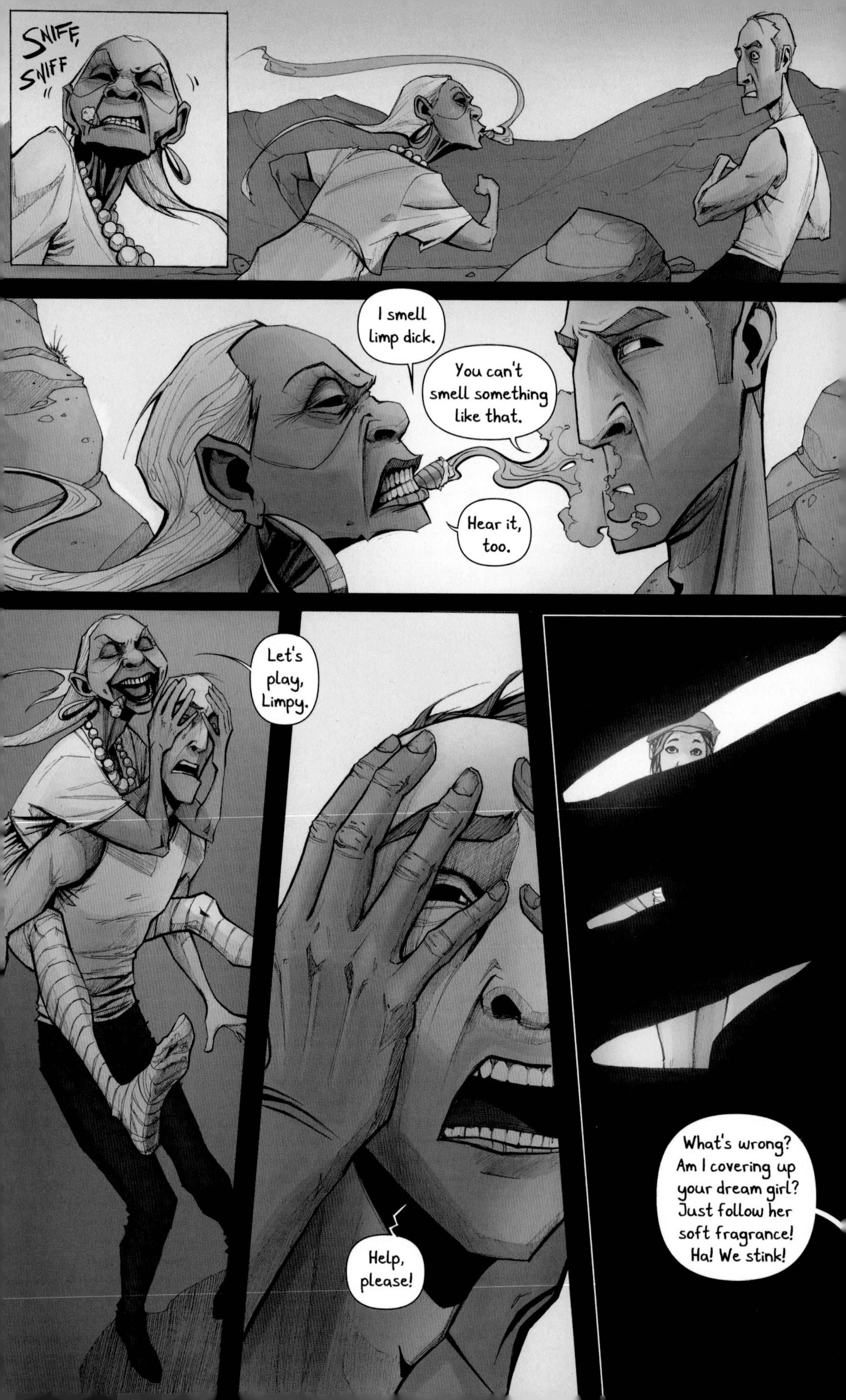
SNIFF, SNIFF
I smell limp dick.
You can't smell something like that.
Hear it, too.
Let's play, Limpy.
Help, please!
What's wrong? Am I covering up your dream girl? Just follow her soft fragrance! Ha! We stink!

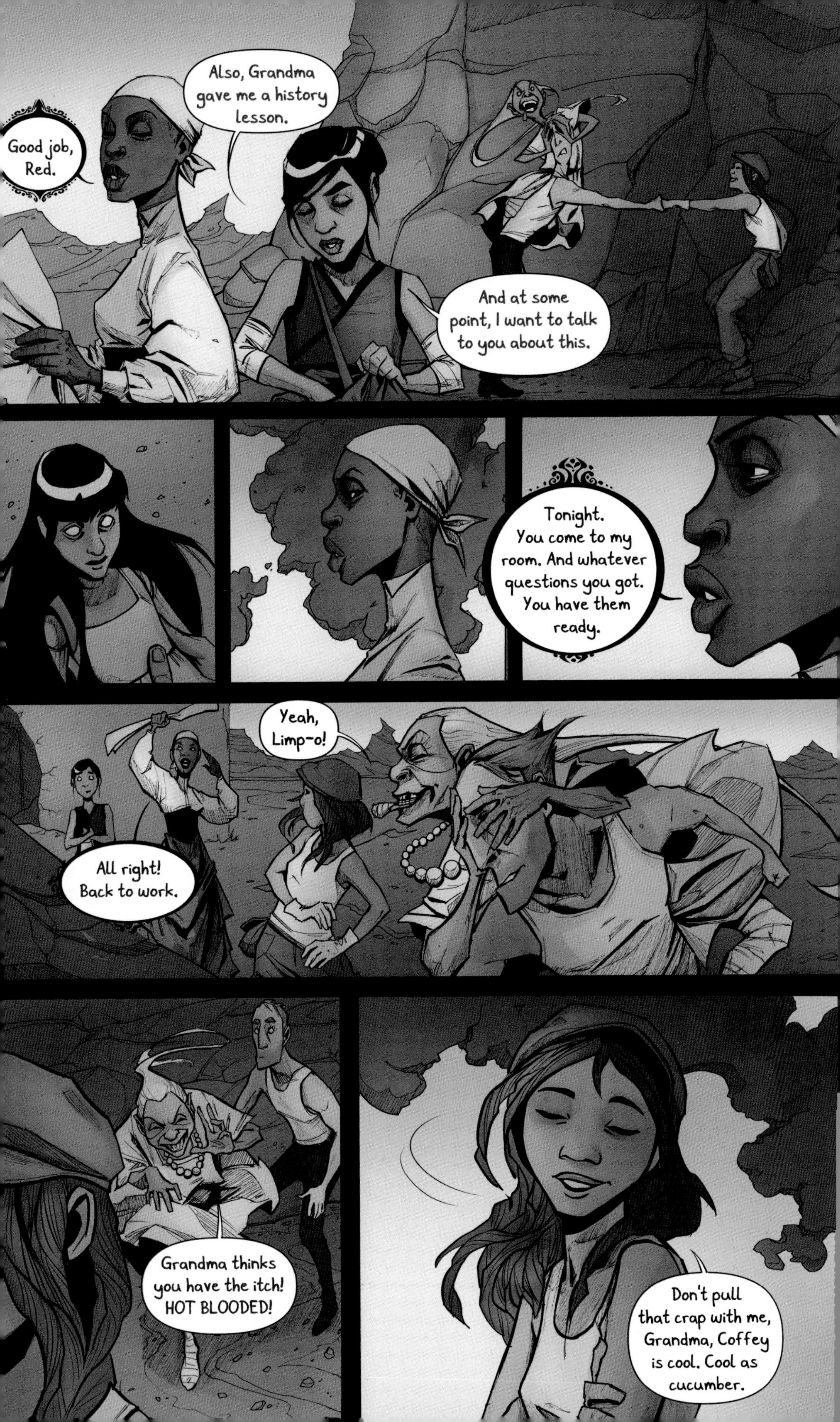
Good job, Red.
Also, Grandma gave me a history lesson.
And at some point, I want to talk to you about this.
Tonight. You come to my room. And whatever questions you got. You have them ready.
Yeah, Limp-o!
All right! Back to work.
Grandma thinks you have the itch! HOT BLOODED!
Don't pull that crap with me, Grandma, Coffey is cool. Cool as cucumber.

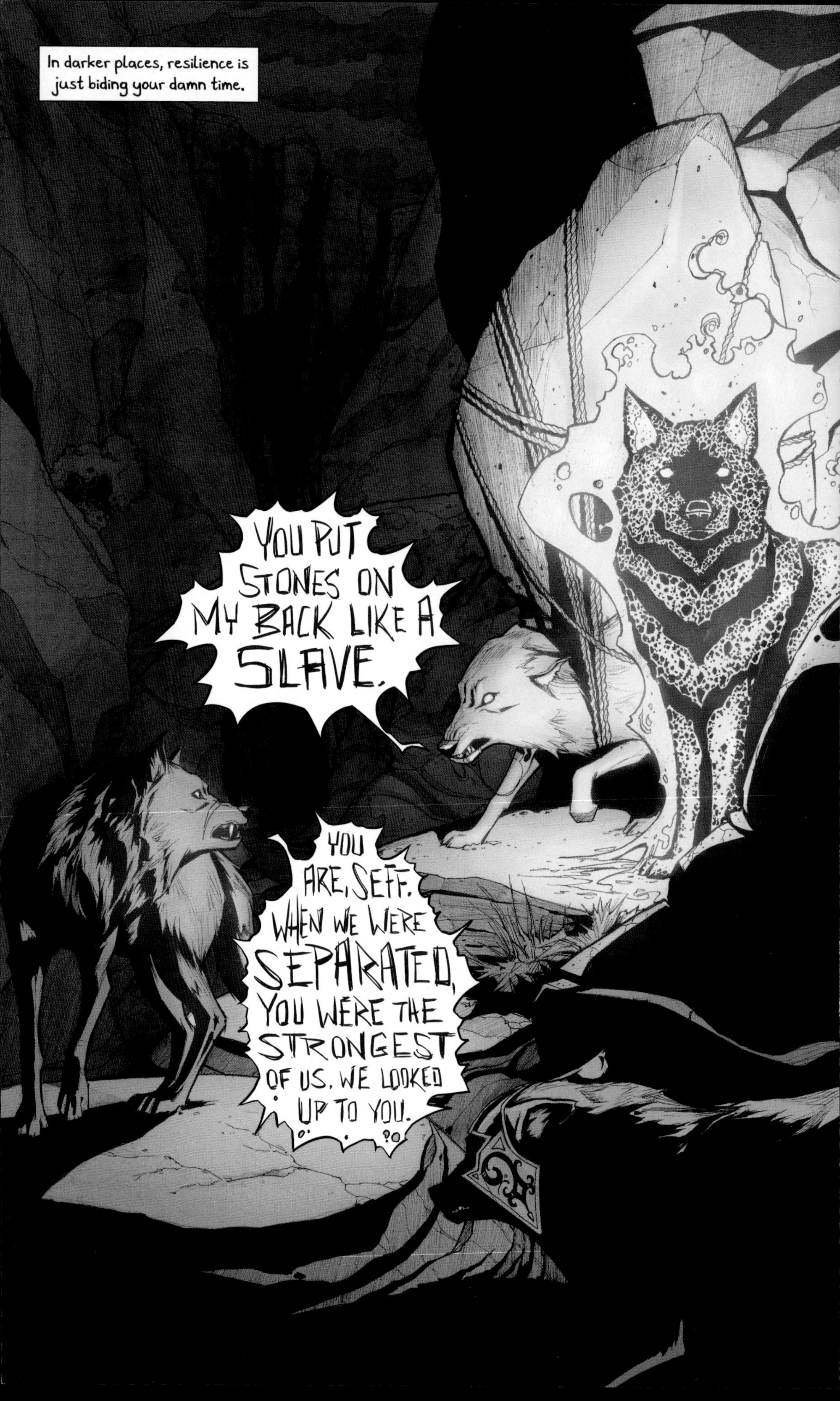
In darker places, resilience is just biding your damn time.
YOU PUT STONES ON MY BACK LIKE A SLAVE.
YOU ARE, SEFF. WHEN WE WERE SEPARATED, YOU WERE THE STRONGEST OF US. WE LOOKED UP TO YOU.

WE THOUGHT YOU WOULD LEAD US TO FREEDOM.
BUT A LITTLE GIRL.
DEFEATED BY A CHILD.
ENOUGH! YOU SAID GAIA WAS WEAK.
SHE IS. WE ALL FELT IT IN THE WIND.
AND WE HOWLED.
WE HEARD WHAT HAPPENED TO YOU. AND WE LAUNCHED.

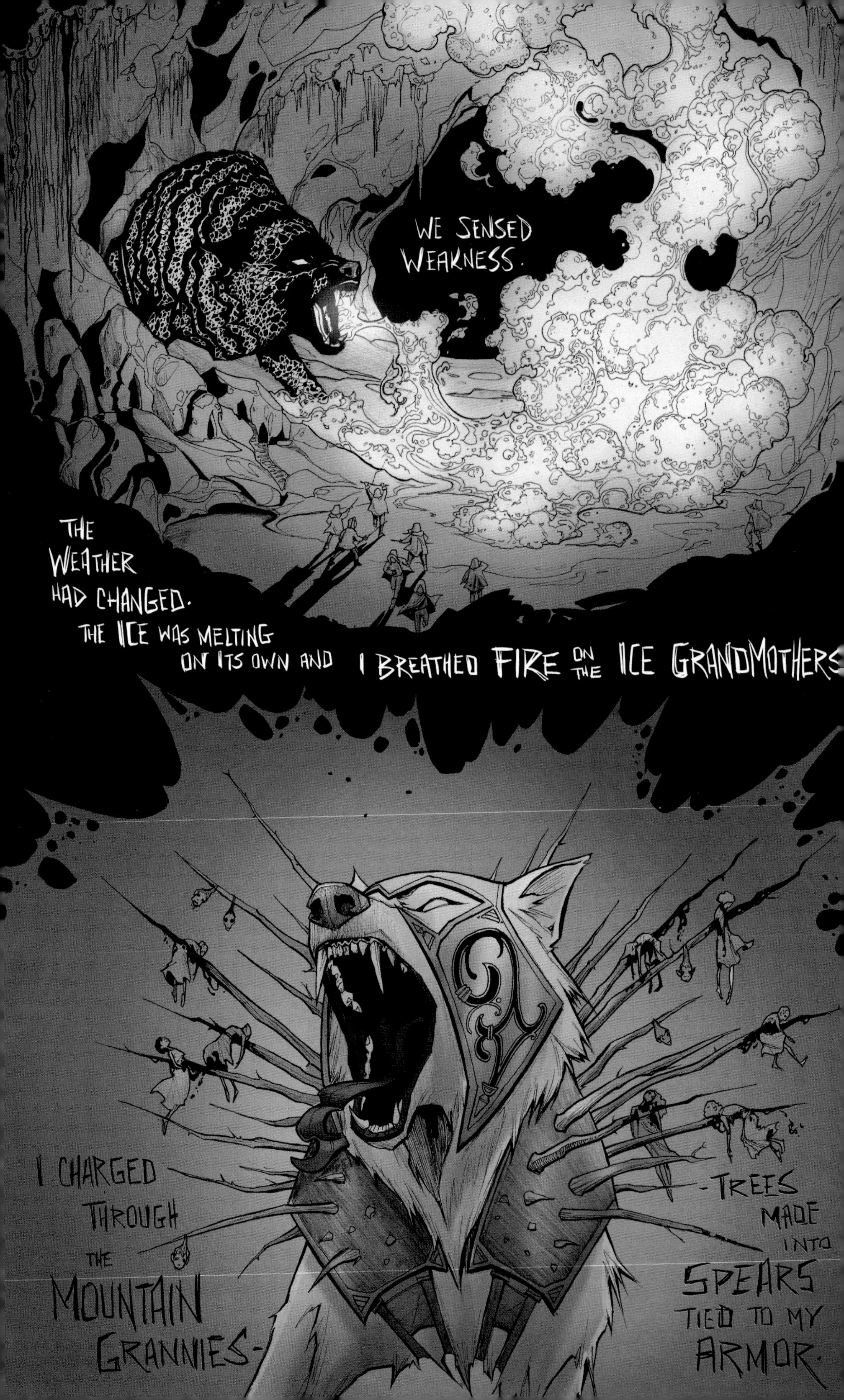
WE SENSED WEAKNESS.
THE WEATHER HAD CHANGED.
THE ICE WAS MELTING ON ITS OWN AND I BREATHED FIRE ON THE ICE GRANDMOTHERS
I CHARGED THROUGH THE MOUNTAIN GRANNIES-
-TREES MADE INTO SPEARS TIED TO MY ARMOR.

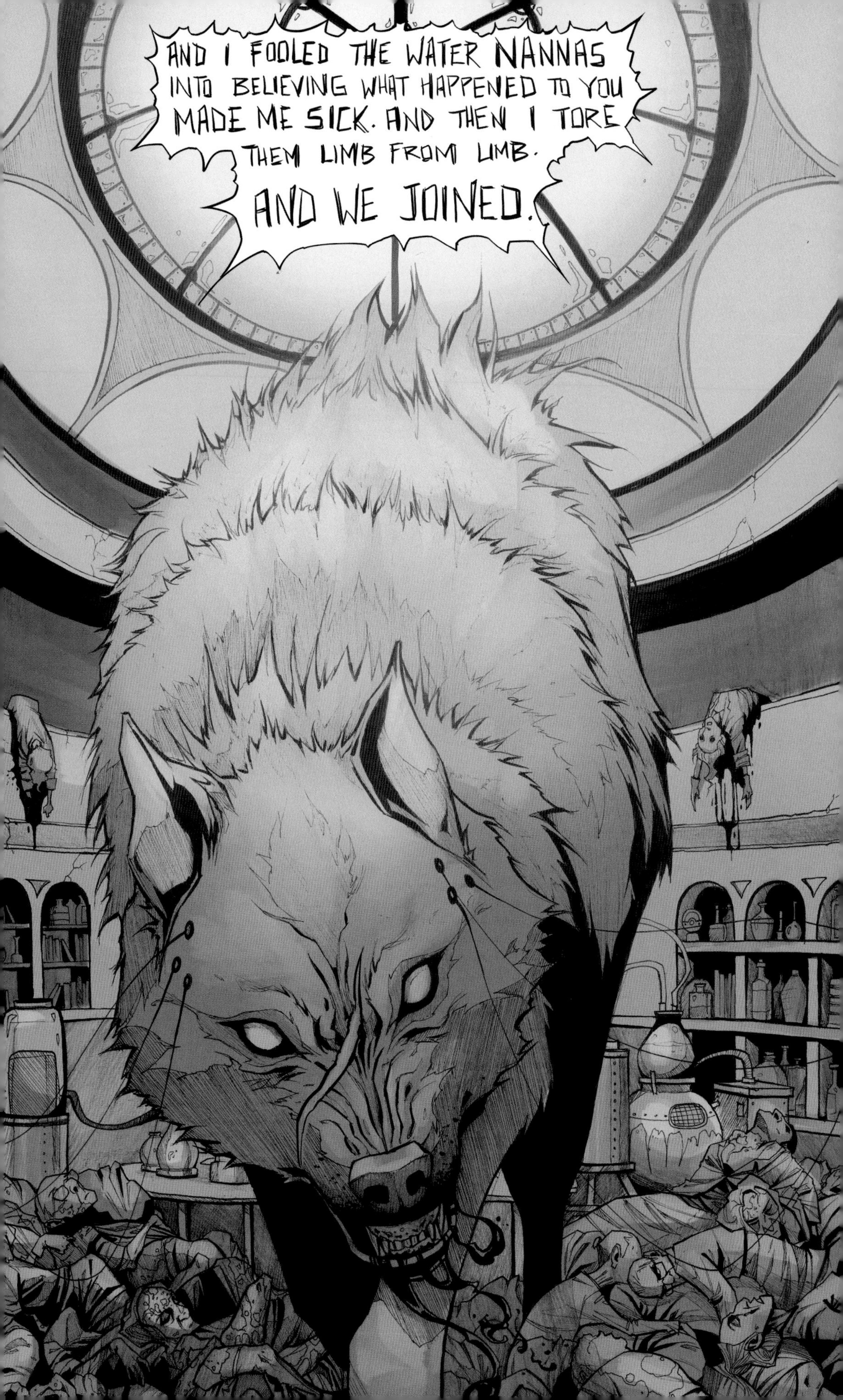
AND I FOOLED THE WATER NANNAS INTO BELIEVING WHAT HAPPENED TO YOU MADE ME SICK. AND THEN I TORE THEM LIMB FROM LIMB.
AND WE JOINED.

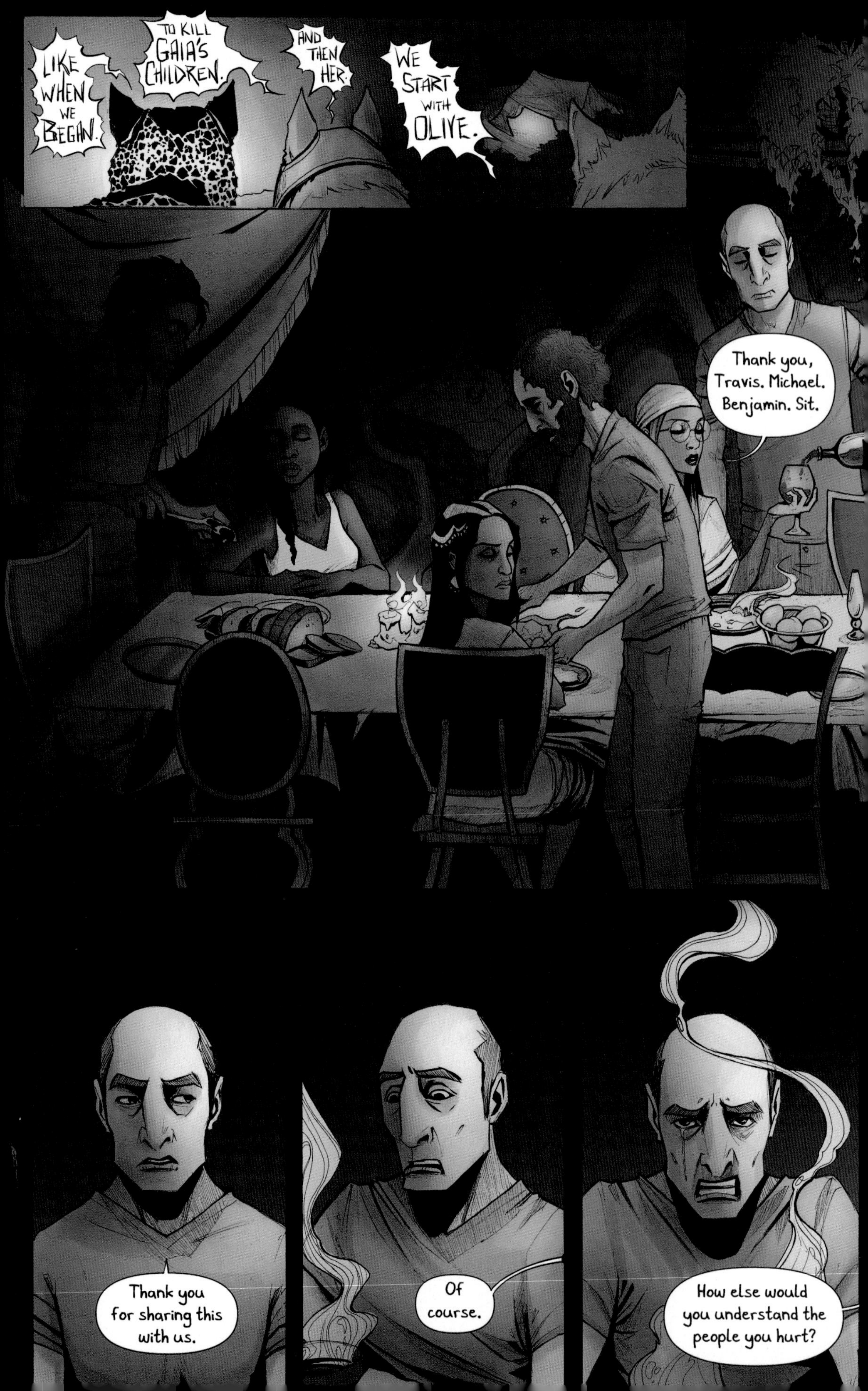
LIKE WHEN WE BEGAN.
TO KILL GAIA'S CHILDREN.
AND THEN HER.
WE START WITH OLIVE.
Thank you, Travis. Michael. Benjamin. Sit.
Thank you for sharing this with us.
Of course.
How else would you understand the people you hurt?

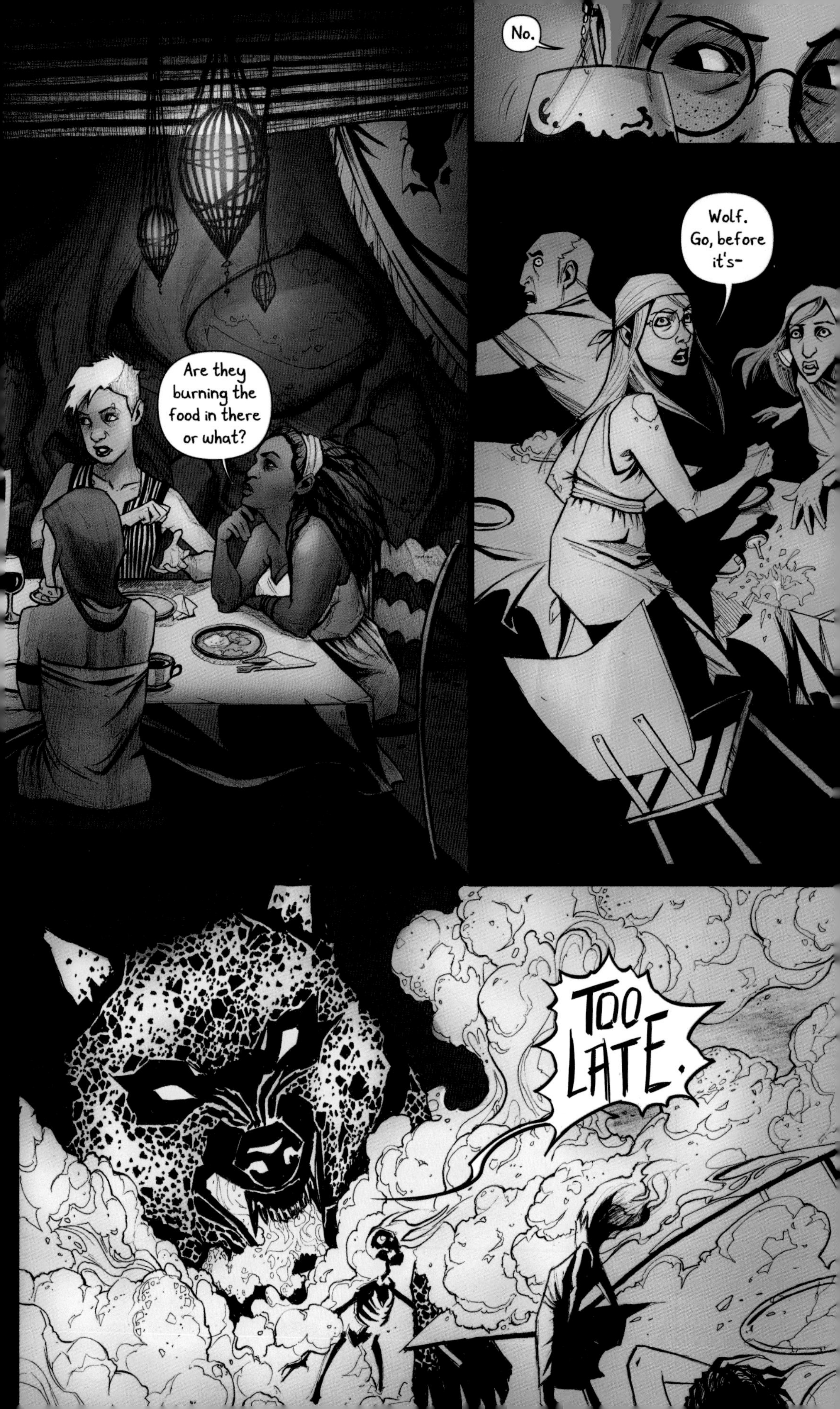
Are they burning the food in there or what?
No.
Wolf. Go, before it's-
TOO LATE.

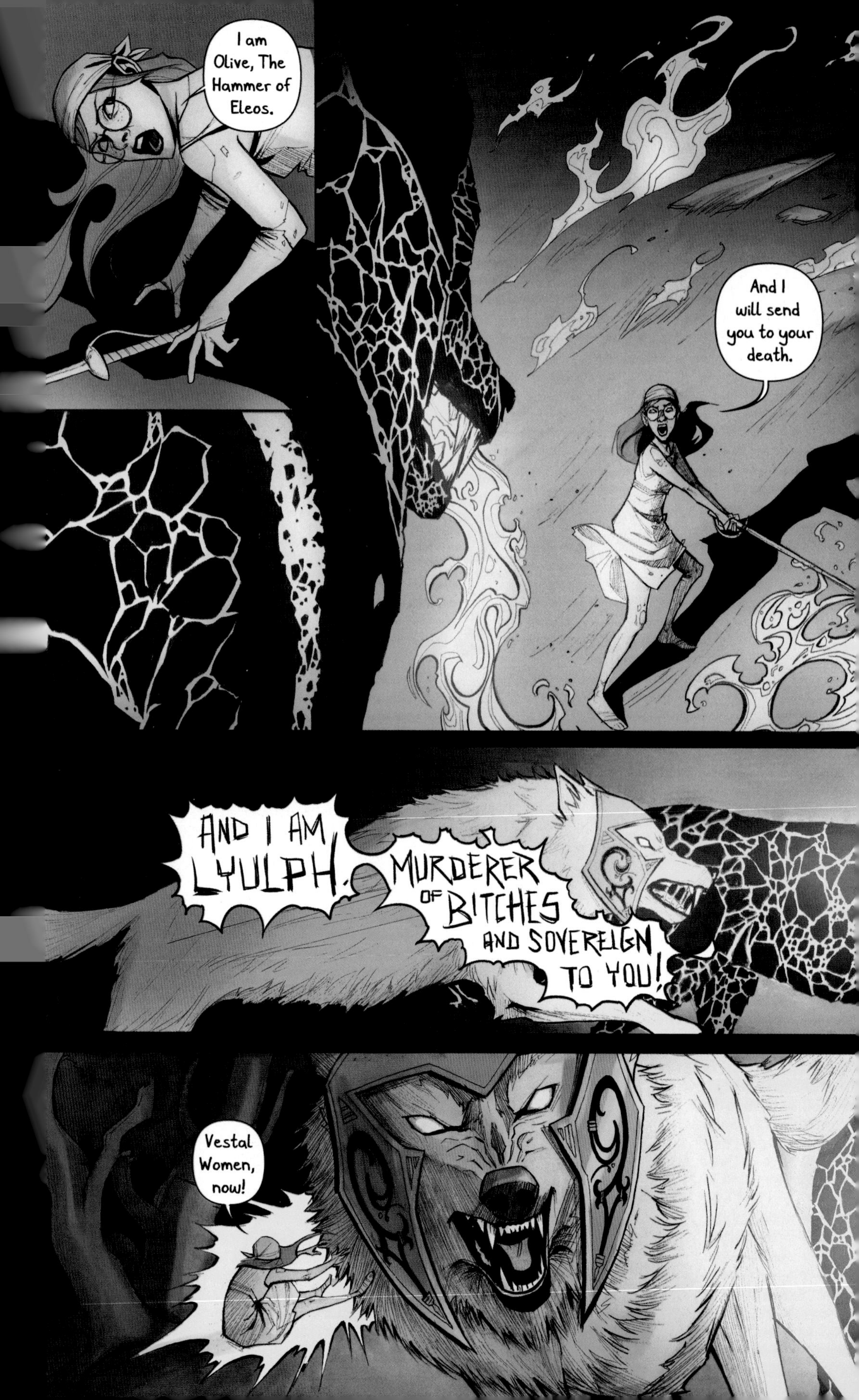
I am Olive, The Hammer of Eleos.
And I will send you to your death.
AND I AM LYULPH.
MURDERER OF BITCHES AND SOVEREIGN TO YOU!
Vestal Women, now!

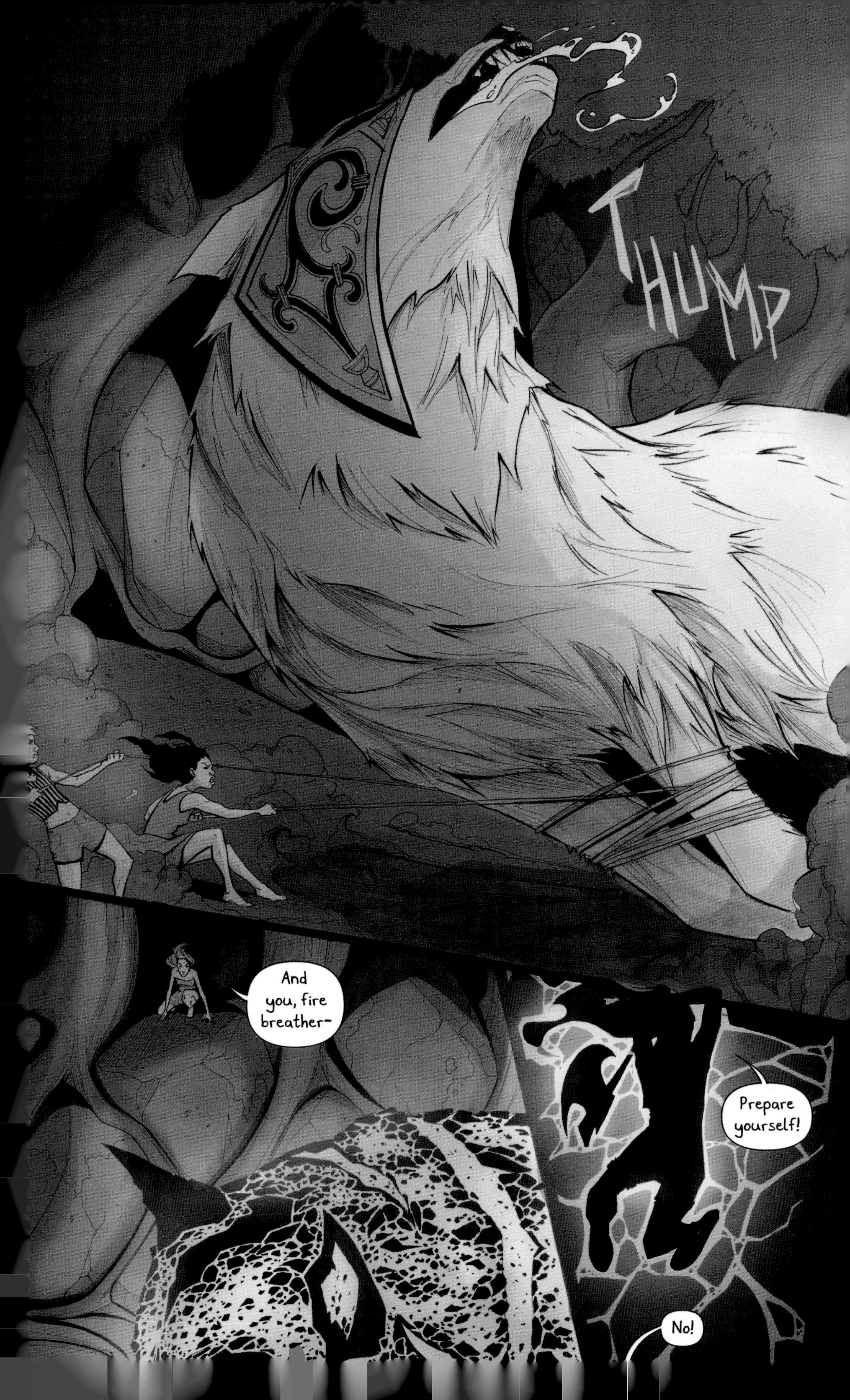
THUMP
And you, fire breather-
Prepare yourself!
No!

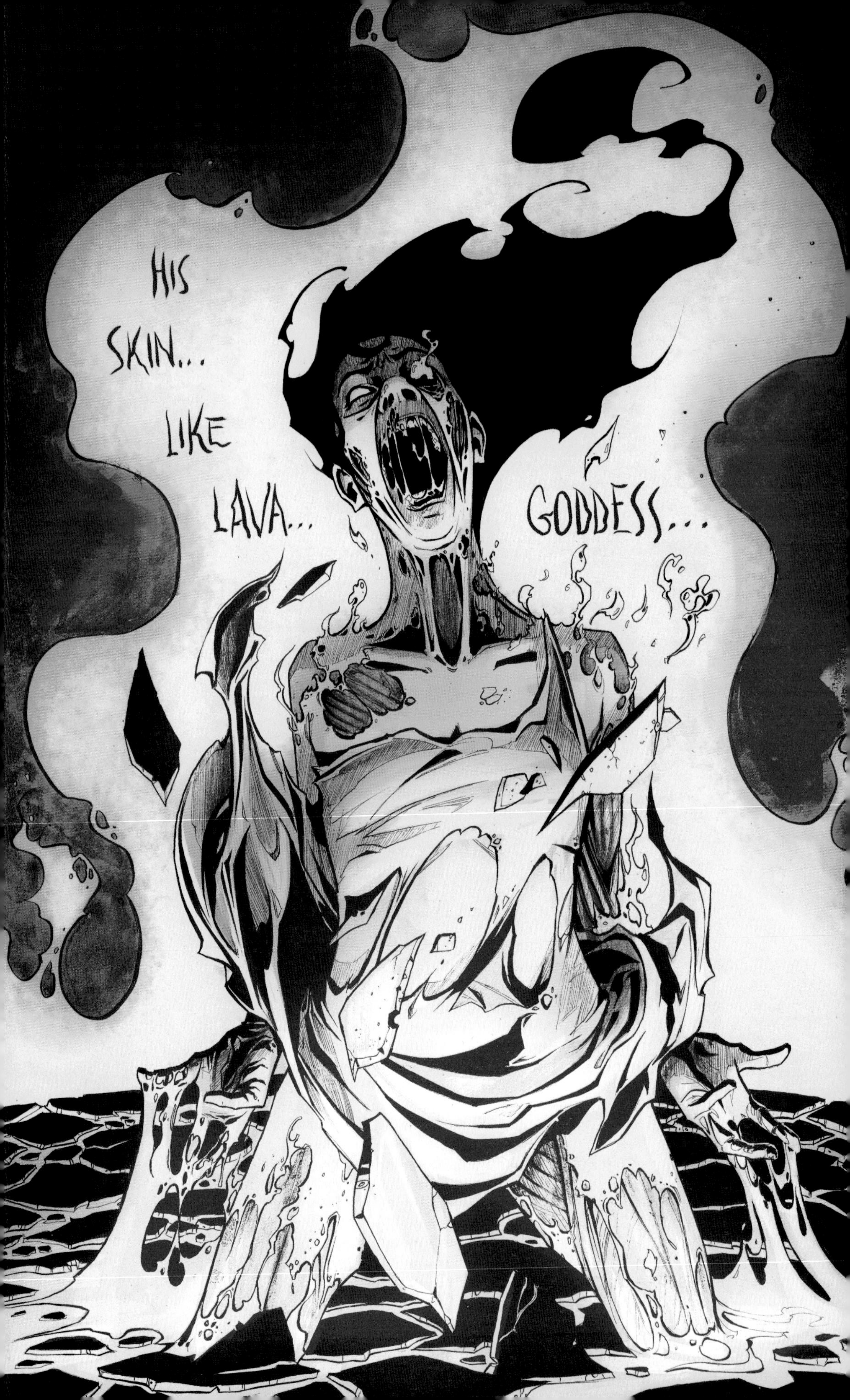
HIS SKIN... LIKE LAVA...
GODDESS...

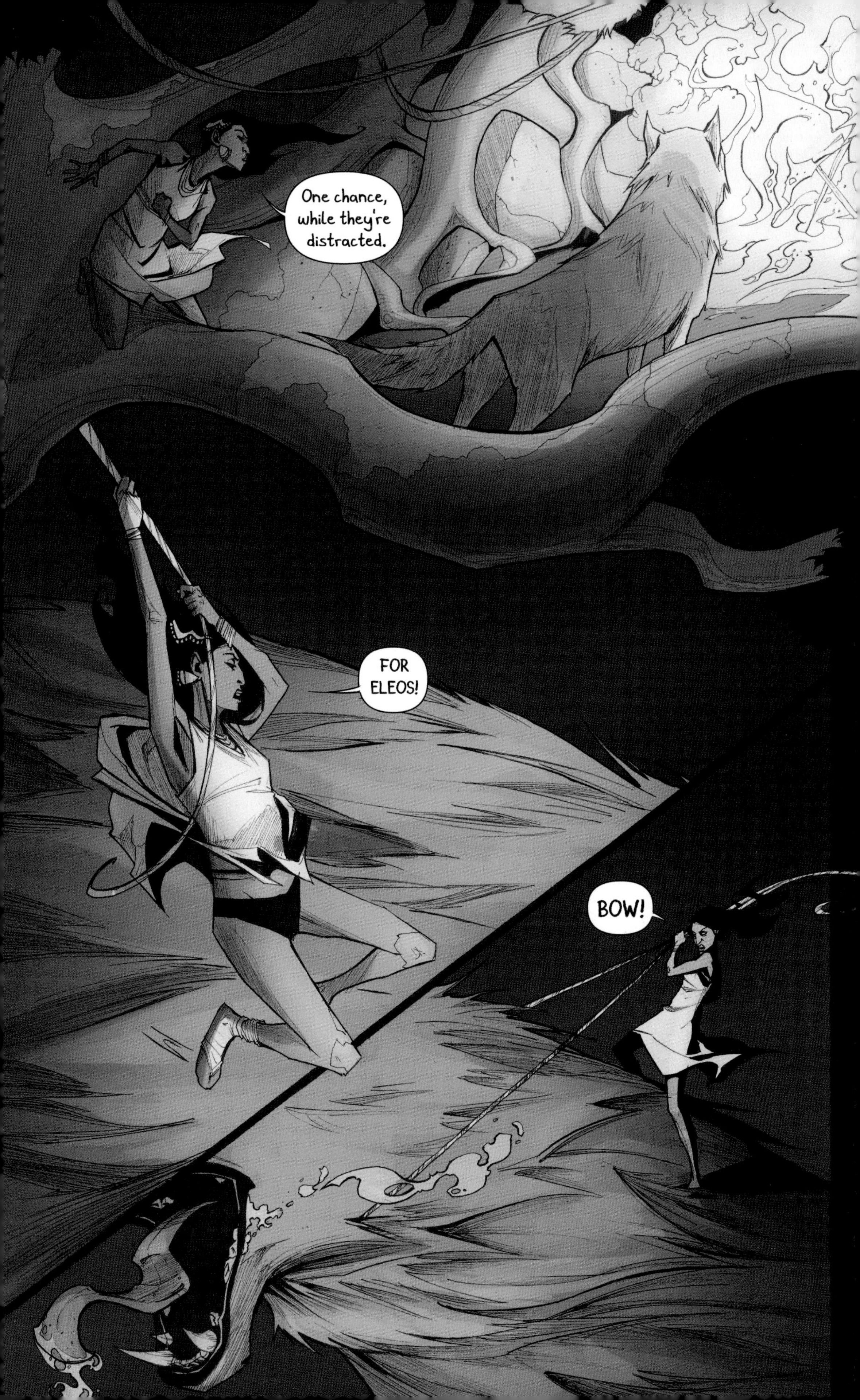
One chance, while they're distracted.
FOR ELEOS!
BOW!

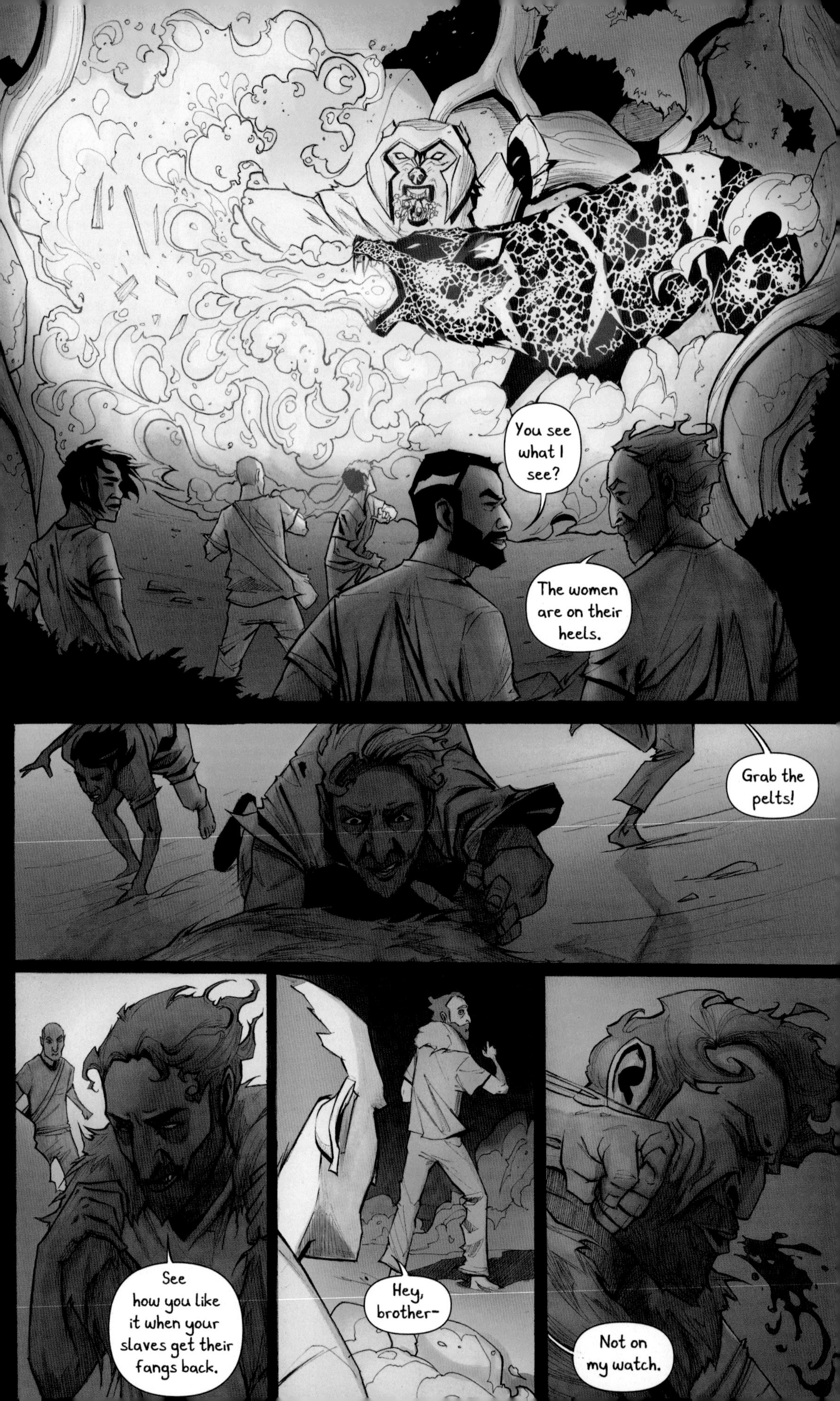
You see what I see?
The women are on their heels.
Grab the pelts!
See how you like it when your slaves get their fangs back.
Hey, brother-
Not on my watch.

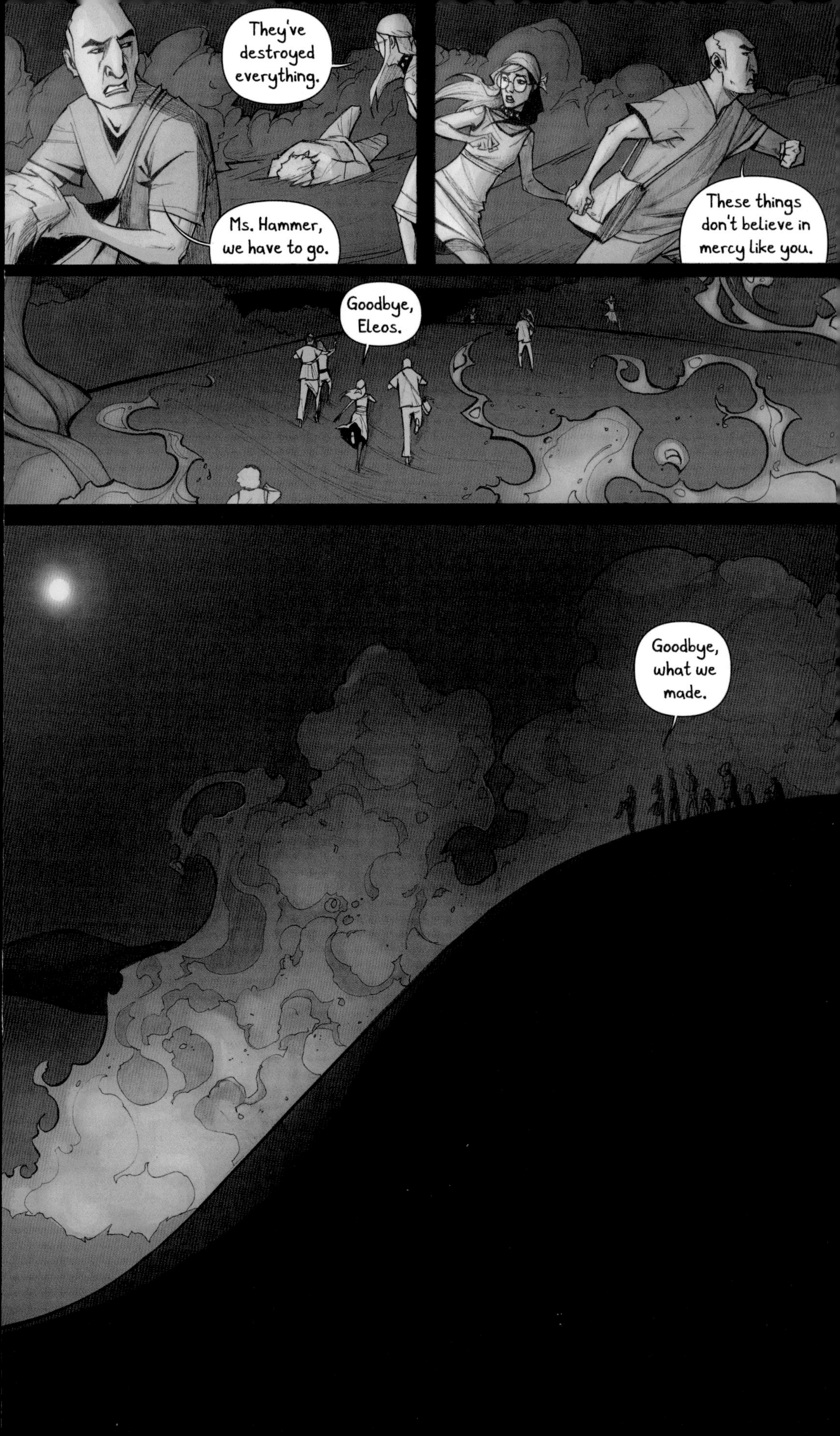
They've destroyed everything.
Ms. Hammer, we have to go.
These things don't believe in mercy like you.
Goodbye, Eleos.
Goodbye, what we made.

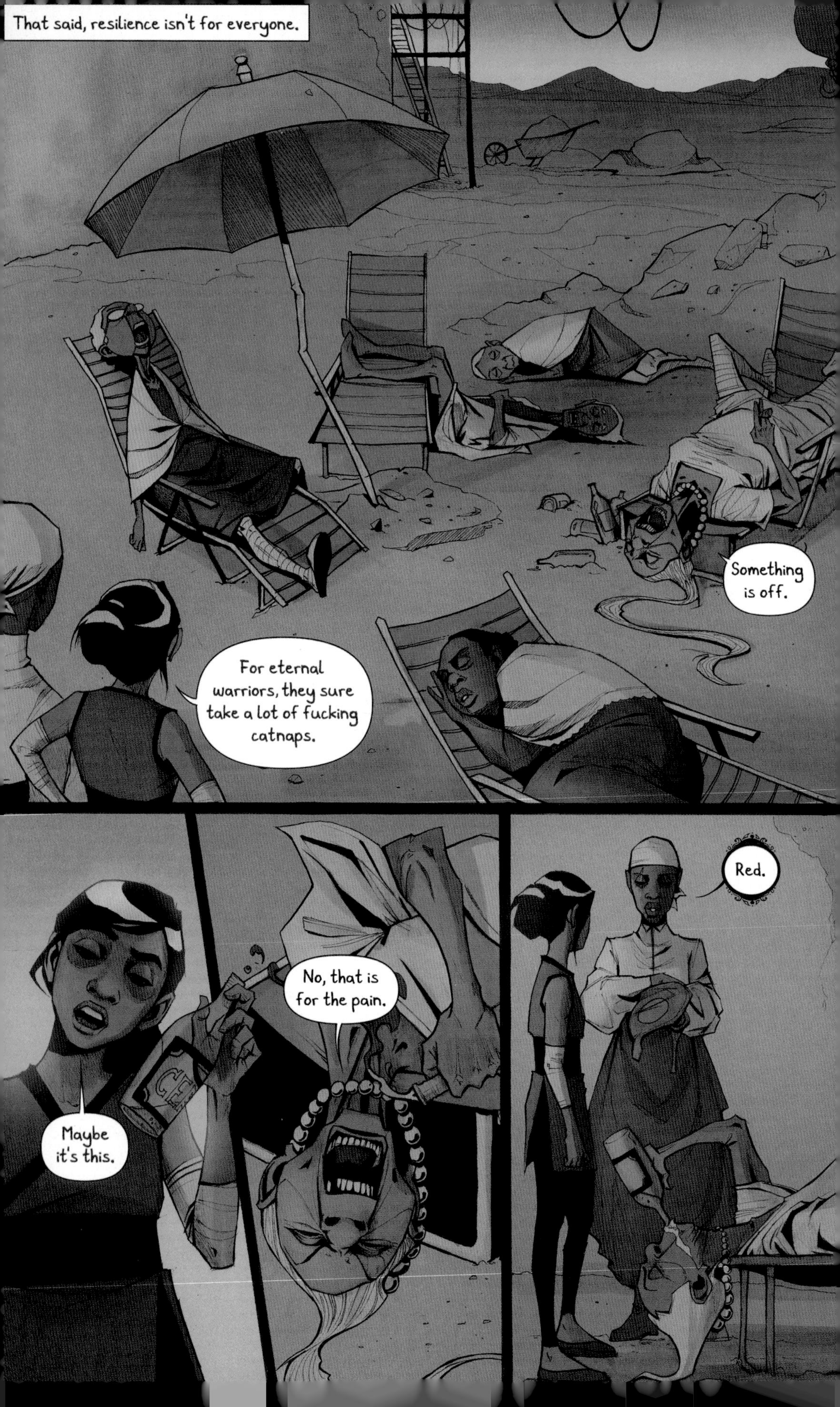

That said, resilience isn't for everyone.
Something is off.
For eternal warriors, they sure take a lot of fucking catnaps.
Maybe it's this.
No, that is for the pain.
Red.

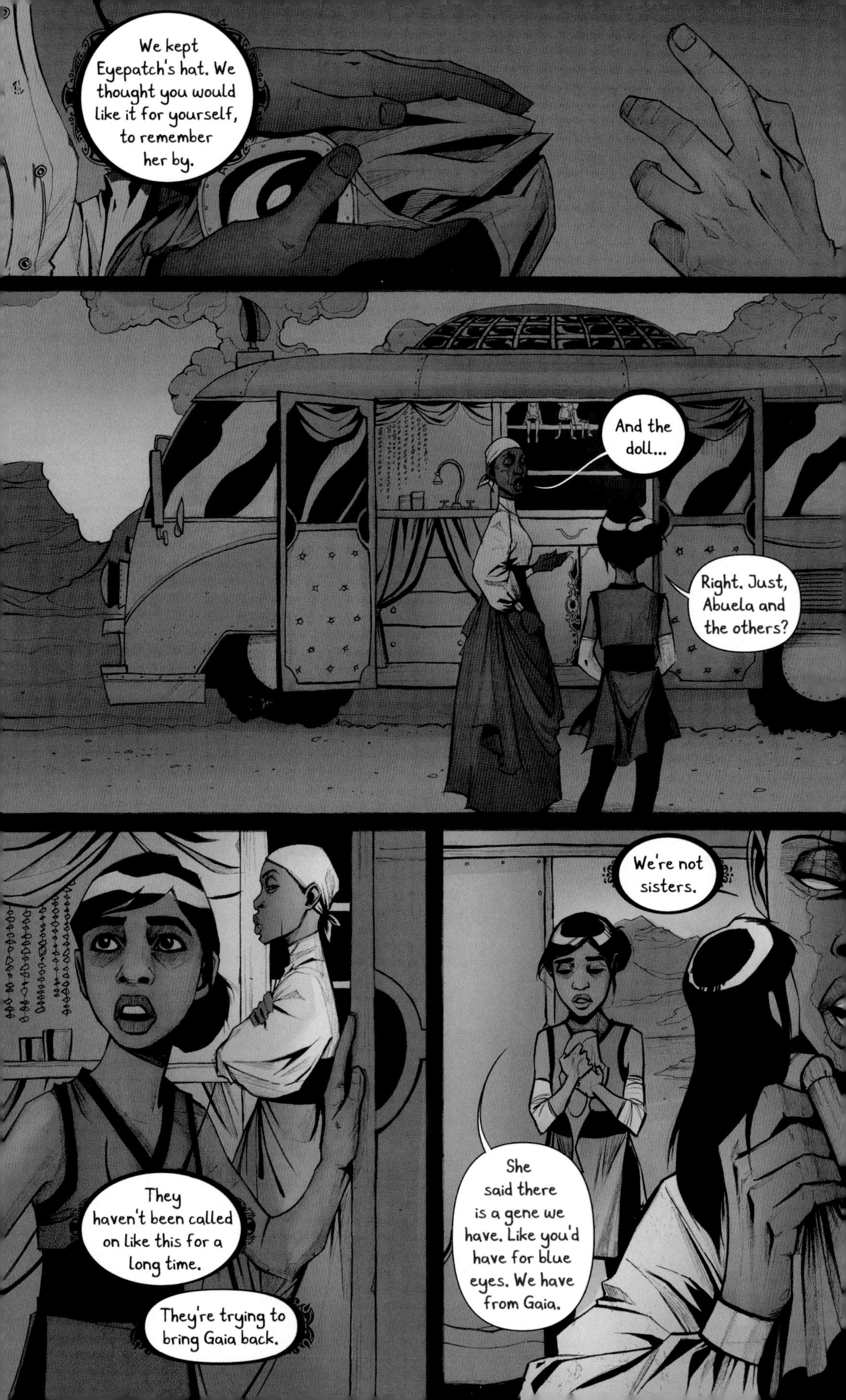
We kept Eyepatch's hat. We thought you would like it for yourself, to remember her by.
And the doll...
Right. Just, Abuela and the others?
They haven't been called on like this for a long time.
They're trying to bring Gaia back.
We're not sisters.
She said there is a gene we have. Like you'd have for blue eyes. We have from Gaia.

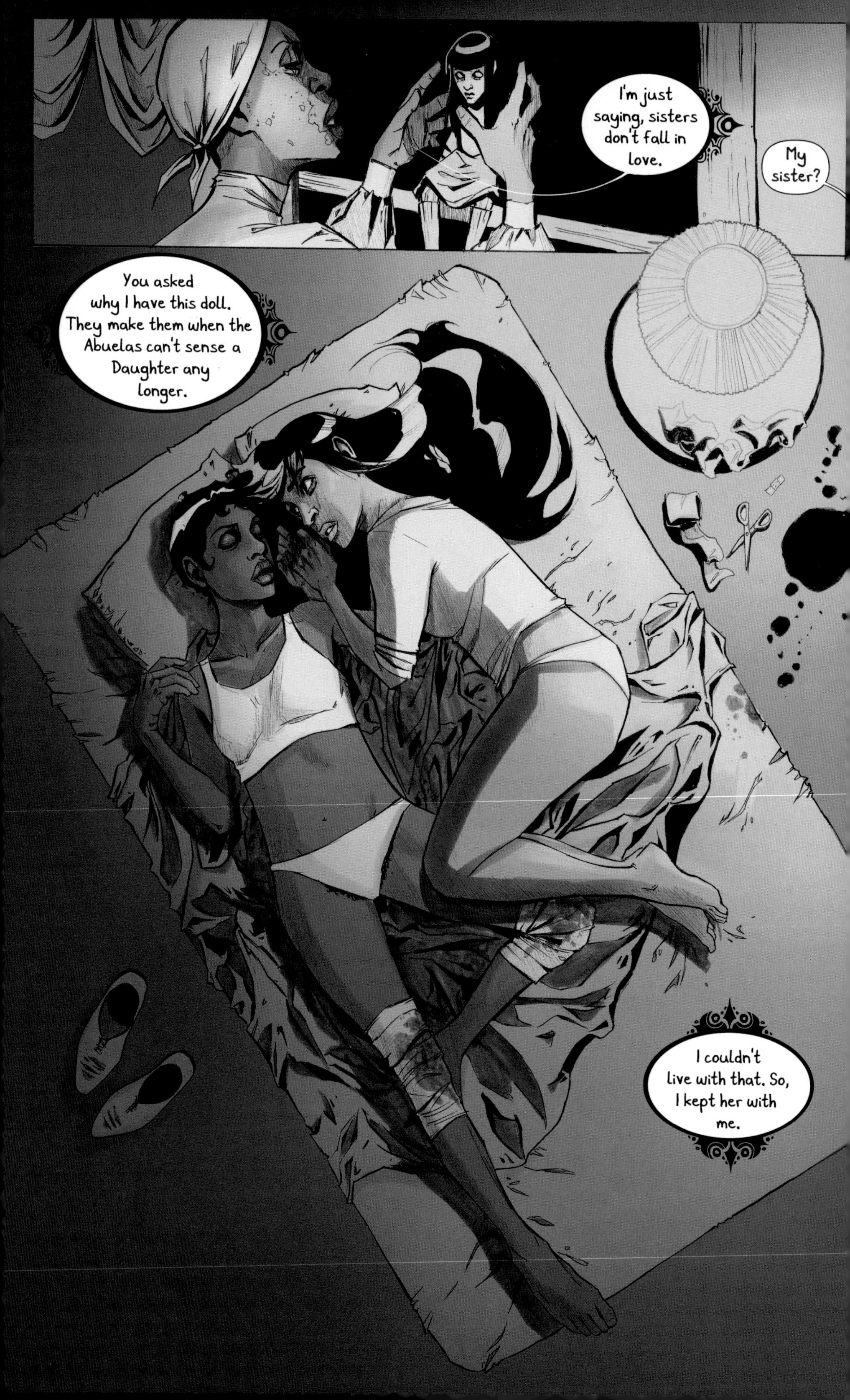
I'm just saying, sisters don't fall in love.
My sister?
You asked why I have this doll. They make them when the Abuelas can't sense a Daughter any longer.
I couldn't live with that. So, I kept her with me.

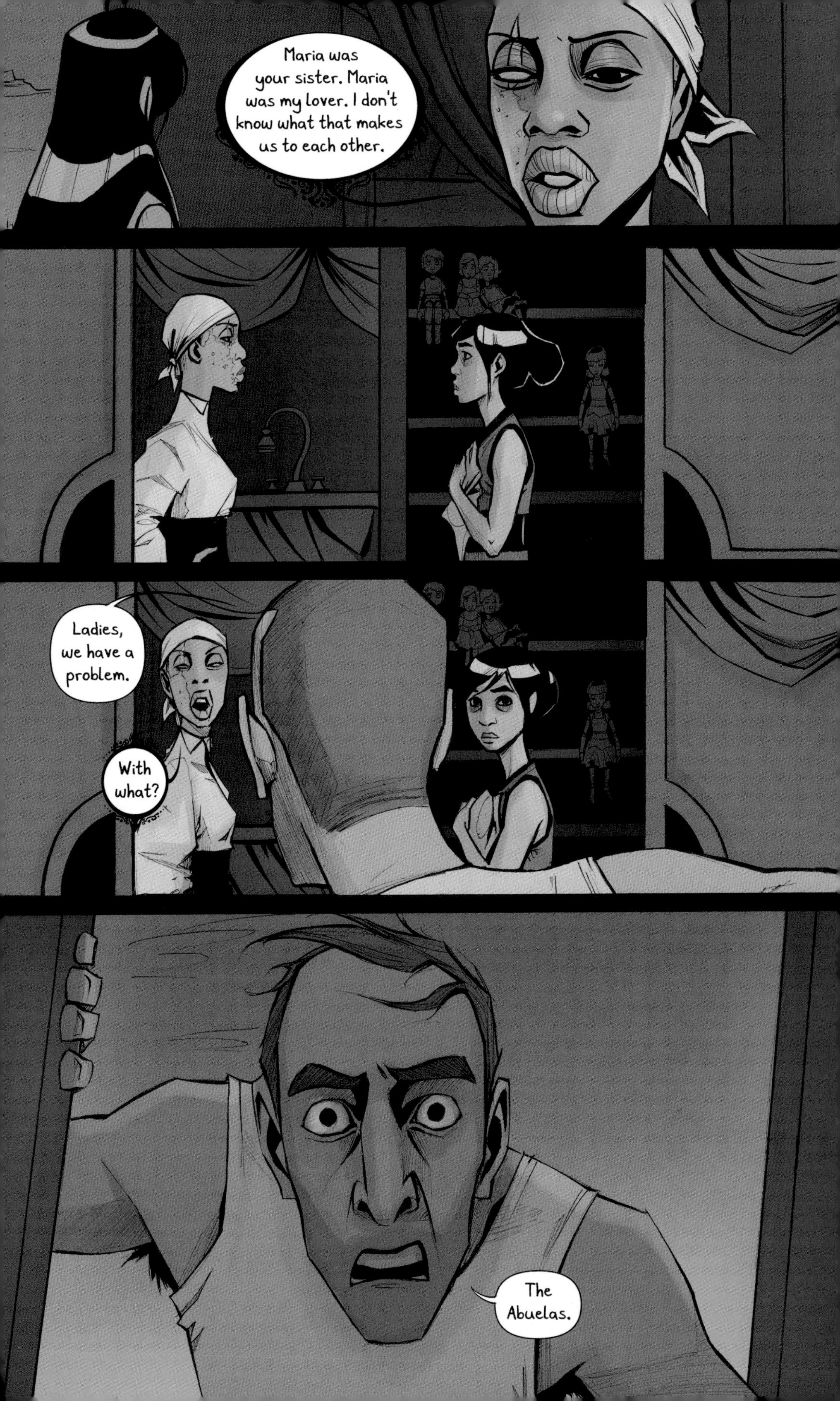
Maria was your sister. Maria was my lover. I don't know what that makes us to each other.
Ladies, we have a problem.
With what?
The Abuelas.

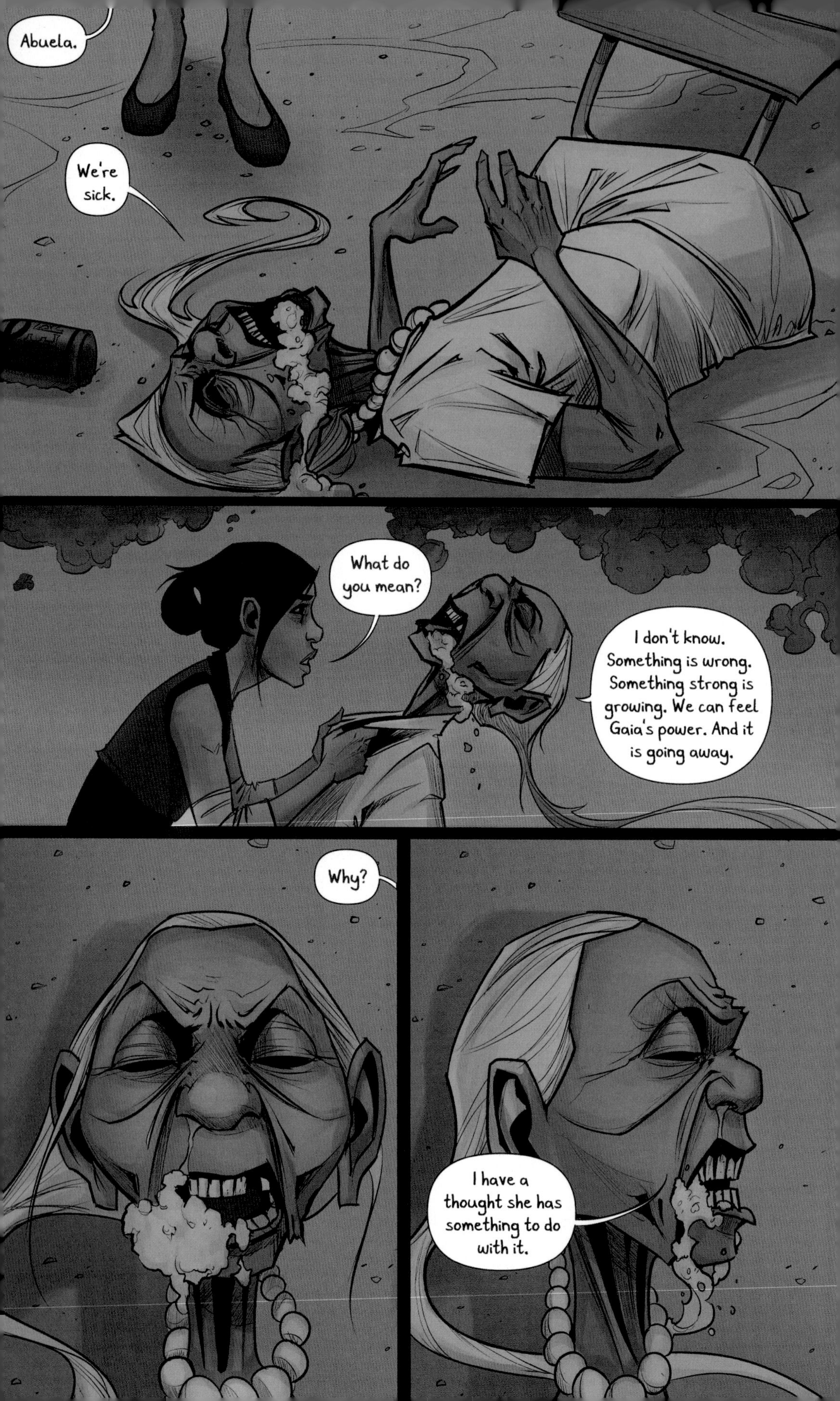
Abuela.
We're sick.
What do you mean?
I don't know. Something is wrong. Something strong is growing. We can feel Gaia's power. And it is going away.
Why?
I have a thought she has something to do with it.

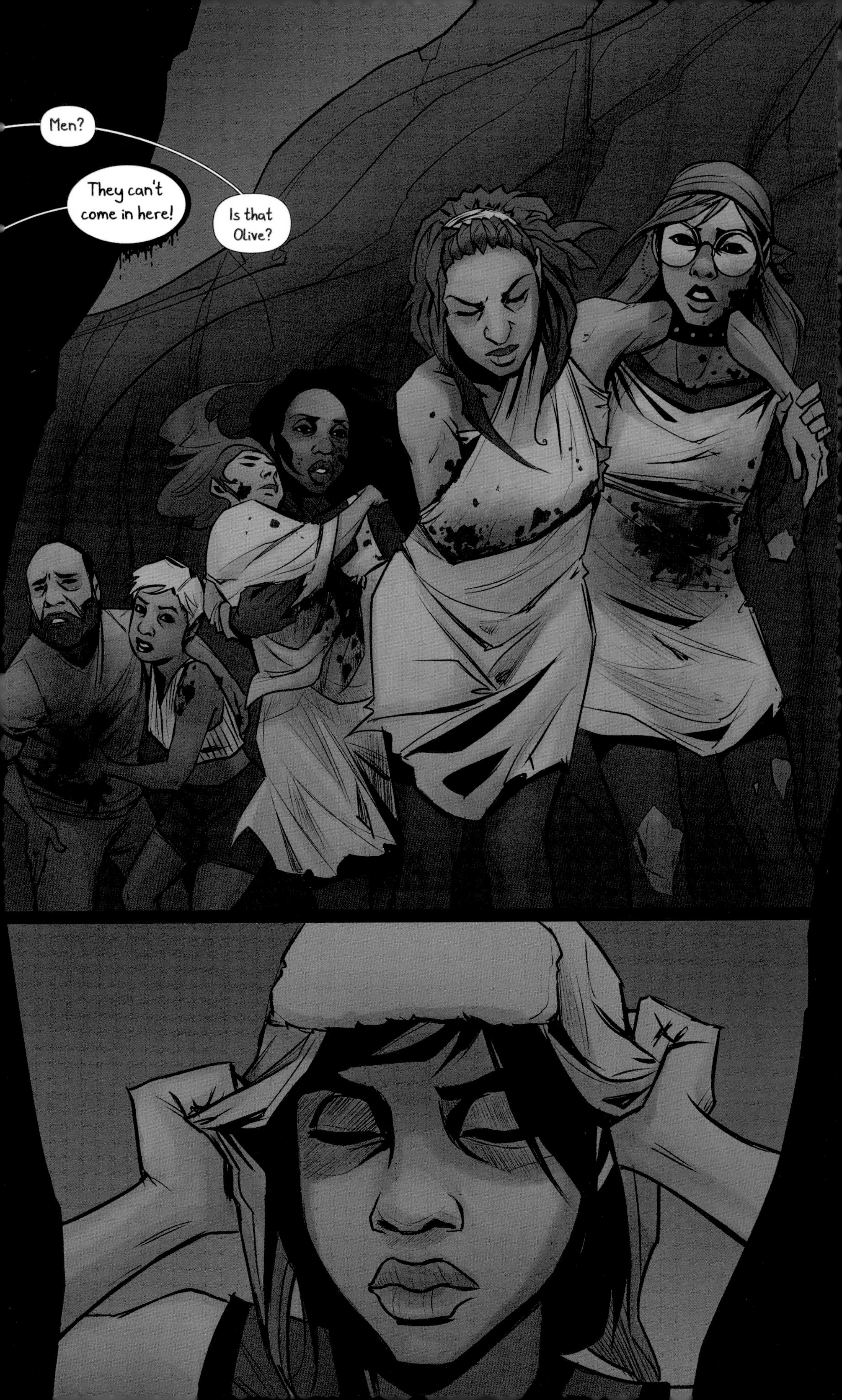
Men?
They can't come in here!
Is that Olive?

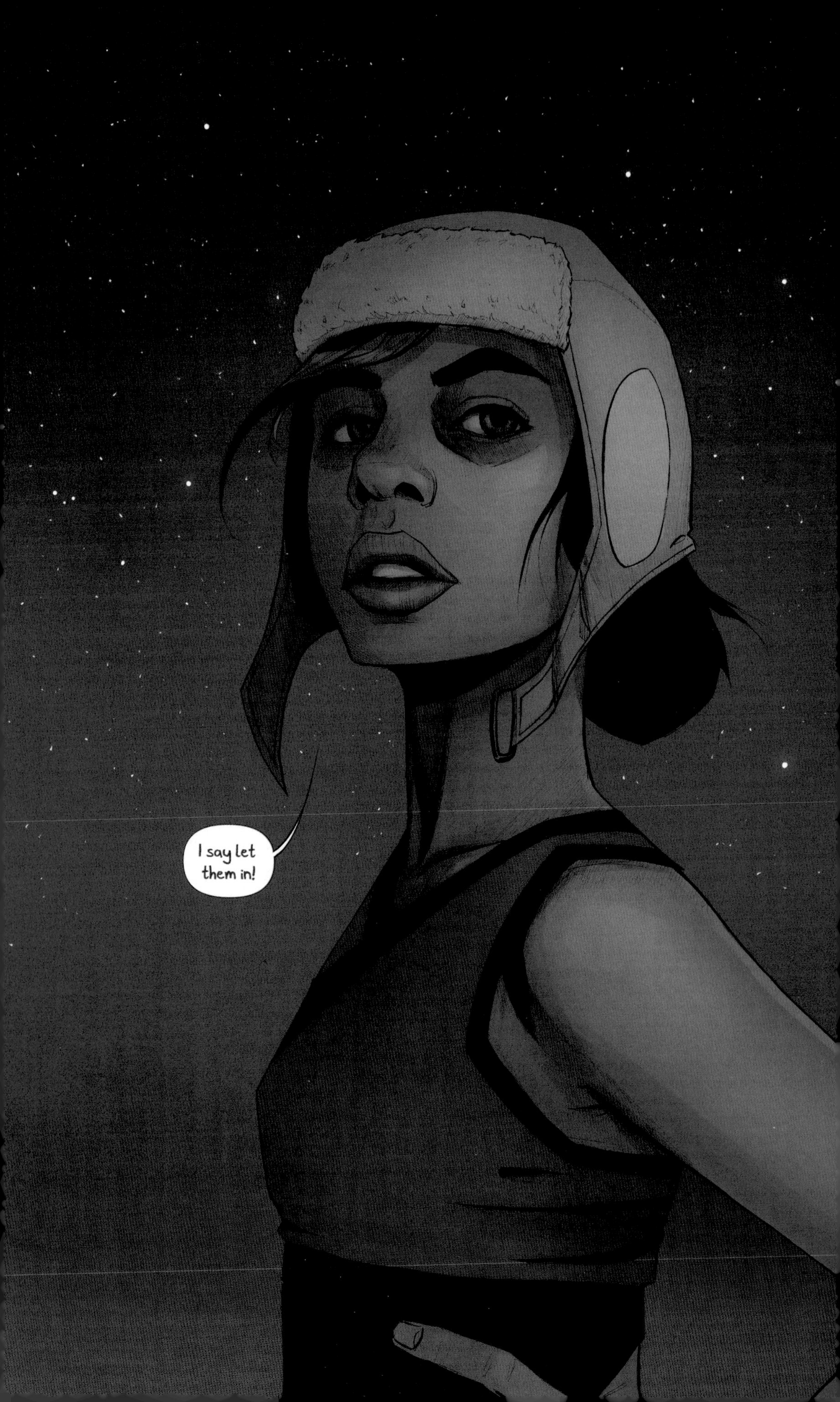
I say let them in!

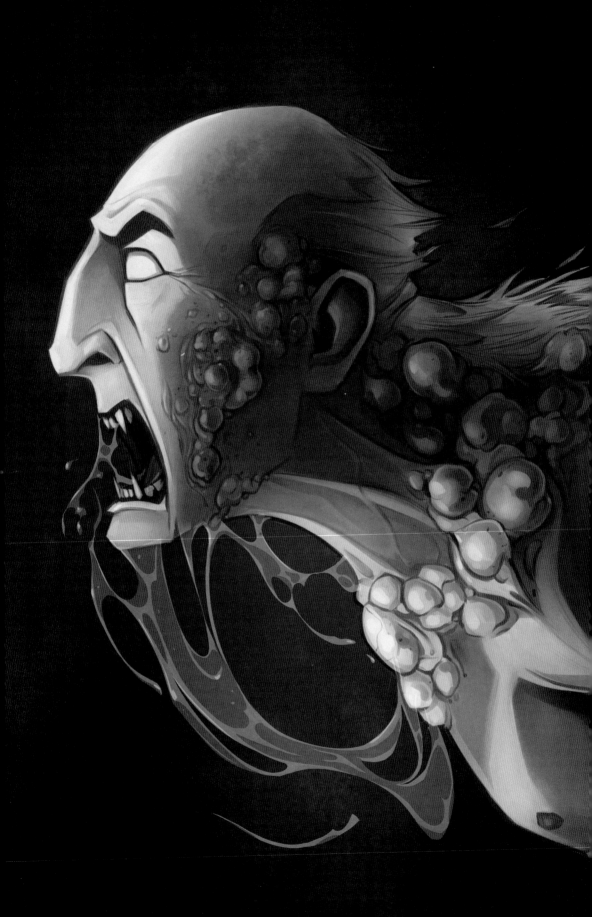

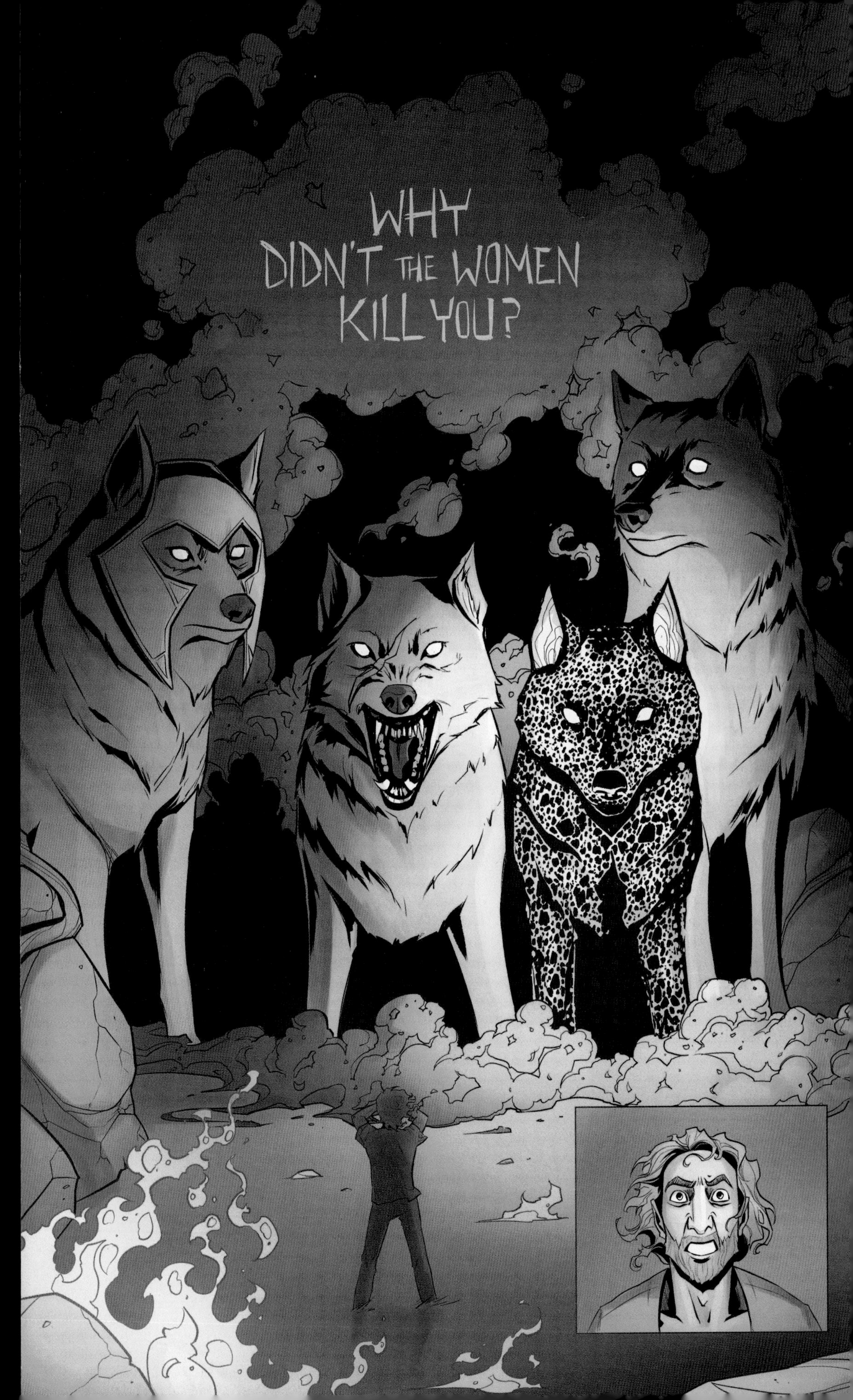
WHY DIDN'T THE WOMEN KILL YOU?

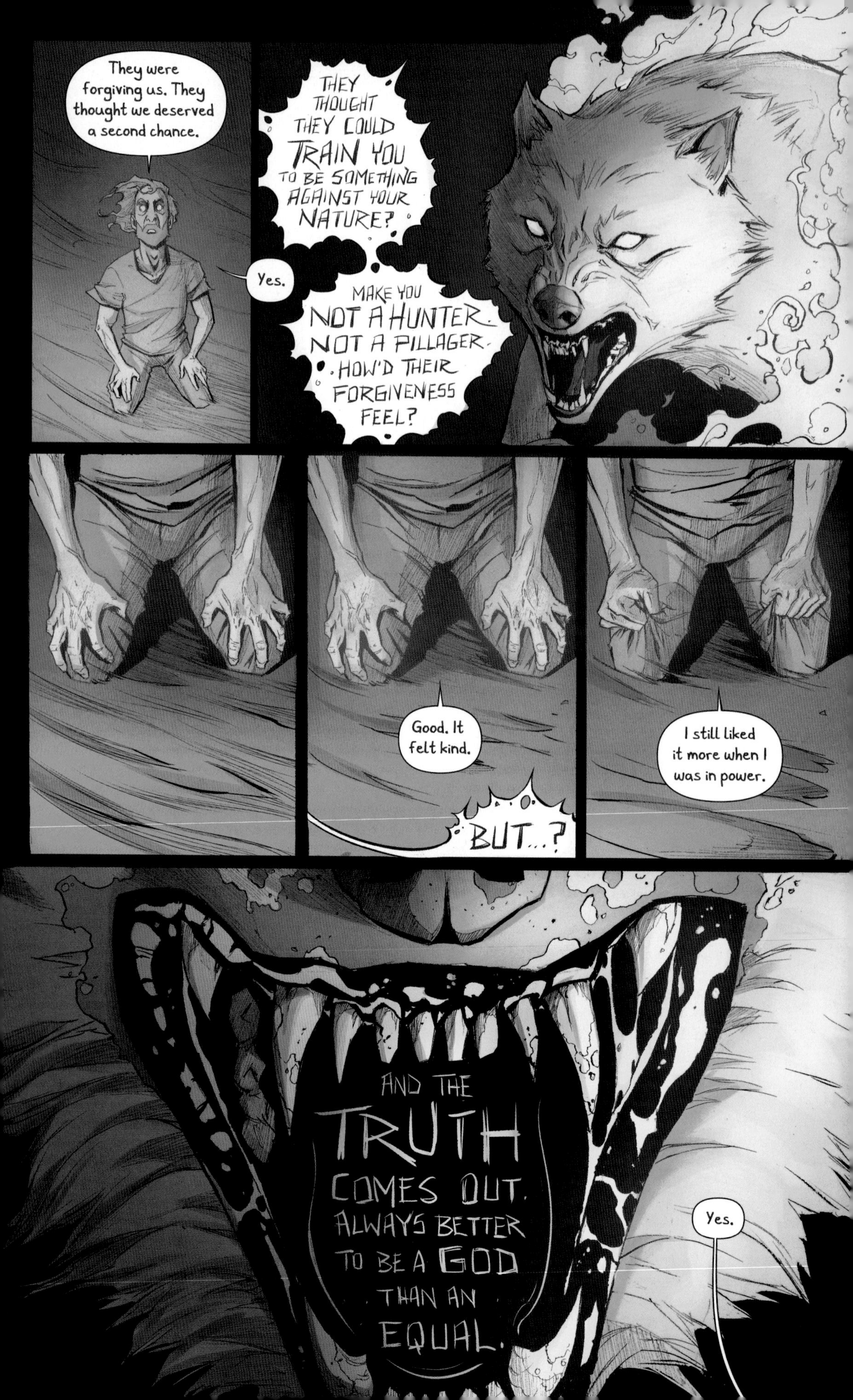
They were forgiving us. They thought we deserved a second chance.
THEY THOUGHT THEY COULD TRAIN YOU TO BE SOMETHING AGAINST YOUR NATURE?
Yes.
MAKE YOU NOT A HUNTER. NOT A PILLAGER. HOW'D THEIR FORGIVENESS FEEL?
Good. It felt kind.
BUT...?
I still liked it more when I was in power.
AND THE TRUTH COMES OUT. ALWAYS BETTER TO BE A GOD THAN AN EQUAL.
Yes.

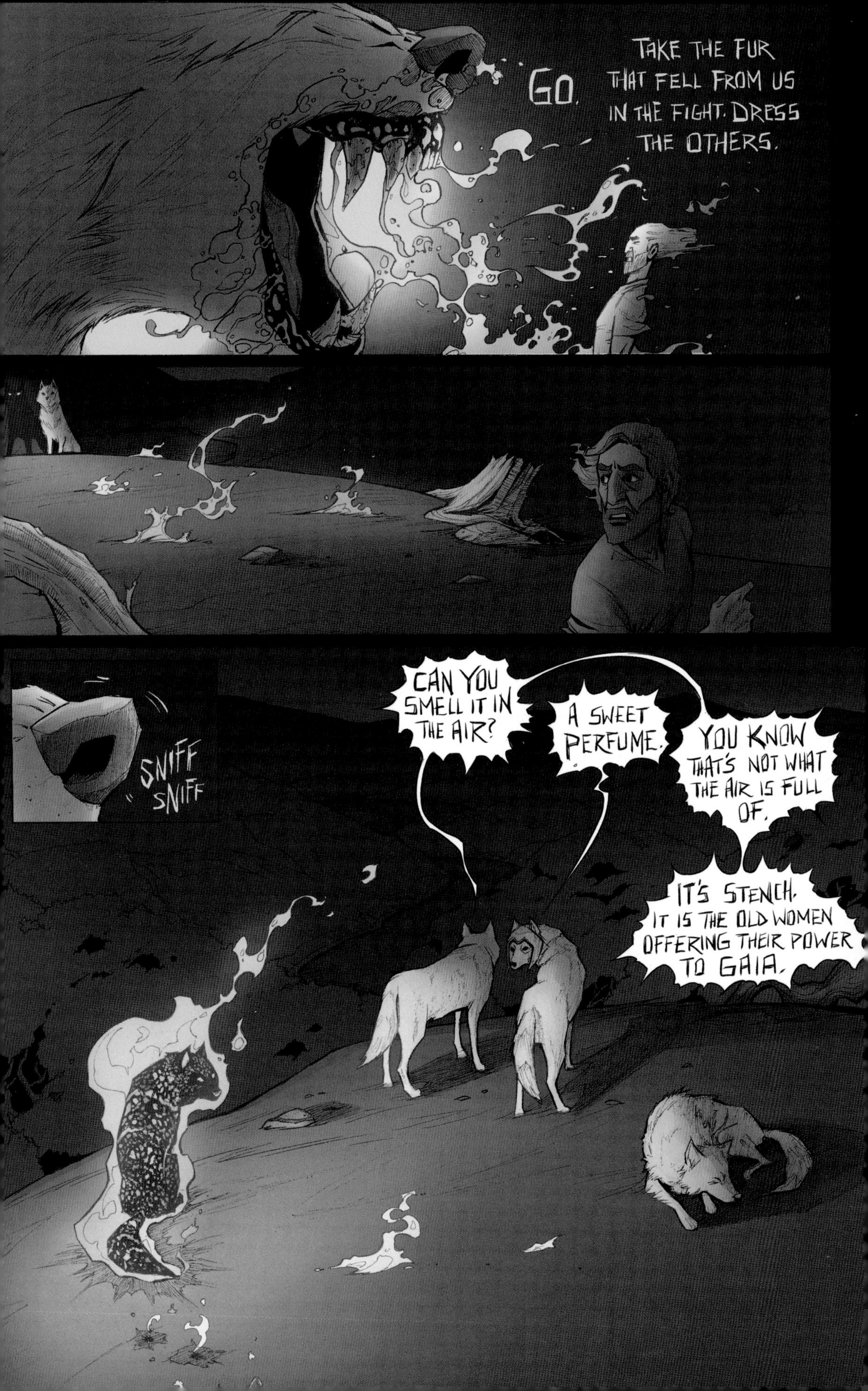
GO.
TAKE THE FUR THAT FELL FROM US IN THE FIGHT. DRESS THE OTHERS.
SNIFF SNIFF
CAN YOU SMELL IT IN THE AIR?
A SWEET PERFUME.
YOU KNOW THAT'S NOT WHAT THE AIR IS FULL OF.
IT'S STENCH. IT IS THE OLD WOMEN OFFERING THEIR POWER TO GAIA.

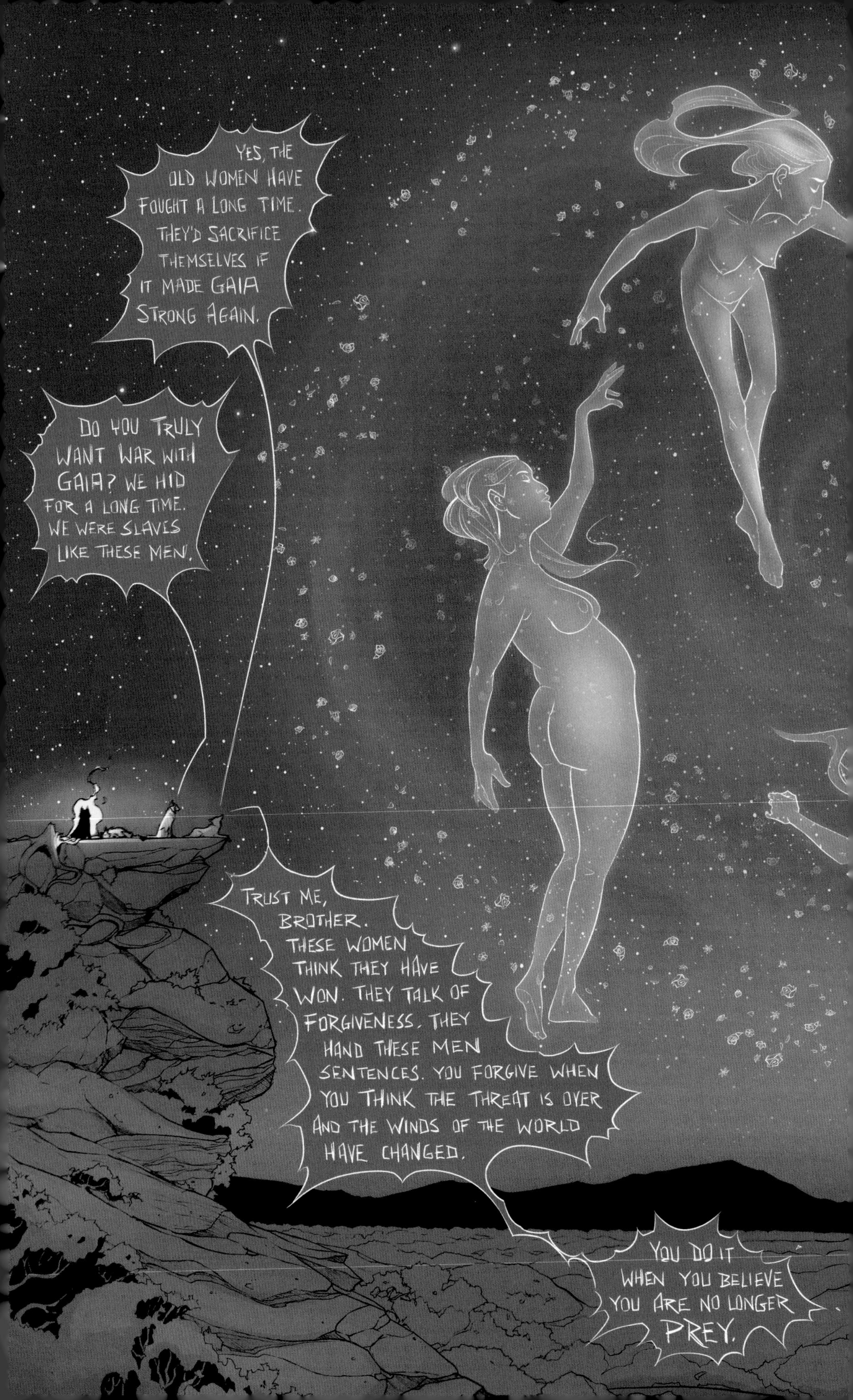
YES, THE OLD WOMEN HAVE FOUGHT A LONG TIME. THEY'D SACRIFICE THEMSELVES IF IT MADE GAIA STRONG AGAIN.
DO YOU TRULY WANT WAR WITH GAIA? WE HID FOR A LONG TIME. WE WERE SLAVES LIKE THESE MEN.
TRUST ME, BROTHER. THESE WOMEN THINK THEY HAVE WON. THEY TALK OF FORGIVENESS. THEY HAND THESE MEN SENTENCES. YOU FORGIVE WHEN YOU THINK THE THREAT IS OVER AND THE WINDS OF THE WORLD HAVE CHANGED.
YOU DO IT WHEN YOU BELIEVE YOU ARE NO LONGER PREY.

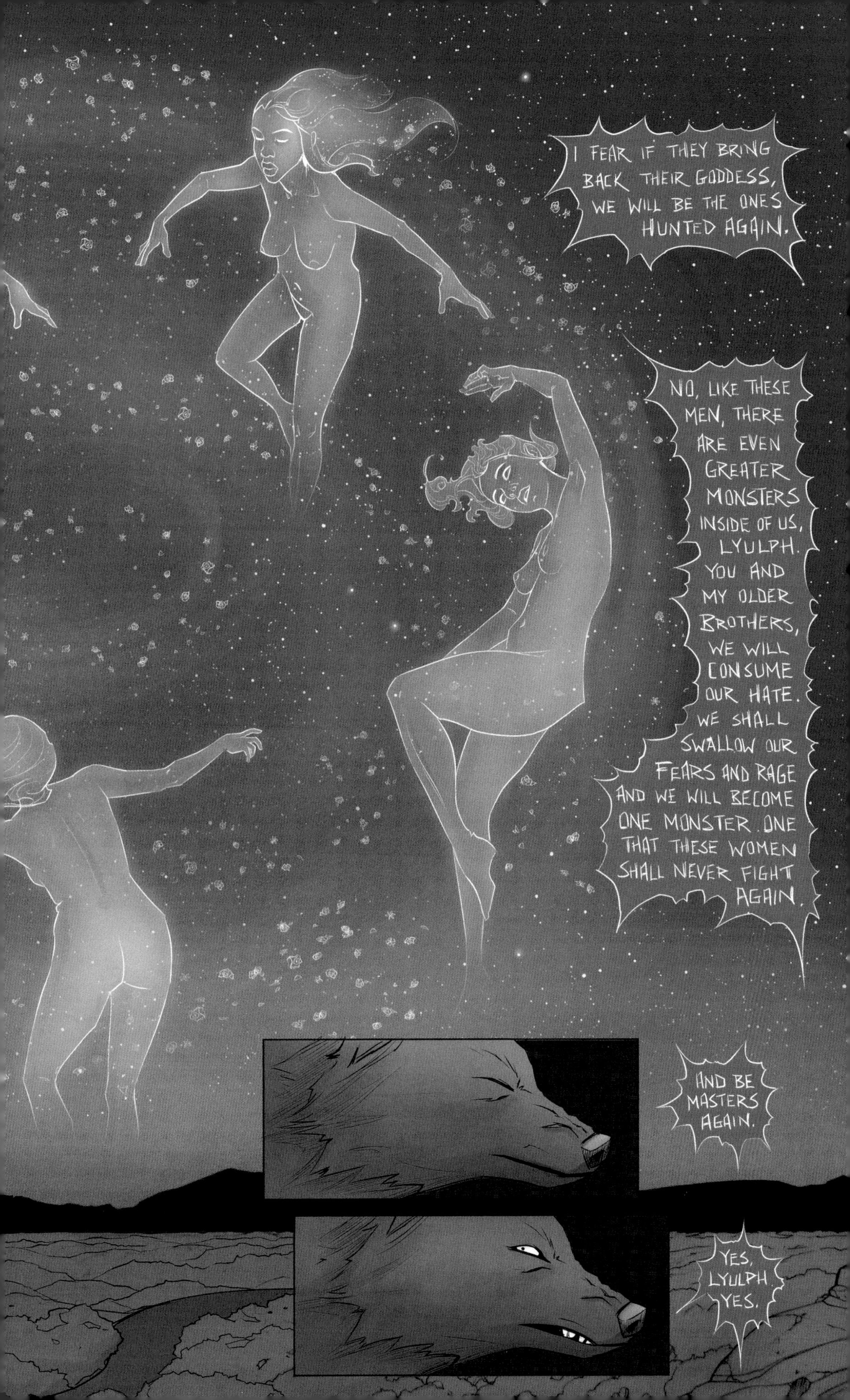
I FEAR IF THEY BRING BACK THEIR GODDESS, WE WILL BE THE ONES HUNTED AGAIN.
NO, LIKE THESE MEN, THERE ARE EVEN GREATER MONSTERS INSIDE OF US, LYULPH. YOU AND MY OLDER BROTHERS, WE WILL CONSUME OUR HATE. WE SHALL SWALLOW OUR FEARS AND RAGE AND WE WILL BECOME ONE MONSTER. ONE THAT THESE WOMEN SHALL NEVER FIGHT AGAIN.
AND BE MASTERS AGAIN.
YES, LYULPH. YES.

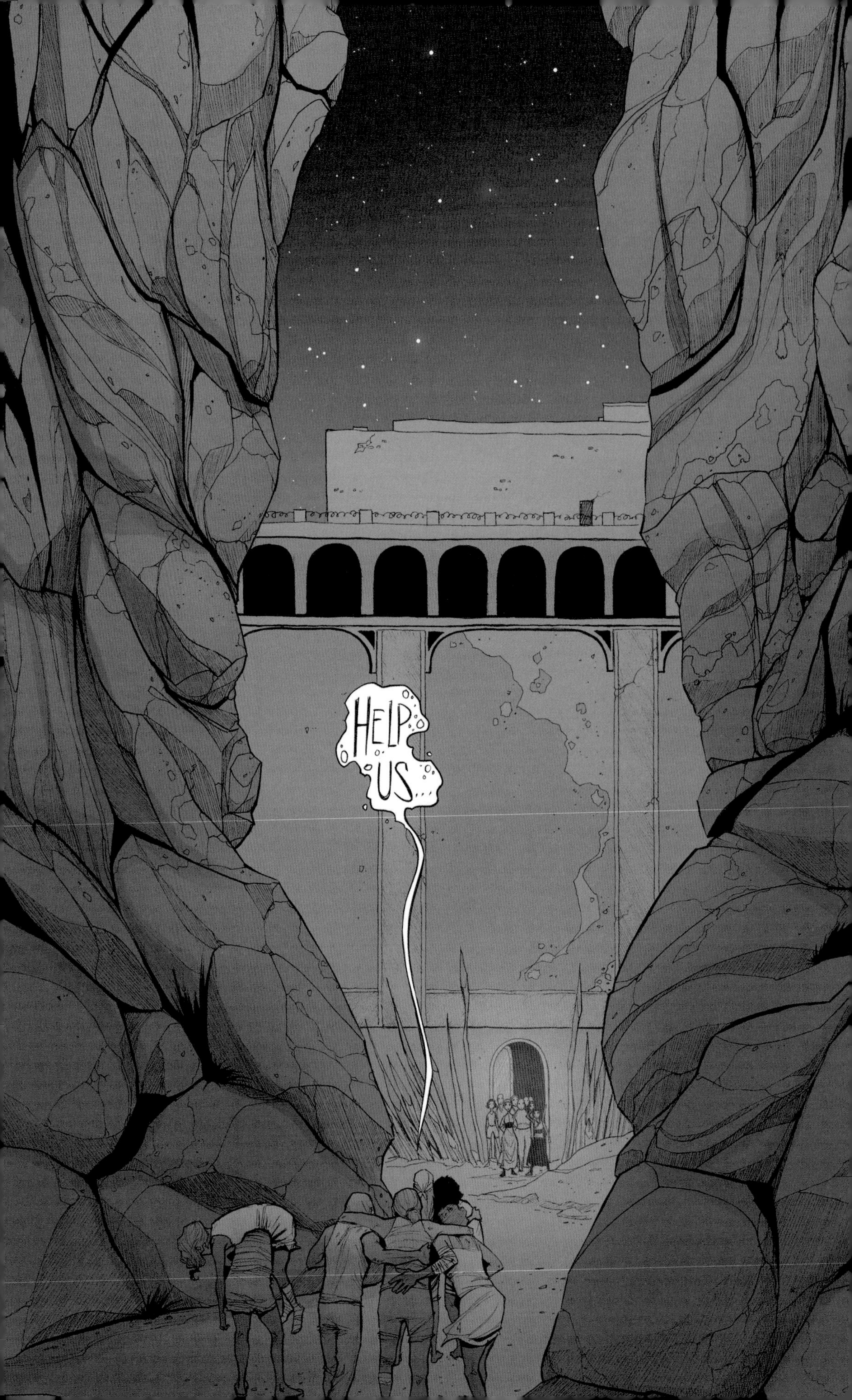
HELP US...

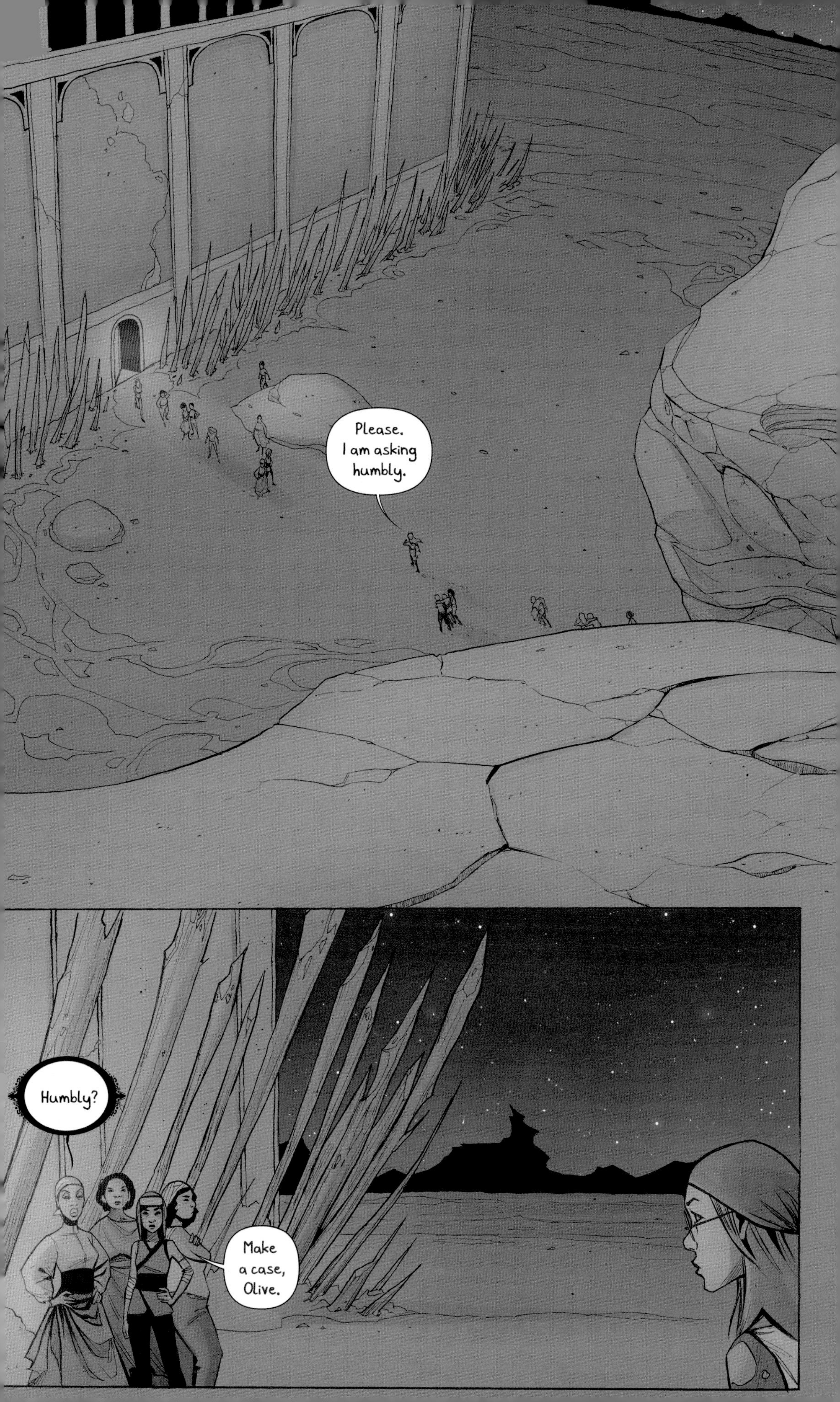
Please. I am asking humbly.
Humbly?
Make a case, Olive.

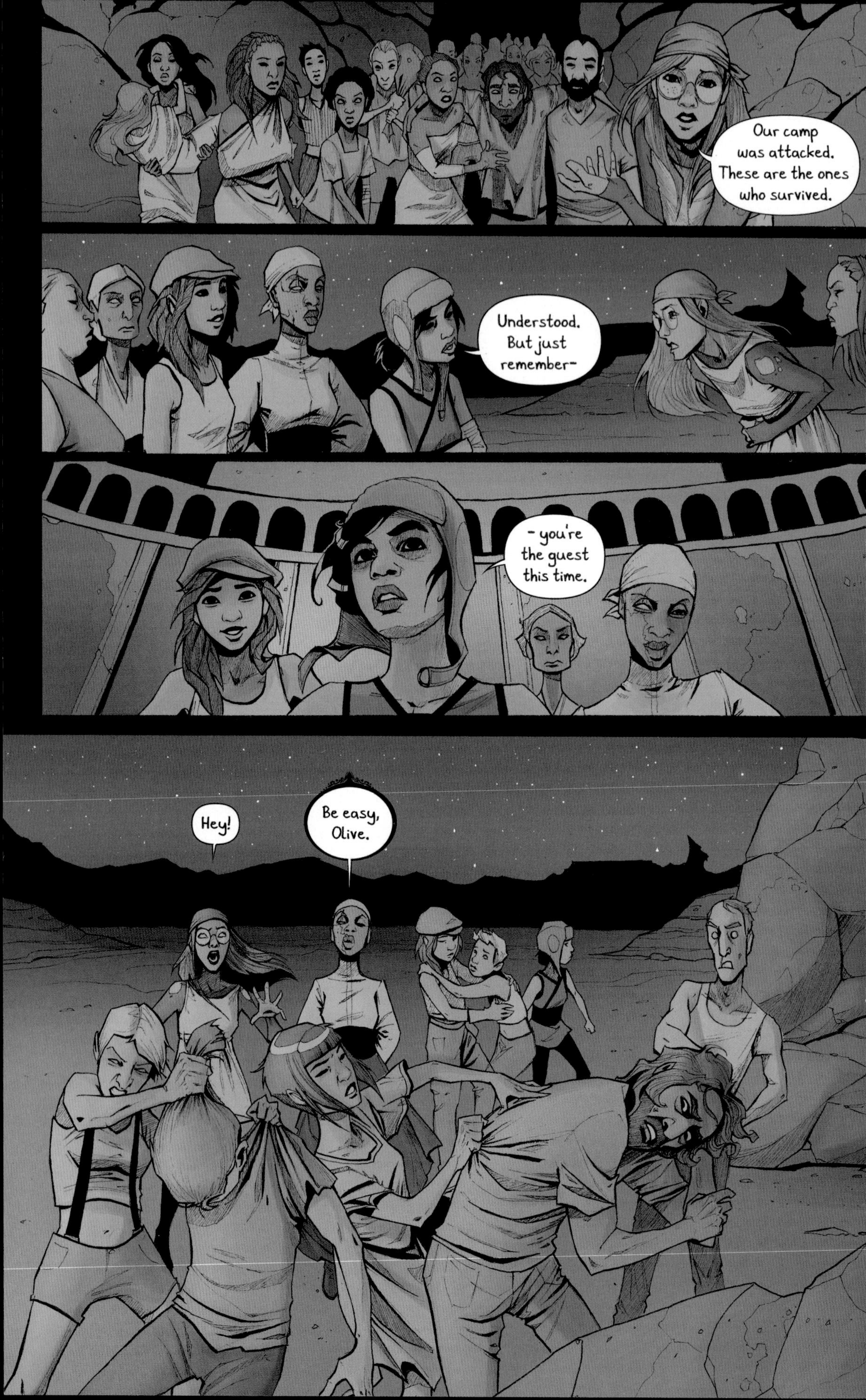
Our camp was attacked. These are the ones who survived.
Understood. But just remember-
-you're the guest this time.
Hey!
Be easy, Olive.

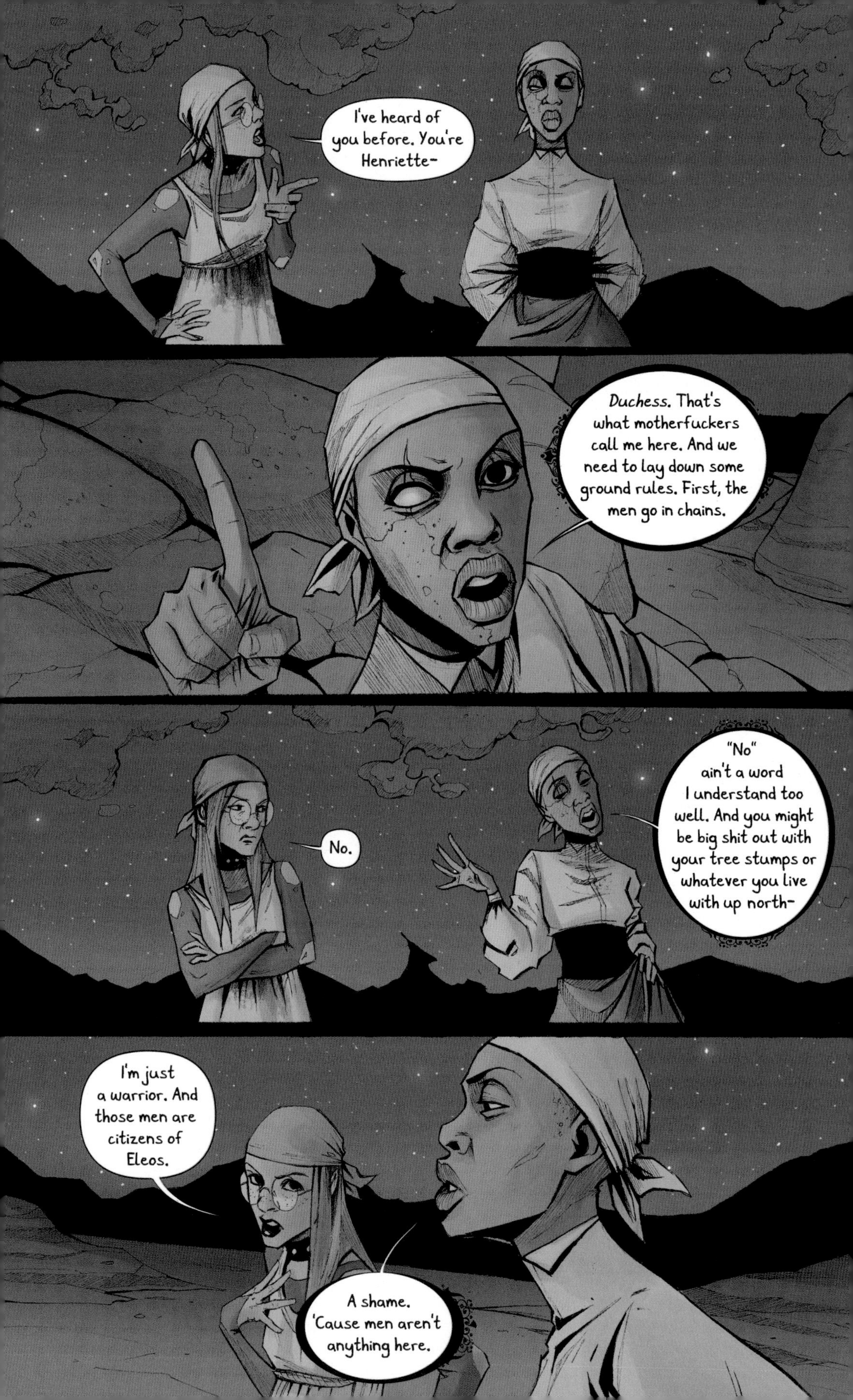
I've heard of you before. You're Henriette-
Duchess. That's what motherfuckers call me here. And we need to lay down some ground rules. First, the men go in chains.
No.
"No" ain't a word I understand too well. And you might be big shit out with your tree stumps or whatever you live with up north-
I'm just a warrior. And those men are citizens of Eleos.
A shame. 'Cause men aren't anything here.

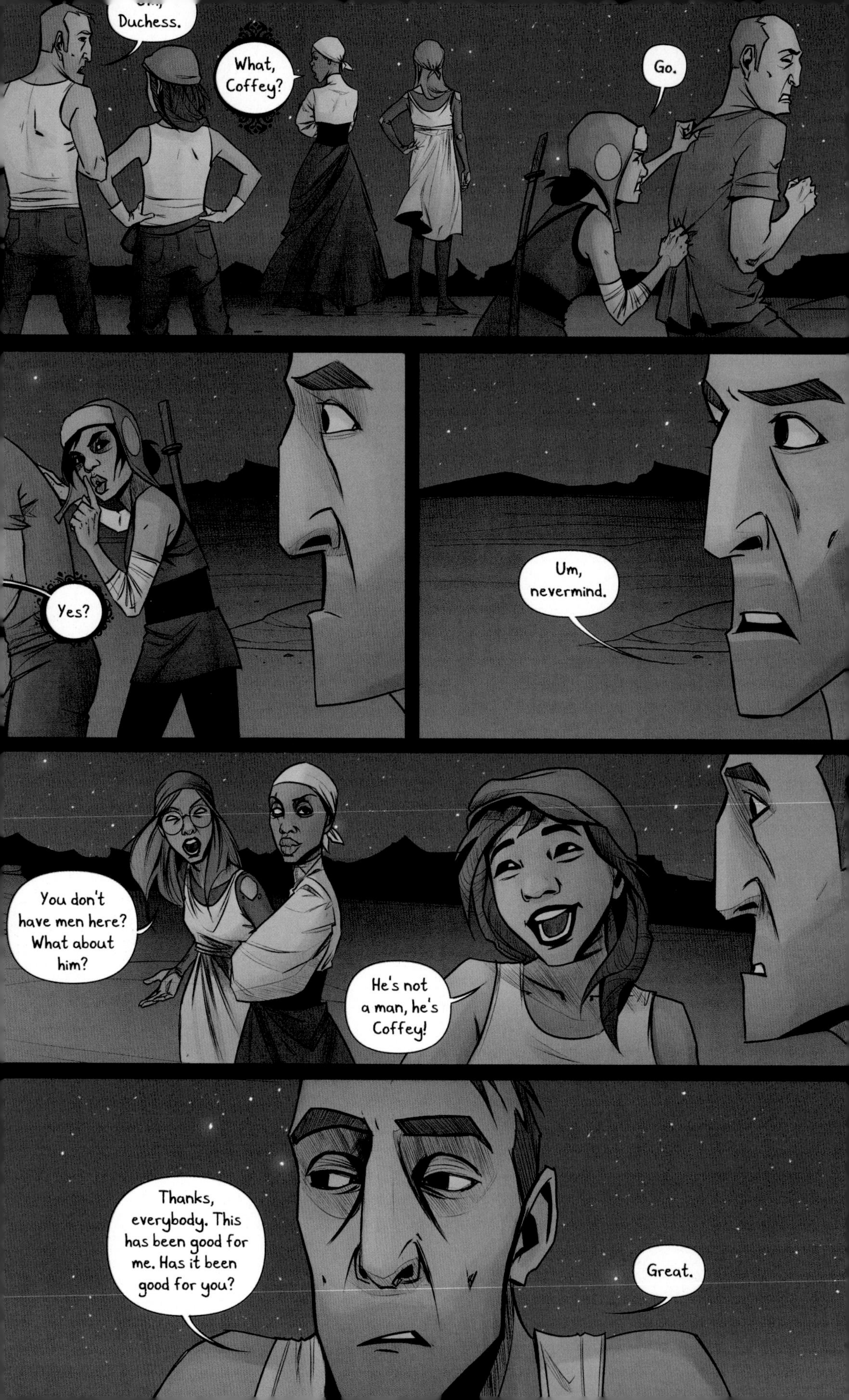
Duchess.
What, Coffey?
Go.
Yes?
Um, nevermind.
You don't have men here? What about him?
He's not a man, he's Coffey!
Thanks, everybody. This has been good for me. Has it been good for you?
Great.

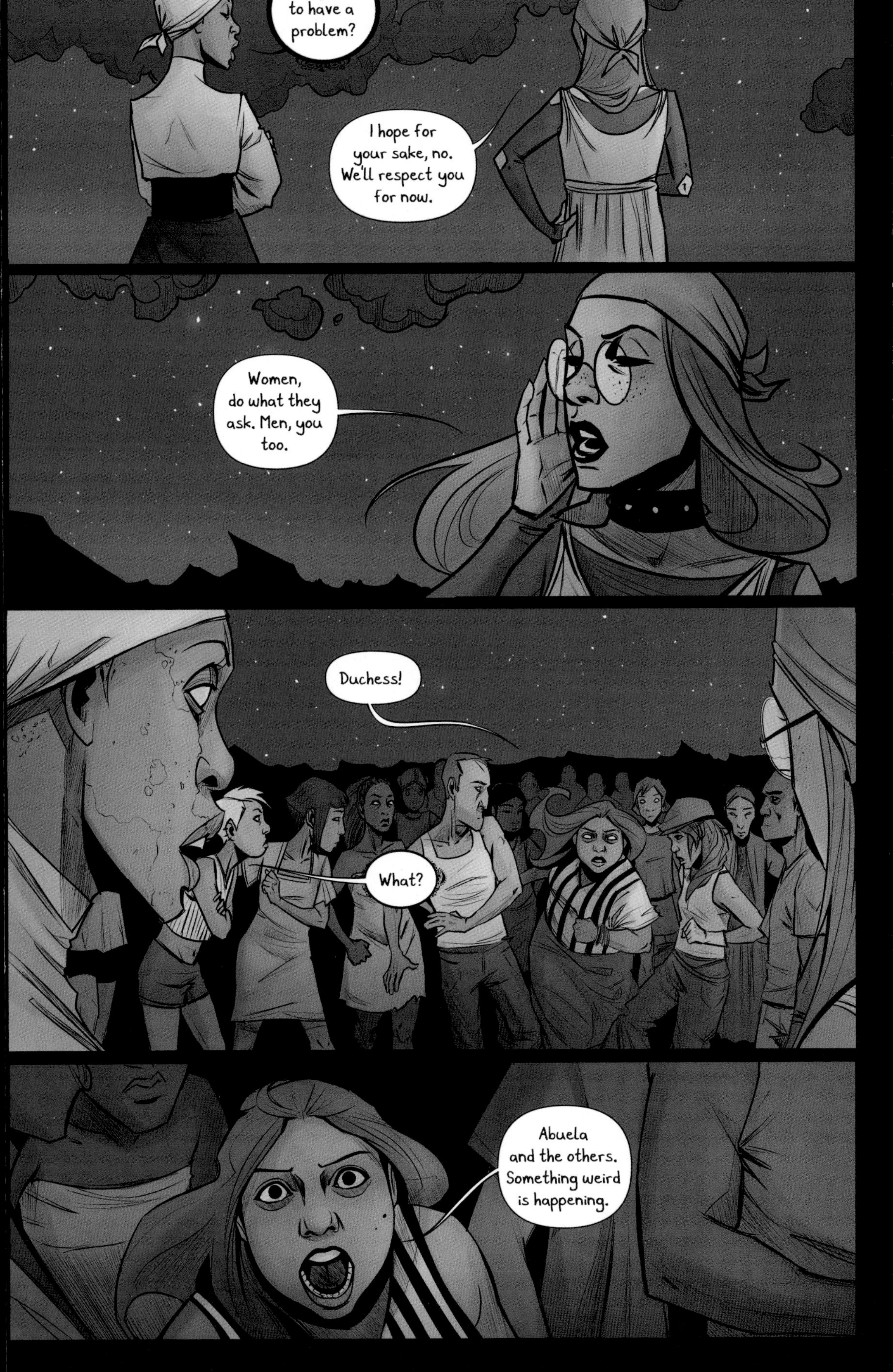
to have a problem?
I hope for your sake, no. We'll respect you for now.
Women, do what they ask. Men, you too.
Duchess!
What?
Abuela and the others. Something weird is happening.

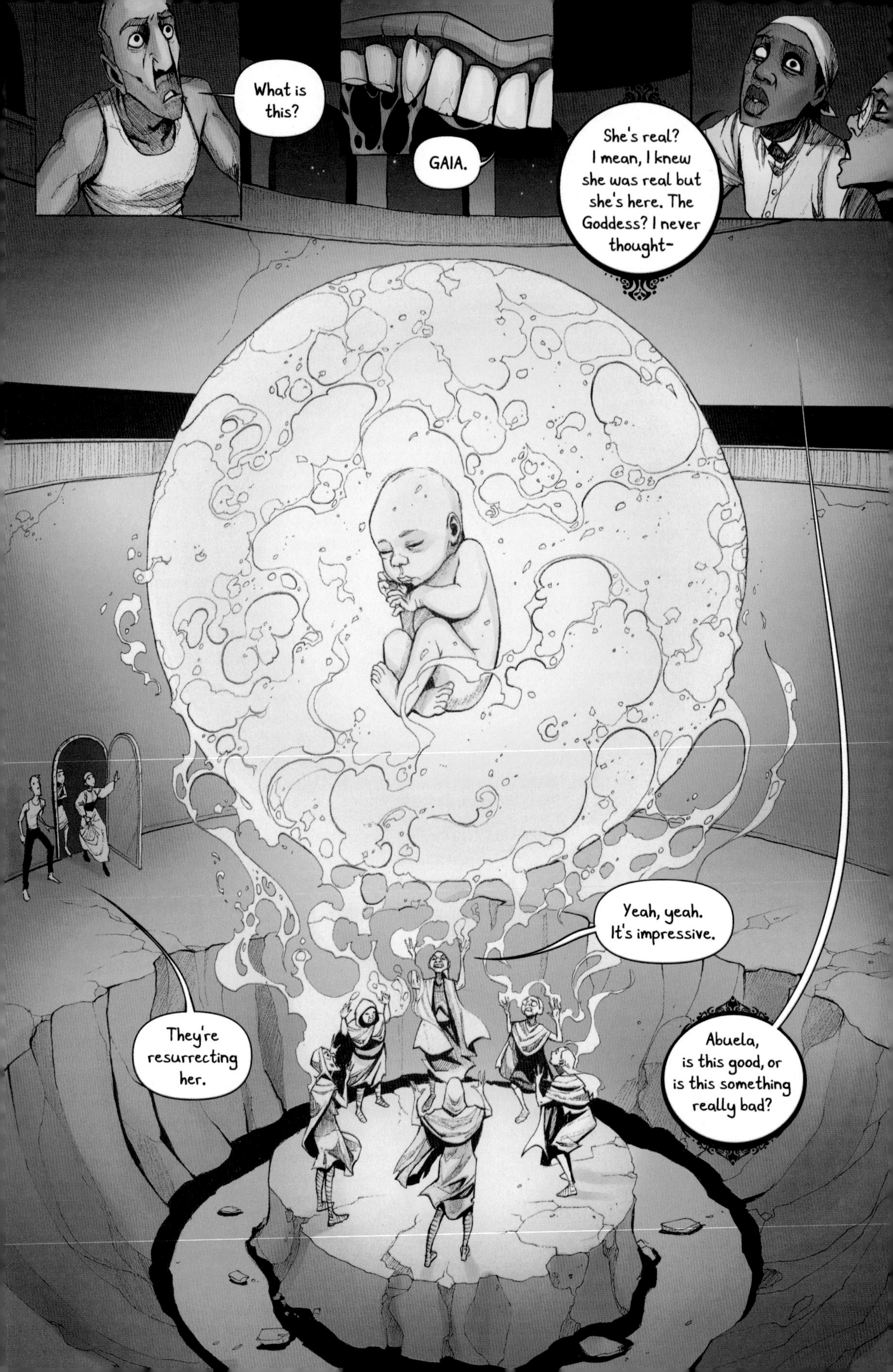

What is this?
GAIA.
She's real? I mean, I knew she was real but she's here. The Goddess? I never thought-
Yeah, yeah. It's impressive.
They're resurrecting her.
Abuela, is this good, or is this something really bad?

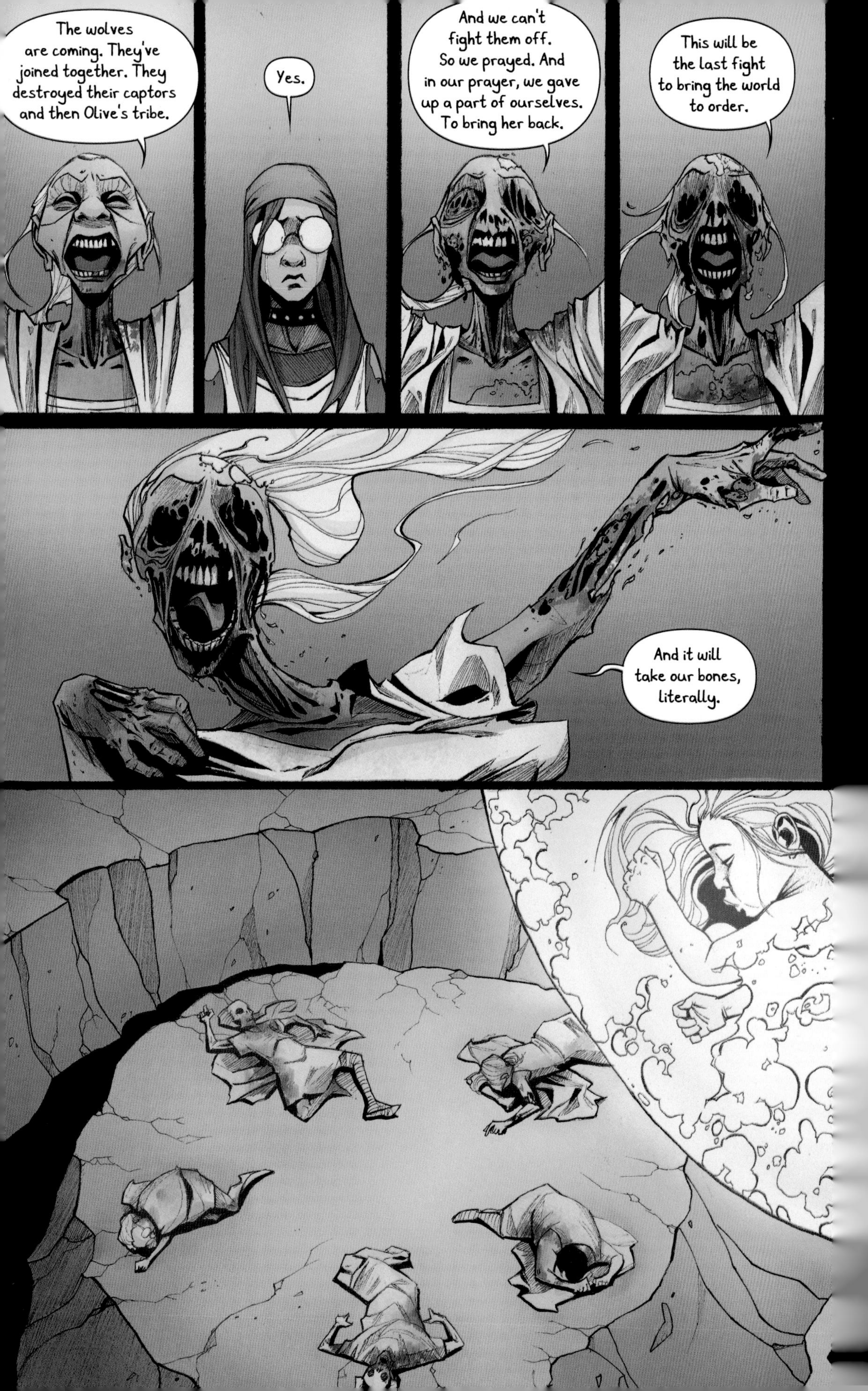
The wolves are coming. They've joined together. They destroyed their captors and then Olive's tribe.
Yes.
And we can't fight them off. So we prayed. And in our prayer, we gave up a part of ourselves. To bring her back.
This will be the last fight to bring the world to order.
And it will take our bones, literally.

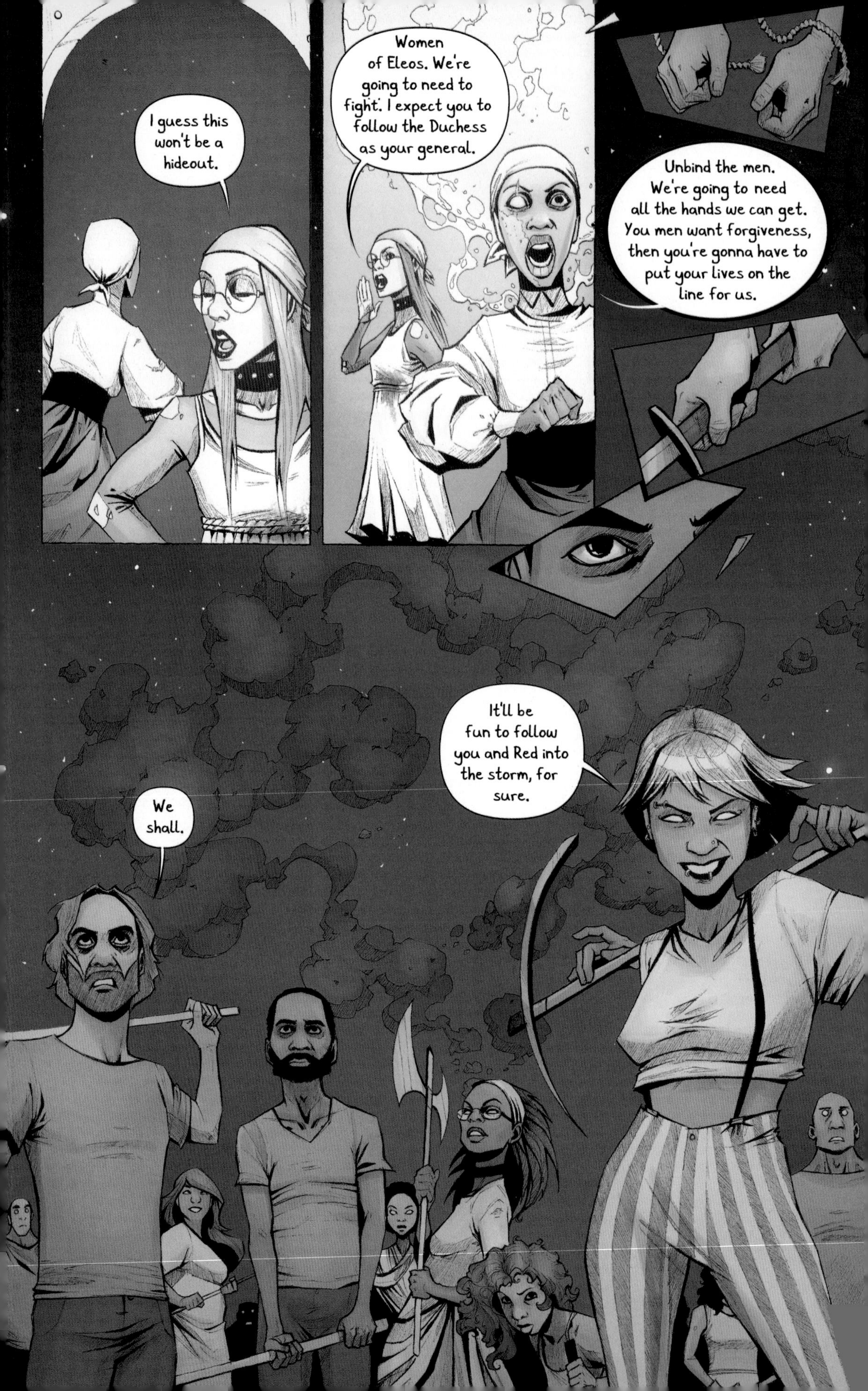
I guess this won't be a hideout.
Women of Eleos. We're going to need to fight. I expect you to follow the Duchess as your general.
Unbind the men. We're going to need all the hands we can get. You men want forgiveness, then you're gonna have to put your lives on the line for us.
It'll be fun to follow you and Red into the storm, for sure.
We shall.

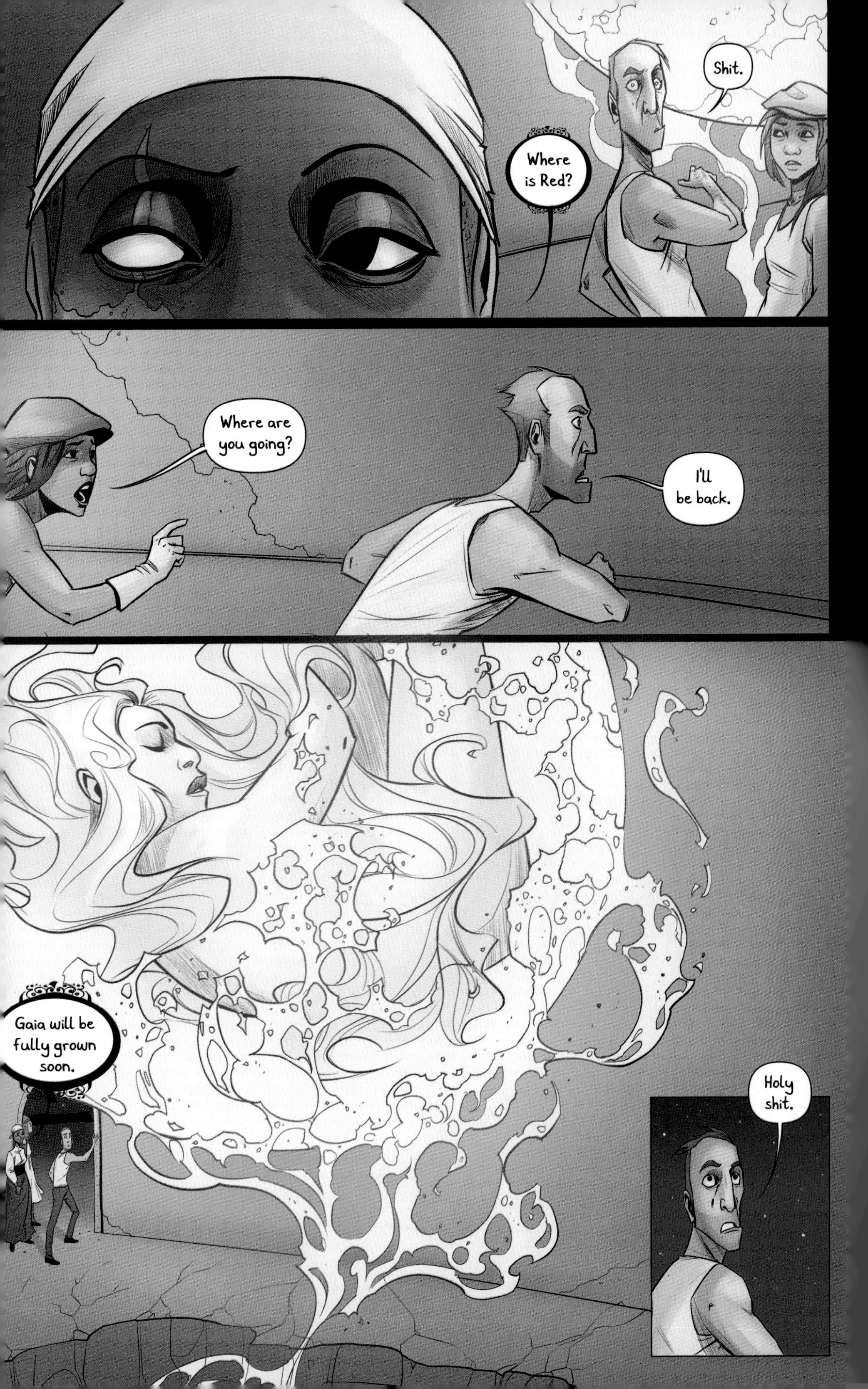
Shit.
Where is Red?
Where are you going?
I'll be back.
Gaia will be fully grown soon.
Holy shit.

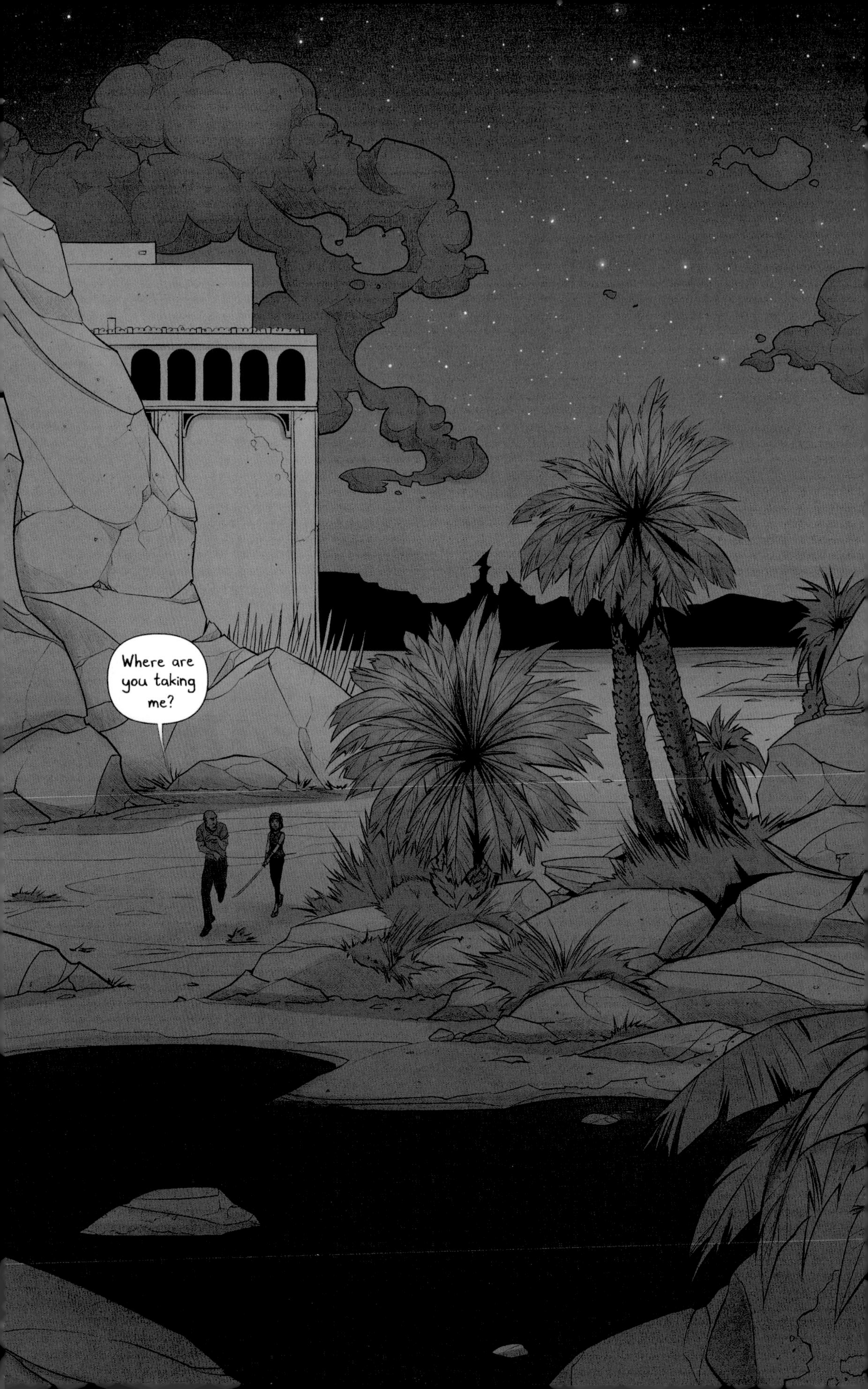
Where are you taking me?

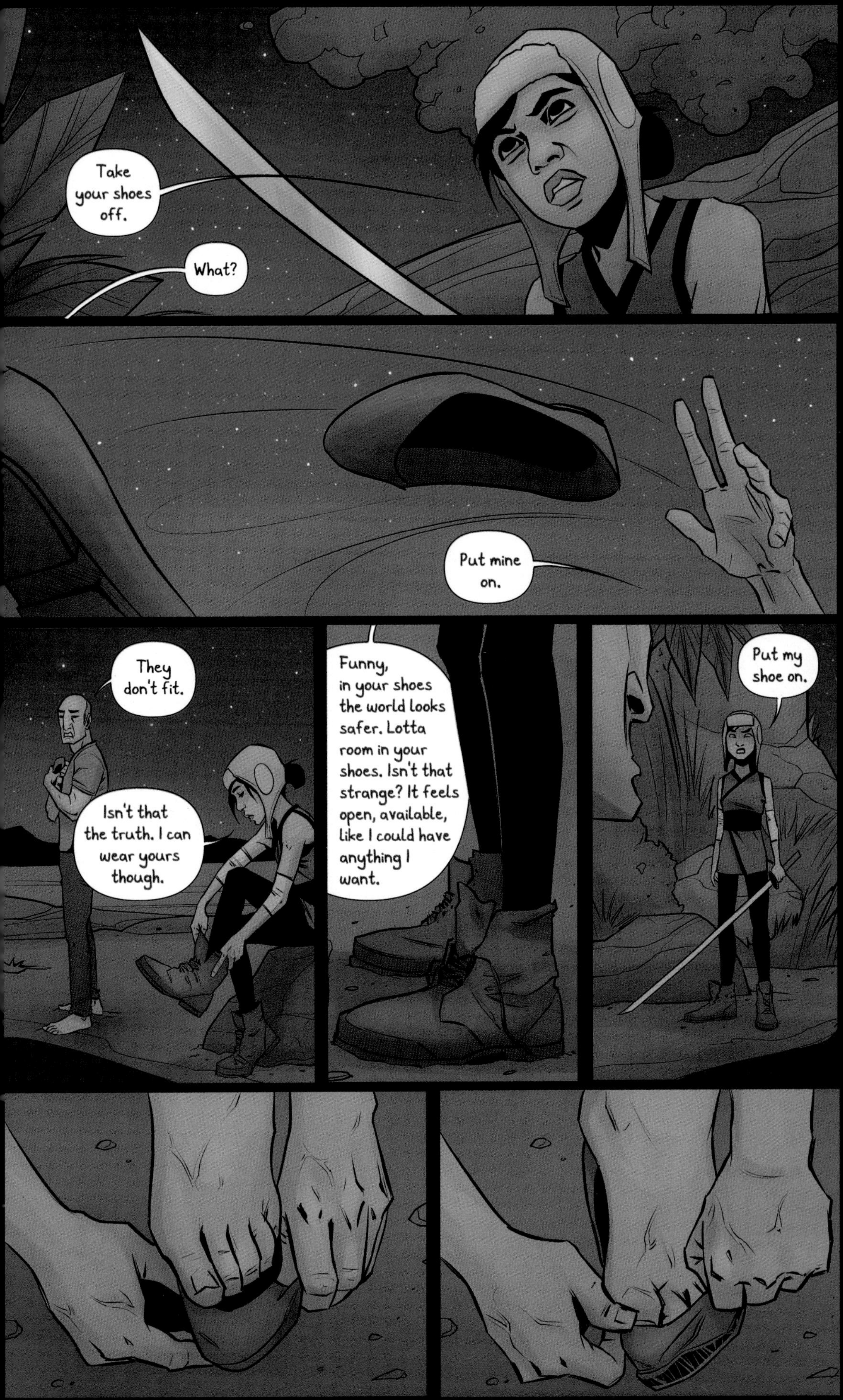
Take your shoes off.
What?
Put mine on.
They don't fit.
Isn't that the truth. I can wear yours though.
Funny, in your shoes the world looks safer. Lotta room in your shoes. Isn't that strange? It feels open, available, like I could have anything I want.
Put my shoe on.

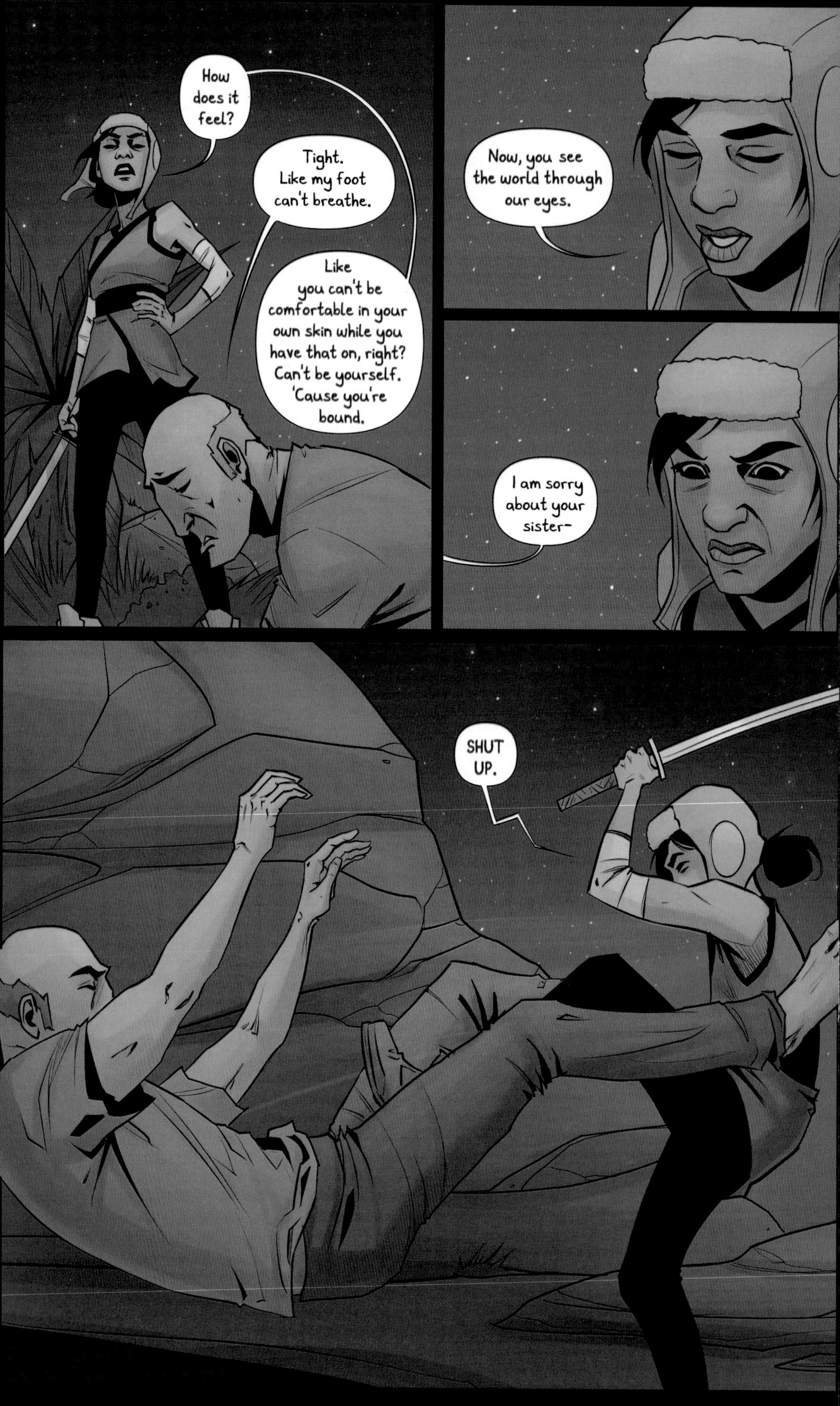
How does it feel?
Tight. Like my foot can't breathe.
Like you can't be comfortable in your own skin while you have that on, right? Can't be yourself. 'Cause you're bound.
Now, you see the world through our eyes.
I am sorry about your sister-
SHUT UP.

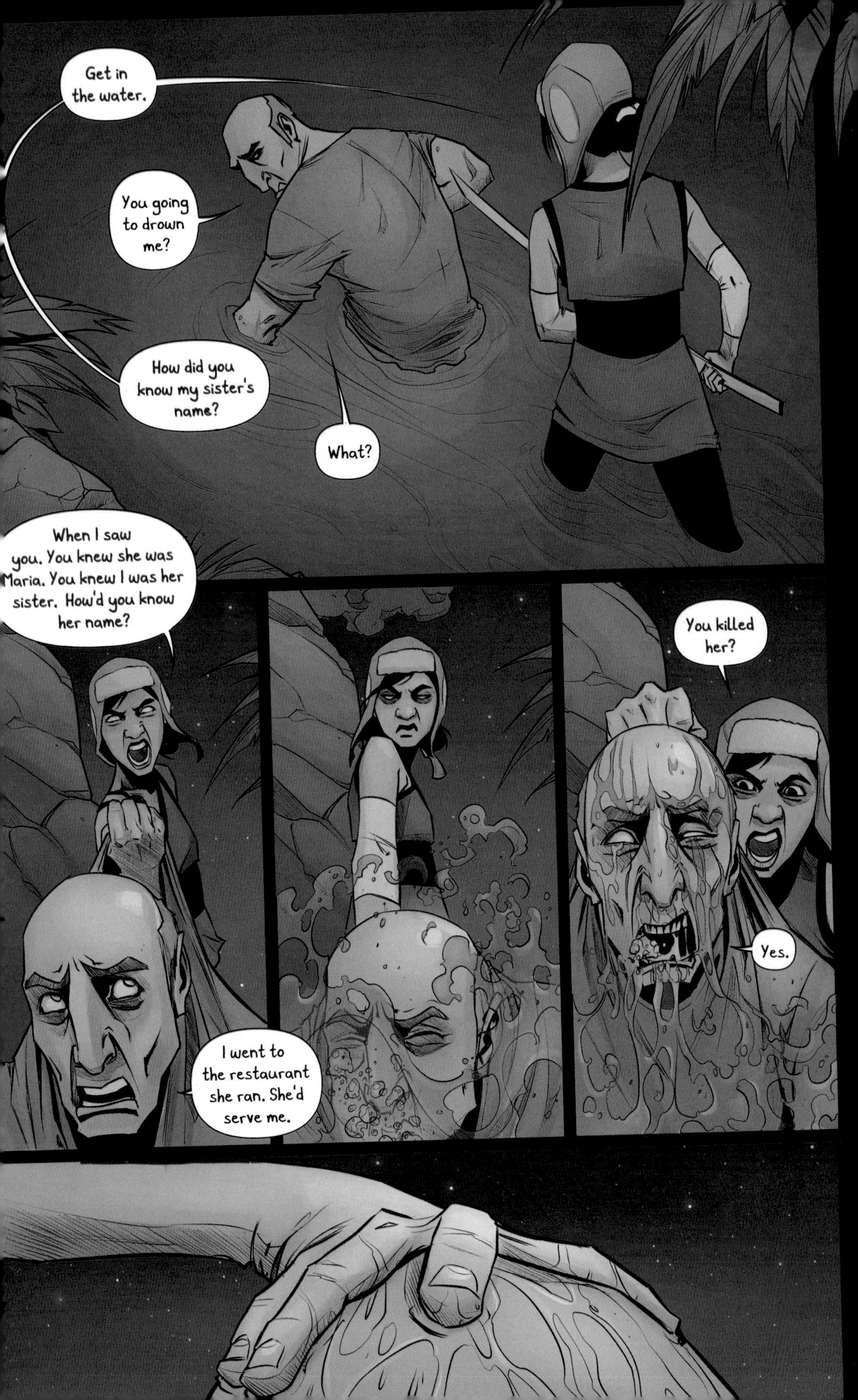
Get in the water.
You going to drown me?
How did you know my sister's name?
What?
When I saw you. You knew she was Maria. You knew I was her sister. How'd you know her name?
I went to the restaurant she ran. She'd serve me.
You killed her?
Yes.

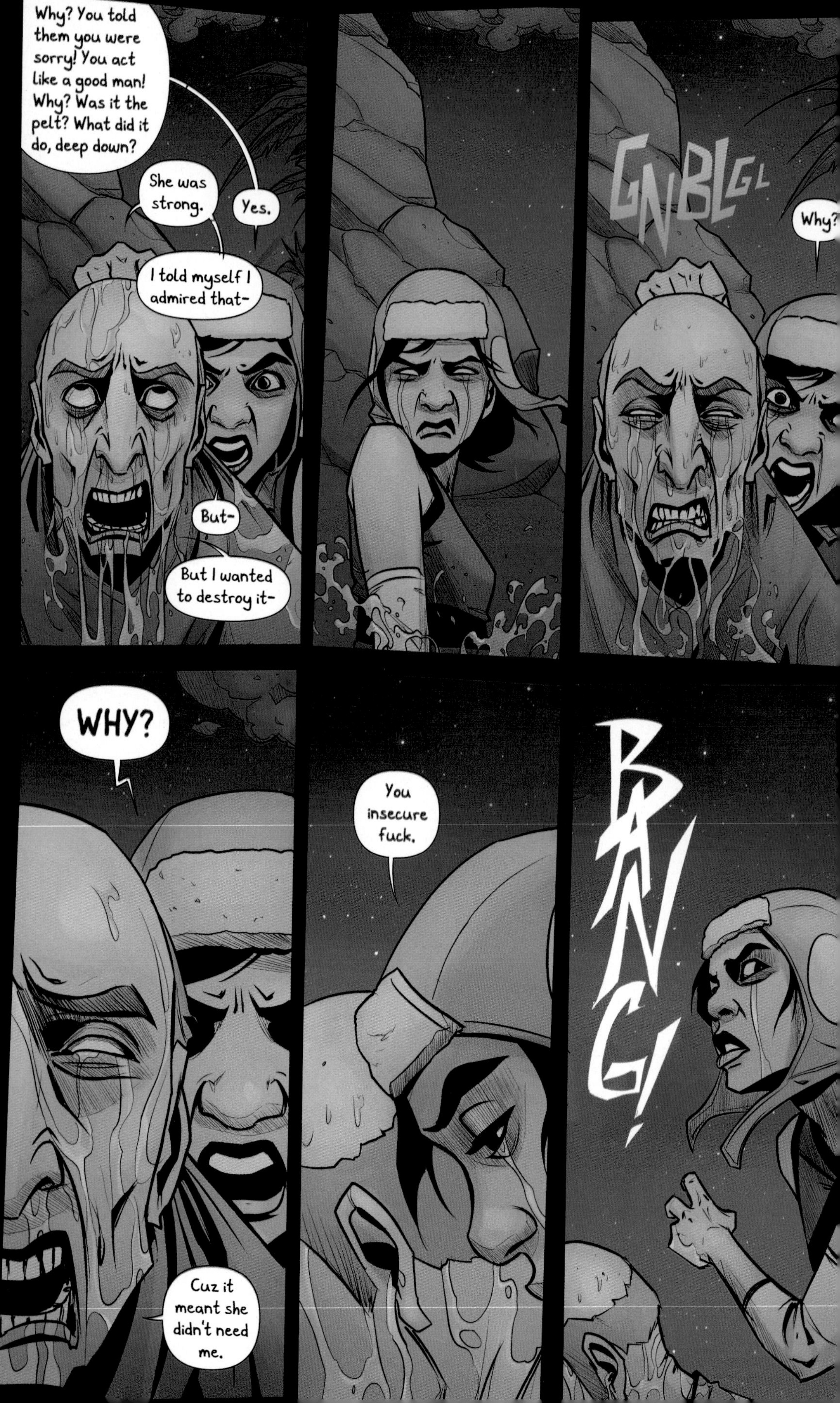
Why? You told them you were sorry! You act like a good man! Why? Was it the pelt? What did it do, deep down?
She was strong.
Yes.
I told myself I admired that-
But-
But I wanted to destroy it-
GNBLGL
Why?
WHY?
Cuz it meant she didn't need me.
You insecure fuck.
BANG!

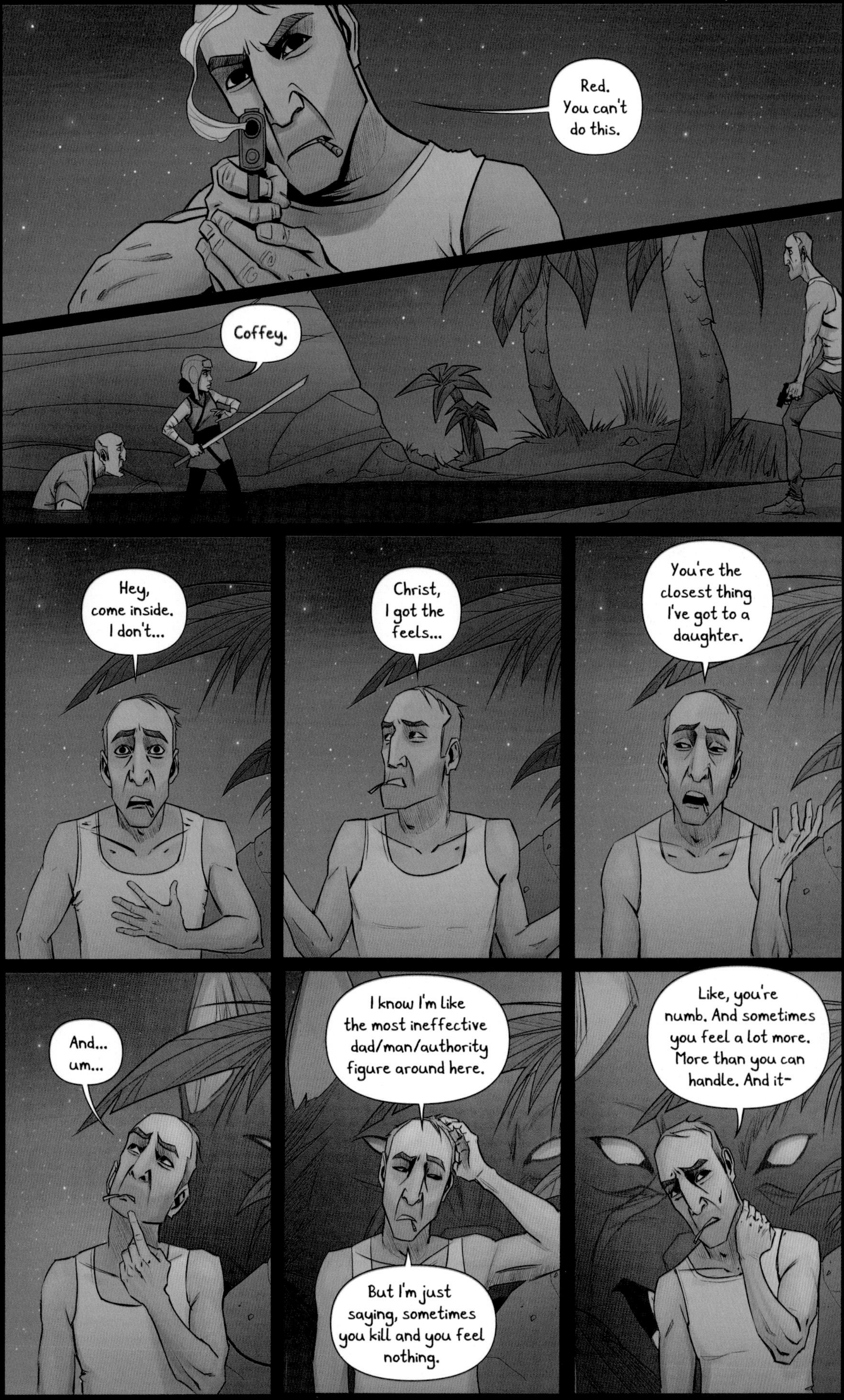
Red. You can't do this.
Coffey.
Hey, come inside. I don't...
Christ, I got the feels...
You're the closest thing I've got to a daughter.
And... um...
I know I'm like the most ineffective dad/man/authority figure around here.
But I'm just saying, sometimes you kill and you feel nothing.
Like, you're numb. And sometimes you feel a lot more. More than you can handle. And it-

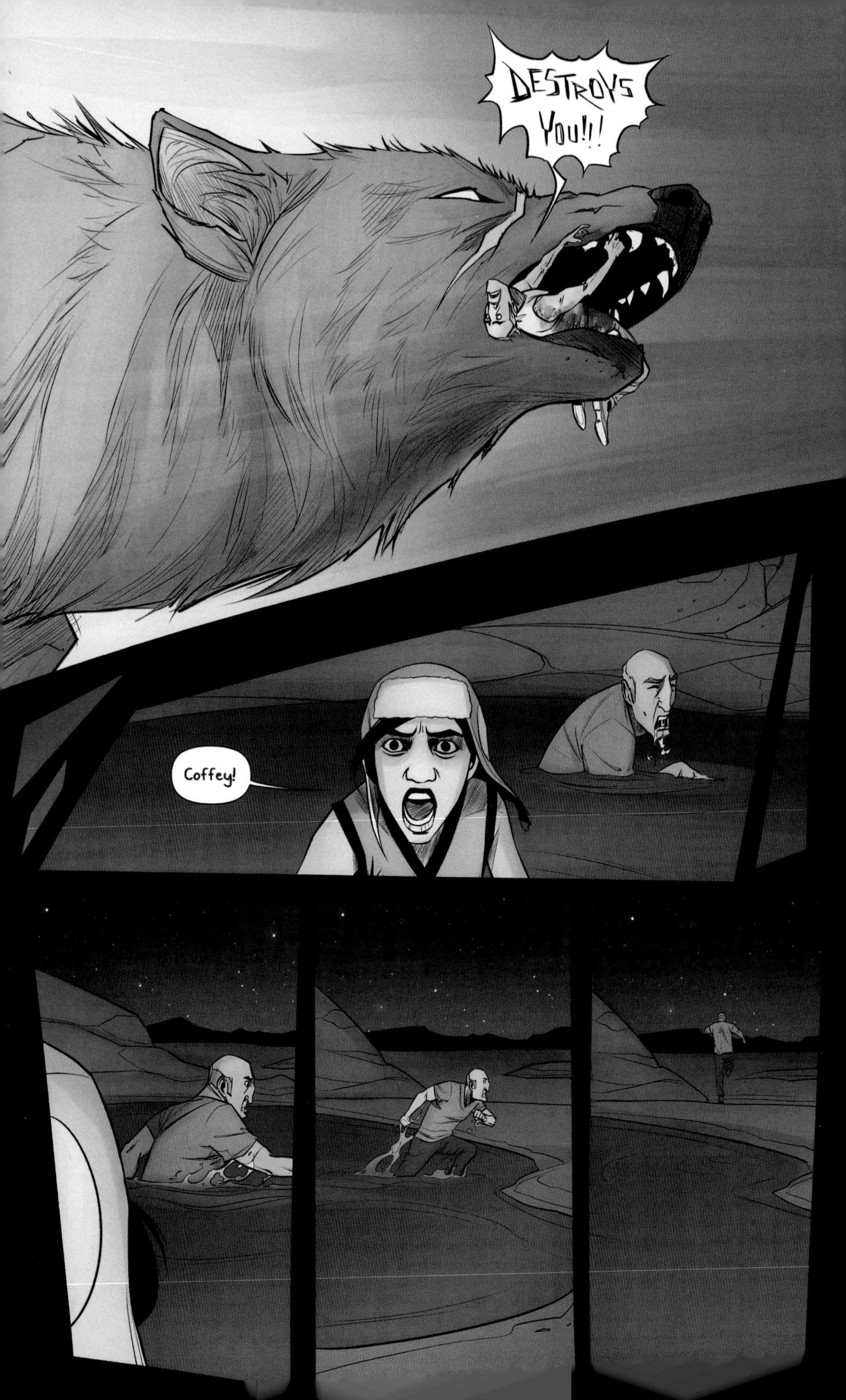
DESTROYS YOU!!!
Coffey!

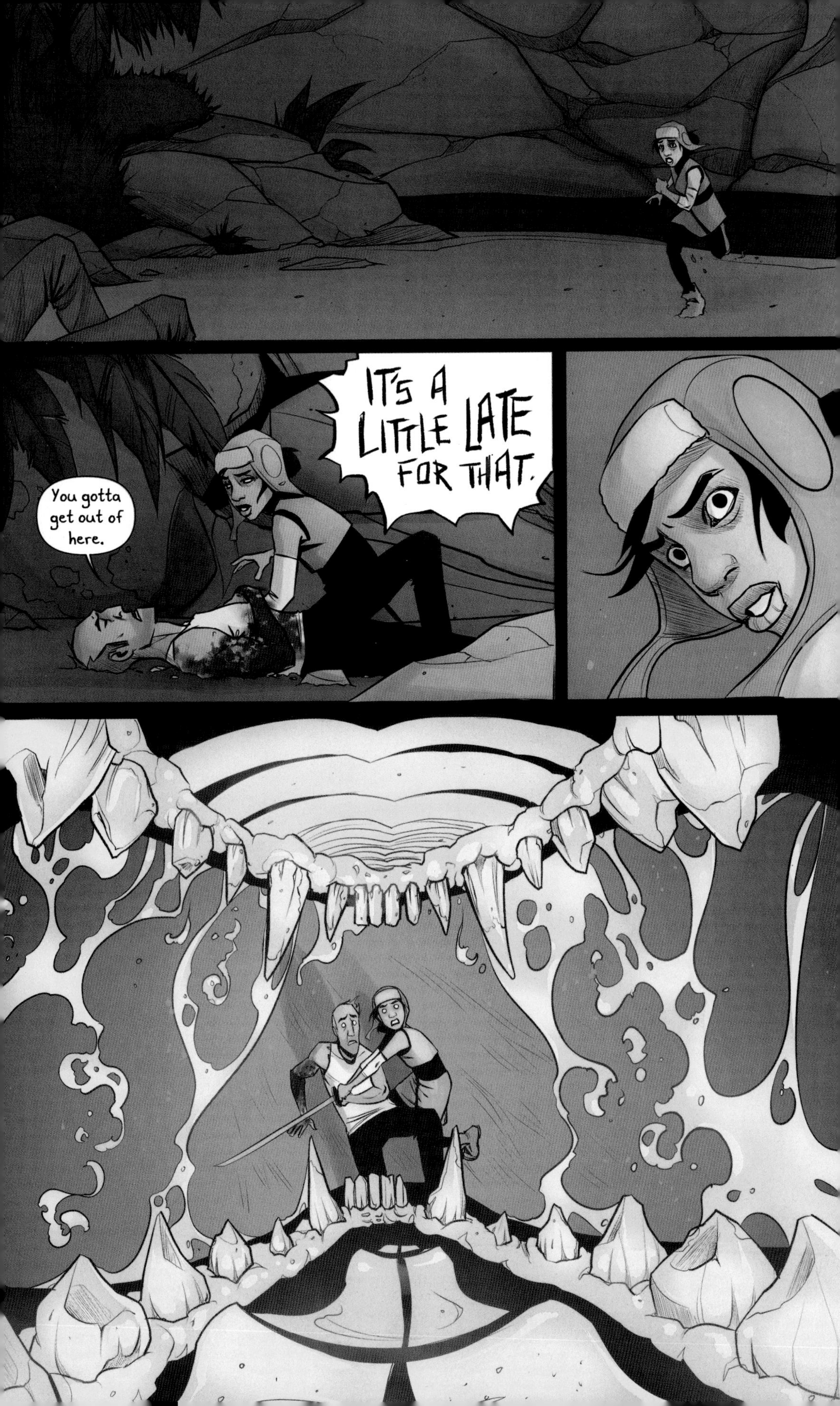
You gotta get out of here.
IT'S A LITTLE LATE FOR THAT.

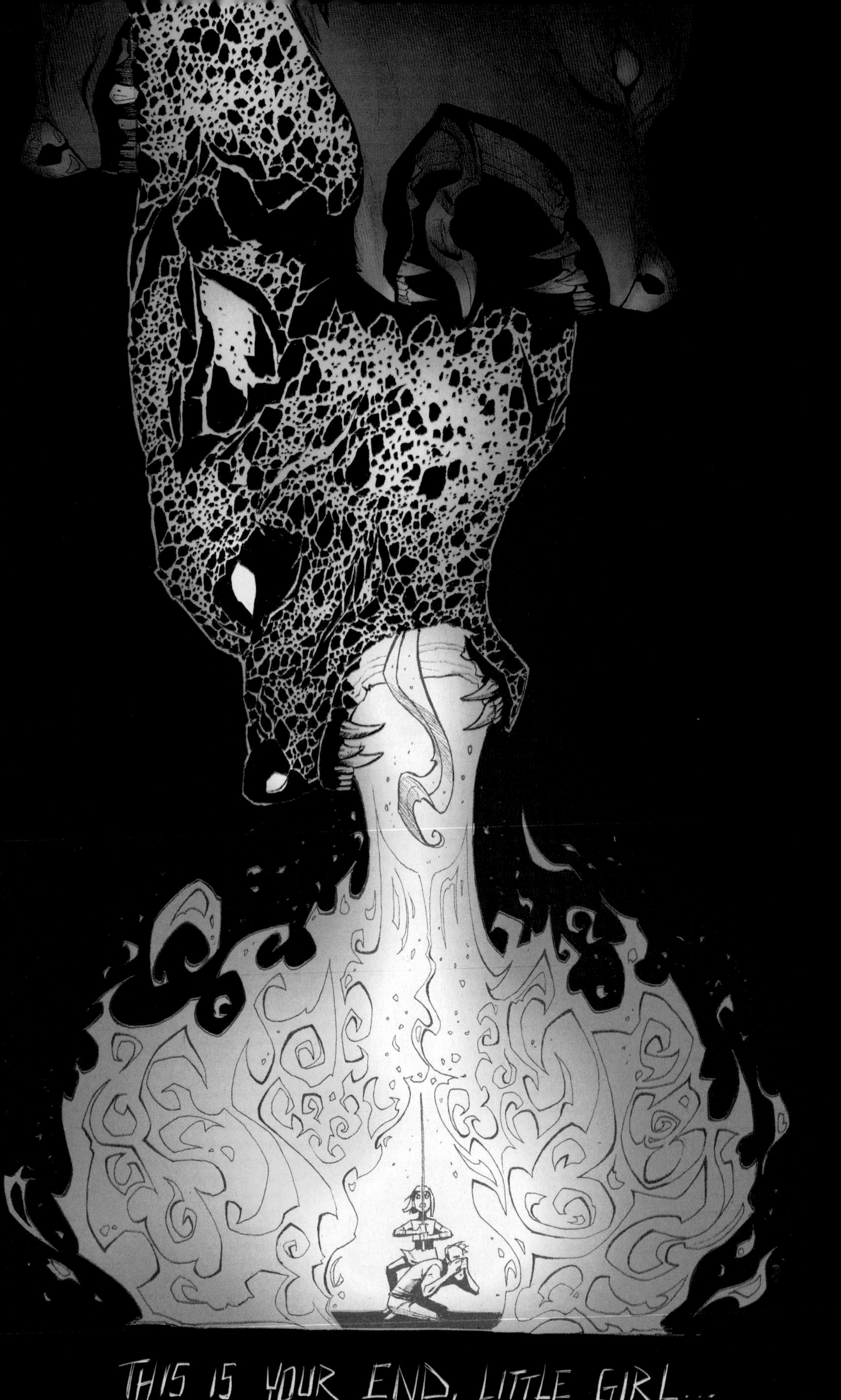
THIS IS YOUR END, LITTLE GIRL...

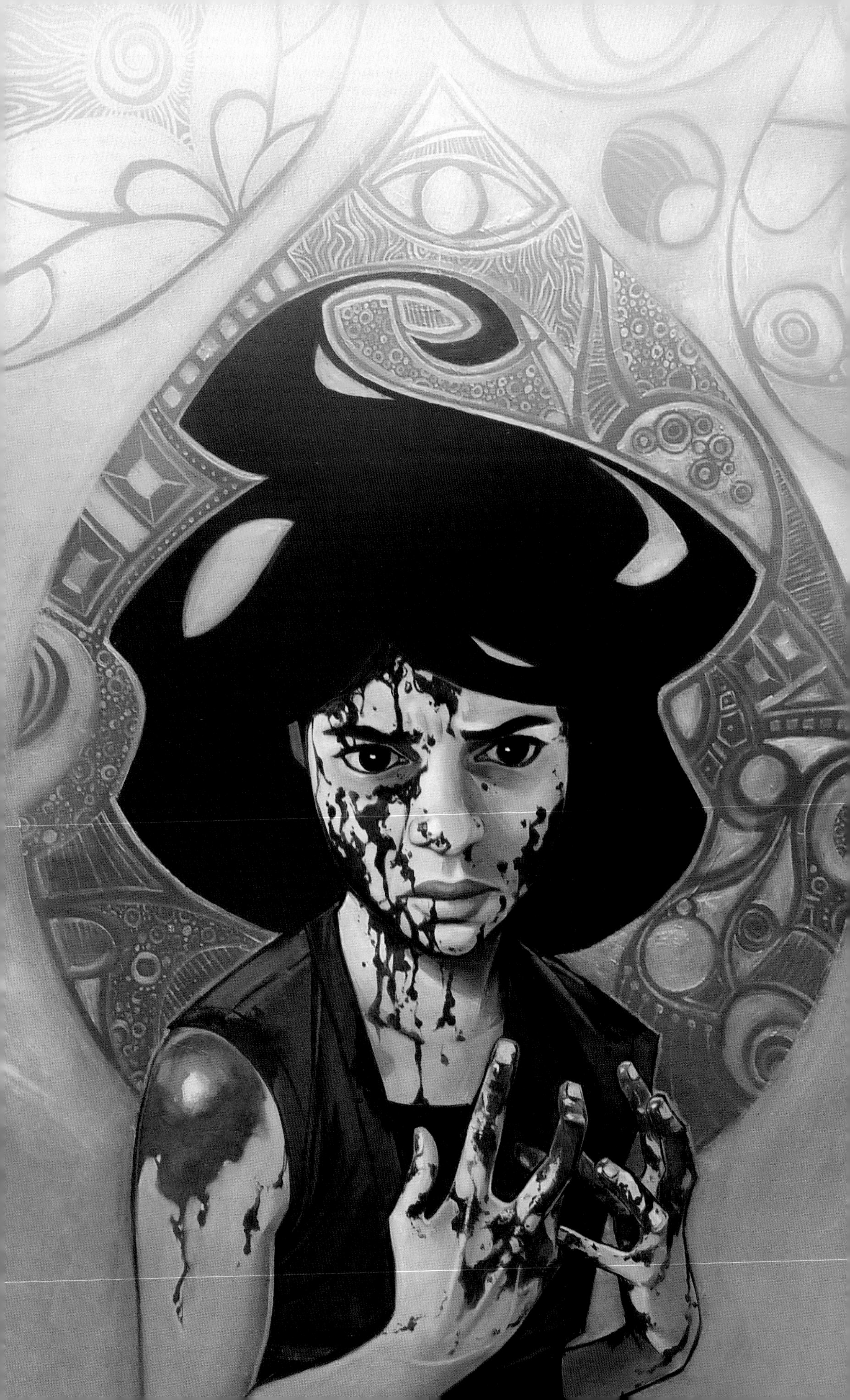

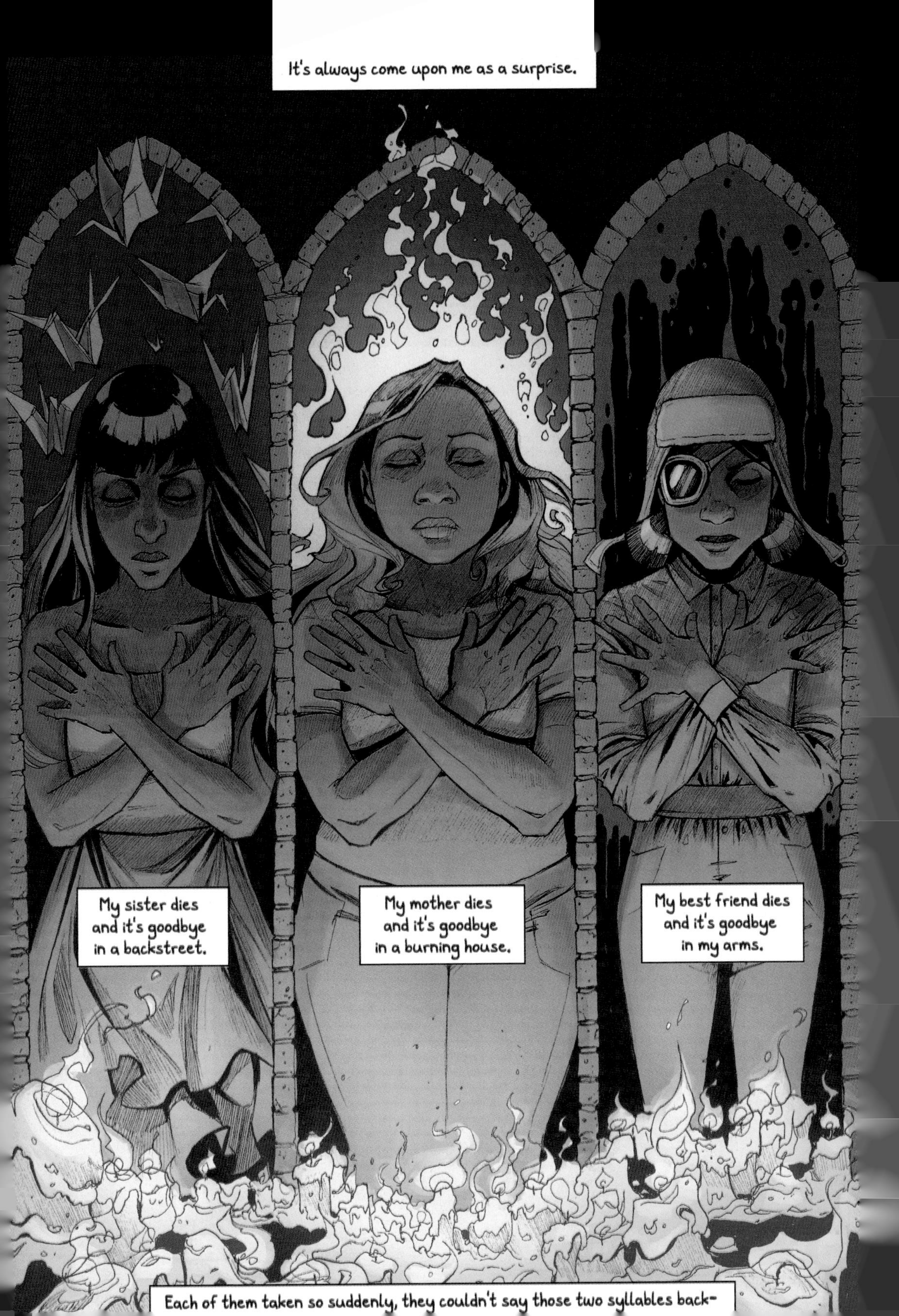
It's always come upon me as a surprise.
My sister dies and it's goodbye in a backstreet.
My mother dies and it's goodbye in a burning house.
My best friend dies and it's goodbye in my arms.
Each of them taken so suddenly, they couldn't say those two syllables back-

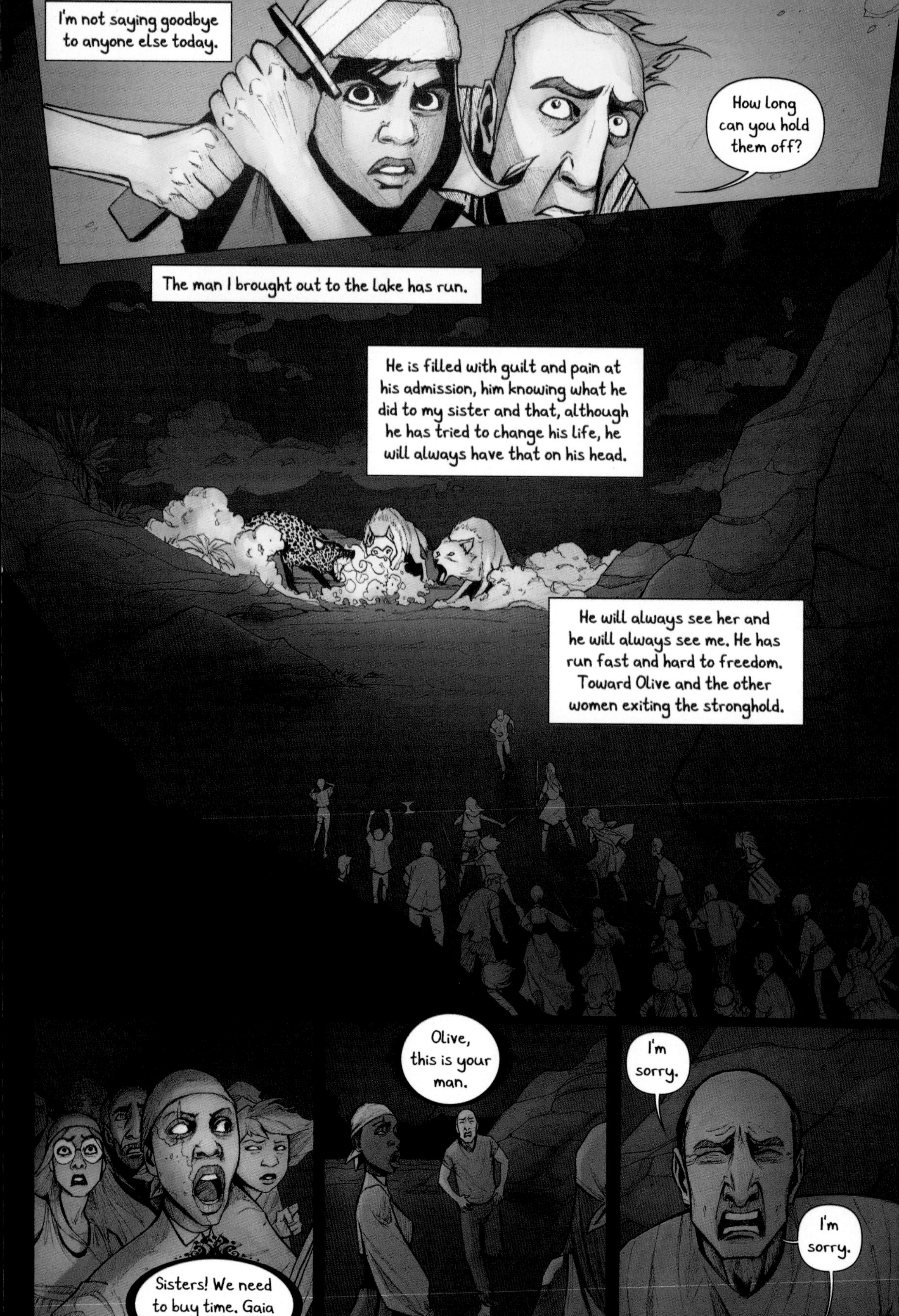

I'm not saying goodbye to anyone else today.
How long can you hold them off?
The man I brought out to the lake has run.
He is filled with guilt and pain at his admission, him knowing what he did to my sister and that, although he has tried to change his life, he will always have that on his head.
He will always see her and he will always see me. He has run fast and hard to freedom. Toward Olive and the other women exiting the stronghold.
Sisters! We need to buy time. Gaia
Olive, this is your man.
I'm sorry.
I'm sorry.

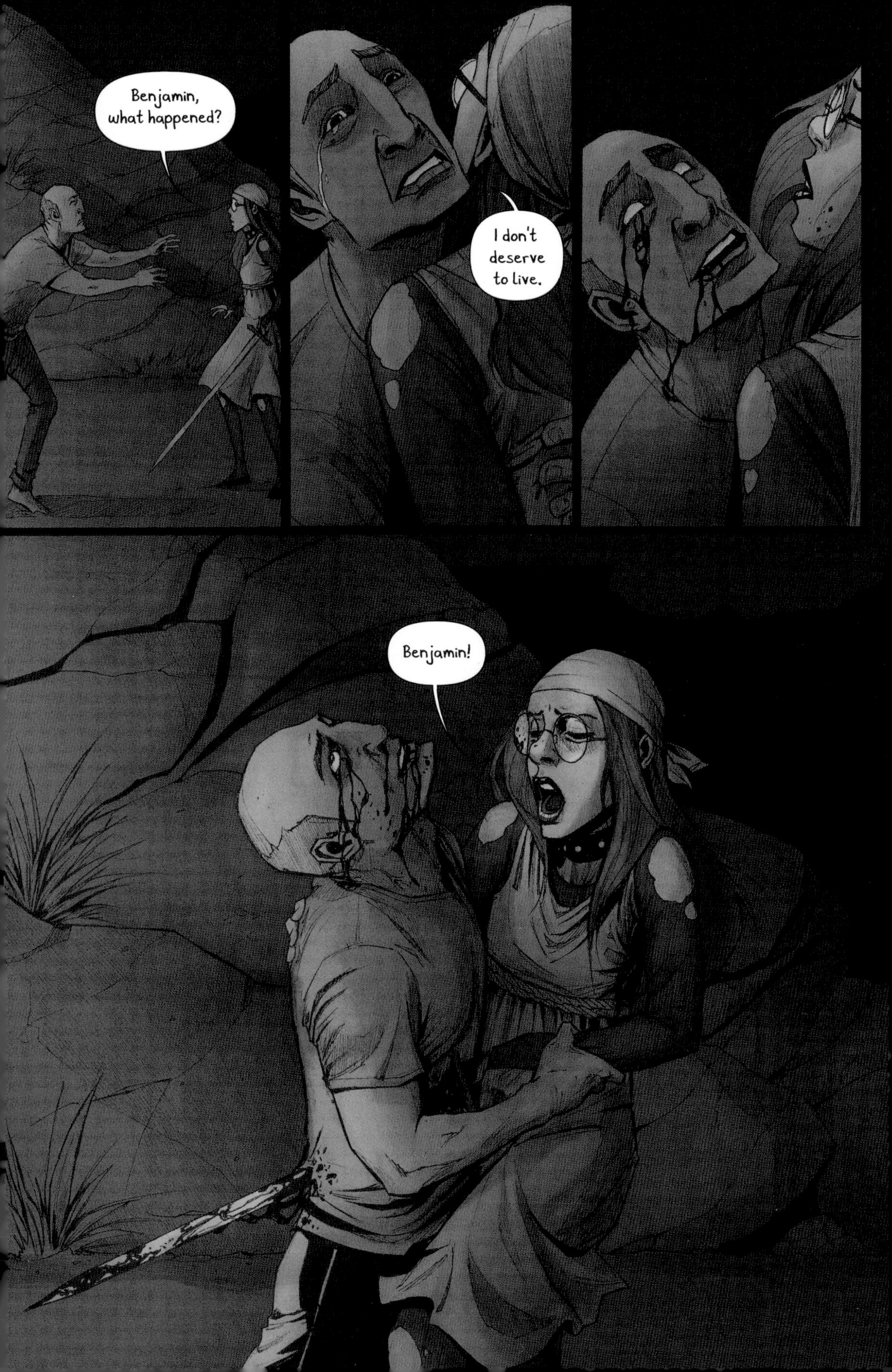
Benjamin, what happened?
I don't deserve to live.
Benjamin!

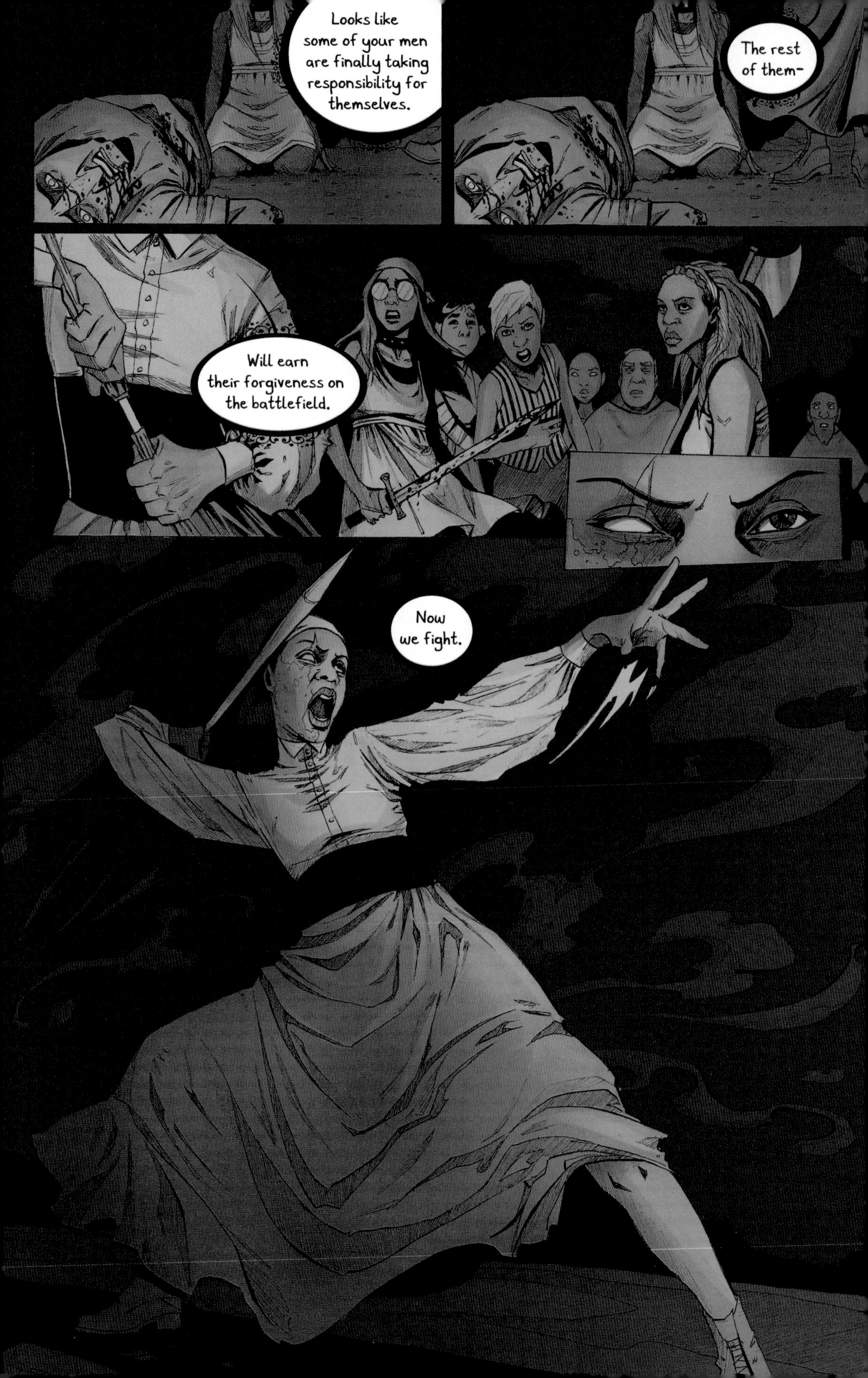
Looks like some of your men are finally taking responsibility for themselves.
The rest of them-
Will earn their forgiveness on the battlefield.
Now we fight.

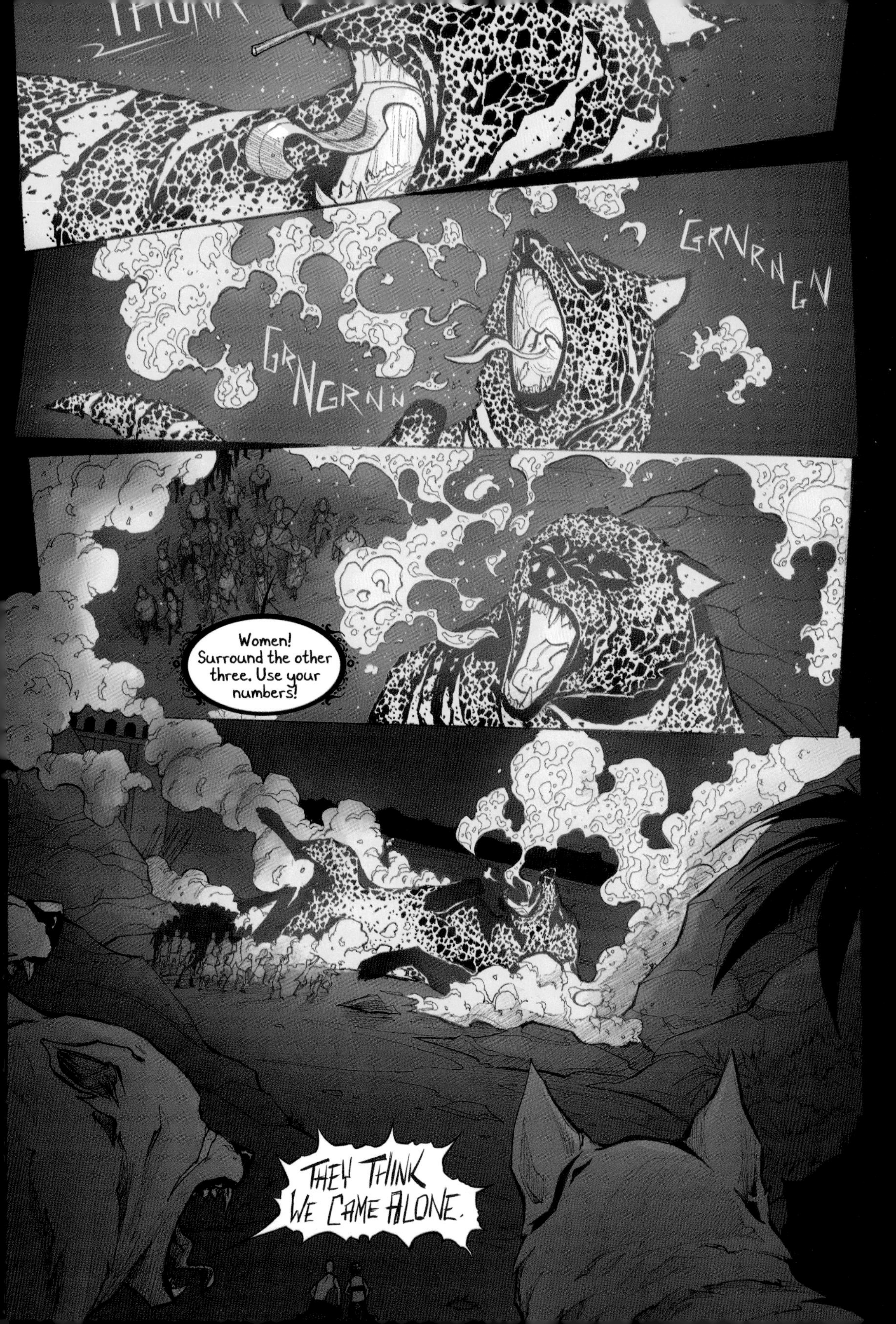
GRNGRNN
GRNRNGN
Women! Surround the other three. Use your numbers!
THEY THINK WE CAME ALONE.

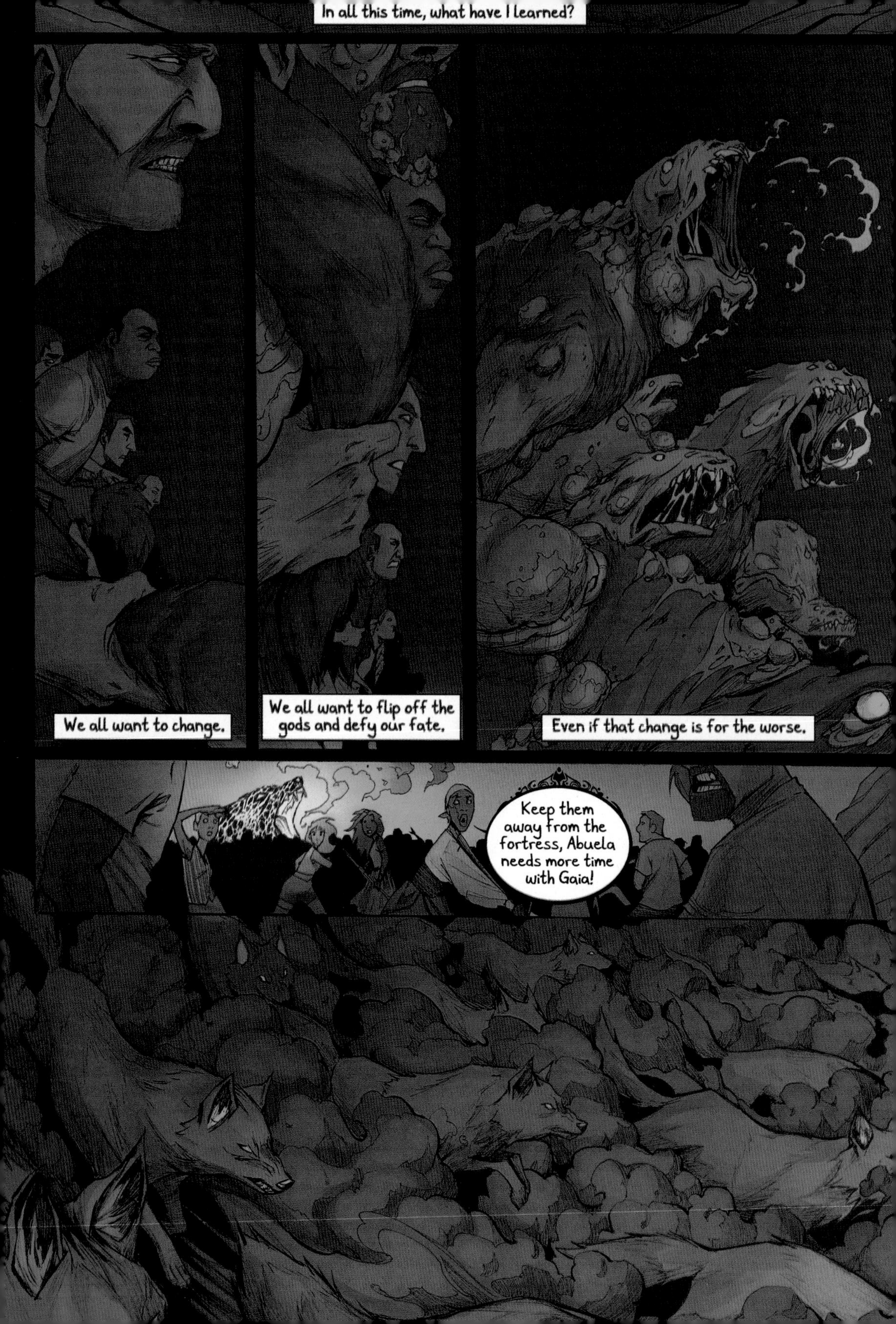
In all this time, what have I learned?
We all want to change.
We all want to flip off the gods and defy our fate.
Even if that change is for the worse.
Keep them away from the fortress, Abuela needs more time with Gaia!

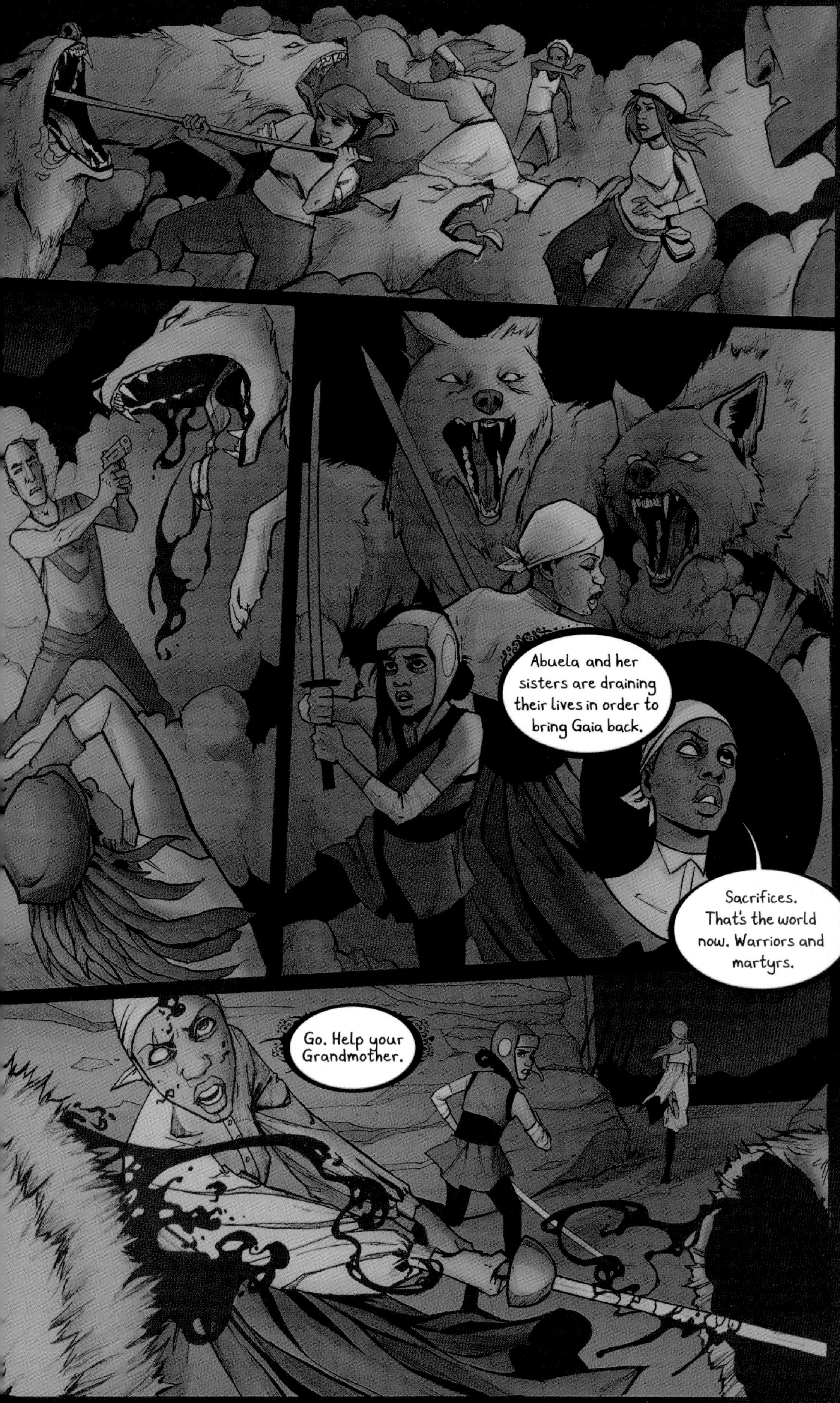

Abuela and her sisters are draining their lives in order to bring Gaia back.
Sacrifices. That's the world now. Warriors and martyrs.
Go. Help your Grandmother.

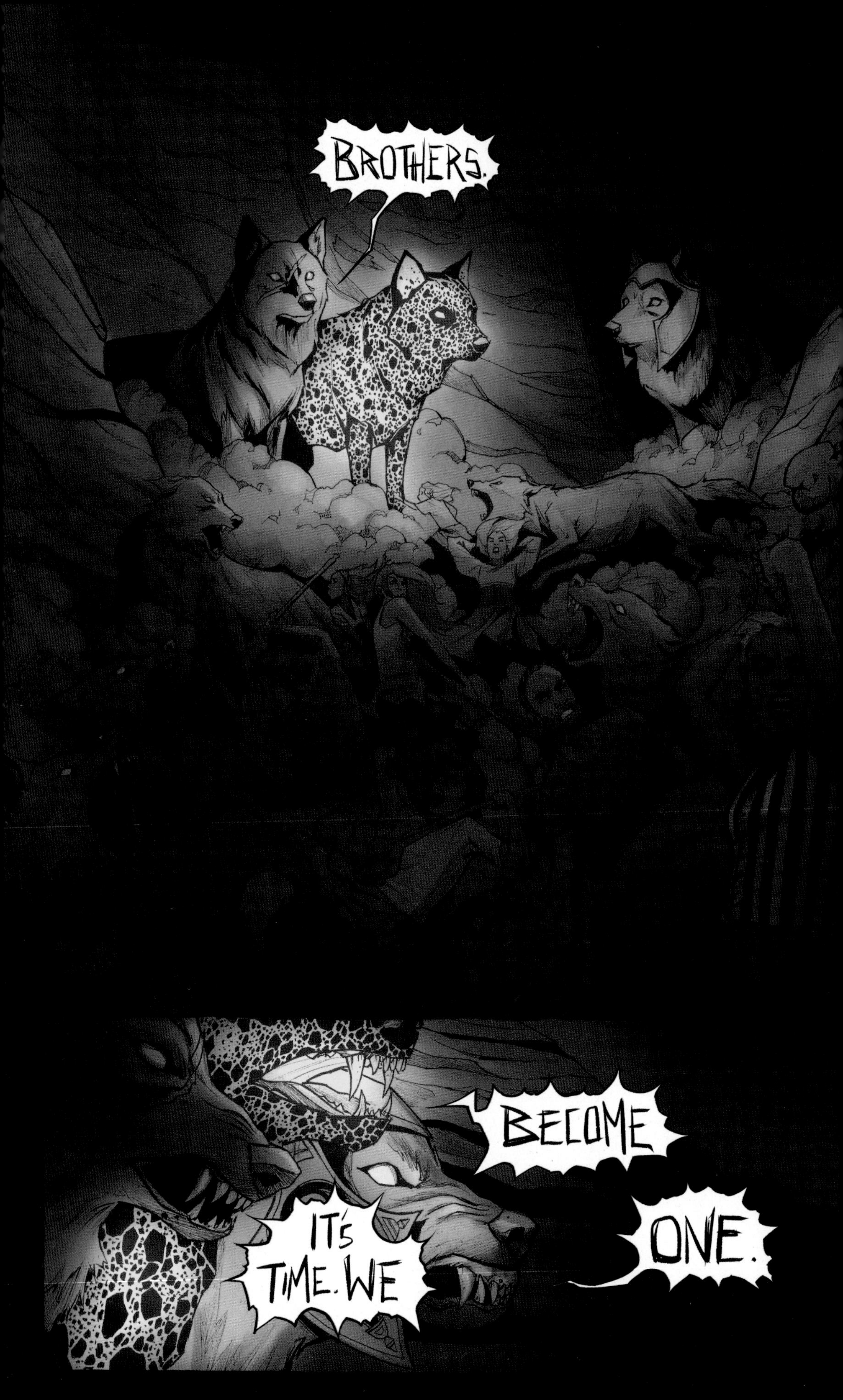
BROTHERS.
BECOME
IT'S TIME. WE
ONE.

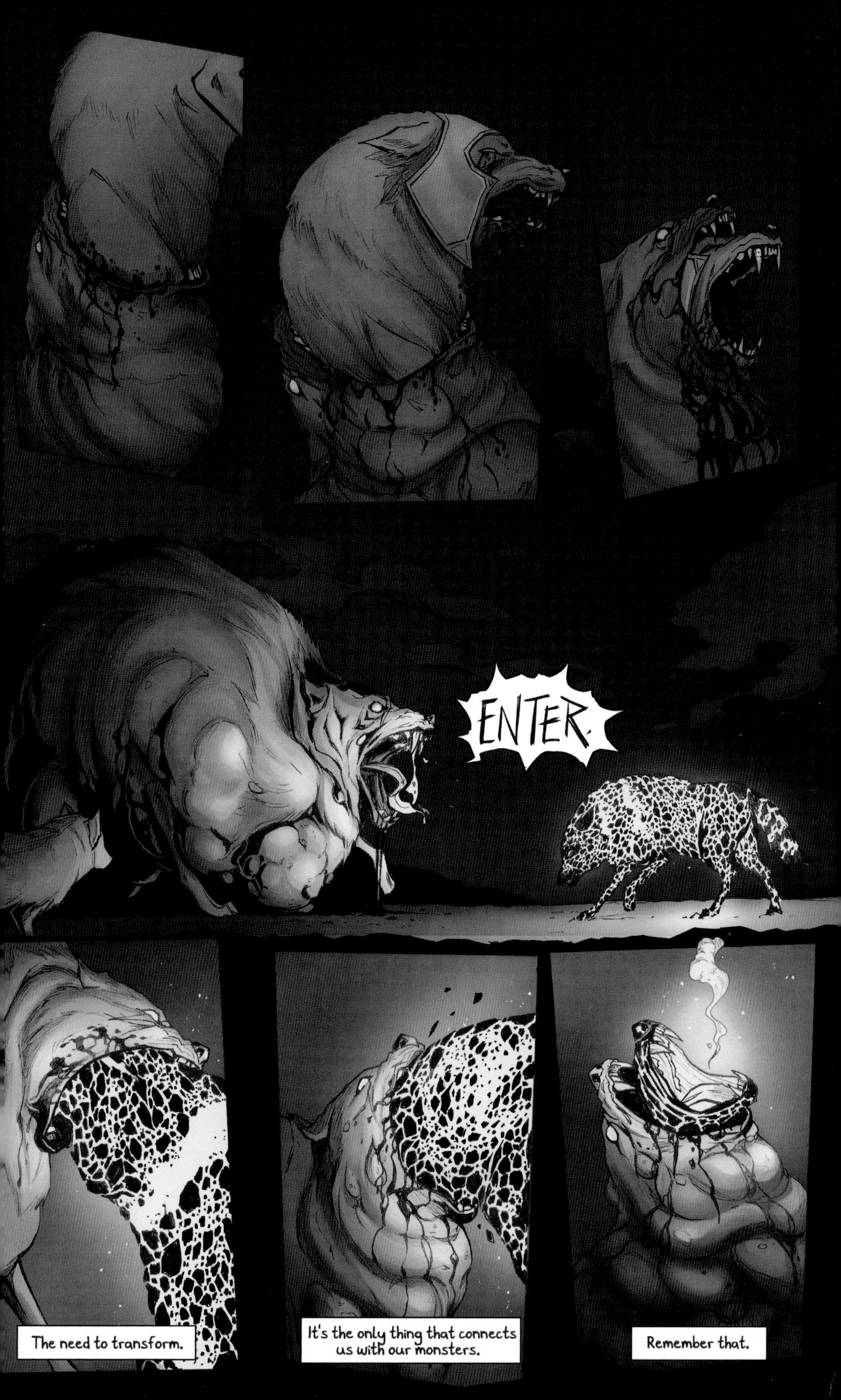
ENTER.
The need to transform.
It's the only thing that connects us with our monsters.
Remember that.

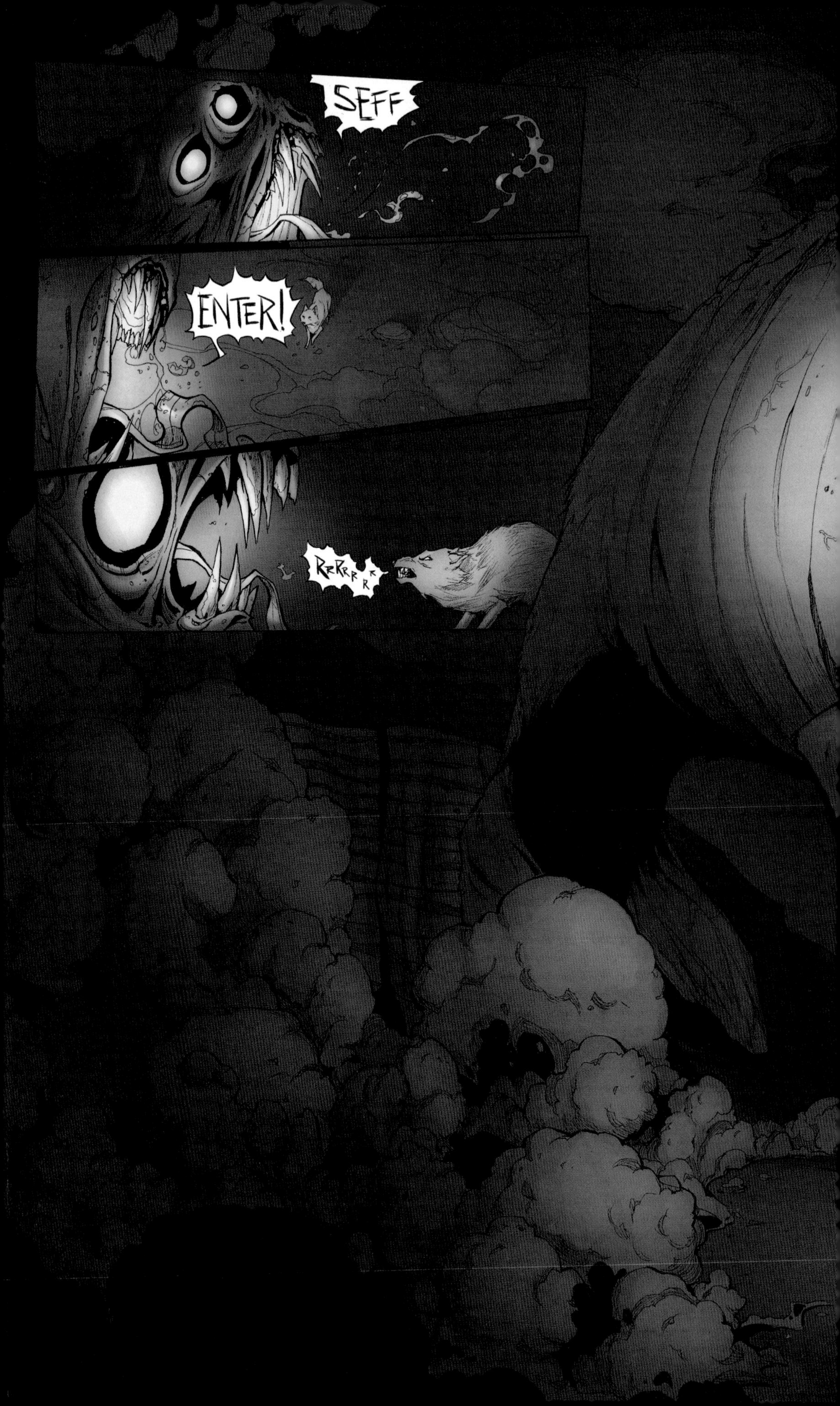
SEFF
ENTER!
RRRRRRR

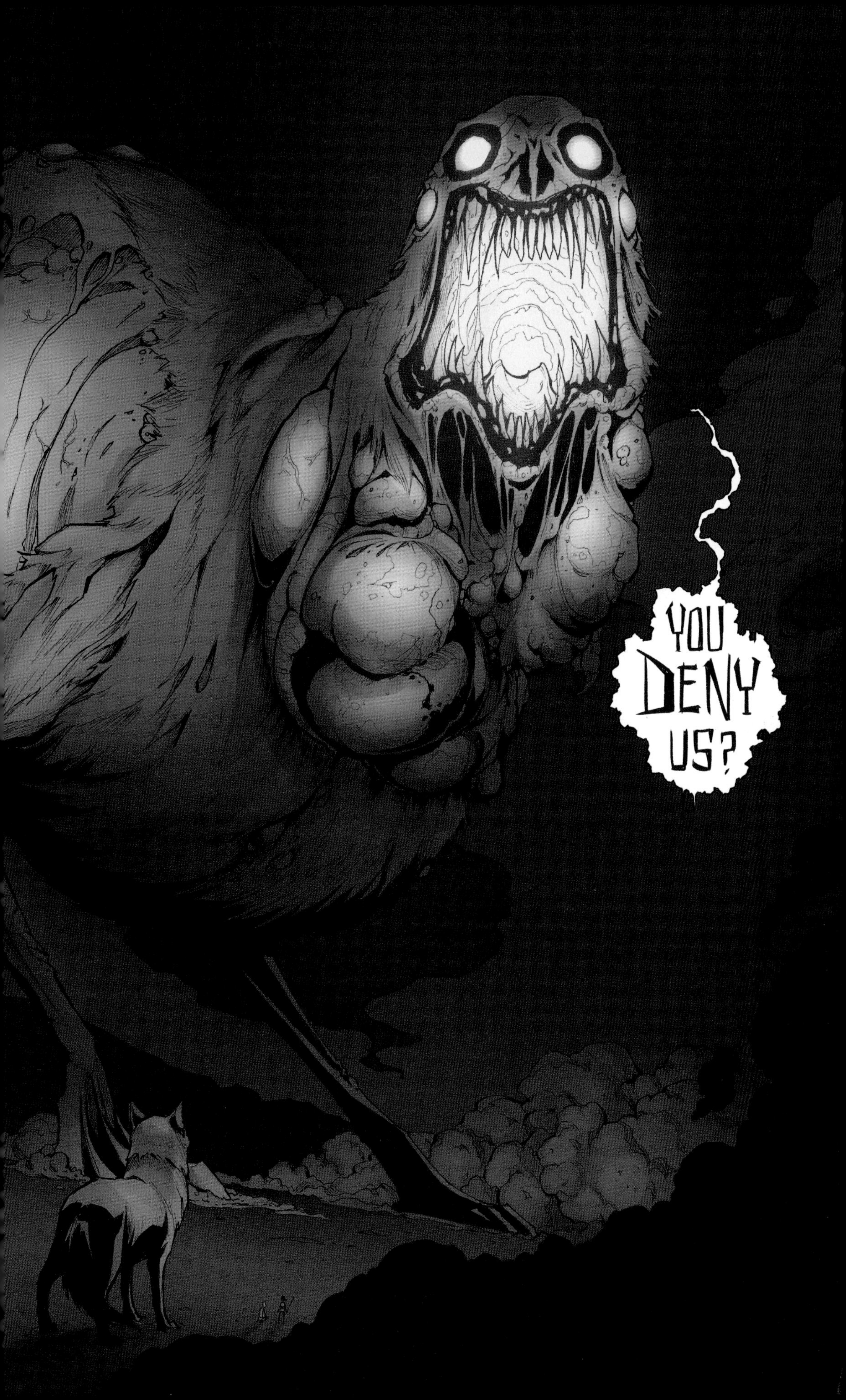
YOU DENY US?

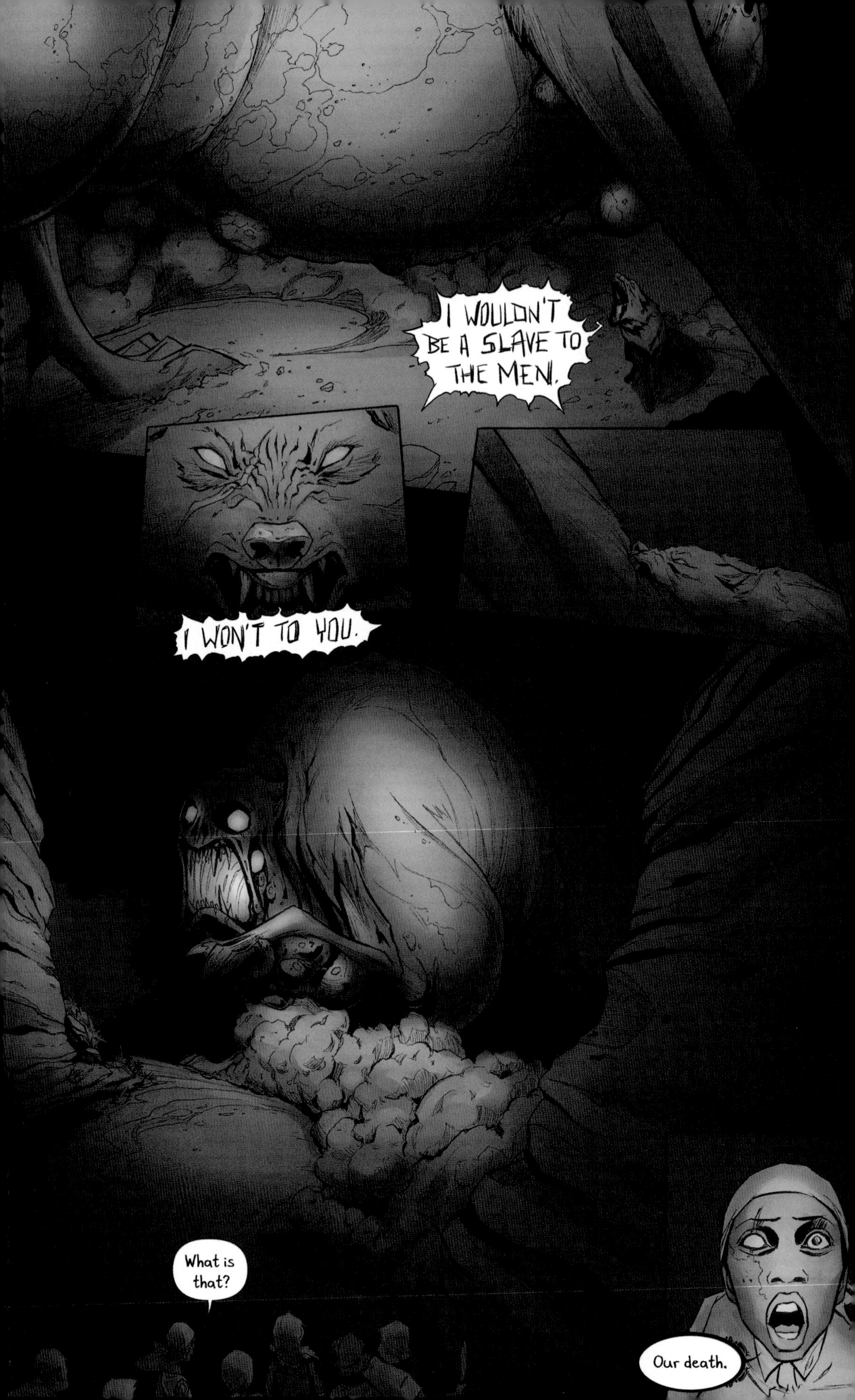
I WOULDN'T BE A SLAVE TO THE MEN.
I WON'T TO YOU.
What is that?
Our death.

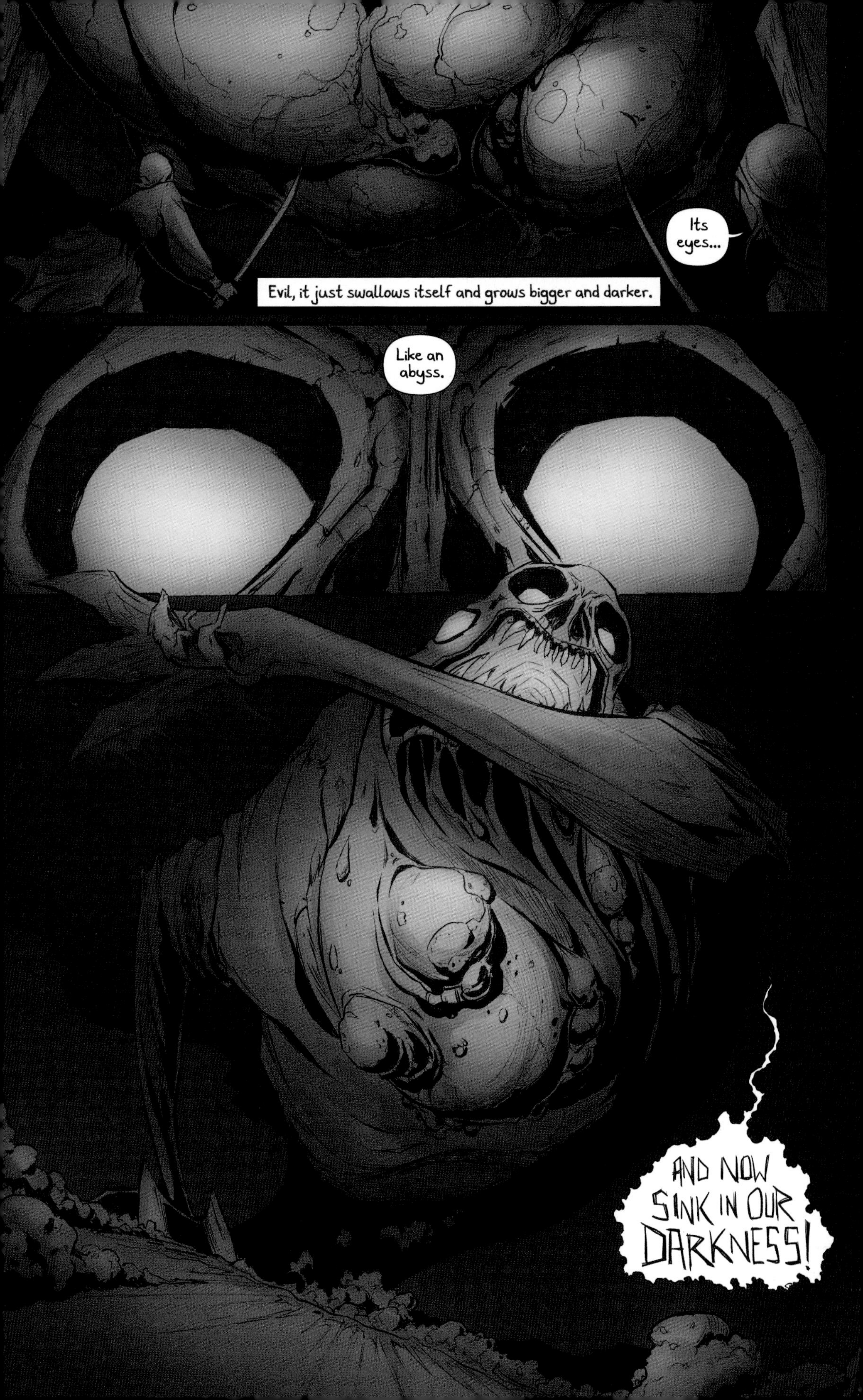
Its eyes...
Evil, it just swallows itself and grows bigger and darker.
Like an abyss.
AND NOW SINK IN OUR DARKNESS!

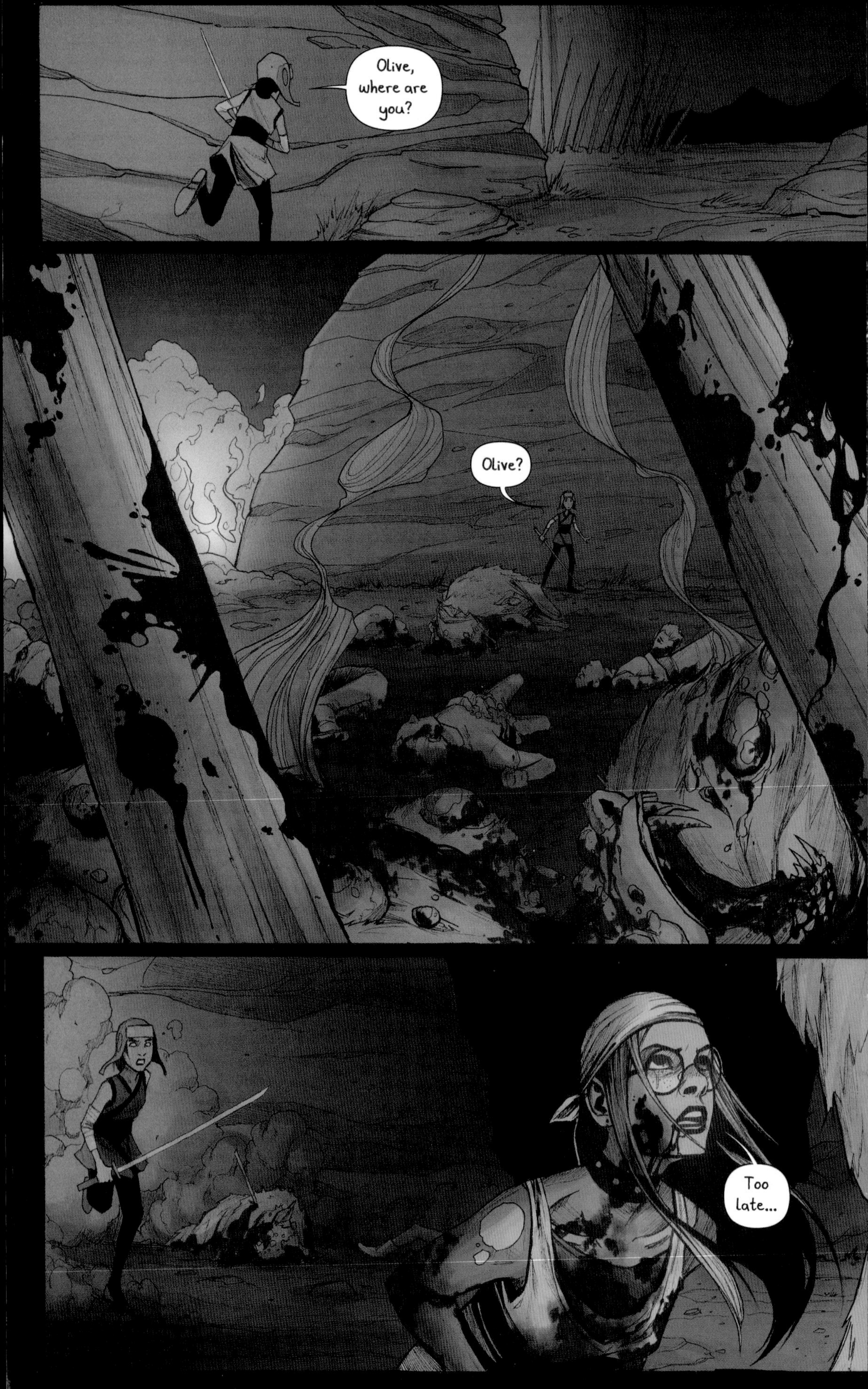
Olive, where are you?
Olive?
Too late...

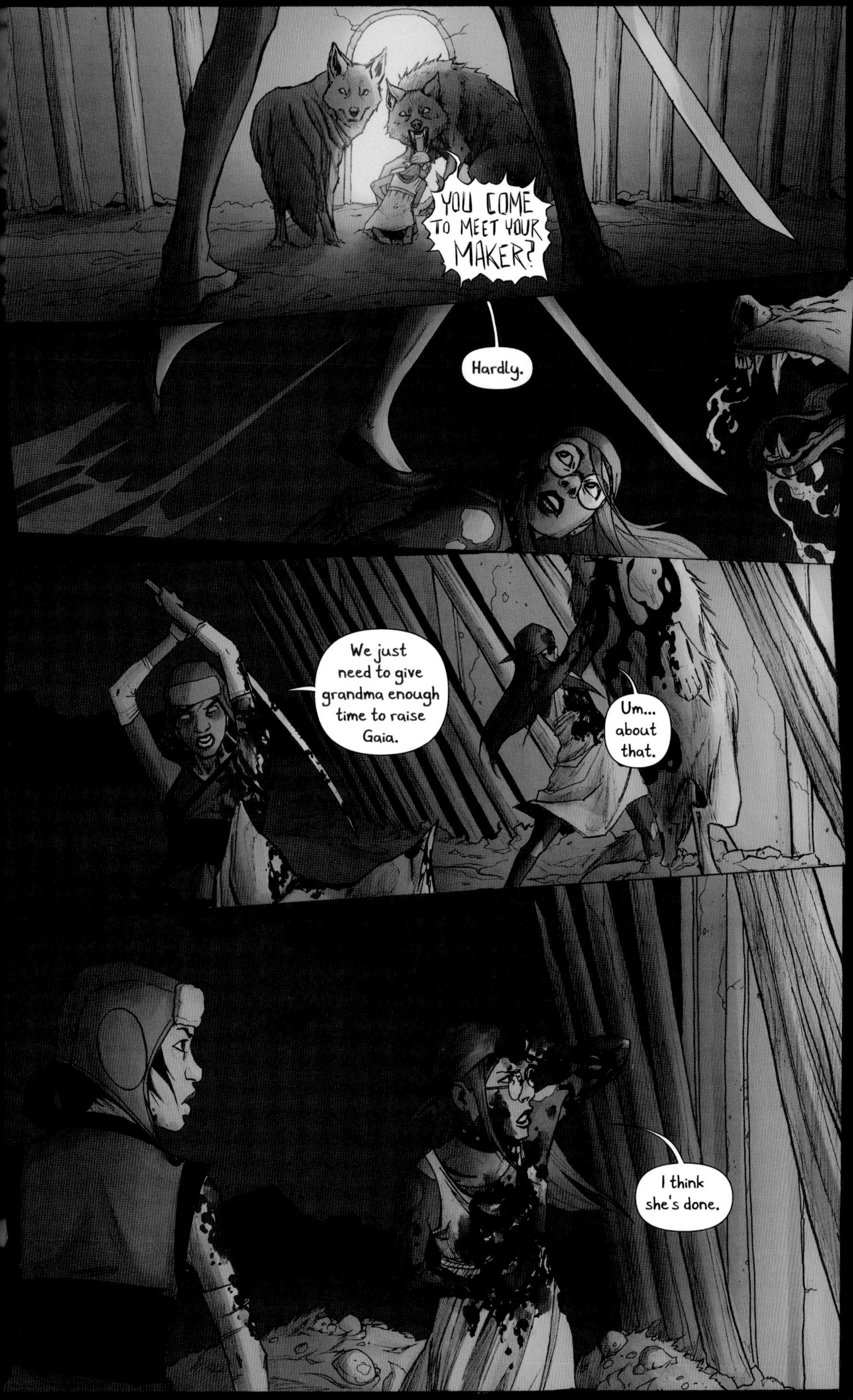
YOU COME TO MEET YOUR MAKER?
Hardly.
We just need to give grandma enough time to raise Gaia.
Um... about that.
I think she's done.

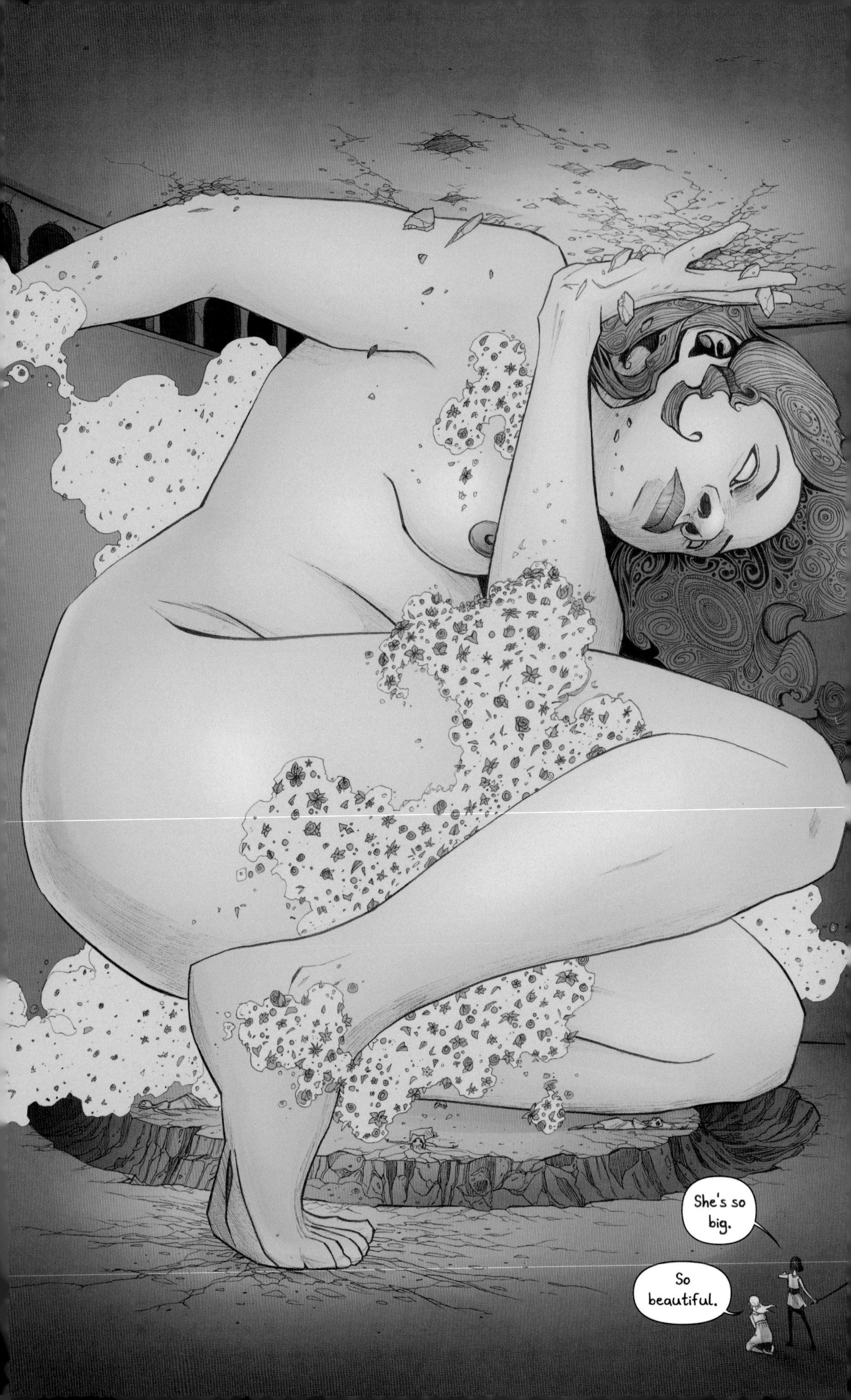
She's so big.
So beautiful.

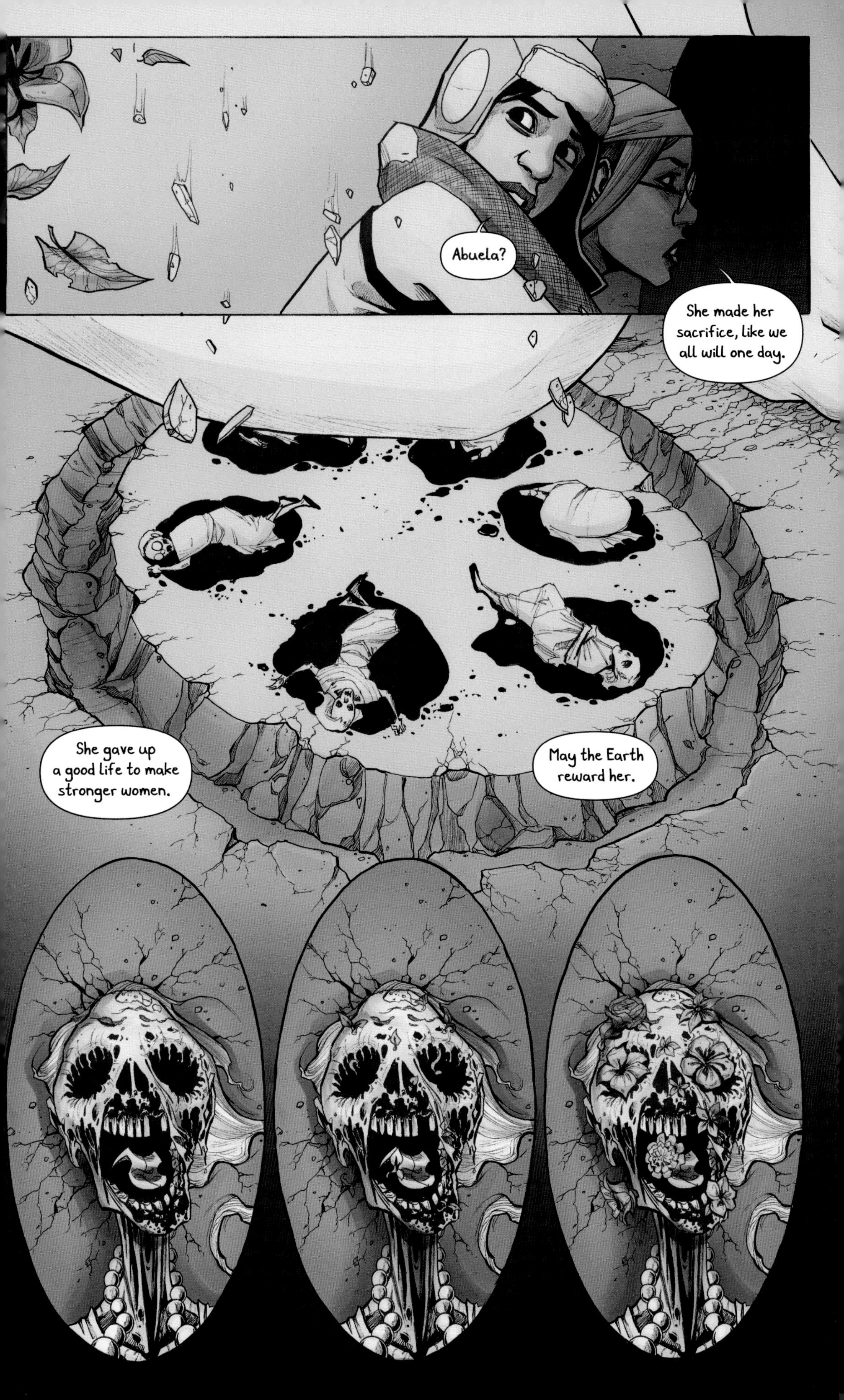

Abuela?
She made her sacrifice, like we all will one day.
She gave up a good life to make stronger women.
May the Earth reward her.

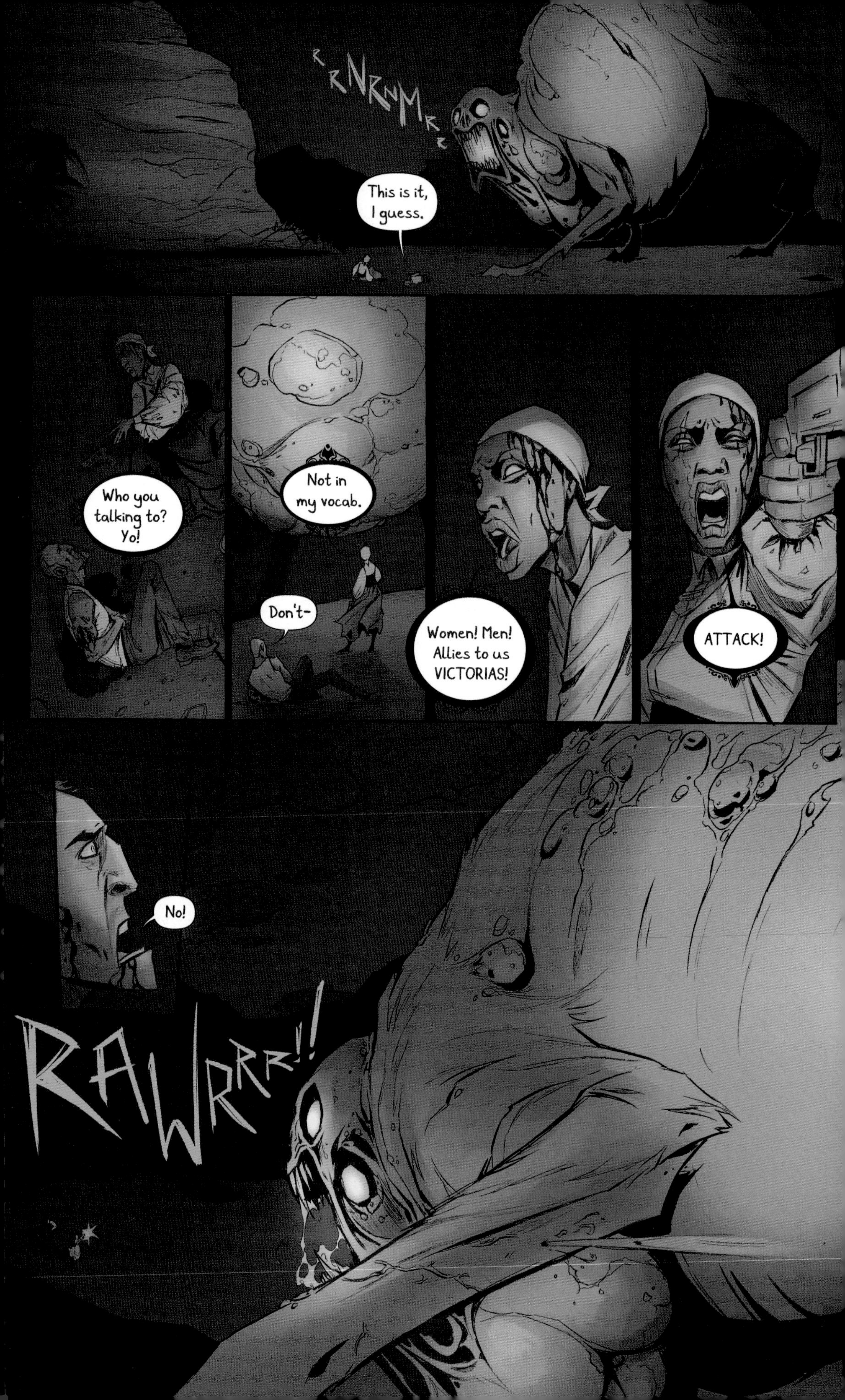
RRNRNMRR
This is it, I guess.
Who you talking to? Yo!
Not in my vocab.
Don't-
Women! Men! Allies to us VICTORIAS!
ATTACK!
No!
RAWRRR!!

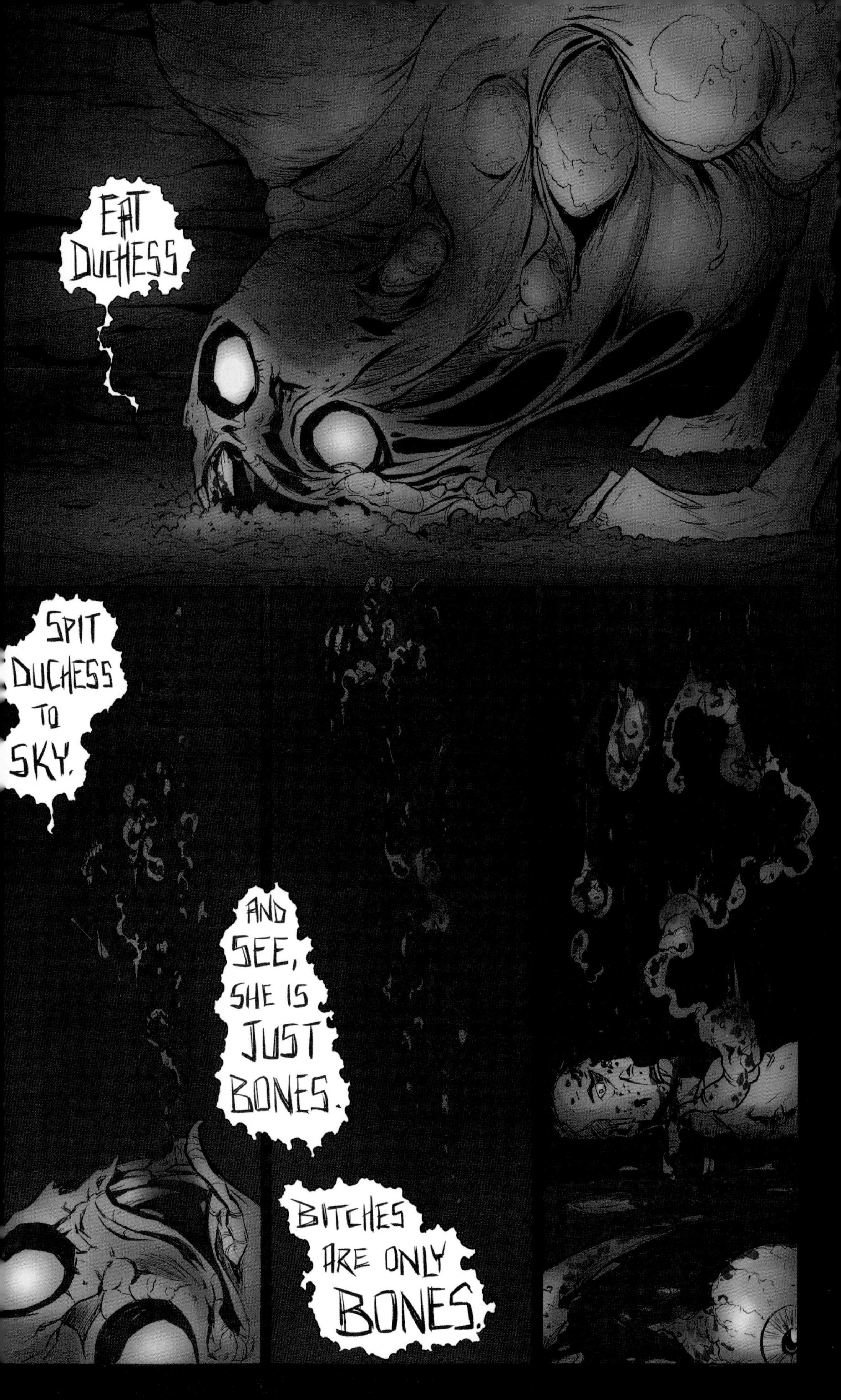
EAT DUCHESS
SPIT DUCHESS TO SKY.
AND SEE, SHE IS JUST BONES.
BITCHES ARE ONLY BONES.

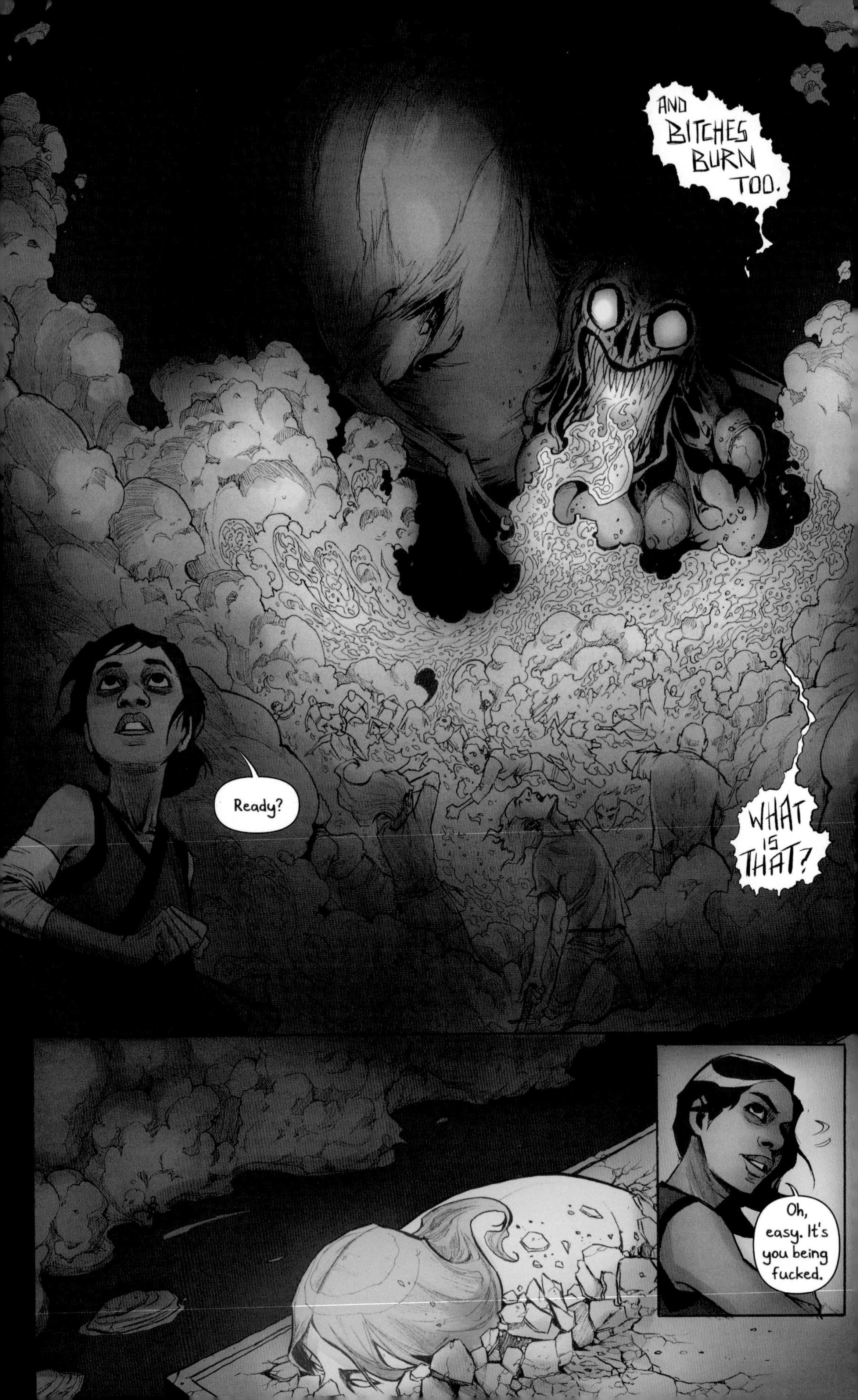
AND BITCHES BURN TOO.
Ready?
WHAT IS THAT?
Oh, easy. It's you being fucked.

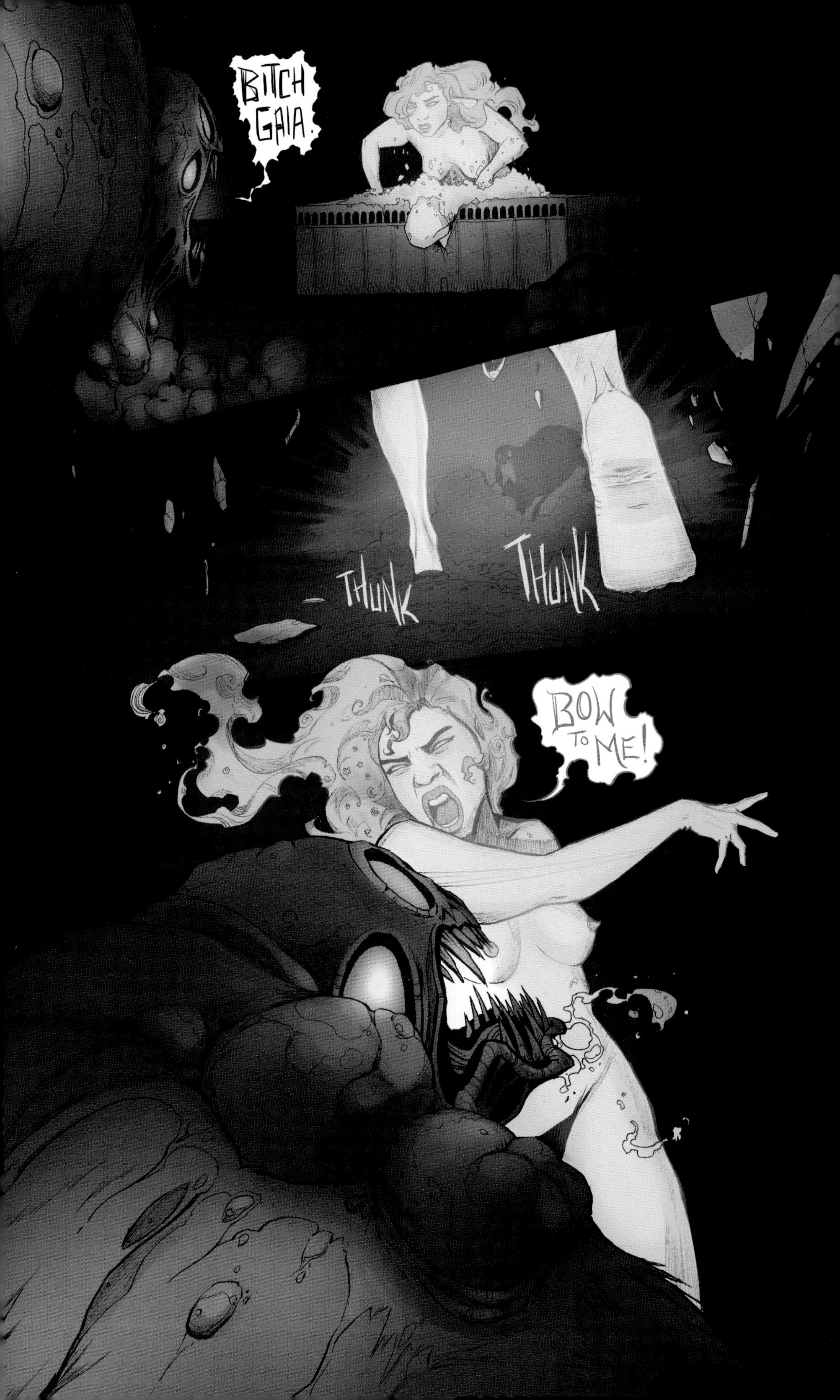
BITCH GAIA.
THUNK
THUNK
BOW TO ME!

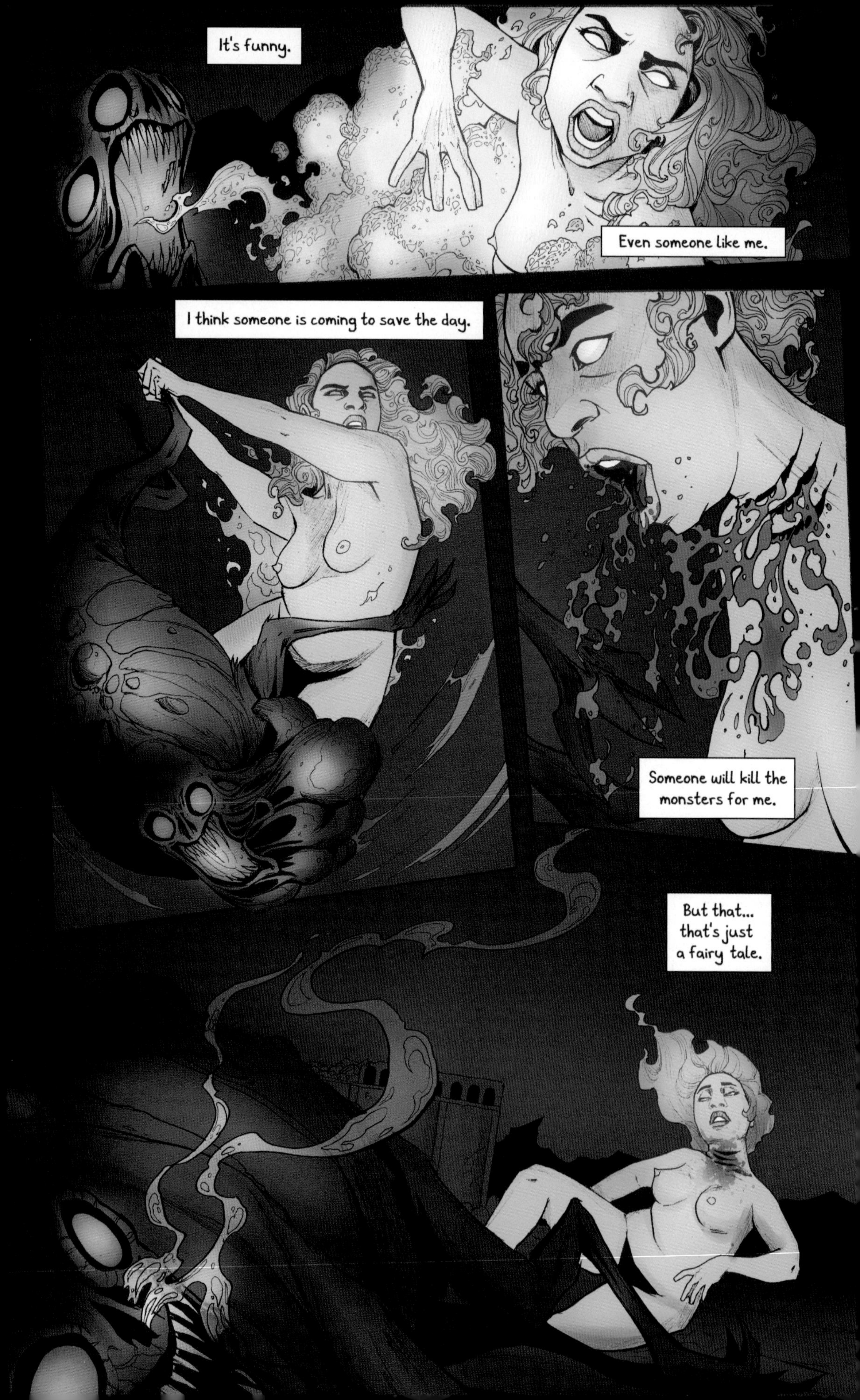
It's funny.
Even someone like me.
I think someone is coming to save the day.
Someone will kill the monsters for me.
But that... that's just a fairy tale.

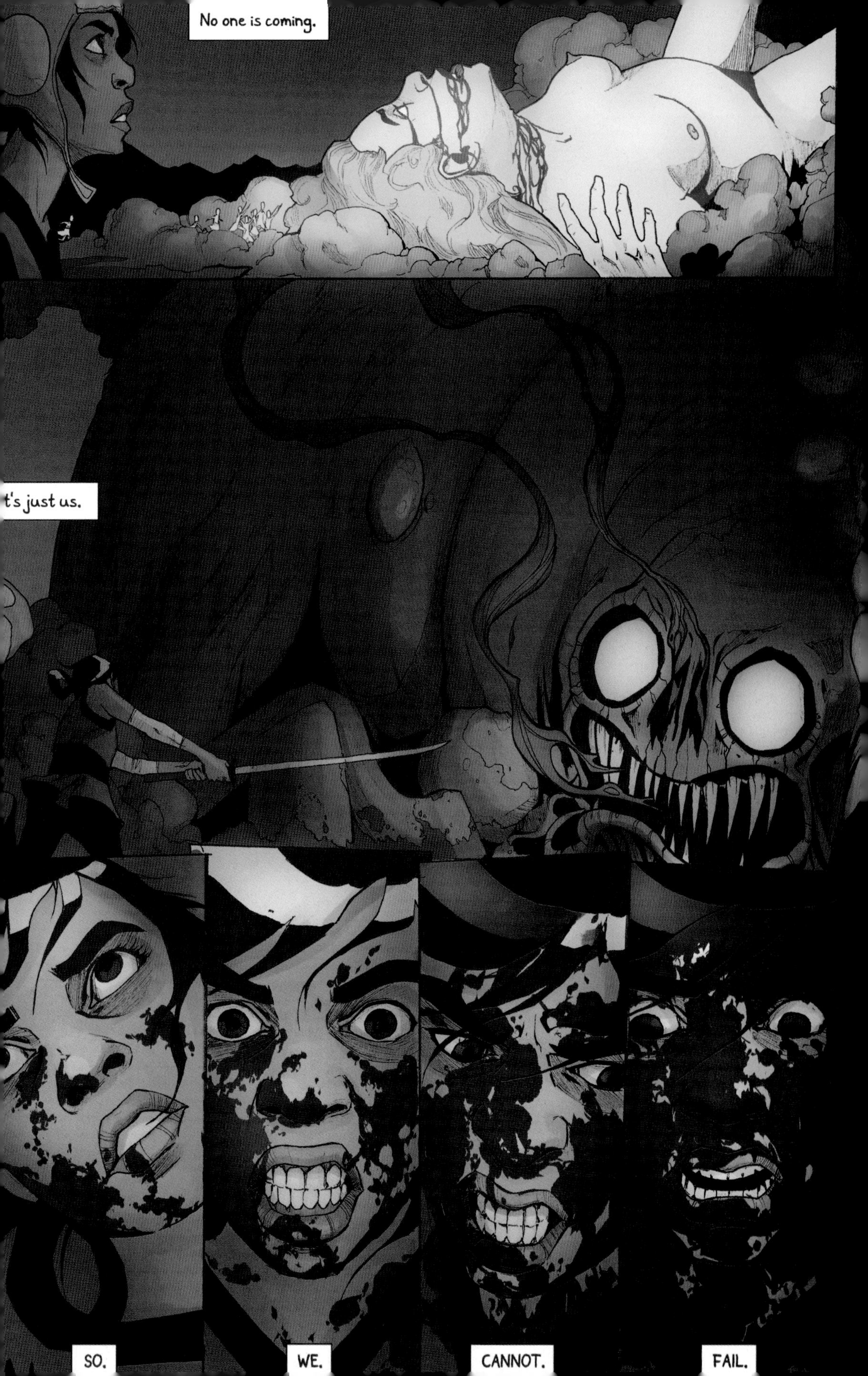
No one is coming.
t's just us.
SO.
WE.
CANNOT.
FAIL.

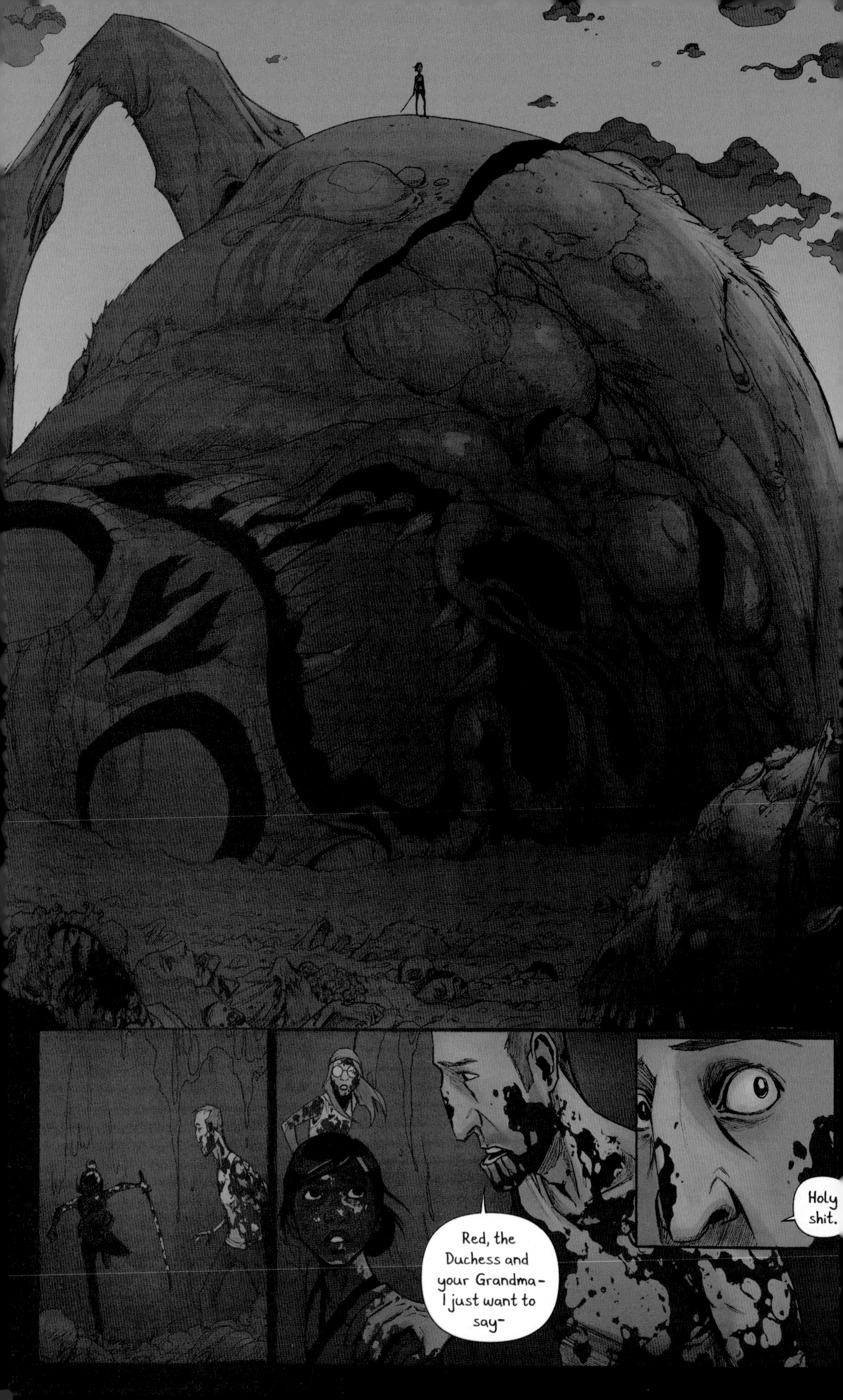
Red, the Duchess and your Grandma-I just want to say-
Holy shit.

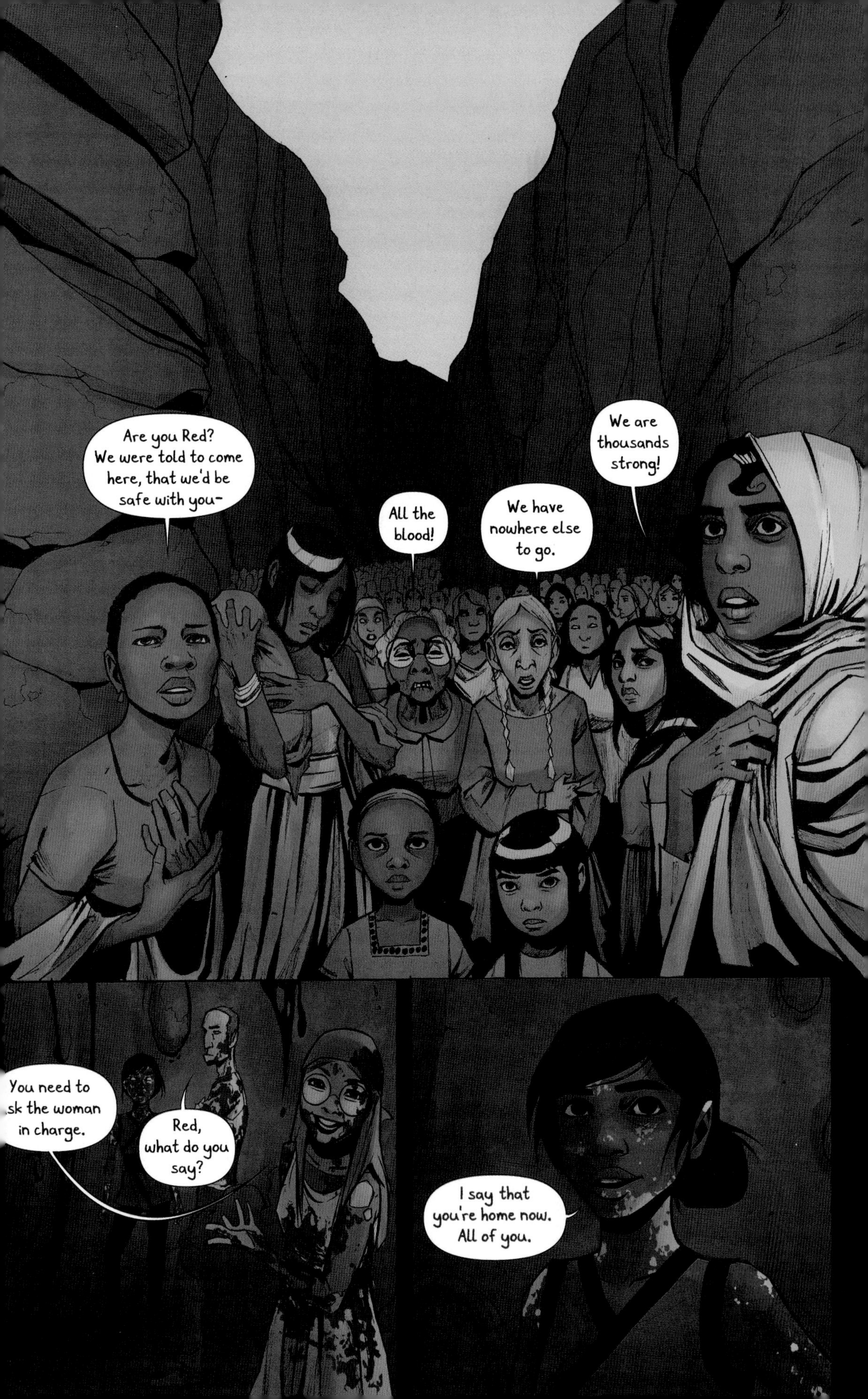
Are you Red? We were told to come here, that we'd be safe with you-
All the blood!
We have nowhere else to go.
We are thousands strong!
You need to ask the woman in charge.
Red, what do you say?
I say that you're home now. All of you.

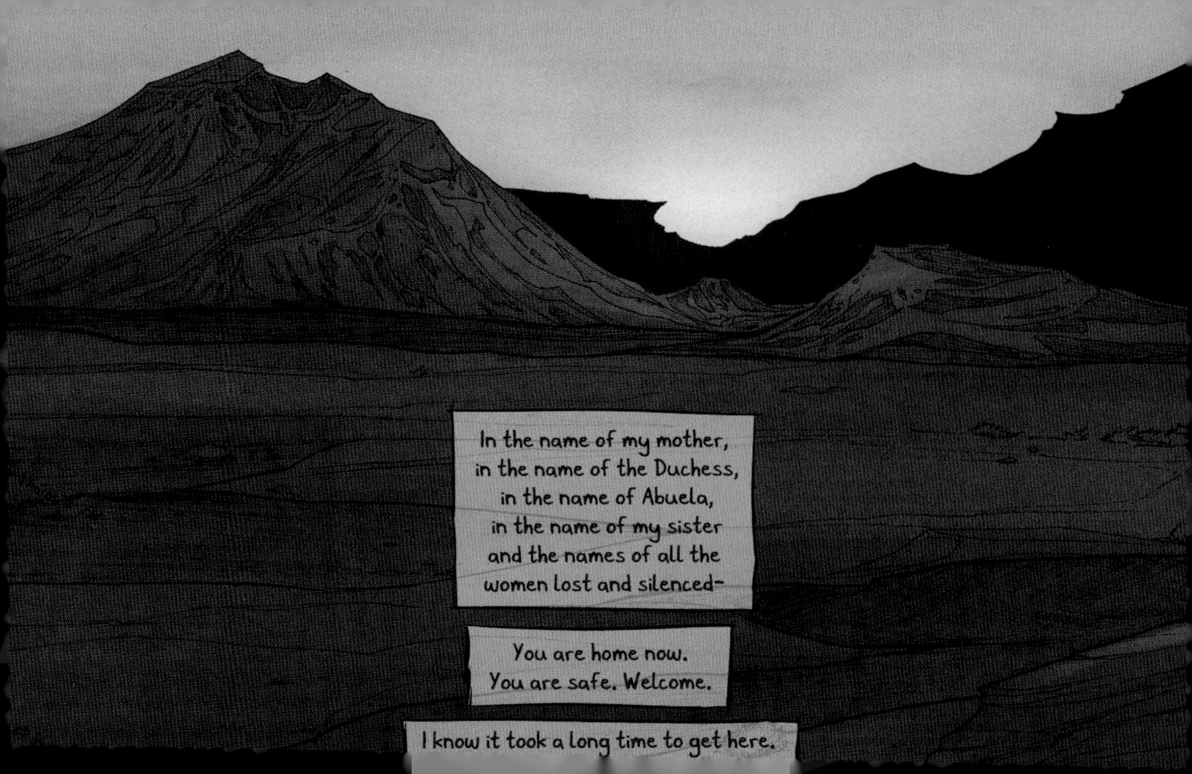
In the name of my mother, in the name of the Duchess, in the name of Abuela, in the name of my sister and the names of all the women lost and silenced—
You are home now. You are safe. Welcome.
I know it took a long time to get here.

I just wanted to write a thank you from Caitlin and I for the time you've spent with this crazy book of ours. We conceived of it three years ago, and it's been three years of a wild ride. It has gotten us both a lot of attention, and, more importantly, connected us to new readers with amazing backgrounds and stories of their own.

A comic book is a way to create new myths in the traditional sense: stories that are about our lives- the most confusing, upsetting and terrifying aspects of them- that need something greater than us for deeper understanding.

There was something swirling in the air when we began talking. It grew as the book did. And it brought up new questions: what is rage? What is forgiveness? What is the price we as a community pay, and what is the judgment we seek? I don't pretend to know the answers to these questions, but RED was a myth I needed. It taught me a lot of things, myself.

It's also been amazing to team with Cait for three years: to see our work grow, to go from collaborators to friends, to travel across the country in buses and trains to sign comics and meet fans...it has been a kind of fairy tale, and that is because of all of you.

As this last chapter starts off- goodbyes are hard, and we often don't get the opportunity to say the ones that are meaningful to us. I don't want to say goodbye to Red. But I like that she is leaving on her terms.

Thanks,

Sean and Cait

SKETCHES AND PROCESS

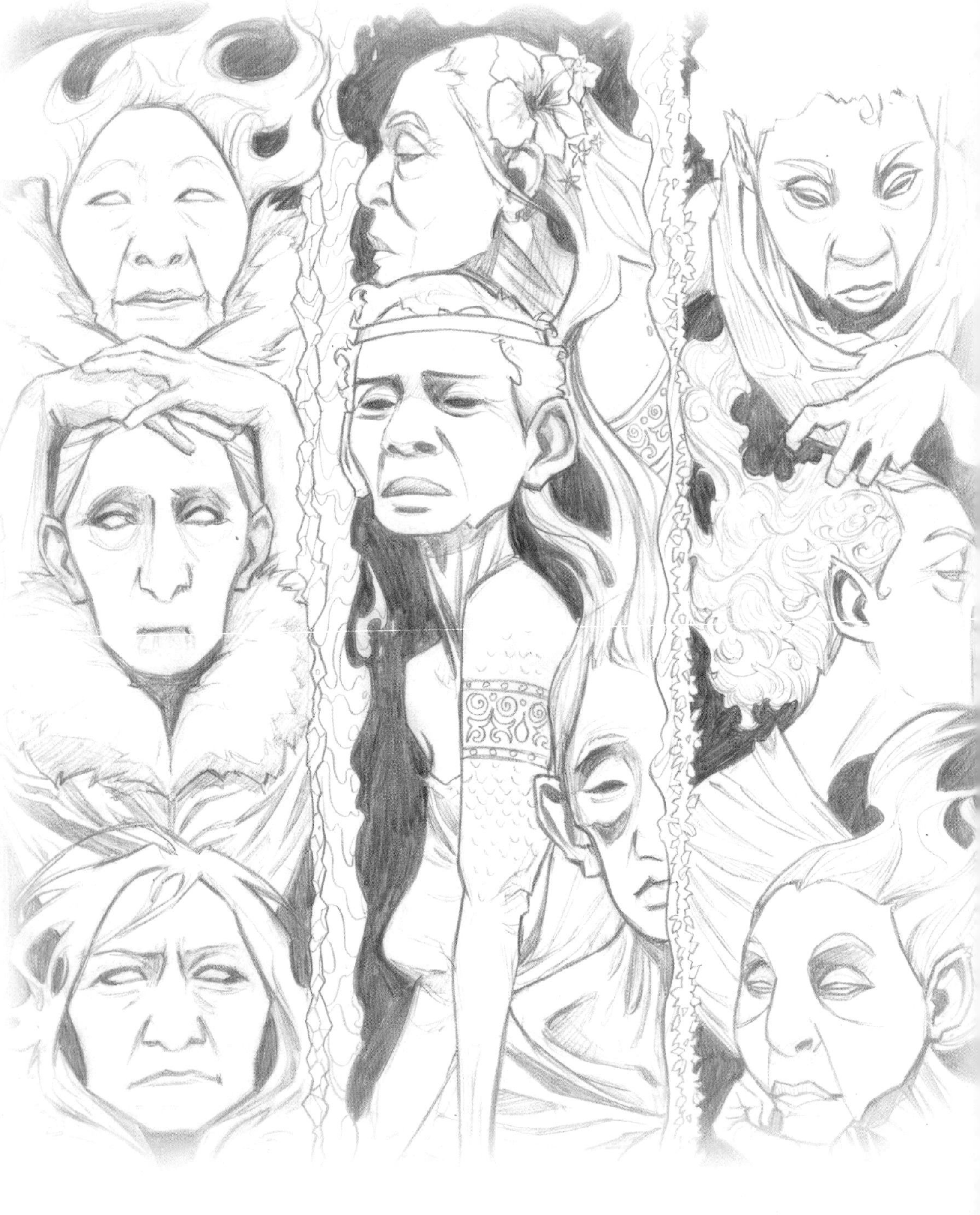

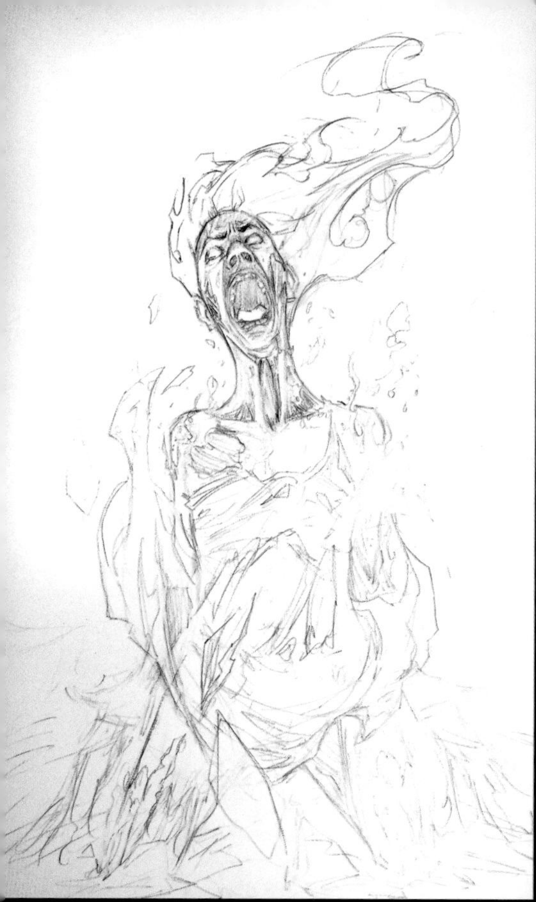
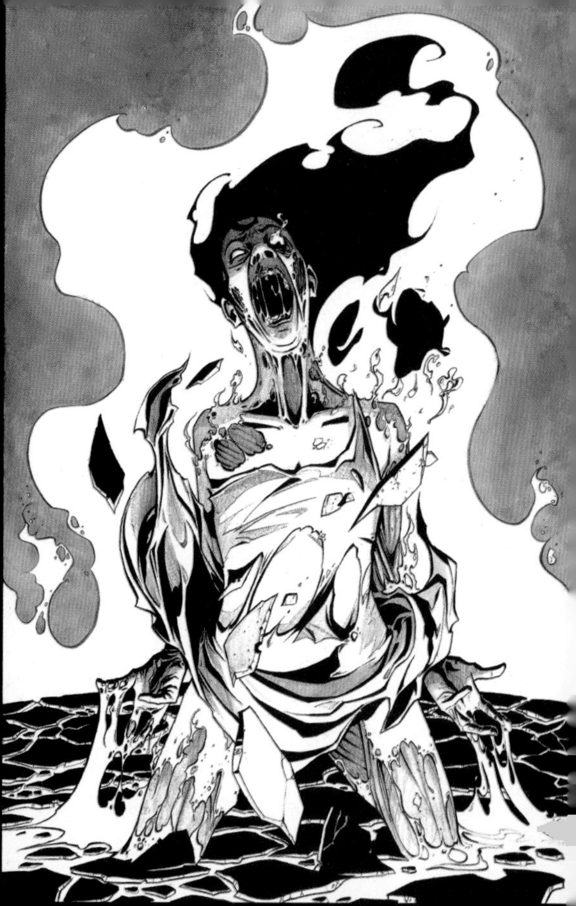
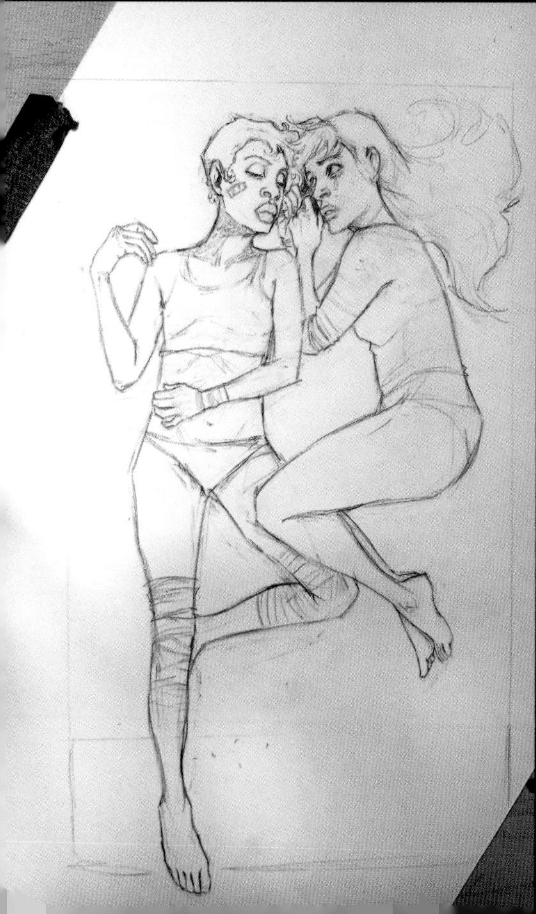
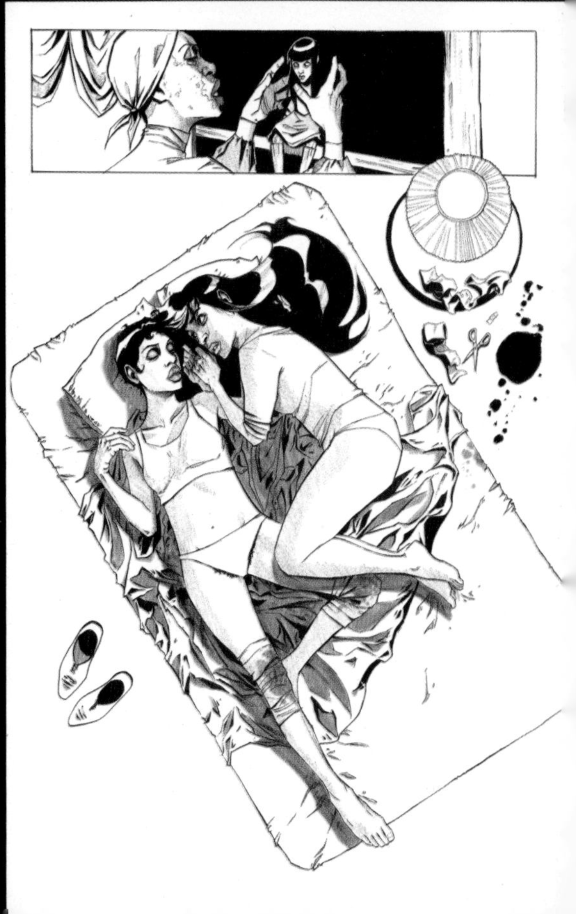

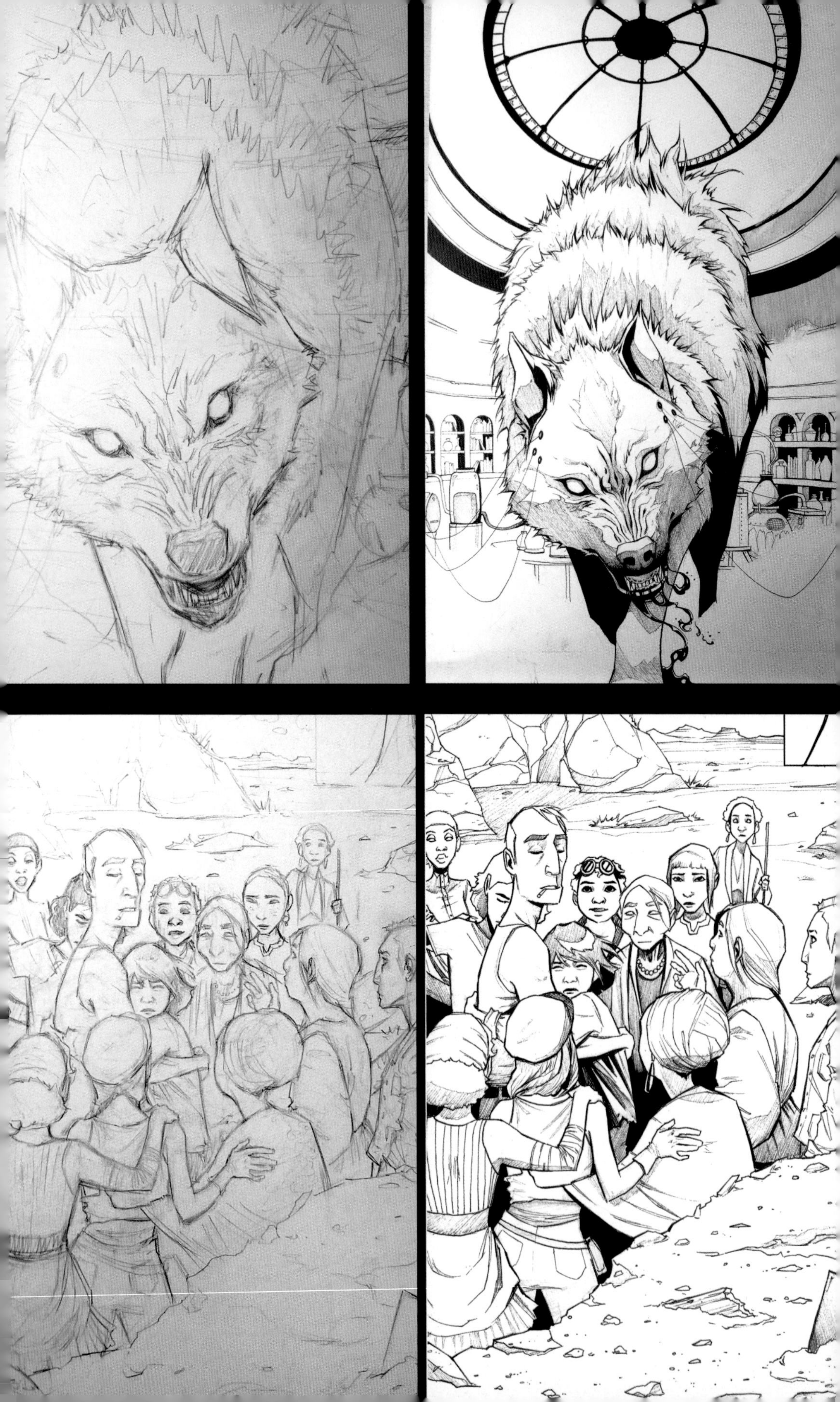

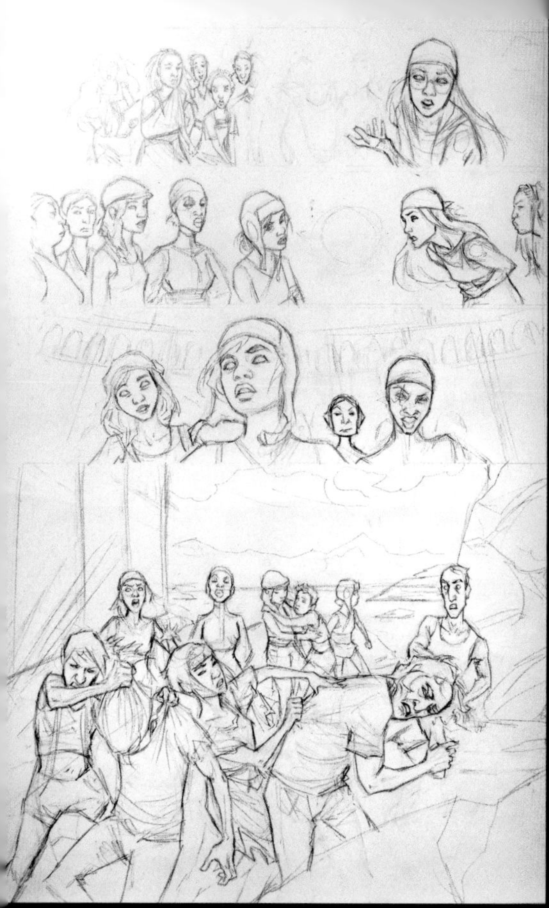

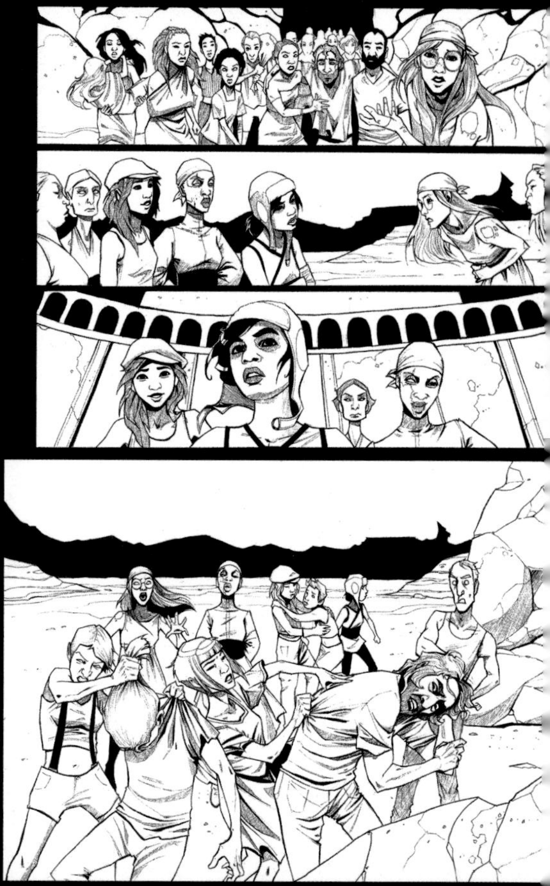

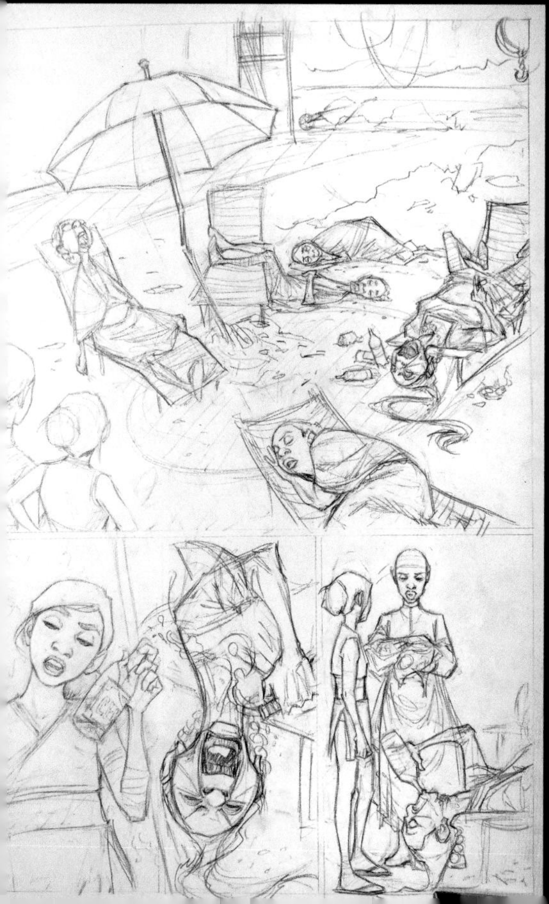

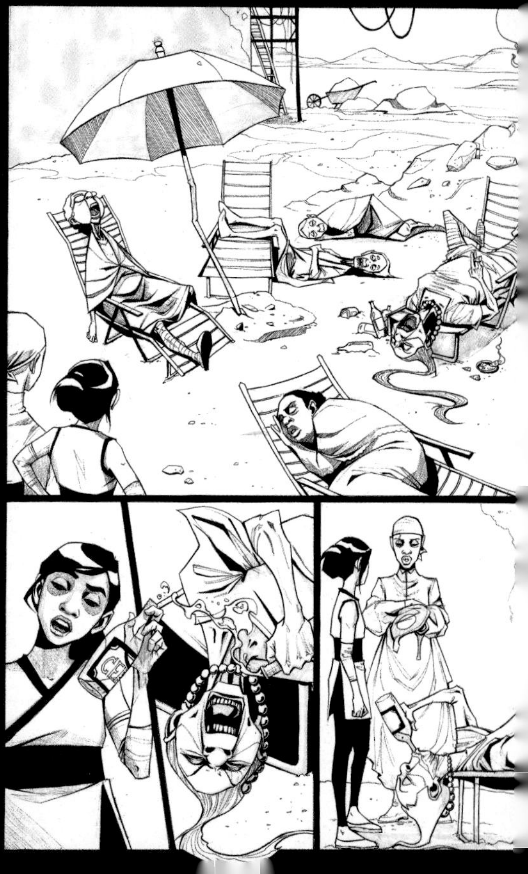

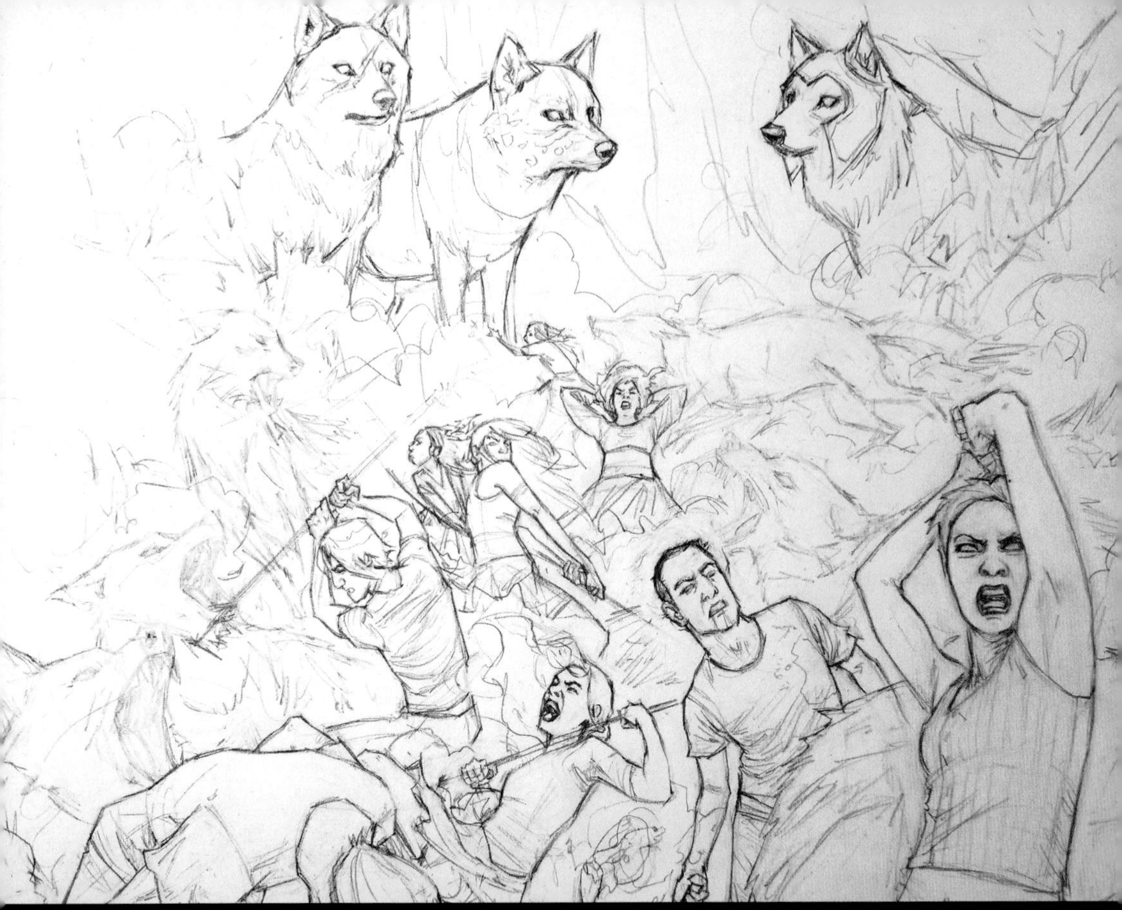

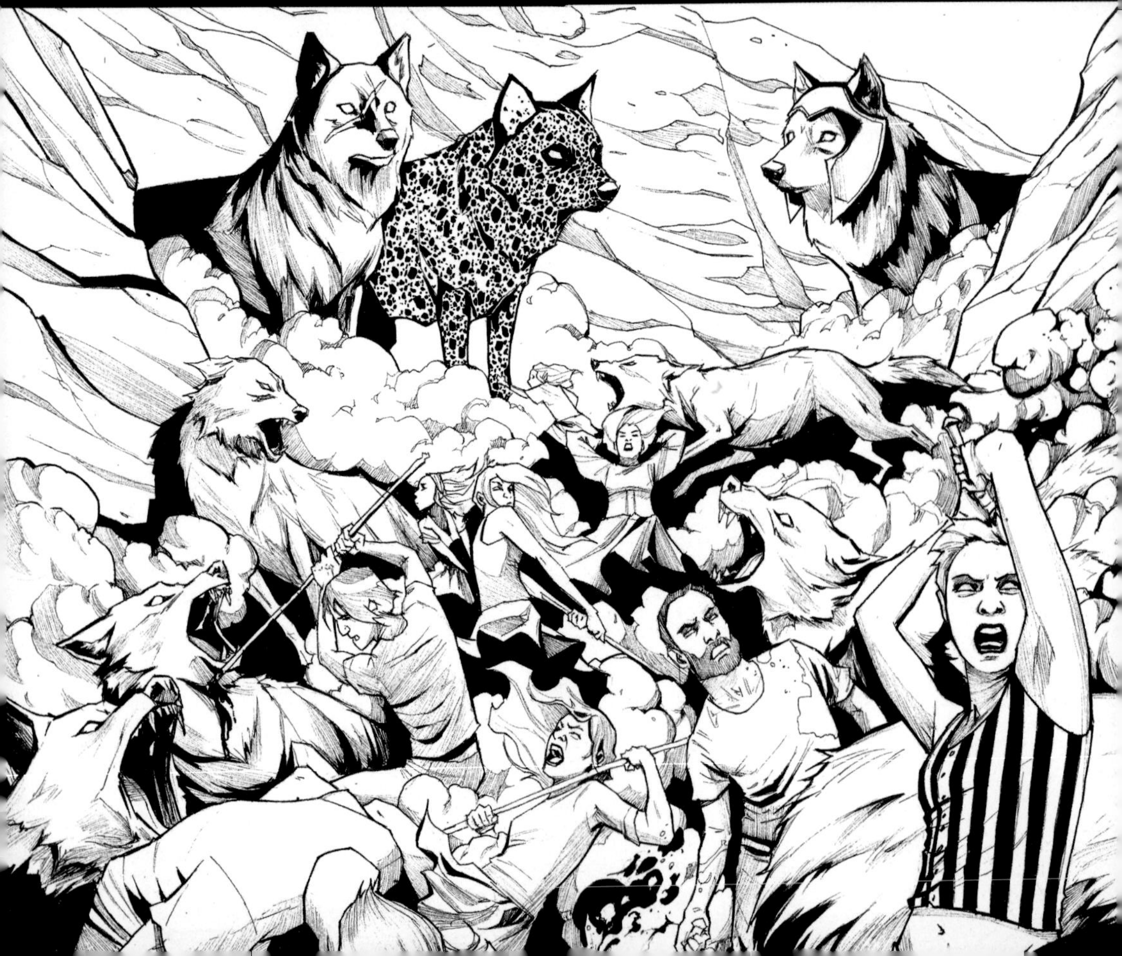